Ever So Silent

Ever So Silent

AN EMMA THORNE MYSTERY

Christopher Little

HP

Honeysuckle Publishing, Norfolk, Connecticut

First published in 2019 by Honeysuckle Publishing
PO Box 485
Norfolk, Connecticut 06058
www.honeysucklepublishing.com
www.christopherlittle.com

Book design and jacket photographs © Christopher Little

Manufactured in the United States of America

10 9 8 7 6 5 4 3 2 1

Ever So Silent/Christopher Little -- 1st edition

ISBN-13: 978-1-7339738-0-9
ISBN-13: 978-1-7339738-1-6 (eBook)
Library of Congress Control Number: 2019904591

For Betsy Kittredge

There are crimes of passion and crimes of logic.
The boundary between them is not clearly defined.

—Albert Camus,
The Rebel (*L'Homme révolté*), 1951

1

A Cop's Nose

Emma had witnessed Will's condition deteriorate week by week. She didn't need to be a psychotherapist to recognize his swelling hell. Will was Emma Thorne's husband. She worried so much about him that it was affecting her work. She shook her head, trying, for the moment at least, to minimize her obsessing.

She started by scanning the traffic around her cruiser.

As she turned onto Hampshire's River Street, Officer Emma Thorne drew behind a Cadillac Escalade SUV. Over the next few minutes, the driver of the Escalade kept checking his rear view mirror, which wasn't in itself out of the ordinary. A lot of guys get antsy with a cop on their tail. Emma observed him slow to five miles below the speed limit on Main Street, which was only thirty to begin with. Next, he put on his blinker and slid into the right lane.

Emma parroted him. Something about the dude smelled. The un-emancipated would call it feminine intuition. She liked to think of it as street smarts.

Based on nothing more than her cop's nose, she radioed his marker tag to her dispatcher. "6 to Dispatch. Run Massachusetts tag X3B 2LR for wants or hits."

From the dispatcher, an immediate reply: "Standby, 6."

The Escalade's driver continued to check his mirror while she awaited a response.

Emma, who had five years in, enjoyed patrol work. Some of her colleagues complained about the very routineness of patrol, but Emma got a kick out of owning her territory and busting bad actors.

The radio crackled. "Be advised, X3B 2LR comes back to a 2018 Cadillac Escalade, color black, reported stolen this a.m. in New Marlborough, Massachusetts. Do you request backup?"

"Roger that."

Emma ignited her light bar and flicked her siren to Wail.

The Escalade immediately jogged into the passing lane and shot forward. *Perfect*, she thought, *a good high-speed pursuit.* The adrenaline kick sent shock waves through her body. Very little about police work intimidated her. She had inherited her bravado from her father, who happened to be Hampshire's chief of police.

She floored her cruiser. There was traffic on Main Street, and the black Escalade weaved wildly. Emma chased him.

He reached his first intersection. Naturally, the light was red. He blew his horn and kept blowing it until he was safely through the crossroads. Emma paused, checking both ways before re-accelerating. She had a little ground to catch up, which she managed to do.

She knew that in about two miles she would reach the town line. Steering with her left hand, she spoke into the mic, "Permission to continue pursuit past the town line?" The law said that she would have to break off pursuit when she reached the state highway unless she received a go-ahead from the Connecticut State Police.

"6, we are in contact with C.S.P. They are deploying stop sticks at the intersection of State Route 88 and Tower Hill Road. You have authority to maintain pursuit."

"Roger."

The Escalade was doing about eighty now with Emma's cruiser close on its tail.

There was one more stop light at the west end of town. Again, the light was red. The Escalade increased speed rather than slowing, the driver blasting his horn.

In an explosion of glass and steel, the black Escalade T-boned a U.S. Postal Service delivery truck. The truck rolled over, skidding across the intersection on its side. An oncoming car slammed into it before it struck a parked car on the far side of Main Street and stopped. Meanwhile, the Escalade sailed end-over-end landing on its roof with a screech of metal on asphalt. Smoke came from the engine of the Escalade. Another car swerved to avoid it.

Emma fishtailed to a stop beside the Escalade. She grabbed the mic and tried to modulate her voice, because she was pretty pumped. "Two-car MVA. Main and Winthrop Streets. SUV vs. utility truck. Request fire, ambulance. Hot. Probable injuries."

"Roger, 6. Dispatching ambulance, fire, and additional backup."

She threw open her door and jumped out.

Incredibly, the driver of the Escalade crawled through the broken driver's side window. He slowly rose to his feet. He appeared to be in his mid-thirties. She recognized him. Hampshire was a small town. She had recently arrested Joe Henderson for driving under the influence. His obvious injury was a gash to his forehead. Blood seeped down his face. His left eye was closed. He didn't appear to have a weapon.

Emma faced him, about ten feet away.

"Place your hands on your head, sir. Get down on your knees," she shouted.

The driver walked slowly toward her, challenging her with his eyes.

Emma felt for her service weapon, a Glock, then changed her mind. She unholstered her Taser and aimed it at his abdomen. "Stop where you are, goddammit, or I'll Tase your ass." No more Sir.

The driver kept coming, his hands clearly visible at his sides. Still no apparent weapon. She heard sirens approaching. The guy kept coming. About five feet now. "If you do not stop, I will be forced to Tase you."

"Fuck you," he said, the first words out of his mouth. "I'm just trying to save Sophie from your fucked-up family."

Emma had no idea what he was talking about. He sounded crazy. There was no Sophie in her family.

It hardly mattered, because he was now within striking distance. "Final warning," she said. He kept coming. She pulled the Taser's trigger.

There was a crack and the snapping sound of the Taser's two barbed electrodes pumping 50,000 volts into his body. Except nothing happened. No convulsions, no incapacitation, no nothing. He kept moving closer. The barbs clung to his shirt, yet … nothing. Maybe the Taser was defective.

She re-holstered the Taser and drew her Glock, yelling for him to stop.

He didn't.

She shifted her aim toward his thigh. He was within striking distance. He was unarmed. Cop or no, Emma wasn't the type of person who could shoot an unarmed man. Had he been brandishing a gun, yes, but not like this.

The guy launched into a flying tackle. His outstretched arms flew toward her gun hand. His hands locked around her wrist, and they both went down to the pavement. Wrestling for her life, she fought to keep his hands away from her weapon. He managed to roll her onto her back. His right hand was now on the barrel of her weapon. Slowly he was loosening it from her grasp.

They rolled further. When she felt he was in the right position, Emma resorted to the defensive technique to which all women are entitled. She kneed him in the balls.

A nearby siren died. Officer Caroline Stoner joined her. Joe was now writhing on the ground beside Emma. Together they rolled him onto his stomach and Stoner jammed her knee into his back. "Jesus, he's wearing body armor," she said.

"Check him for weapons," Emma shouted.

After Caroline Stoner handcuffed him, she patted him down. "Clean! He's got an empty holster."

His weapon must have fallen out when he flipped the stolen Escalade.

Emma said to Caroline, "Thanks, partner. Score one for the girls."

She decided to wait until he stopped moaning before reading him his rights. When he had partially recovered, she Mirandized him and placed him under arrest.

Joe mumbled, "You will pay dearly for this."

"Whatever you say, pal," she said.

2

The Goddaughter

S HE LOOKED OVER at the Escalade. Black smoke escaped from underneath the hood. The upside-down vehicle, its undercarriage fully exposed, looked to her like a great beast felled, its tires pointing upward in submission.

Her police training kicked back into gear. At an MVA, always account for potential passengers, even ones who might have been ejected. *Was there a Sophie in the vehicle?*

She looked through the broken driver's side window. There was no one in the passenger seat. She tried to look through the rear window, pressing her hands against the glass to shield the light. She couldn't see through the tinted glass. In a pouch on her Sam Browne belt was a tool specifically designed to break auto glass—a spring-loaded punch. She used it to good effect. The safety glass spider-webbed and dissolved into thousands of tiny pieces that cascaded onto the top of the Escalade.

"Sweet Jesus!" Emma said aloud. Trapped inside was an upside down, seat-belted female.

Behind her Emma heard someone shout, "Get away, Thorne, the engine's on fire."

Emma shouted, "Stoner, help me! I've got a vic in the back."

Without regard for the girl's potential injuries, they rescue-dragged the body outside and away from the vehicle, the fire. The fire moved from the engine compartment to the body of the Escalade.

It was a teen-aged girl. She was dazed and bloodied.

Emma said, "Where do you hurt, sweetie?"

The girl sobbed and shook.

"What's your name?" Emma tried again.

"Sophie King. I want my mother."

"We'll get to that, but first I need to know where you hurt."

"I'm okay," she sobbed. "Just get my Mom. I really need her."

The EMTs arrived and pulled Emma away from Sophie. "We'll take it from here."

"Okay," Emma said, "but I will need to speak with her in the ambulance."

Emma watched the EMTs do a rapid trauma check and pronounce her okay. They dressed her wounds, mostly cuts and scrapes. When they loaded her into the ambulance, Emma got in beside her. Sophie was a healthy looking, pink-cheeked teenager. Her blue jeans were ripped in all the right places. She wore a ridiculously revealing tank top like all girls her age seem to do. Her straight black hair reached halfway down her back. Her affect mixed worldly wisdom with teen-aged naïveté.

"What's your mom's phone number?" Emma asked. "I'll call her and have her meet us at the hospital."

She got Karen King on the line, told her about the accident, and assured her that Sophie was going to be fine.

Emma held her hand. "Sophie, I need to know what happened here. Can you tell me what he did to you?"

Still weeping, she said, "Joe's my boyfriend. At least he was." She managed a sheepish smile. "He hates my family, and they hate him. He didn't really do anything to me. We were just going over to his studio."

"What were you going to do there?"

"Um, hang out, I guess." Emma read into her expression that she expected to do a little more than just hang out. "Joe's into photography. He wanted to take some photos of me ... and for me to meet some of his friends. He has a photo studio down in Lincoln."

Like a firehouse receiving a dispatch, alarm bells clanged.

She remembered that she had Joe's wallet in her pocket. Stoner had taken it before she'd placed him in the back of her cruiser. Inside, Emma found a valid Connecticut driver's license for a Joe Henderson, born 3/24/1984. She did the math: Joe was thirty-six. He also carried a valid Connecticut State Police carry permit.

"How old are you?" asked Emma.

"I'm fifteen."

Emma lifted an eyebrow.

"Don't you think that Joe's a little old for you?"

She grimaced, "That's what my mom says."

"Why were you in the backseat?" Emma asked.

"I have no idea. Joe's kind of weird that way."

"Do you have any idea why Joe took off when I tried to pull him over?"

Sophie said, "He recognized you. He said you'd arrested him for driving DUI. He said he was only a little buzzed. He also said he was going to show you who's boss. He's not the kind of dude who likes to be beaten by a woman. He was laughing the whole time, and I got scared."

Emma said, "You must've been very frightened. Do you know why Joe was wearing body armor?"

"What's that?"

"Not important," Emma said, thinking it was very important.

"Wait a second," Sophie said, surprise in her voice, "I just figured out who you are. You're married to Will Foster, Georgia's brother. Georgia Foster is my godmother."

So that was what Joe meant by her "fucked-up family."

Emma couldn't quite parse the Sophie-Joe relationship.

"What attracted you to an older guy like Joe?"

"He's really good looking, and he's got awesome clothes," Sophie said, sounding very teen-aged. "Plus, he's really smart and really rich. He owns a Corvette. Um, I guess that sounds kinda shallow, huh?"

"If he owns a Corvette, why did he steal the Escalade."

"No clue."

Shaking her head, Emma concluded, "Well, I guess you've been through a lot."

Through the rear doors of the ambulance, Emma and Sophie watched Hampshire firefighters foam the Escalade.

Suddenly, they heard explosions within the vehicle. From experience, Emma knew that car fires could produce explosive sounds, as when tires explode and when water hits burning magnesium wheel rims, but she was pretty sure that this was ammunition. An EMT closed the back doors of the ambulance. A moment later, Emma heard the fire chief say over the radio, "Command to Units, be advised we have ammo in the vehicle, use caution." The firefighters immediately widened the circle around the Escalade and raised their hose nozzles, lobbing water into the fire.

Everyone else backed away, too, and watched the vehicle burn to a charred skeleton.

3

"To the land of gloom and utter darkness"

The weeks following Emma's discovery of Sophie King in the backseat of Joe Henderson's stolen Escalade should have been a happy time for her.

Except there was her husband Will.

The press and the townsfolk showered her with accolades. The *Hampshire Chronicle* lauded her "stunning rescue" of Sophie under the headline "Heroine of Hampshire." WFSB, the CBS affiliate in Hartford, sent a crew to interview her. There was a story in the *Hartford Courant*.

Chief of Police Archie Thorne, Emma's dad, was beside himself with pride.

Sophie and her parents stopped by police headquarters one morning to thank Emma. The *Chronicle* sent a photographer to happy-snap the occasion. Sophie declared herself "un-traumatized" by the event. Although childless, Emma liked kids, and she was happy for Sophie.

The post office worker suffered a pelvic fracture and several broken ribs. Joe Henderson was locked up in the Connecticut Department of Correction's Hospital in Somers. Joe faced a number of charges. He was in way deeper shit than his previous DUI.

Even Georgia Foster, her husband's reclusive twin sister, telephoned.

"Thank you so much for saving Sophie's life. Since you and Will don't have any children, she's as close to a niece as I'm likely to get." Then Georgia added, "Sophie being rescued from abduction was a life-changing event for me."

A strange thing to say. But Emma's relationship with Georgia was fraught enough already. Emma didn't bother to seek an explanation. Instead, she thanked her and ended the conversation.

On the work front, at least, Emma basked in her brief celebrity.

At home ... another story entirely.

Will seemed to be getting worse each day. He either didn't or couldn't understand his wife's micro-moment of glory. She didn't blame him. When he didn't react to the *Chronicle's* headline, she dropped the subject.

That Friday—the day Will Foster vanished—was otherwise perfect.

Emma steered her cruiser onto River Street, where the chase had started two weeks ago. The leaves were such a vital green that it was no wonder folks in the northwest corner of Connecticut spent their winters longing for the month of May. The former mill town would never be pretty. But the way the sun felt on her face that day and the way the whipped cream clouds distracted her from the shuttered mills and their broken windows gave Hampshire its best shot.

Emma Thorne liked to think that Hampshire, Connecticut, had four spines. Together, they formed the backbone of the town. Main Street, which ran east-west, had four lanes, divided by a median strip. Hanging from the lampposts, purple banners proclaimed, "Hampshire has Heart." The Broken River paralleled Main Street. A row of dilapidated mill buildings cluttered the south shore. River Street ran along the back of the mills, where, generations ago, employees had arrived for work. Despite the cheery signs, the truth was that much of the heart had left Hampshire.

A call came over her mobile radio. A minor MVA on the other side of town. Minor injuries. Another officer on patrol, Max Beyersdorf, took the call. The car crash dispatch interrupted an increasingly rare, peaceful moment. She wasn't sure what caused her jarring reaction: memories of her recent car chase or her husband.

The frail threads that suspended Emma's life intruded once again.

Rarely did Hampshire seem sweeter than her marriage. That day it did. There was plenty of evidence that her husband's depression was worsening. His was an inky hole. After five years as a cop, Emma had always looked forward to her next call. Today, she was dismayed that a dispatch not even meant for her could upset her. Will's misery was becoming contagious.

Earlier, Will's therapist had told them that his sudden-onset depression was "eminently treatable." When she upped the diagnosis to "treatment-resistant major depressive disorder," both Will and she had despaired.

She checked the dashboard clock. It was 4:30 p.m. Worries about Will busied her brain. She wasn't doing her job. She wasn't scanning the other vehicles or pedestrians on the sidewalk looking for mischief-makers.

Emma decided to do something she had never done before: ask for personal time. She called Sergeant Weeks on her cell phone.

"Weeks," her grumpy sergeant replied.

"Sarge, Thorne here—"

"Well if it's not the Heroine of Hampshire," she said. "What's up?"

"I need some personal time. Okay if I cut my shift short today and head home?"

"Oh, fuck me. Who'm I going to get to cover the rest of your shift?"

She hated groveling to Sergeant Stella Weeks, but she said, "Sarge, I really need to get home."

"Okay, Emma, you go home, but you'll have to make up the time."

Emma dismissed Stella as she made a U-turn in the middle of Main Street.

W ill," she called from the front door, "it's me. Where are you?" No answer, but she didn't expect one.

Before going upstairs, she glanced in the living room, where they used to read, watch TV, and snuggle; into the dining room, which they hadn't used in months; and through the kitchen, where breakfast's dirty dishes triggered a wash of guilt. In their bedroom, Will sat on the floor with his back against the wall. In one hand, he held a book. His other hand covered his face. Will's brown hair was matted and unkempt. He wore a bathrobe, a pair of sweat pants, and white athletic socks. He hadn't taught his class at Yale—Literature and the Environment—in three months.

"Oh, it's you." He did not look up.

Emma knelt beside him and gathered him into her arms. To her surprise, he wrapped his arms around her and held on tightly. For a spell, they stayed like that not saying anything. His hair smelled like sour milk.

"Bad day?" she finally whispered.

She caressed his hair and his cheeks. He muttered, "Worse than yesterday."

Right or wrong, she tried to present a strong face to Will in the belief that he would gain strength from that. When she heard him say those words, though, she felt tears pop out of her eyes. She hugged him to hide them.

"Cry all you want. That's all I do." He began to cry, too. She kissed each of his eyes in turn and tasted his salty sadness.

"What are you reading?" she finally asked.

He held the book for her to see. She was surprised to see the *Holy Bible*. Bits of torn paper marked specific pages. In the years of their marriage, she had never known Will to enter a church, funerals and weddings excepted. They had said their own vows in the City Clerk's Office in Hampshire before her father, the chief of police and a justice of the peace.

"Is it helping?"

"Not in the least. I'm reading the Book of Job."

"Are you sure—?"

"What else should I be reading?" he said. "I'm not looking for the part where Jesus makes the blind man see."

"Maybe you should," she said tenderly.

"Here, listen to this." He opened to one of the marked pages. "Job says, 'My face is red with weeping, and on my eyelids is deep darkness.' How effing relevant is that? And this: 'Although I am blameless, I have no concern for myself; I despise my own life.'" Will's voice rose a notch. "Or *this* from Job 10:21, 'Before I go to the place of no return, to the land of gloom and utter darkness.'"

"Don't say that. You're going to get through this. *We're* going to get through this. You'll see. I promise."

Before I go to the place of no return, Emma repeated in her mind. *That wasn't Job speaking.*

She rose to her feet and helped him up. He dropped the Bible. "Let's go upstairs. We can take a bath together."

Will acquiesced, as hollow as a dead tree.

Upstairs, in the tub, he zoned out. He submitted to a body wash with no more connection than a thousand-yard stare. Emma turned him around so that he was between her legs and washed his hair with shampoo and a pitcher. As much as she wanted it to be different, theirs was a moment of intimacy which lacked any intimacy.

Late in the afternoon, she fed him Campbell's Healthy Request Chicken Noodle in bed. She would have cooked him her best stab at a gourmet meal, but he hardly ate anything she served him. He finished half the soup.

He surprised her when he broke the silence. "Georgia stopped by this morning. She is so inappropriate."

"How so?"

"She brought me a book."

"What's inappropriate about that? Seems thoughtful to me. Maybe, a new book'll take your mind off—"

Angrily he said, "She gave me that book about Charlie Manson, *Helter Skelter.* Think that's appropriate?"

He threw his spoon onto the tray and announced that he was ready for bed.

Emma had to agree with Will. Georgia's internal governor had slipped again.

She served him his evening cocktail of psychoactive drugs—the shrink called the rationale *antidepressant polypharmacy*—and a zolpidem sleeping pill. Will slept about twelve hours a day.

Will said with a smile, which momentarily reminded her of the old Will, "The quack says, 'You can't get better if you don't sleep.'"

She climbed into bed, spooning him. Although she was dressed, he was naked. They hadn't had sex since Christmas. Will was a generous lover. She missed the pleasures he gave and those she returned: the way he would kiss her breasts, the way she would stroke his stomach. Mostly, she missed the intimacy after climax, when the security of a cuddle overwhelmed any desire to talk.

In time, Will's breathing slowed as the sedative numbed his misery. Minutes later, he was in the embrace of what he called his Blessed Oblivion.

Twilight fell on Hampshire.

Job's phrase—*before I go to the place of no return*—haunted Emma. Could Will actually do it? Would he?

Deerfield Street, in the New Forest section of Hampshire, was quiet in the evening. The kitchen, where she poured herself a glass of wine, was in the back, garden-side. She swirled the wine, creating a mini-whirlpool in her wineglass.

There was no denying that Will was making her miserable, too.

Yet she still believed, heart and soul, that she could help him recover. She didn't understand the root of his depression, but perhaps that was incomprehensible.

Emma's dad, who had raised her by himself, had given her the greatest gift a parent can bestow: self-confidence and a can-do attitude. She had depended on these gifts throughout her life. Emma knew how to solve problems … with one frightening exception.

She dialed the home telephone number of Will's therapist, who accepted the after-hours call without complaint. She took Emma's report of Will's suicidal thoughts seriously and suggested that Emma bring him in for an unscheduled appointment the next day.

Emma poured herself another glass of wine, appreciating the calming buzz.

She stared at the phone in her hand.

God, I'm thirty-six years old, and the only person I want to phone is my Dad.

She dialed Archie's number. It was 9:00 p.m.

He sounded groggy. "Hey, Baby, I'm hoping this is about Will, since you just woke me up."

"I'm sorry, Dad, I had to talk to somebody." She began to cry, and she didn't bother to muffle her sobs.

"Hey, hey, Baby. What's going on?"

"I think Will is considering suicide. Dad, I don't know what to do anymore."

"I'm so sorry. I truly am. Will's good people. Have you called his shrink?"

"I called her just before I called you. I have an appointment for Will tomorrow."

"Then I think you're doing all you can for tonight. Do you want me to come over?"

"No, I'll manage. Thanks, though. I'll check on him every once in a while, but he's taken a sleeping pill, so I doubt he'll wake up."

Archie said, "I'll talk to Sergeant Weeks in the morning, tell her you won't be coming in."

Emma couldn't help an involuntary laugh. "That'll piss her off."

"You let me worry about that. You just take care of Will. And more importantly, take care of yourself, Baby. Call me if you need me. I will always be here for you. I love you. Bye."

"Bye, Dad," she said.

Left on her own, Emma realized that she hadn't been shopping in over a week. Food and household supplies were low. She decided to drive over to Hampshire's only 24-hour market.

Before leaving, she checked Will. He was sawing logs, that was for sure. He was gone to the world … in more ways than one.

Emma left the house, not worried about him for the time being.

Around 10:00 p.m., Emma, with armfuls of grocery bags, unlocked her door on Deerfield Street. She put all the groceries away and poured herself another glass of wine.

Driven by months of overthinking all things Will, she again checked on him. Unusually, the door to the bathroom was closed. Will never closed the bathroom door. Assuming he was in there, she sat on the bed to wait until he was finished. The Bible, which had recently been tearing into him, rested on his pillow, squared off so that it was precisely lined up with the pillow's edges. She stared at it. It struck her as odd. She looked back at the bathroom door. She couldn't hear running water, the sloshing of tub water, or the stream of pee. She stared at the closed door as she had stared at the book: uncertainly, but with a growing feeling that today would be different.

Finally, she sprang into action.

The bathroom was empty.

Frantically, she searched the rest of the house. She raced from room to room. She burrowed under every bed. Sweeping aside clothes on hangers, most of which dropped to the floor, she checked the closets. She ran down to the basement, looked behind the furnace and the hot water heater. She kept shouting Will's name over and over until her throat hurt. Emma somehow knew she was not going to find Will, but she couldn't stop looking. She went to the garden in the back. She threw open the door to the garden shed and looked inside, anywhere a human being could fit. She re-checked the kitchen. Will, who had not left the house without her in three months, had disappeared.

She re-searched the house until she finished in the bedroom where she had started. There was no sign of a struggle; the front door had been locked as usual, as had the kitchen door to the garden. His bureau was full, and his wallet, which he hadn't carried in months, was on top of the bureau. Credit cards, ID, and cash all inside. His cell phone was there, too. She checked the top drawer. His passport was where he kept it. Will, stoned to unconsciousness by zolpidem, had somehow left the house with nothing.

How was that even possible?

She could only fear the very worst. Yet, where was he?

Emotions gut-wrenched her thinking—horror, impotence, fear, sadness, and, yes, guilt for leaving him alone. Again, where was he?

What had he done? Had he hurt himself? How would he be able to? And, yet again, where the hell was he? Her despair only increased her fear. She leaned her back against the bedroom wall. Her knees buckled. As she slid to the floor, her shoulder knocked a picture off the wall. The shatter of glass on the wood floor was too much. She looked at the ruined frame. The jagged glass had cut into a photograph she had taken of Will. She battered her temples with her fists until they hurt.

With Will gone, Emma couldn't imagine anything worse could happen, but she was wrong.

4

Silver Alert

The bedroom grew smaller and smaller. Emma felt she couldn't breathe. She had this horrendous lump in her throat, which she would carry with her for days. She later learned that there was a name for it, a globus, the same thing shrinks called "the lump of grief." Then, frightful chills overwhelmed her, even though the bedroom was warm. Her whole body shivered as if a sudden fever had spiked. She knew, absolutely, that the life she'd lived and loved was over. Bitter and angry tears came again and wouldn't stop. *Will, where are you?* She couldn't stand her bedroom for another second. She hauled herself to her feet and crunched over broken glass, ran downstairs and out the front door.

Taking deep breaths of the May air, Emma sat on the front steps. She shut her eyes. Her head dropped into tremulous hands. She couldn't stop shaking.

Eyes closed, she imagined Will getting into his car. He was wearing a bathrobe and sweat pants. He backed carefully out the driveway and drove away. He drove right, left, then right again until he reached the State Highway, Route 88. He was talking to himself, but Emma couldn't hear what he was saying. At the town line, he gradually increased his speed. There were no cars in front of him. Fifty, sixty, then seventy. He maxed out at eighty-eight. Flying without due regard, he crossed the Broken River. At the west edge of Simpson's cornfield, a railroad bridge, long disused, spanned the highway.

He unclipped his seatbelt.

Will pressed the accelerator until it contacted the floor, and he aimed his car at the concrete abutment on the north shoulder of 88.

The impact forced the engine into the passenger compartment. It crushed his legs. At the same moment, the instant deceleration—ninety-miles-an-hour to zero in .001 seconds—threw his body forward. His head crashed through the front windshield. Simultaneously, it struck concrete, twenty-feet-thick.

Like a watermelon dropped from a skyscraper, Will's head exploded.

Emma screamed. She jerked her head upright. In the driveway, Will's Audi rested in the shade of a maple tree, untouched for months.

She called Dad first, of course. He was all she had. After voicing his sympathies over the phone, it didn't take Archie long to get down to business: "Wait for me outside the house. Do not go back inside the house. For the time being, we'll treat it as a crime scene until we know more. I'll be there ASAP. On my way, Baby. Hang tight!"

Already outside, Emma felt useless. Continuing to blather wasn't helping. After a few quiet minutes, her spine straightened. Anger gradually pushed her despair into a corner of her brain. Putting feelings aside was never easy for Emma. She was naturally an emotional person. No histrionics usually, but she cared deeply about the things that mattered to her. Will was foremost among them. Her only task going forward was to save him if she could … and find him if she couldn't.

There was enough of the cop in Emma to work the angles, come what may. She saw only three possibilities. Will had gone to the place of no return, to the land of gloom and utter darkness. He'd been considerate enough to not make a mess in the house. Or, someone had kidnapped Will. His parents were wealthy. Everyone in Hampshire knew that. Even if Emma didn't have the money, his parents would pay anything to get their only son back. Finally, some person or persons unknown had murdered Will and removed his body. There was no evidence of that, besides which it was patently inconceivable. Until recently, Will had lived a charmed life. Emma had never met a soul who didn't immediately warm to him.

Emma couldn't help parsing all the possibilities, however hideous. She loved Will more than life itself. She could not imagine going forward without him. She would find him. She knew it.

She heard a siren approaching. Archie swung into the driveway skidding on the turn. His LEDs, concealed in his grill, strobed red and blue, bright in the nighttime. His unmarked car shuddered as he threw the shift lever into Park.

Pepper, Archie's stalwart Belgian Malinois police dog, bounded across the lawn and gave Emma enough love to make her feel one-quarter ready to face what was to come.

Archie ran toward Emma. Out of breath, he threw a big bear hug around her. He enveloped her, and she sobbed anew. Emma was tall, but when she pressed her cheek against him, her head fit comfortably under his chin. Patting her back, as fathers do, he muttered, "There, there. We'll sort this out."

Emma heard another siren approaching, then another, and then a third. The whole department was responding.

Detective Larry "Buzz" Buzzucano was right behind Archie. A cop's cop, Buzz could intimidate the shit out of the most insufferable suspect. Officer Caroline Stoner was right behind Buzz.

The last to arrive was Sergeant Stella Weeks, Emma's *bête noire* on the force, but Emma was still glad she'd responded. Weeks had clearly come from home.

They stood in a jumpy group on the front lawn. Archie directed Buzzucano and Stoner to canvass the neighbors north and south of Emma's. "See if anybody saw anything, anything at all," he ordered.

To Weeks, Emma, and Pepper, he said, "Let's go inside."

Archie found a sock of Will's in the downstairs laundry hamper. He called Pepper over. She sat in front of him, her ears pricked. "Search, Pepper," he commanded.

While Pepper bounded off and methodically searched the house room-to-room, the rest of them made the same inspection that Emma already had completed. Except for the dirty dishes and the broken picture in the bedroom, there was nothing to find. No evidence, and no Will. Pepper came up empty, too.

"Shit," Archie said.

"Yeah," Emma agreed. "What now?"

He took a last look around the living room where they were standing. "Sarge, do you mind stepping outside?"

When Weeks left the house, Archie said, "Tell me exactly what happened between you and Will."

"Oh, Dad, this is so completely awful. I don't know—"

"I understand, Baby. But let's just concentrate on the here and now. Finding out what happened is all we should be thinking about." Archie was now sounding more like a policeman than a dad.

"I get it," Emma replied. "There was no trouble between us if that's what you're inferring. Just Will's depression and my concern for him." She paused and tried to answer the other part of his question, "Okay, I gave Will a bath and an early supper. He ate very little. No surprise there. Before that, he was reading crazy passages from the book of Job. That's what scared me the most. After I gave him his meds, I got into bed with him until he went to sleep. Then I had a glass of wine, after which I decided to use the time to do some shopping. The shelves were bare. At most, I think I was out of the house for ninety minutes. No more. When I got home, he was gone."

"Listen, Emma, we gotta talk frankly here. But only if you're up to it. Are you?"

"Yes, Dad."

"Based on what you told me tonight and Will's psychiatrist's reaction, I think we have to face the fact that Will might have tried to hurt himself or is going to. Do you have any idea where he might go? Did he have a quiet place where he liked to take walks? In the woods? In the state park? Someplace private?"

"Will wasn't a big outdoors guy, but he did like to walk around New Forest Lake, but that's not exactly private. Lots of people walk there."

Archie scratched his head. "There is that patch of woods on the north side of the lake. We could start there."

There was a knock on the front door. Stoner and Buzzucano.

Stoner said, "We canvassed the neighbors. Everyone who was home claimed they didn't see a thing. The lady across the street saw Emma leave, but she didn't see her come back. Sorry, Chief. We got zilch."

"All right, let's go back to headquarters and rally the troops. Emma, you come too. We'll call a meeting. All available bodies. I want patrol units off the street, too. I mean everybody."

The headquarters of the Hampshire Police Department was in the center of town and shared its space with the town administration and the city council. Across Main Street, the Broken River flowed, swollen by spring rains. The abandoned mills crowded the south bank.

HQ looked like a hellish Victorian prison. Inside was no better. The roll-call room was shabby. Church basement chairs in haphazard lines faced a podium. Emma entered with the other officers and detectives. A grim venue, she thought, for a grim meeting. But when she saw off-duty officers arriving as well, she felt gratitude. The Blue Line was solid.

Behind the podium, there was a hand-scrawled sign which spoke volumes about her father's tenure: "Archie's Three Rules: No Floozy, No Boozy, No Snoozy."

Archie and Pepper arrived through a separate door at the front of the room. Archie took his place behind the podium. His face held a grimace. Pepper sat down next to the podium and gazed at her master.

Emma studied her dad. Will's disappearance had clearly caused him more distress that she had realized. His typically ruddy face was gray.

Before beginning, Archie scanned the room. He made eye contact with every single officer. "You all know why we are here," he began. "Your colleague, Emma, needs your help. I do too. As some of you know ..." Archie sent Emma a questioning look. She nodded. "... Will Foster, Emma's husband, has been suffering from depression and has been out of work for some months. Some of you know Will; some of you don't. For those who have never met him, my son-in-law is a standup guy. Will would do anything for any of you. I can't imagine anyone wishing him harm. That said, we are the police. So, we are going to investigate every possibility.

"But the first possibility we have to consider ..." He glanced at Emma again. "... is that Will intends to harm himself. This afternoon, he said some disturbing things which could be construed as suicidal feelings. We are going to split up and conduct area-specific searches for him. I will also ask the public via social media to muster tomorrow morning at oh-nine-hundred for a town-wide search. I've also issued a Silver Alert with state authorities. Any questions before I continue?"

Officer Pete Sinclair said, "I thought Silver Alerts were for Alzheimer's patients."

"They are, but they're also for folks over the age of eighteen who have a mental impairment. I stretched a little and included depression."

Sinclair followed up with, "What is Will driving, sir?"

"We don't know if he is driving anything. Both of the family vehicles are accounted for."

Emma glanced around the room. There were thirteen officers, sergeants, and detectives present. Virtually the whole department. They were all attentive, hanging on Archie's every word.

Archibald "Archie" Thorne had been chief of Hampshire, Connecticut's fifteen-person police department for as long as anyone bothered to recall.

He was very much the "town father" type. A master of "aw shucks," most people in town and all his cops loved him. Emma was his only child, and he had wanted her to join the police department since, as he might've said, she was knee high to a night stick.

"I want Stoner and Beyersdorf to drive down to New Haven and interview Will's colleagues in the English department at Yale. I know the chief of the Campus Police. Introduce yourself to him, and he will look after you. Good guy. His name's Conor McCarthy.

"Sinclair and Smith will take friends and associates of Will's around Hampshire. Emma can give all you guys a list of people to talk to."

Archie continued, "As for one of the other possibilities, Detective Buzzucano is going to set up a trace on Emma's cell phone, her home phone, and whatever phones the Fosters, Will's parents, use. We will be prepared if this turns out to be a kidnapping for ransom, which I highly doubt. As I said before, we are Will's friends, but we are also the Hampshire Police Department."

Archie looked up from his scribbled notes and said, "That's it, guys. We are going to find Will Foster whatever it takes. Right?"

The members of the department shuffled out of the room thoughtfully, leaving Emma alone with Archie and Pepper.

"He's dead, isn't he?"

Archie put a hand on each of Emma's shoulders and looked her straight in the eye. "Too early to say that, Baby, way too early. Hang in there."

Emma nodded her head, but her instincts screamed the opposite. He pulled her into a hug.

"By the way," her dad said into her ear, "do the Fosters even know yet?"

Emma shook her head.

"You'd better go see them, then, before Buzzucano does. Can you do that? I'd better stay here and organize the searches." He looked at his watch. "It's late. Why don't you go tomorrow morning? I'll wave off Buzz until then. You can take Pepper with you. She's a reliable companion ... and a good one to have for a mission like this."

5

On the Veranda

On Saturday morning, Emma procrastinated. She didn't head over to the Fosters until eleven o'clock. Will's parents, Frank and Joan Foster, lived in a shingle-style house on New Forest Lake. A sprawling, custom-built home, it faced west toward the water. Frank liked to call that his "cocktail light." He had made a fortune in insurance in the days when Hartford Insurance meant real money. Joan liked to call herself a housewife/philanthropist. They were card-carrying Conservatives.

Frank and Joan had never cottoned to Emma. Their dream for a daughter-in-law hadn't been a cop's daughter ... let alone a cop herself ... let alone a left-leaning cop. Nor did it satisfy them that their Yale professor son had married a girl with a degree in Police Science from the University of New Haven. A hard-won master's degree in Criminal Justice didn't make the grade either. Emma took it as well as she could, but it didn't make for the coziest of Thanksgiving dinners.

With Pepper at her side, Emma rang the front doorbell. She was surprised when Georgia, Will's fraternal twin, opened the door. Georgia rarely left her house. Will used to say that his sister had "issues." If Emma had a problem with Will's parents, she enjoyed a complete disconnect with Georgia.

"This a surprise," Georgia began.

Her long blonde hair was done up in an elaborate braid-bun. Although she was convinced of her irresistible beauty, Will once whispered to Emma, "I hate to say it, but my sister has a million-dollar body and the face to protect it." Emma thought he said that just because he loved to be funny. Georgia wasn't a conventional beauty, but the combination of her lustrous hair, her widow's peak, her stature, her wide mouth and full lips, and her intense blue eyes combined to leave people, men in particular, with a powerful impression.

"Hello, Georgia. It's been a while. How's Sophie doing?"

"Fine. Thanks to you. You know, I never really thought of you as a real cop. I thought it was more of a nepotism kind of thing,"

"Are your parents home?"

"They're on the veranda."

Pepper and Emma followed Georgia through to the side of the house that faced the lake.

Joan and Frank were sipping from glasses of white wine. Frank wore a country squire tweed jacket. He rose to greet her, giving her a kiss on the cheek and a lukewarm pat on the shoulder. Joan switched her wineglass to her left hand and extended a bony right hand. Georgia sat next to her mother and retrieved her wineglass.

Emma was surprised to see Sophie King standing behind Joan Foster's chair. She waved to the girl. Sophie didn't look any the worse for wear after her ordeal. Mostly she looked young. She wore a pair of shorts and a Justin Timberlake tee-shirt. Her long black hair was tied in a ponytail.

"Do join us. Wine?" Frank said.

"No thanks."

"What brings you here," Frank said, "on this splendid spring day? Where's Will? He doesn't teach on Fridays, does he?"

Were these people clueless? Will hadn't been to work in months.

Emma found herself forestalling the inevitable. "I'm sorry I haven't been around to visit. I've been pretty busy."

Joan said, "Keeping the public safe, I presume. Hey, what's with the dog? He's not dangerous, is he?"

Emma might have corrected her. *Pepper is a she, and she's not dangerous unless I tell her to throttle your scrawny neck.* But she refrained.

She already knew that this was not going to end well.

Emma sat fidgeting, stalling. She couldn't bring herself to trigger the vituperation she knew would inevitably follow. "It's been ages since

Will stopped by. Yale sure keeps him busy," Joan mused.

"He's such a star," Frank said, "We're so proud of our Will."

Emma knew that Will avoided his parents as best he could. She also knew why. Through confidences, which Will had shared with her early in their marriage, she couldn't understand why Georgia didn't avoid them, too.

"I'm afraid I have some disturbing news," she finally said, "Will has gone missing."

Joan leapt to her feet. "What does that even mean? Gone missing?"

"For the first time—it was yesterday—Will began to hint at suicide. I called his psychotherapist last night, and she agreed to see him today. When I got home from shopping, Will was gone. My department has not found any trace of him so far—"

They all spoke at once.

Frank shouted, "What the hell! Why didn't you tell us? This happened *yesterday?*"

"You went *shopping* while our son was threatening to kill himself?" Joan shrieked.

Georgia summed up, "You're to blame for this, Emma. You alone."

Emma felt herself begin to snap. It wasn't as if this hadn't been bad enough. She'd already known these people would give her no comfort. She couldn't believe her dear, sweet Will was even a part of this family.

But she tried to be reasonable. "Look, Georgia, I know you blame me for Will's state of mind. You've made that clear enough but I—"

"You're goddamn right I blame you. Will was the happiest man alive until he met you—"

Alert to the contretemps, Pepper rose from her sitting position. Emma said *no* under her breath.

"That's not fair, and you know it. That's just not fair." In spite of herself, Emma felt tears looming. She tried to hold them back. On top of everything, their reactions pissed her off. "I did everything for Will, when he was well and when he became sick. The only thing I couldn't give him, which we both wanted more than anything, was a baby." Her voice rose. "Do you blame me for that, too?"

"I do," Joan said.

"Me, too," Georgia echoed.

Emma straightened her back and turned on her heel in a tactical retreat.

In the forecourt of the house, she heard the crunch of pea stones behind her. She whipped around, half expecting Georgia to be pursuing her with more hurtful words. It turned out to be Sophie King.

"Mrs., um, Thorne, I'm sorry I didn't say anything before. The Fosters, they, like, creep me out. I never feel like I say the right thing. Like they're always so critical."

"Tell me about it," Emma said.

"I just want you to know that I appreciate you saving my life the other day. Joe is such a loser. I must've been crazy to look twice at him."

"The good news is that *you* seem okay. I guess we can both agree that your "incident" could've had a different ending."

Sophie looked as if she had something more to say.

Sophie said, tentatively, "Um, ever since the deal with Joe, Georgia's been acting all weird-like. It's like she's different. Like suddenly she's my mom or something."

"Maybe she's just worried about you—"

"No, it's different. She keeps asking me if Joe, you know, touched me. And keeps asking me. She wants to know all the gory details. She won't let it alone."

"I just think she's concerned. That's what it sounds like to me. I suppose you could just say you don't want to discuss it any more, that it's upsetting to talk about."

Sophie said, "That's a great idea. Thanks, Mrs. Thorne."

Emma thought for a minute and decided to go ahead. "Have you heard that Joe is back on the streets? He hired an expensive New York lawyer and paid a hefty bail to get out."

"I told you he was rich."

"Yeah, well, tell me if he gets in touch with you. Will you do that for me?"

Sophie said, "Sure thing Mrs. Thorne!" as if such a promise was a mere triviality.

Sophie skipped back into the house, acting like she'd shrugged off a great weight.

6

No Shock Advised

The week after Will vanished felt like a forced march through mud season. The cops' slog was unyielding and enervating.

The department pulled together. Overtime flew out the window. Archie stayed at headquarters day and night fielding reports and directing his troops.

The town rallied on the Saturday morning after Will's disappearance. Archie sent them out in search parties with specific instructions and predetermined search areas. Over eighty people showed up on Saturday. On Sunday, more than 100 people pitched in. The outpouring cheered Emma, but only slightly. The townspeople found nothing.

Max Beyersdorf and Caroline Stoner, who was so pretty nobody could understand why she didn't have a partner, returned from New Haven with nothing to report. No one in Will's department had seen or heard from him.

Pete Sinclair and Chuck Smith interviewed everyone in Hampshire on Emma's list. Every single person denied any knowledge of Will's whereabouts. They reported to Archie that they believed them.

Emma continue to despair.

On Friday, one week after the disappearance, her dad showed up on her front door.

He looked pallid and disheveled, like an unmade bed.

She studied his face. "You're going to give up, aren't you?"

"Give me a hug," he said instead of answering. They embraced on the threshold. Pepper inserted her snout between their legs.

"We're not getting anywhere, Baby," he continued. "The department is exhausted. I confess, I'm exhausted. And, well, as I said, we're just not getting anywhere."

Not meaning to be unsympathetic, Emma said, "So that's it? No Will. And the department resumes its daily chores?"

"I'm afraid so."

"Well, I will continue to search for Will—"

"And I will help you. It's the department I'm forced to worry about."

"I understand, Dad," she said, not sure she meant it.

"Thank you for that. I know how hard this is. Not just for you."

"Dad, what do you really think happened?"

Her father rarely couched important matters. She didn't expect him to do so now.

Archie raised an eyebrow. "Truthfully, I think Will was in complete despair. I think he found a secret place where we might not find him for a long time and committed suicide. I think he did that to spare you the trauma of discovering his body."

"I disagree. Will would never do that to me. I know him. He would have suffered for as long as it took for him to get better rather than hurting me like that."

Archie looked at her for a long time. He smiled. Then he said, gently, "You know you'll have to go back to work? I can't spare you anymore."

"I understand."

Archie drove back to headquarters, leaving Emma alone with her thoughts.

She remembered the first time she'd brought Will home to meet her dad. *University of New Haven introduces Yale to Hampshire's Chief of Police*, she recalled with a rare chuckle.

That afternoon Connecticut was in the embrace of a dramatic autumn. Oranges, yellows, and reds dazzled the eyes as they drove up Route 8. As the splendid colors flew past, she realized that she had never brought home someone she was really serious about.

Will and she had danced around the marriage topic, but the music was still playing.

Dad greeted them at his front door with the undisguised scrutiny that a girl's father reserves for a first prom date. He didn't offer them a drink, and he quizzed Will for the first hour. Emma knew that Archie didn't particularly like Will's father. There was some ancient history about Frank Foster trying to coerce Archie into fixing a speeding ticket.

Will remained unfailingly charming throughout and answered Archie's questions without a sniff of sycophancy. Eventually Archie seemed to relax. He said to Emma, "Baby, why don't you mix us three martinis?" To Will, he said, "You do like martinis, don't you?"

When Emma returned ten minutes later with a tray of martinis, both men were smiling.

"What's so funny?" she asked.

"Will turned the tables on me and asked me a question I couldn't answer. It is a question only you can answer."

Emma blushed crimson as Will dropped to one knee right in front of Archie and said, "Emma, I love you. Will you marry me?"

The next week, Emma resumed patrol duty with a sodden heart. Not much happened for the first few days. A few traffic stops, a burglary, one domestic ... little of importance.

On Thursday, Emma decided to surprise her dad by taking him out to dinner. At the end of her shift, she returned to headquarters and climbed the steps to Archie's second floor office. She knocked on the door, but there was no answer. She let herself in. Archie was sprawled in his reclining office chair, his head cocked back, fast asleep. Pepper had her snout rested in his lap. An endearing sight. She closed the door quietly and went back downstairs to the locker room where she changed into her civvies.

Caroline Stoner walked in after a shower, drying her hair with a towel. Emma was once again struck by how beautiful she was. At roughly 25-years-old, she turned eyes wherever she went, and not just men's. She was more than noticeable. Half Portuguese, with an American mother, she had coal black hair. If the light was right, hints of blue appeared like Wonder Woman's hair in the original comic books. Emma envied her luscious red lips. The word around headquarters was that Caroline was actively looking for a guy. Why she hadn't found one was beyond Emma.

Emma liked her, as did the whole team.

They rehashed the arrest of Joe Henderson, finding a few things to laugh about. "What an oxygen thief," said Emma. Nothing bonded officers together more than a hairy take down.

Half an hour passed before Emma went upstairs. On the first floor, she passed the glass-fronted dispatcher's room. The dispatcher on duty motioned her in. She said, "Have you seen the Chief? Mayor Wardlaw has called three times. You know what *he's* like—"

"Yup, I sure do." Emma laughed.

"Anyway, every time I put a call through to your dad's office, he doesn't pick up."

"Last time I looked he was fast asleep, but I doubt he would've slept through three phone calls. Maybe I should go wake him up."

Emma took the steps two at the time. Archie was in the same position and Pepper still had her snout in his lap. But this time Pepper whined.

"What is it Pepper?" she asked from the doorway. She walked over and shook her dad by the shoulder. His head lolled. "Oh, Jesus," Emma cried.

She felt for his carotid artery. No pulse. She put the back of her hand close to his mouth. Archie wasn't breathing either. She hauled him off the chair onto the floor. She started chest compressions. With her left hand she reached for her radio, but it wasn't there. She'd changed out of her uniform.

She paused compressions to grab the phone. The dispatcher answered.

"My dad's down. Call the ambulance. Request a paramedic," Emma shouted. She dropped the phone, dropped to her knees, and resumed compressions. "Dad, Dad, don't go. Please don't go."

Shit! She'd forgotten the defibrillator. She grabbed the receiver again. "You still there?"

"I'm still here, Emma. Ambulance is on its way—"

"Get an AED up here right away."

Emma continued pumping Archie's sternum until Stoner arrived with a defibrillator. They ripped off his shirt and attach the pads. The machine's disemboweled voice intoned, "Stop CPR. Do not touch the patient."

There was an agonizing pause.

"No shock advised," said the machine.

"Fuck," Emma wailed.

There was a good kind of "no shock advised" and a bad kind.

Emma knew which one this was.

They continued CPR. Emma pummeled his chest. She felt a rib crack. Caroline Stoner performed mouth-to-mouth.

But they both knew that Archie Thorne was dead.

The last two to arrive in Archie's crowded office were the brothers, both in blue suits, who co-owned Hampshire Funeral Services. The cops made way for them. They wheeled in a gurney and lowered it next to Archie's body. On the gurney was a black, rubbery bag with a long zipper.

When they approached Archie, Pepper growled at them. Emma had to quiet her.

They finished zipping him up.

Emma said, "Wait." She knelt next to the bag, unzipped it to expose her dad's head. She kissed him on the forehead. "Goodbye, Dad, I love you." He was already cold. Pepper joined her and licked Archie's lips.

Emma nodded to the brothers. With help from a couple of the cops, they loaded Archie onto the gurney and wheeled him out the door.

Emma looked around the room. It seemed like the whole department had crowded into the office. Everyone looked on in disbelief. No one said a word.

Emma said, "Would everybody mind? I need a moment."

They all left with murmurs of condolences.

When she was finally alone, she sat in Archie's chair and dropped her head to his desk. A lifetime of tears flowed.

Eventually, she lifted her head and blew her nose. Pepper was pacing the perimeter of the office like a tiger in a cage. She called her over. "He's gone, I don't know what else to tell you. I know I can't replace him, but I promise I will try."

7

Double Jeopardy

I despise disorder.

Three **P**s rule my life: preparation, plotting, and pulling it off.

Before I go to bed, I set the breakfast table. After polishing the silver with a soft cloth, I place the fork one inch to the west of my plate. The knife and spoon go one inch and two inches, respectively, to the east. My juice glass goes one and a half inches southwest of the northeast corner of my placemat. Then I'm all set for breakfast.

I have my house—and it's a damn fine house—all to myself.

Every once in a while, I think it is a useful exercise to take stock, to take a moment to look over the past and plan for the future. Recent events make this especially useful.

My last plan, I executed perfectly, which is no big surprise if you know me. I am highly intelligent, organized, and competent. Planning and executing is what I am best at. (I know, you're not supposed to end a sentence with a preposition, but, if you already know the rules, it is permissible to break them.) As Winston Churchill said, "This is the sort of English up with which I will not put!"

I suppose a psychiatrist would diagnose me as a narcissist. Considering the strengths of my personality skills, why wouldn't they? I have every right to think highly of myself. On the other hand, I believe that psychotherapy is contraindicated for me in particular. Why fix what ain't broke? (It is okay to use slang where such usage improves the strength of the message.)

It is all about the planning, and then there is nothing on earth more satisfying than the successful avenging of a wrong.

"You kill my dog, you better hide your cat," Mohammed Ali said.

Did I mention that I served my country ("My country, right or wrong.") as a navy corpsman in the U.S. Marine Corps (*Semper fi!*)? Unless you were once a hospital corpsman, and I was, there are few skills you do not possess. Like learning to think "outside of the box."

Did I mention that I am highly intelligent? I'm also introspective. Many highly intelligent people are not. When something goes wrong (which rarely happens to me), I understand why. Ordinary People (film reference intended) don't possess this skillset. This makes me very powerful and successful at my current mission, which is to right a wrong.

This morning, I retrieve the Hampshire Chronicle from my front door. The headline draws me up short.

Wow!

> *Archibald Thorne Dies*
> *Heart Attack Suspected*

> by Virginia Hobson, Staff Reporter
> Archibald "Archie" Thorne, 61, Hampshire's widely admired Chief of Police, was found unresponsive by his daughter, Officer Emma Thorne, at Hampshire Police Department headquarters. Officers Thorne and Caroline Stoner attempted CPR, but Chief Thorne was pronounced dead by paramedics on scene. Chief Thorne began his career ...

Not much point in finishing the article. I know the rest.

I am not ashamed to say that a small smile escapes my lips. Between Will and Archie, Emma must feel like she's being convicted twice for the same crime.

8

A Bear Hug

Emma could find no instructions for her father's funeral, although she searched his house and office. Archibald "Archie" Thorne was a lapsed Catholic. Emma chose St. Michael's Catholic Church anyway, because it was Hampshire's largest. Mock Gothic, the nave of St. Michael's was cavernous, and she knew that every seat would be filled. Like Hampshire, St. Michael's was shopworn, but Father Ben insisted that his congregation was growing.

When Mayor Dick Wardlaw found out that Archie had left no special wishes, he promptly took over the preparations. Rather than being annoyed, Emma accepted the state of affairs with relief. She honestly couldn't face the arrangements on her own.

Moreover, she couldn't believe that she was attending her father's funeral without Will by her side. It was so goddamn unfair.

Saturday, the day of the service, dawned gray. She hadn't slept much the night before. She and Pepper arrived early, so as to miss the crowds. It would be hard enough to face people at the reception without doing it twice. She waited in the sacristy with Father Ben's blessing. Her two best friends from high school, Deb Barger and Vanessa Mack, sneaked in to buck her up.

At 10:05 a.m. Father Ben cracked the door of the sacristy. "It's time, Emma. Are you ready?" She dabbed her eyes with a handkerchief and followed him into the church proper. Although she knew that Archie was popular in the community, she was stunned by the size of the crowd. Every pew seemed to be filled, and there were people standing at the back and along the sides. The entire department in their dress blues was lined up on either side of the coffin in front of the altar. As Acting Chief, Stella Weeks stood slightly apart. Her chief's hat, with scrambled eggs on the visor, was way too big. Emma fleetingly wondered if she had expropriated it from Archie's coat rack.

The eulogists included the lieutenant governor, the commanding officer of the Connecticut State Police, State Senator Ethel Davidson, and Mayor Dick Wardlaw.

While they spoke, she thought about how fabulous her dad had really been. When she was seven, a doctor had diagnosed her mother with a virulent form of cancer. She died in less than three months. It was so long ago that Emma needed photographs to remember what she looked like. In those days, her dad was a patrol officer like she was today. His life flipped the moment Mom was diagnosed.

Virginia Thorne had been an unapologetic housewife who dedicated her life to caring for her only child. Overnight, Dad became Emma's sole caregiver. Mom and Dad, all rolled into one. Archie had met the challenge with characteristic enthusiasm. He'd loved and cuddled her, cooked her meals, taken her to the playground, organized birthday parties (even baking cakes), tucked her in every night after a story, even took her to the pharmacy to buy her first box of Kotex for Teens.

Mayor Dick Wardlaw was the last person to speak.

Dick Wardlaw stepped up to the mic, his favorite place to be.

Bald and overweight, Wardlaw could have been the clone of a certain disgraced Hollywood producer. She had heard some unsubstantiated rumors, and she'd often speculated that his personal behavior might follow the same script. She wouldn't be surprised, because he was a powerful man. Nobody in town could figure out how Wardlaw seemed to have every member of the City Council in his pocket.

"I first met Archie Thorne in grade school," Wardlaw began.

Beware of eulogies that begin with the word I, Emma thought.

"I was in the playground of Hampshire Elementary. I was a little overweight then ..." He gave the self-deprecating shrug of the experienced politician. "... Anyway, the playground bully, I kid you not, threw sand in my face. I didn't know Archie at the time. But guess who was the first person to intervene? You're right! Archie Thorne punched the bully right smack in the nose." He paused expectantly for a laugh. He got one, albeit more of a collective chuckle. "Since that time, up until Archie's untimely death last week, we have been the closest of friends."

Wardlaw droned on. After ten minutes of down-home folksiness, he got to his punchline.

For Emma, it was more of a punch than a punch line.

In a conclusion completely inappropriate to any funeral speech, Wardlaw ended by saying, "With the unanimous backing of the entire City Council, I'd like to announce that we have selected Emma Thorne to succeed her father to be the next chief of police of Hampshire. Congratulations, Emma!" He started the applause, and the assembled congregants followed wholeheartedly.

Emma was blindsided and furious. But she kept her expression impassive. She patted Pepper on the head to distract herself.

Father Ben organized the recessional. Led by Sergeant Stella Weeks, who looked shell-shocked, six members of the force lifted Archie's coffin to their shoulders. They marched slow-time toward the narthex. Emma left her pew and followed the coffin with Pepper glued to her left knee.

Shifting her eyes from side to side, she smiled at friends, neighbors, and many strangers.

Yet she felt completely alone.

The reception in the Barbagallo Community Room overflowed with well-wishers. Congratulations and condolences mixed in a Waring Blender blur. Kisses, handshakes, and hugs. A woman she'd never met before told her that it was a tribute to Archie that he had so many friends even though he was the chief of police. It was an odd thing to say, but it resonated with Emma.

She looked around for Dick Wardlaw. She had a few things to say to him. For the moment he wasn't anywhere to be found.

Emma felt a tap on her shoulder. "Um, hi. Guess it's been a while. How've you been? Except for all this, I mean." He waved an arm awkwardly.

She recognized him immediately. Ethan Jackson was still a good-looking guy. They had dated their junior year in high school. It was pretty easy to remember the first guy you slept with.

Before their "first time," Ethan had kept increasing the pressure on her. He'd cajoled. He begged. He swore he'd "done it" before. *Whatever it took in his seventeen-year-old mind.* Eventually she'd relented, and they'd had clumsy sex in the back of his mother's Honda Odyssey. It wasn't the end of the world, but Emma felt used, and she dumped him the next day.

"Emma, I just want to say that I'm, well, sorry about what happened, you know, back then." On the continuum of inappropriateness, Ethan had Dick Wardlaw beaten by miles. "And, of course, about your dad, too. And Will. Actually, things aren't going too well at home—"

"Ethan, this is not a good time," she said, keeping her voice low but pointed. "Actually, *really* a bad time. I'm burying my dad here. Right?"

When she saw her friend Deb Barger coming over, she gave Ethan the slip.

Deb brought her a cup of punch the color of lime Jell-O. Vanessa Mack gave her a restorative hug. The three agreed to meet soon.

The Fosters stopped briefly and offered cool condolences. Emma said, "Thank you so much for coming. It means a lot to me." But she said it to their backs, they moved away so quickly.

Will, ever polite, would have been aghast.

Emma excused herself from an informal line of people waiting to speak with her. She found the ladies room in the back of the community room. Thankfully it was empty. It gave her a chance to think about Wardlaw's "nomination." At first, she had been angry. Angry at being blindsided. And, truth be told, scared. There are only two people whose advice she needed to undertake such a daunting task. Neither one was available. Suddenly, she realized what would've been obvious to anyone else. Both Will and Archie would have, unequivocally, urged her to take the challenge. But she still wasn't sure. Being chief would be life-changing. But would it be good for her? She honestly didn't know. Oh, sure, she was flattered. That was only human. Still, she needed more time to think. She splashed water on her face; there was no makeup to ruin. Then, she marched back into the fray.

Almost immediately, she ran into Dick Wardlaw. He bear-hugged her, squashing her breasts against his chest. She was sure she felt him tilt his pelvis forward to make contact with hers. Defensively, she arched her back, keeping air between them. If it hadn't been Archie's funeral, she would've called him out on it. She took a backwards step. Wardlaw said, "Congratulations, Emma. I hope you're as happy as we are." His breath was foul, and she took another step backwards.

"I need to think about this, Mayor Wardlaw—"

"Dick! Please! Call me Dick. We're in this together."

"It's not that I'm ungrateful. You just took me by surprise." She tried to be as polite as possible under the circumstances. Hell, in the end she might just accept.

"Have to tell you the council's been pressing me to form a search committee. I had to go out on a limb offering you the job. You weren't exactly top of everyone's list. I'm sure you'll understand that I need your answer by tomorrow morning. That shouldn't be a problem, should it? Here, let me give you a kiss to encourage you to make the right decision." He aimed for her lips. She gave him the back of her head.

Finally, the ordeal was over. The kisses, the hugs, all the words … she needed a shower. Emma retrieved Pepper, who was waiting obediently by the door, and quickly drove home.

There was one other person whom Emma trusted to give her good advice.

She took off her funeral dress and put it into a pile for dry cleaning. Bra and panties went into the laundry hamper. She finally took that shower. Not an especially vain person, she still checked herself in the mirror. At thirty-six, she thought that she looked pretty good. She was slim and thin-waisted. Her girls, as Will affectionately called them, weren't too big and weren't too small. Just about right, she thought. Not exactly an hour-glass figure, but hey. Her overflowing brown hair was longer than your typical female cop's.

Tonight, she dressed down for a trip to her favorite bar. She just wanted to be alone, chill, and talk to Phil. She wore blue jeans and a navy turtleneck. Pepper and she drove to Hampshire's busiest bar, which was called Group Therapy.

Pepper was welcome at Group Therapy, despite a state law to the contrary. Phil Masters, the owner, was the welcoming sort. He wore a beaming smile and a handlebar mustache worthy of Wyatt Earp and didn't give a shit about rules. He greeted Emma with an extravagant wave. At 6:30 p.m. on a Saturday night, the joint was jammed. Emma glanced at the TVs. Baseball was on—Red Sox vs. Baltimore—no wonder it was busy. She took a stool at the bar. Pepper went off to greet humans she knew.

They were regulars.

Phil brought over a bottle of Lagunitas India Pale Ale ("homicidally hoppy" and "ruthlessly delicious" according to the brewer) and poured it into a frosted mug. "So sorry to hear about your dad. He was one-of-a-kind, old Archie. Broke the mold. I went to the service. Didn't get a chance to talk to you, though. By the way, congratulations, I guess. Archie's gonna be a tough act to follow."

"Thanks, man. I have to tell you, it's been tough."

Phil patted her hand. "No doubt it's been tough, but you're tough, too. You aren't Archie's girl for nothing. Have you decided yet?"

"How do you know I haven't decided?"

"Occupational hazard."

Phil had been a psychotherapist at the state prison in Rosedale before opening Group Therapy.

"What do you think I should do?"

"Let's look at the downside first. First, it'll wreck your life. You'll be on duty 24/7. You'll never be able to kick back your heels and get shit-faced. Second, the warm friendships you've enjoyed with some of your colleagues will cool. A few will resent your promotion, but everyone will treat you with wariness and keep their distance. Third, Archie's shoes are pretty damn big.

"On the upside, you have no choice, because it's what Will and Archie would've wanted."

Emma laughed out loud for the first time in forever. "Easy as that, huh?"

At the other end of the bar, someone banged his empty beer bottle on the bar. An out-of-towner, no doubt.

"Hold your horses!" Phil shouted. "Can't you see I'm talking to a lady?"

"You good?" Phil asked with a kind smile.

"Go take care of your business. Thanks, Phil."

9

An Untimely

Monday morning, while Emma was outside waiting for Pepper to pee, Mayor Wardlaw telephoned. He didn't trouble himself with pleasantries. "Are you ready to give me your decision?" Before she could answer, Wardlaw continued, "Honestly, how hard can being a police chief be? You just boss other people around."

"Yes," she said.

He prattled on as if she hadn't spoken.

"Frankly, I'd rather have someone with a degree in criminal justice running my department than a cop who rose through the ranks. Well, what's it gonna be?"

"Yes," Emma said again.

"Why that's just super!" Wardlaw exclaimed. "We are going to be a great team. Friends, too. We'll have this whole town by the balls." He chuckled. She could almost smell his breath.

It was more than a little freaky, but Will, in complicated ways and even more than Archie, had a lot to do with her decision. Other than the offer itself, Mayor Wardlaw had nothing to do with it.

Her swearing-in was scheduled for Wednesday afternoon at City Hall, in the same building as her new police department.

Monday and Tuesday, Emma continued her patrol duties, but she took the time to speak to as many of her colleagues she could button-hole, hoping to smooth any ruffled feathers and reassure folks that no dramatic changes were imminent. Ruby Sato, Archie's long-time administrative assistant and secret weapon, scheduled a fitting for her new uniform early Tuesday morning.

The swearing-in was brief, ending with two unavoidable kisses from Mayor Dick Wardlaw, one on each cheek. A few friends attended, Vanessa Mack, Deb Barger, and Phil Masters among them. The ceremony was mandatory for the department, except for those on patrol. The *Chronicle* photographer took a photo of the Mayor, Emma, and Pepper.

Thursday morning, outside her new office, Ruby handed Emma the *Hampshire Chronicle*. "Good morning, Chief, and welcome," she said. "Don't hesitate to let me know if there's anything I can do for you."

"Thanks. Please feel free to continue calling me Emma."

"With respect, you are Hampshire Car One now, and I'll call you Chief. I hope you'll expect everyone else to do the same." Ruby gave her a meaningful look.

Inside her new office, Emma sat in the very chair which Dad had occupied for so long. She felt pride and sadness at the same time.

Ruby had been busy. A prism-shaped, plastic name plaque was already on the desk: Emma Thorne, Chief of Police. Emma honestly thought it should read Emma Thorne, Rookie.

She picked up the paper.

Archie Thorne's Daughter Sworn In:
Hampshire's First Female Police Chief

She didn't mind that her name hadn't made the headline, but the omission reminded her of Phil Masters's remark about Archie's shoe size.

She didn't know quite what to do, her first day on the job. She'd brought with her a couple of personal items. A framed photograph of Will, her favorite fountain pen, a hairbrush, some deodorant, and a toothbrush and toothpaste. Pepper ran into the office in front of her. She placed her forepaws on Archie's chair and sniffed long and hard. Pepper, a fully certified police dog, now belonged to Emma. The Belgian Malinois had a black mask, a fawn coat as sleek as mink, and she wore four black leggings.

Watching her longing for Archie broke Emma's heart.

Emma looked away and studied her new office. It was definitely all-male, but she wouldn't be redecorating anytime soon. A collection of antique, model police cars gathered dust on one shelf. On another, a Red Sox baseball signed by David "Big Papi" Ortiz.

His brag photos, as she thought such photos ought rightly to be called, lined the walls: Dad in dress uniform with four gold stars on his collars standing with the governor, Dad with the state attorney general, and Dad, six years ago, proudly posing, a master and his police dog, at Pepper's graduation from K-9 school.

Emma had also brought last weekend's Sunday *New York Times Magazine*.

If anyone dropped by, she hoped they would knock before entering. She didn't want to get caught noodling a crossword her first day as chief. Emma liked to start with the long, theme clues, which, today, all had something to do with "Conquest." The clue to twenty-three across was Director Leni's 4th Film (sixteen letters, four words). She chewed the end of her ballpoint and thought for a moment, but there was no reason to hurry anymore. There was nobody to compete with. Before their former lives came to a cataclysmic end, Will and she had reserved Sunday mornings for a rollicking crossword puzzle race. Pencils prohibited. They played it in bed.

Emma had reason to remember the film's title. She printed the answer. "Triumph of the Will."

She remembered, in the early days of their marriage, she used to participate in a three-way race. Georgia, Will, and Emma. When Emma beat them both, as she often did, Georgia became so angry she quit coming.

Emma glanced at the portrait of him she'd brought to work. It was taken on their wedding day. The desiccated leather of the frame was as worn as the hope that she would see him again. She still could not accept that he was dead. The only other explanation was that Will had run away. But that was the unlikeliest reason of all, because Will was too accustomed to his creature comforts. She didn't mean to be unkind, but, without his Platinum card, Will would be like a cop without a gun.

As she often did, she stared at his picture, asking the same questions over and over. The beautiful man in the picture remained mum. As the camera's shutter had opened that day, their future had seemed impossibly auspicious. Will of the wavy brown hair, leading-man good looks, and the easy, ready smile. He was a yummy man. They had been invincible. No more. She missed him so much. She loved him more.

A new idea was percolating, but it would have to wait until she'd eased into her new job.

It was a Sunday morning, and Emma had volunteered for duty, primarily to set a good example. She was still easing into the responsibilities of her new job. She retrieved the unfinished crossword puzzle from a pile on her desk looking for another theme clue to answer.

From the radio mounted on her desk, a stutter of static interrupted. "Car 4, respond to number 103 Hickam Street for an untimely. 46-year-old male. Cold response."

In the well of her desk, Pepper pounded her tail against the floor. She had heard the dispatch, too. Worried that Emma wouldn't bring her along, Pepper nuzzled Emma's leg.

A moment later there was a rap on the frosted glass of her office door. She quickly stashed the puzzle. From the silhouette, it was Sergeant Stella Weeks, who was as short as Lady Gaga, and more manipulative than Lady Macbeth.

Weeks opened the door. Perhaps to compensate for her stature, she wore her blue uniform blouse a size too small, thus emphasizing her generous chest. Attached to her Sam Browne belt were more accoutrements than any cop should have to carry: a good twenty-five pounds-worth. Glock 19, handcuffs, flashlight, latex gloves, collapsible baton, portable radio, pepper spray, a bubblegum-pink Taser, and enough magazine pouches to hold off SEAL Team 6.

She believed that as senior sergeant, she was Archie Thorne's obvious successor. Stella had been openly hostile after the funeral. She bore her defeat with uncompromising bitterness. Tennessee Williams wasn't the only reason that Emma wanted to scream *Stella!* every time she saw her.

"I'm responding to the untimely. We just got a second 911, turns out it's Ethan Jackson. I understand you knew him. Just sayin'." She winked at Emma.

She heard the clamor of Stella's boots on the stairs.

But the dispatch got her attention. Time to start being a police chief.

What on earth could have happened? She remembered Ethan had seemed shaky at Archie's funeral.

She swung her feet off the desk and grabbed her once-worn chief's cap. Followed by Pepper, whose tail was cork-screwing, she went downstairs to her unmarked police interceptor sedan. Even as a beginner police chief (which, when she thought about it, was a pretty funny oxymoron), Emma thought it was silly that her car was known as a "police interceptor sedan," when everyone knew it was just a gussied-up Ford Taurus.

103 Hickam Street was in the Northwood section of Hampshire. Newish construction, the central part of Ethan's house was A-framed with a cathedral ceiling and a wall of windows facing Hickam Street. It reeked McMansion. Emma preferred older, smaller houses. Behind Ethan's was the golf course of the Hampshire Country Club.

Stella Weeks's SUV was in the driveway along with another HPD vehicle and the ambulance. The dispatch had been for a "cold" response, which meant no lights, no siren, but Stella's light bar was lit up like a Walmart at night. It was raining, but a small group of neighbors rubber-necked at not a whole lot.

She let the dispatcher know of her arrival. As she parked, Max Beyersdorf opened Ethan's front door and walked toward her car. Emma thought Max was the smartest of her bevy of officers. Max was built like a linebacker, but he was charmingly anxious to please. He sported a fuzzy crewcut, making him look like a Bichon Frisé with a pet trim.

"Uh, Chief, he's BART—"

"Pretty stinky, eh?"

Bart was cop-speak for a Body Assuming Room Temperature.

Max offered her a small jar of Vicks VapoRub.

After she dabbed a dollop of Vicks under each nostril, Emma asked, "How did he do it?"

"Poor bastard hung himself."

"Hanged," she corrected reflexively.

"Either way, he's dead."

10

A Sharpie

Sergeant Weeks met Emma at the front door. She handed her paper booties and a pair of purple nitrile gloves. Pepper walked in barefoot, keeping her shoulder next to Emma's left knee. Dad had explained: "Dog heels on the left, it keeps your gun hand free."

She remembered the course she'd taken at the University of New Haven, Crime Scene Processing. The teacher had emphasized, "Treat all suicide scenes as crime scenes."

Sergeant Weeks said, "A suicide is treated as a crime scene. Follow me, and please don't touch anything."

Yes, Stella.

"It's pretty cut and dried. Suicide by hanging. No note. At least, we can't find one. I let the medical examiner's office know. They may send somebody, or they may not. After that, the funeral home will remove the body and hold it until the ME picks it up for autopsy. All suicides get an autopsy."

Emma listened to Stella without comment.

Not including the deceased, Emma counted six people and a dog in the living room. There were two Hampshire EMTs, Detective Larry "Buzz" Buzzucano, who was taking photographs with a Canon Rebel, Sergeant Weeks, and Max. She gave Pepper the command Down. Without a flicker of hesitation, Pepper extended her forelegs, folded her haunches, and lay motionless.

Under Stella's watchful eye, Emma directed her attention to Ethan. She hadn't had any contact with Ethan since high school, excepting Archie's funeral. She knew that he'd made a boatload of money on some tech company. She'd never loved Ethan, but she couldn't walk back that they had once been intimate. She now regretted her dismissal of his overtures at the funeral. What had he said? Something about things not going well at home. They sure weren't.

She was viewing the body from behind. He had tied the suicide rope around a ceiling truss. His body hung from a classic hangman's noose with the knot placed against the left side of his head. He wore boxer shorts. The rest of his clothes were neatly folded on the sofa. A pink sweater, pressed khaki pants, tasseled loafers, and red socks. He looked like he had been dressed for a country club brunch.

Ethan must have measured carefully, because his toes were no more than six inches above the carpet. An eight-foot step ladder lay on the floor where it had smashed through a glass-topped coffee table. Looking at the body was disturbing, but she found herself adjusting to the reality that she was in charge. That she, Emma Thorne, was actually the Chief of Police. No one else's decisions, not even Stella's, mattered. The scene (and future scenes) were hers and hers alone. She bore the responsibility for success as well as all the risks of failure.

On another note, Emma was grateful for Max's VapoRub. Ethan had shat in his boxers, excrement stained his thighs, and the camphor and menthol helped mask the smell.

His tall corpse swayed almost imperceptibly at the end of the long rope, giving the scene the eerie quality of a *tableau vivant*. But Ethan's eyes and mouth were squeezed permanently shut. She guessed he no longer wished to see or taste his world.

Not surprisingly, her thoughts turned to Will. Had he found some secret place in the middle of a state forest? There were plenty around Hampshire. Was he hanging from some tree, already infested with maggots, not to be found for months, maybe even years?

She barely managed to shake that thought away.

She did a 360 around Ethan's corpse. Stella was right: Ethan's death seemed straightforward. She must be hardening to the scene. Speaking of hardening, Ethan had an erection underneath his boxers. Noticing her stare, one of the EMTs stepped forward. "It's called a postmortem priapism, Chief. It's pretty common in hangings. When you see one, it's an indicator that the death was swift and violent, whatever the cause."

"Thanks for the tutorial. And I'm not being sarcastic."

"No sarcasm taken." He smiled. "By the way, EMTs call it Angel Lust."

"I never heard that one."

Emma turned to Pepper and gave the Search command. Her nose to the floor, Pepper started with the outside of the room. She made ever smaller concentric circles, sniffing doggedly, until she was right under the corpse. She took some deep sniffs of Ethan's bare feet. Emma didn't think that Pepper had found anything conclusive, but she knew that the smells in that room were permanently imprinted in her memory banks.

"Hey Buzz," she called, "do you have all the photographs we're going to need?"

"Should be good to go, Chief. How about fingerprints? Want me to dust the place?"

"That shouldn't be necessary," Stella piped up.

Emma thought about that and tended to agree. "Alright, I guess."

Emma poked around the living room. She spotted a framed, black and white photograph of Ethan sitting beside a very attractive woman and a blond boy who looked about ten. Picking it up, Emma asked Stella if she had been able to contact Ethan's wife.

"Sure have, Chief, she and her son are upstairs in the bedroom."

"What? It would have saved me some worry if you'd mentioned that."

"I've already spoken to her. Naturally, she's very upset—"

"*I* would like to talk to her."

"I'll show you the way." Stella started for the stairs.

"Alone," Emma said.

Stella said, "Considering your past relationship with the deceased, you might want to consider recusing yourself and letting me handle this."

Emma saw this for what it was, her first test. "As I said, alone."

She didn't want to pour gasoline on Stella's flame, but Stella needed to know who was in charge.

The bedroom door was ajar, and she could hear two people weeping. She tapped softly with a gloved knuckle. Mrs. Jackson invited her in. She was holding her son in both arms as they sat on the edge of the bed. Emma studied Ethan's wife, who was as attractive as her photo. She wondered if Mrs. Jackson had any inkling that she was Ethan's first sexual partner.

"Mrs. Jackson, I'm Emma Thorne. May I have a word with you?"

"Of course, I understand," she said. "Call me Mary, and this is Julian. We call him JJ." She dabbed her eyes with a well-used Kleenex. Julian didn't look up. "I heard that you'd gotten Archie's job."

Outside the window, Emma could see a copse of greening saplings behind the house on the border with the golf course. The trees looked like they had been recently planted. Does a man plant trees and then commit suicide?

"I am very sorry for your loss—"

"There is absolutely no way Ethan would have done this," she began. "No effing way. Somebody killed him." Her voice rose. "We were so happy. Jesus, we were planning to go hiking this afternoon! Weren't we, JJ? I'm telling you, somebody did this to Ethan."

"Do you feel up to answering a few questions? Or, would you rather I come back later."

She gave her a sharp look. "What do you want to know?"

"Who found Mr. Jackson?"

"JJ has baseball practice on Sunday mornings—the Northwest League—we left early. I usually get Ethan to take him, but I let him sleep in this morning. JJ is the star of his team. His dad is so proud of him."

"Were you the one who found your husband, Mary?"

"We stopped for breakfast in Waconia. JJ really likes eggs, bacon, and home fries after practice." She spoke of her son as if he were 8-years-old, although he looked considerably older. Emma guessed fifteen. "I suppose we got home around 11:00, maybe 11:15. That's when we found him." She dabbed the corners of her eyes again. Julian still hadn't raised his head from her bosom. Mary stared at her. She was a remarkably beautiful woman. Her blue eyes unwavering. "I want you to find out who did this ... to him ... to *us*."

"I can promise you we will find out everything we can."

"Is that it?"

"I have a few more questions. Would you like to speak in private?"

"No! JJ stays with me." She hugged him tighter. Emma still hadn't seen the kid's face.

"Alright then. Your decision. Has your husband been feeling himself lately? Any depression or changes of mood? Headaches? Deviations from routine? Anything that might make you think he would want to hurt himself?"

"Look, just stop it. Ethan is the happiest man I know. He's successful, handsome, well-liked. He drives a goddamn Porsche. No, we don't have any financial problems or marital problems or any other kind of problems. And don't you people always ask how our sex life is? *Well, we have fantastic sex all the goddamn time!"*

She stood up. Julian rolled away from her, sobbing.

Her eyes squinted and hardened. "You of all people should know how good a fuck Ethan is."

"Mary—"

"Now please leave us alone! You've upset my son. We want to grieve in peace."

Emma felt terrible for her, but felt she had to speak plainly.

"I'm sorry I've caused you anguish, both then and now. But, as to the matter at hand, we will fully investigate your husband's death. I promise you."

"Please, would you just leave!"

Downstairs, the EMTs were still hanging around. Detective Buzzucano was packing his camera away. He said, "Chief, the medical examiner's guys will be here soon." Max stood by the door.

Sergeant Weeks said, "We heard some shouting. You handling everything okay?"

"She's as upset as anyone would be."

Emma reexamined Ethan, doing another, slower 360.

She studied him more closely this go 'round. He seemed a little less smelly.

Sergeant Weeks said to the EMTs, "Why don't you guys take off? We're all set here."

While they were leaving the room, Emma noticed something she had missed earlier. On the inside of Ethan's left ankle, there appeared to be a tattoo. She peered closer. It was red; it looked like the numeral 7; yet it wasn't faded like a typical tattoo. She took his ankle in her gloved hand and pulled it toward her nose. The odor was unmistakable. She was certain that the 7 had been freshly drawn with a Sharpie.

"Hey, Buzz," she called. "Did you get a shot of this?"

Detective Buzzucano stepped forward. "I think so."

To Emma, that sounded like a no. "Do me a favor then," she said, "can you give me a nice, new close-up of that with a ruler in the frame?"

Sergeant Weeks stepped forward, too. "What do you make of it?"

"I dunno," Emma said. "Did you notice it before?"

"Of course."

"I'm wondering why a suicide would draw a number on his ankle. And why he would draw it upside down, so we could read it as a 7. If he drew it for himself, wouldn't it be an **L**?"

"Chief, with all due respect, you're not making a helluva lot of sense."

"All I know is it must be important. Why, I'm not yet sure."

Stella harrumphed.

Emma looked around the living room some more, poking through the drawers and cabinets, but did not turn up a Sharpie. She stripped off her gloves. She wondered if Mary Jackson's words were the hope-against-hope sentiments of a suicide-widow-in-denial, or was Ethan a truly happy guy with no reason to kill himself? She would have to think on that ... and find out.

"Okay, guys," she finally said, "We're done here. What time are the body snatchers coming?"

Buzz said, "About an hour, the M.E.s office said."

"Let's cut him down, then. Get him ready."

11

A Moist Palm

Stella Weeks took the wheel of her cruiser and steered back to Police Headquarters. The roads were slick. It was still raining, and the wipers squeaked annoyingly, leaving streaks on the windshield. Buzz Buzzucano sat in the passenger seat. Max sat in the backseat, where the prisoners are kept behind a barricade of Plexiglas with holes in it known as the "cage."

Stella resumed her daily diatribe, "She's so fucking annoying. Why's she want to go investigating the poor bastard's death. The guy offed himself. End of story."

Buzz grunted.

"And she sits around doing crossword puzzles in ink, thinking she's so smart."

"No shit," Max said, "she does 'em in ink?"

"Not to mention bragging about this college degree and that grad school degree every other time she opens her mouth like she could win on 'Wheel of Fortune.'"

"I've never heard her brag about her degrees," Max piped up.

"Shut up, Kraut," Buzz and Stella said, more or less simultaneously.

"My personal feeling is that if you're smart enough to go to college," Stella said, "and you end up a cop, there's something definitely off about you."

Max said, "She is the chief, guys, at least give her that. And she's smart."

Stella turned half-way around in her seat. "Kraut, if you can't contribute to the on-going topic of this conversation, kindly zip it. Okay? Anyway, she shouldn't be the chief."

"And that's the rub," Max muttered, "because you're sounding like a five-year-old."

"I heard that."

"On another subject," Buzz said, "what do you make of that mark on Ethan's ankle? You noticed it, didn't you?"

"Of course, I did. Said so, didn't I?"

"I didn't spot it. But, whatever. It does seem sort of weird. I have a hunch she might be onto something there."

"Doubt it," Stella said.

There was another reason Stella had it in for Emma, but it was not something she would ever share with Buzz. And certainly not Max.

Stella turned right onto Main Street. Without saying anything, she flicked on her light bar, tapped her horn twice, causing the siren to whoop-whoop, and pulled over a red Toyota Tacoma.

Max asked, "Why're you pulling him over?"

"It's raining."

"So?"

"No headlights. Sections 14-96a to 14-96aa, inclusive."

E mma stopped at Broken River Park to give Pepper a run. The rain was sheeting. They braved the park alone. Thoughtfully, Pepper peed and pooped without taking her sweet time about it. "Good girl, Pepper."

They drove toward headquarters. On the north side of Main Street, which included Town Hall and Police Headquarters, a variety of commercial establishments, some open, many closed, stretched for several miles. She passed The Gibson, the movie theater where she and Will went for their first date. They hadn't watched much of "American Beauty," as they were busy kissing in the back row.

Main Street was a strip-mall before they had a word for it.

She noticed a new sign on one of the derelict mill buildings: "Artist Lofts for Rent." The landlord had some work left. Most of the windows were broken.

Emma thought about the town she had sworn to protect and keep safe. Hampshire was fifty miles square with a population of twenty-four thousand. Despite the griminess of downtown, there was a rich section. At the top of the township sat the enclave of Northwood, where well-to-do folks like Ethan Jackson lived.

Her sister-in-law Georgia lived on the outskirts of town in an even more exclusive and secluded area called Wentworth.

Sooner or later, Emma knew that she would have to try to repair the open rift between her and her sister-in law. Georgia had been clear enough that she blamed her for Will's depression and, worse, for his disappearance. Emma's last encounter with Georgia at the Fosters' lake house still rankled.

At the corner of Main Street and Sachem Avenue, Emma witnessed a fender-bender: a teen-aged boy in a beater struck the rear end of a sedan driven by an elderly gent. She flicked on her concealed LEDs and pulled protectively behind the accident. After ascertaining there were no injuries, she called it in. "1 to dispatch. On scene with a two-car MVA, negative injuries. Dispatch Car 4 to take the call. She should be in the area."

She had barely taken her thumb off the transmit button when she heard Stella broadcast: "Negative, dispatch. We're on a 10-59. Unable to respond." *Damn*, Emma thought. A 10-59 was a minor traffic stop. She would have to wait on-scene until another cruiser arrived.

B ack at headquarters, Emma poured herself a cup of coffee in the empty canteen. Pepper and she climbed the steps back to her office.

She took a sip of muddy coffee, picked up her ballpoint, and re-opened the *Times* magazine section to the puzzle page. Emma would have been horrified if she had known that Stella Weeks had noticed her using a ballpoint pen. The next themed-clue (sixteen letters, four words) was "King Riggs." She quickly penned in "Battle of the Sexes." She filled out a few more answers. By the time she had completed the upper left quadrant, she lost her focus and turned her attention back to Ethan Jackson.

The unexplained mark on his ankle tugged at the suspicious gene which she had inherited from her father. She made a decision. First thing tomorrow morning, she would telephone the state medical examiner and discuss it with him.

At 5:45 p.m., Emma decided to call it a day. After changing out of her uniform, she and Pepper ducked out through the underground garage where the cops brought in arrestees. In her town-issued Taurus, they drove home.

She uncapped a beer and sipped it outside in the garden. Pepper joined her. She rolled over on her back exposing her tummy for a rub, which she received. Luxuriating, she snorted with pleasure.

Meantime, Emma reveled in the warm, late afternoon. She loved when the days became longer. Spring was a glorious time in Hampshire. Her newly mowed grass smelled delicious and peaceful. She was able to put work and worries aside.

She took a last sip of beer "Want to go to Group Therapy?"

Pepper was too relaxed to move.

"Well I'm going anyway."

Emma laughed as Pepper leapt to her feet.

Phil Masters greeted Emma with a kiss, which was unusual but welcome. She kissed him back. As usual, Pepper wandered off.

"How goes it?" Phil asked. "Awful news about Ethan Jackson. I didn't see that coming."

"Had he been in recently?"

"Yeah. Friday night. I have to say, he did not seem on the brink." Phil raised an eyebrow. "Actually, he was having drinks with a lady I didn't recognize."

"Really?" Emma raised an eyebrow.

"I wouldn't read too much into it. Looked pretty innocent to me."

"Doesn't sound like a guy on the brink, to use your word."

Phil didn't hear that last bit. He was off to serve other customers.

Emma heard someone say to the guy sitting next to her, "Hey, man, do you mind giving up your stool. I'd like to sit next to this beautiful lady here."

Dismayed, she recognized the voice of Dick Wardlaw.

Her next-door neighbor moved without complaint. Wardlaw had that effect on people.

"Hi, Emma, how goes it?" he said.

Mayor Wardlaw was pushing seventy and had an elaborate combover. He had a gray mole on his upper lip, for which he couldn't be blamed, but nor could it be called a beauty mark. He was famous for glad-handing everyone and taking credit for anything good that happened in town.

"Oh, hi Dick, please do have a seat." Wardlaw was immune to sarcasm.

"How're you getting on, Chief?"

"I'm taking things day by day. I have lots to learn, and I'm learning a lot. Right now, I'm just trying to chill."

"Well, let me 'chill' with you. Call it a boss's prerogative," he added, baring yellow teeth in what passed as a smile.

Pepper returned from her walk-about, sniffed the trousers of Dick's tweed suit, refrained from wagging, and curled up next to Emma's stool. Dick didn't seem to notice.

"That was a big shame about Ethan. His wife called me about an hour ago. She said she was a little put off by your questions. She also said she's sure Ethan didn't kill himself. What do you think?"

"I can't discuss an open case. You of all people should know that."

"You can with me." He placed a moist palm on top of hers. "You can always talk to me."

She pulled at her hand, but he had it clamped to the sticky bar top.

Wardlaw plowed ahead undaunted. "You're a very beautiful woman, Emma. I love the way you do your hair. It's so sophisticated for little old Hampshire. You and I could be better friends. You know that, don't you?"

"Dick, I am married—"

"Not really." The yellow teeth made her reel.

"That is a despicable thing to say," she said. "Please let go of my hand."

He lifted his hand and stood up. Then he leaned over and whispered to her. She could smell whiskey and tooth decay. "You may regret speaking to me in that manner. Good night, Emma."

Phil sidled up. "Looks like you need another."

"No, I think we'll head home."

"Stop it. Don't let that pig get to you. Besides, he's gone."

"Thanks Phil, you always give me good advice. I think I *will* stay."

No matter, Phil was already pouring her another IPA.

"Any of my predictions come true yet?" Emma knew what he was talking about.

"Stella Weeks hates me. But you weren't quite right about that, because Stella's always hated me. You know Stella, right?"

Phil guffawed. "The spark plug with tits? Sure do."

The door to Group Therapy opened. It was the kind of place where everybody turned to check out a new arrival. Phil and Emma did too.

"Speaking of tits …" As he moved away, Phil added, "Good luck."

Georgia, Will's fraternal twin, marched straight toward her.

She stood squarely in Emma's personal space. A sneer on her face.

Emma looked up at her from her barstool.

Georgia Foster was the fuck-up to Will's success story. Georgia was nearly as tall as her brother, almost six feet, which made her an imposing woman. She was obsessed about her physique, Emma knew, and had the muscles to prove it. That night she wore a turquoise western-style shirt tapered to accentuate her skinny waist, a fashion mode not often seen in Hampshire. Her biceps strained the sleeves, and her mountainous boobs threatened to pop the front snaps open. Emma thought they looked as hard as boccie balls, but Will swore they were real.

Georgia didn't hold back. "I still can't understand why Will would want to leave a lovely wife like you."

Sighing, Emma said, "I don't want to fight with you. I really don't."

Georgia folded her arms across her ample chest, and, if possible, leaned even closer. "What if *I* do?"

"Do me a favor and let me finish my beer in peace."

"No, I'm not done with you. Will is better off without you. I guarantee he's in a better place, and thank heaven you don't know where."

Standing suddenly, Emma went toe-to-toe with Georgia. "Back off. I am so sick of your shit. Nobody—not Frank and Joan, and certainly not you—is more devastated about Will than I am. So, stuff that right up your ass."

Georgia spat in Emma's face, leaving a glob of phlegm on her cheek. Georgia also spat the hideous word, "Cunt."

Emma heard a low growl at her feet, but, before anything worse could happen, Georgia spun on her heel. Emma was tempted, but she chose not to follow.

Pushing people aside, Georgia stormed out of Group Therapy yelling "Get out of my fucking way!"

From behind the bar, Phil shouted, "Hey, no foul language in my bar, asshole!"

Between Wardlaw and Georgia, Emma had had enough. She signaled to Pepper and left without saying goodbye to Phil.

She drove directly into her garage, leaving the door open. Pepper jumped out and found a spot outside to do her business. Ten minutes later, Emma was under the covers, wishing that was where she'd been all evening. When she couldn't sleep, she took one of Will's leftover Ambiens.

Boom, she was in dreamland.

Emma recognized Will in the distance. He was at the first-class check-in station about to speak with a chicly-dressed Qantas employee, who wore a navy and red uniform with a splash of hot pink the same color as her lipstick.

Will was in the Tom Bradley International Terminal at LAX. Emma moved closer so she could hear. She stood behind a column and peeked through a potted plant, B-movie-style.

"Good evening, Mr. and Mrs. Goodwin. May I see your passports please?"

Mrs.? Oh, Jesus.

Emma separated the plant's leaves further. She didn't care if Will saw her. She had to see what Mrs. Goodwin looked like.

"One way to Sydney? Is that correct?"

"That is true," said Mrs. Goodwin in some sort of Scandinavian accent. Emma got a good look at her. She was stunning. Blonde hair done up in a French twist like she was in a goddamn wedding. There was a gold wedding band on her finger, guarded by a ring with a rock. She was trim, tall, and tanned. Honeymoon in the Seychelles? Bali? Phuket?

Even without her spike heels (red leather), she would have been taller than Emma. Even without makeup, and she wore little, Mrs. Goodwin was more beautiful than any woman had a right to be. Her long straight nose, her turquoise eyes, her fulsome lips … she oozed perfection.

The Qantas lady said, "I'll call the first-class lounge. It's on the fifth floor. Let them know you're coming."

Will said, "That won't be necessary, but thank you. We have a room at the Sheraton. Don't we, love?" Mrs. Goodwin smiled. Her fucking teeth were perfect.

Will collected their boarding passes and passports. They left the terminal and caught a taxi. Emma followed their cab to the Sheraton on Airport Boulevard.

Emma was not a phobic person, but she suffered from a mild form of acrophobia. She was therefore proud that she was able to climb up to their sixth-floor balcony on the outside of the building. They hadn't bothered to close the curtains, and Emma was shocked at the speed at which Will removed Mrs. Goodwin's dress.

She wore the kind of underwear Emma knew Will loved, black and lacy. He had those off in a flash, too. Will's pants quickly followed.

Her crotch was hairless, and naturally her boobs were perfect with zero sag and nipples that aimed impossibly toward the stars.

In a sudden violent motion, Will threw her over the edge of the bed. He slapped her ass hard and repeatedly, leaving red marks on her buttocks. He separated her ass cheeks and drilled into Mrs. Goodwin.

Will kept pounding her until Emma couldn't watch any more.

Emma backed up against the railing of the balcony. She felt herself falling, and she did nothing to save herself. Her spine bent over the balustrade, and she plunged toward the parking lot six floors below.

Her last thought before she hit the tarmac was, if only I'd known what Will wanted ...

12

Fiskars

Emma woke with an Ambien hangover and unpleasant memories of the previous evening. Dick Wardlaw overtly harassing her. Her dustup with Georgia. She'd also had a disturbing dream about Will.

Over breakfast, Emma telephoned the state medical examiner.

Dr. Herbert Mittendorf was a well-known forensic pathologist, in Connecticut and beyond. He had testified at high profile criminal trials. Emma had seen him interviewed on television several times.

She identified herself.

"Yes, I read about you in the paper. You're the new police chief in Hampshire. I knew your dad. He was a fine man. What can I do for you?"

"We had an untimely yesterday—"

"Yeah, I just read the police report. Suicide by hanging. We'll do an autopsy because of the age of the deceased. My guys picked up the body."

"There was something that bothered me, something I wonder if you'd take a close look at? Let me know what you think?"

"Hmm. So, you're thinking there's something hinky going on?"

"Well, as you know, Dr. Mittendorf, I'm new to the job. I feel I need to cover my bases."

"What did you notice?"

She thought for a moment. "There was a mark on the deceased's left ankle. I'm not even sure what it was, but I definitely smelled the ink from a Sharpie."

"I use Sharpies all the time. I know what you mean about the smell. It's distinctive." She heard the shuffle of papers over the phone. "By the way, there's no mention of the mark in the police report."

"You're kidding."

"No, not kidding. No mention of a mark in the police report. I mean, you either saw it or you didn't."

"Who signed the report? I haven't seen it yet."

"Let's see." More shuffling. "It's signed by Sergeant S. Weeks, badge number 41, and a Detective L. Buzzucano, badge number 32."

"Okay, I'll look into the omission."

Even as she fumed, she tried to sound measured.

Mittendorf said, "I have an idea. Why don't you come and observe the autopsy? Then, we can say hello properly. I'd like to put a face to Archie's daughter. I admired your dad."

Emma had never witnessed an autopsy. It was one thing to see your old boyfriend hanging from the rafters but quite another to see him being dissected. But she understood the imperatives of her new job.

"I'll be there. Tell me when and where."

"I've scheduled his procedure for tomorrow at 10:00 a.m."

"Um, Dr. Mittendorf, I have a question for you of a personal nature."

"Shoot."

"Do you know of a good private investigator you could recommend?"

Mittendorf laughed. "Don't you do your own investigations?"

"This is something that the department has already investigated, now a cold case," she said vaguely.

"That sounds mysterious. Although I have never had cause to hire an investigator," he said archly, "I know a guy whom other people respect. Name's Mark Byrne, based in Hartford. I'm sure you can find him online." Emma could hear someone speaking in the background. "Whoops, gotta go. See you tomorrow."

She didn't bother to replace the receiver before making her next call.

"Weeks," Stella answered.

"Sergeant Weeks ..." She usually called her Stella. "... this is the chief. Why didn't you include a description and photograph of the mark on Ethan Jackson's ankle in your report? And, secondly, why didn't I see your report before it went out? Lastly, why did I have to find this out from Dr. Mittendorf?"

"Like I told you, Chief, Buzz and I didn't think it was worth mentioning. I mean, why make this a big deal? The dude's got a mark on his ankle, but he's still swinging in the wind. Know what I mean?"

"In the future, I want to see every report you write before you fax it out of this office."

"Okey dokey, ma'am. Is that all?"

Emma hung up. Pepper snorted as if she had been following the conversation. She gave Pepper a scratch on her backside with the toe of her boot, which made Emma feel marginally less annoyed. But Stella remained the pebble in her shoe.

Stella would drive her crazy if she let her. Her talent for finding which of Emma's buttons to press was uncanny. In retaliation, Emma pushed Sergeant Weeks firmly out of her mind.

Emma felt the need to get back to what made her hurt deep inside.

She knew it was time—one more time—to look into Will's disappearance. For his sake and for hers. She couldn't give up yet. Will was the sinkhole in her life. *God, I miss him,* she thought.

The irony was she could not have taken the P.I. route with Archie still alive. He would have been furious that she'd consider employing a private detective over their own police force.

She found Byrne's number on switchboard.com.

He answered in a gravelly voice, "This is Mark Byrne. Who's calling?" He sounded like pastrami on rye with a kosher dill pickle spear.

She explained that she was interested in finding a private investigator and why. He agreed to drive to Hampshire and meet with her. But he said, "I've got to be honest with you, Chief, if you cops can't find him, I'm not sure what I can do, but I'll give it a try."

She couldn't blame Mark Byrne for not sounding enthusiastic, but somehow Emma felt better for the call.

It was a forty-minute drive to the state medical examiner's office. The entire way her brain swam with grotesque images of squishy organs floating in pools of blood. She had read about the famous Y-incision in Kay Scarpetta novels. She feared it would be quite another matter to witness one.

Dr. Mittendorf's office was in a modern glass and granite building. It was Tuesday morning, a few minutes before ten o'clock. Dr. Mittendorf's assistant led her down a long hallway. They passed a leggy blonde woman, whom Emma couldn't help but stare at. She was attractive, and she wore a gray T-shirt with OCME Investigator silkscreened front and back. The assistant noticed and said to Emma, "Maria's one of our Medicolegal Death Investigators."

"No kidding."

"Actually, it's a very important job," she said huffily. "Our investigators are highly trained and important members of our team."

"I didn't mean any disrespect."

The assistant deposited her in a small room outside Mittendorf's office, where she was asked to wait. Piles of magazines, *People*, *Martha Stewart Living*, and *Architectural Digest*, littered the coffee table just like at her gynecologist's office.

After a short wait, Dr. Mittendorf greeted her. "So, you are Archie's daughter! I'm so happy to meet you. Follow me." He was an older man with shiny button eyes, longish white hair, and a ruddy face.

He led her down another long hall to a flight of stairs that descended to the basement. He stopped in front of a small open-doored closet. Dr. Mittendorf handed her a yellow gown with built-in plastic booties, nitrile gloves, a face mask, and a paper bonnet. She had the devil of a time getting her cop shoes into the booties. Being nervous didn't help.

Mittendorf smiled and held out his hand to help her balance. "Have you ever been to an autopsy before?" He glanced at her face and continued without pause, "Obviously not. Well, don't you worry, we'll take it slow, see how you're making out. Don't be embarrassed if you need to leave. Everyone reacts differently. Here let me help you." She was struggling to tie the paper strings of her mask behind her head. "There, how's that?"

Fully gowned, they pushed through a set of swinging doors. She didn't know exactly what she was expecting. Perhaps a small, quiet room with a human-sized stainless-steel sink and lots of knives, scalpels, and other tools of the trade.

Instead, Emma walked into a chaotic factory. Gleaming white walls, about a million watts of fluorescent candle-power, and she counted five autopsies being performed simultaneously by five teams. "Believer" by Imagine Dragons pounded from a boom box. Corpses in body bags on rolling gurneys were parked every which way. They reminded her of an RV park after a tornado. Behind them was a massive refrigerator door covered with cartoons. Medical examiner humor, she supposed. In the far corner of the room was a human skeleton hanging by a hook screwed into its skull. The skeleton wore a lab coat and a face mask.

A photographer on a rolling ladder was shooting pictures of a corpse she recognized, Ethan Jackson.

Mittendorf said, "Welcome to our little world."

Surprisingly, the room didn't smell. No fecal matter, no formaldehyde. Ethan's living room had smelled worse than the autopsy room did. She followed Mittendorf to Ethan's body. Emma averted her eyes from the work going on around her. She felt queasy and labored to will the sensation away. Sweat drenched her back and armpits.

Mittendorf pointed to Ethan's neck. "You can see the ligature marks from the rope here." Ethan's gruesome necklace had turned the reddish-brown color of a horse chestnut. He moved Ethan's head to the side. "This is the furrow." He pointed to a bruised channel from Ethan's neck up the side of his head. "This proves he was not garroted."

Emma studied Ethan's neck with horrid fascination.

"The victim may have had some medical training, or he did a lot of Googling," Mittendorf said, "because he mimicked a 'judicial hanging,' which the British invented in 1872 to afford victims a more humane death. Here, Emma, you can see the hyperflexion of the neck caused by the British-style eyelet." He pointed. "He positioned the noose under the left angle of the jaw. That, combined with the drop, serves to jerk the person's head backwards and sideways, which causes fractures of the neck vertebrae—ideally between C2 and C3. It leads to immediate unconsciousness and not the agonizingly slow death of asphyxiation. I'm guessing when we open him up, that's precisely what we'll find."

"Oh."

Mittendorf spent more time examining the ligature marks around Ethan's neck, while Jennifer, the photographer, took photographs.

"Okay, Jen, that's enough for now. Let's move him to my station." To Emma, he said, "We'll do a head-to-toe under the lights. Look at your Sharpie mark."

Two assistants wheeled the body over to the work station. They hefted it over the railing of the stainless-steel sink and dropped him. His head thunked on the steel. Emma recoiled, until she thought about it. *Get over yourself.* Ethan's dead. He's just a lump of skin, bones, and meat.

She thought that her revised reaction would help steel her for the cutting to come. She hoped so. She wasn't looking forward to First Cut.

Dr. Mittendorf started a thorough head-to-toe examination.

Emma held her breath when he finally reached Ethan's left ankle.

"Ah, here it is." An assistant handed him a magnifier with a circle of LEDs around the lens. "I have to agree with you, Emma, this is indeed strange." As she had the previous day, he sniffed the mark. "I don't smell anything, but that is not surprising after twenty-four hours, give or take. It does look like the mark a Sharpie can make, the approximate width anyway." He removed a Sharpie from the pocket of his scrub suit and drew a **7** on his wrist. He held his wrist next to Ethan's ankle. "Well, damned if they're not identical. I'll send the ink to the lab, but dollars to donuts, Emma, I think you're right. But it doesn't answer the Why, does it?"

He asked Jennifer to take some more photos. She had a special, macro lens with a large circular flash mounted around the front of it.

Dr. Mittendorf finally arrived at Ethan's feet, which he examined as carefully as every other inch of his body. He even checked between his toes, splaying them apart two-by-two.

"Well, lookee here," he said. "Jennifer, get me a nice, big close-up right here." He separated Ethan's big toe and his second toe. "Jennifer, the photo number?"

She looked at the screen on the back of her digital Nikon. "DSC_0145.jpg."

He pulled out a pocket recorder. "I see a puncture wound, photo number DSC_0145. It appears to have been made by the needle shaft of a syringe inserted one centimeter medial to decedent's long toe." He looked up. "I'll be damned!" His eyes crinkled above his face mask. "Looks to me like you might have a homicide here, Emma. In my experience, a suicide doesn't inject something between his toes, like a heroin addict does to hide his tracks, and then hang himself. Just isn't done. The toxicology lab will tell me what substance was used."

Emma reeled and not just from the surroundings. *A homicide.* How would she handle that? Homicides didn't happen in Hampshire. She couldn't remember the last one. She wasn't even sure Archie had ever had one. Overdoses, yes, uncomfortably often. The occasional suicide. Maybe half a dozen fatal car crashes per year. But, homicides? No.

Emma felt her stress level soar.

Mittendorf hefted an oversized scalpel, which glinted in the surgical light like some instrument of torture in a bad spy film. "Okay, Emma, time to get to the real work. Steady yourself."

Sweat poured down Emma's sides. Her uniform shirt was soaked. She was glad for the gown.

He made a deep cut from Ethan's left clavicle to below his xiphoid process at the bottom of his sternum and back up to his right collarbone. The incision was in the shape of a large **U**.

At the bottom of the **U**, he sliced straight, except for a slight detour around the cadaver's navel, to Ethan's pubic hair. She had the presence of mind to notice that it wasn't the famous **Y** cut after all. But that revelation did nothing to steady her.

Mittendorf unpeeled Ethan's chest and dumped it over his face. She felt herself swaying.

When he used a pair of Fiskars garden shears to sever Ethan's ribs, she lost it.

"I'm sorry ... I have to go."

Emma didn't make it to the bathroom.

13

Measure Twice, Cut Once

On Sunday mornings, I wake up at 6 a.m.

Monday through Saturday, I wake up at 5:30 a.m. I have no need for an alarm clock. My body self regulates. Unlike my brain … but that's another matter altogether.

As I always do, this Sunday I watch "New Day Sunday" with Christi Paul and Victor Blackwell (CNN, out of Atlanta). Christi is pretty and smarter than her co-anchor. At 6:30 a.m., I turn off the show because very little happens in the second half other than recaps and touchy-feely features which bore me. Then I retrieve the Sunday *Hampshire Chronicle* and the Sunday *New York Times* from outside my front door. Although I rarely engage with townsfolk (I admit I occasionally patronize Group Therapy), and I almost never attend town functions, I like to know what's going on.

Before I look at the paper, I make a frittata of spinach, Fontina cheese, onions, tomatoes, mushrooms, kimchi, and pesto mixed with the eggs. And eight ounces of orange juice.

I take care of my body.

After breakfast, I open the paper and read every article. Even the one with the headline:

May Is For Dog Tags
And Transfer Station Permits

I predict that tomorrow's *Chronicle* is going to be much more interesting.

I open the magazine section of the *Times* and turn immediately to the puzzle page. I love the puzzle editor, Will Shortz. He's as smart as I am. Did you know that he's the only academically-accredited puzzle master in the world (Indiana University)? He's an enigmatologist, a person who studies puzzles. I guess you would say that I am an enigmatologist, too. Or an arachnophile, a spider-lover.

Oh, Emma, you're going to love my puzzle-web.

It is now 7 a.m. Time for my workout session. In the basement, I have my own fully-equipped gym. There, I complete my Sunday regimen: dumbbell bench press, hanging leg raise, incline bench pull, barbell squat, and butterfly. Ten sets of ten reps each.

Next to my gym, in a separate temperature-controlled room, I have a Tsunami 300-gallon aquarium, where I keep my collection of exotic fish. It is 96 inches long, 30 inches wide and 24 inches deep. The tank cost $2,204.99. I keep Hawaiian boxfish, lionfish, stonefish, and pufferfish. Every day, after working out, I feed my fish mixtures of salmon, clams, mussels, squid, and unshelled shrimp. That way they don't eat each other.

After a shower, I drive over to Hickam Street. It's a fifteen-minute drive, because my house is in an isolated spot outside of town. That's why I bought it. I park near the country club. I am a member, but I never attend any events. Nor do I play golf or tennis. I prefer to exercise in private.

Then, as I have been doing every day for several weeks, I take a walk along the rough of the golf course, which happens to pass behind my target house. It is raining. As Dolly Parton said, "The way I see it, if you want the rainbow, you gotta put up with the rain."

Triple checking, I pat my pocket, feeling the capped, loaded syringe inside. I pretend to be searching for lost balls, taking care not to annoy the golfers, although there aren't many. I wear a long raincoat and a floppy hat, and nobody seems to pay any attention to me.

From my position on the edge of the fourth hole, I can see the driveway of the house.

I have planned this carefully, and I don't mind being patient until the moment is right. I have prepped my target in advance. He expects me to call him … but only when his wife is out.

I hear a car starting on the other side of the house. I grab my binoculars from underneath my coat. A 740e BMW comes into view. At the wheel of the $98,000 behemoth is none other than Mary Jackson.

My rainbow has arrived.

In a New Haven Walmart, I've bought a prepaid, no-contract cell phone for $19.88 in cash. It has never been used. If all goes as planned, I will only use the phone this time … and one more time.

I dial Ethan's home phone number. I store hundreds of phone numbers in my flawless memory.

"Hi, it's me. I'm sick of waiting. I want you, babe. Let me in the backdoor."

"I'll be right there," he replies. I can tell by his dry, throaty voice that he is one horny bastard. Randy, ripe, and oh-so-ready.

He answers the door. I kiss him right away … before he says a word.

Ten minutes later I kill him.

14

"Do you think he's still alive?"

Thursday was a fine spring day, much warmer than the rainy, chilly, slushy beginning of the month. Emma had scheduled a lunch date with her best friends from Hampshire High, Deb Barger and Vanessa Mack. She looked forward to seeing them.

She needed good friends.

They decided to go on a picnic. In the Northwood section of Hampshire was a large tract of land owned by a wealthy and generous family. They called it The New Forest. The family dedicated the densely-forested land—full of oak, hickory, white and red pine, elm, ash, sugar maple, yellow birch, and American beech—to forestry research, conservation, and public-access recreation. Since her earliest memory, Emma had hiked the trails with her father. It was he who had taught her about the forest and its creatures.

As she drove to the trailhead, she thought about Dr. Mittendorf. She had his toxicology report to look forward to. The mark on Ethan's ankle still itched like a deerfly bite. Unfortunately, on that front, Dr. Mittendorf hadn't had a better theory than she had: he'd had no theory at all.

In spite of her lackluster performance at the postmortem, Emma felt a new sense of empowerment.

A homicide.

A Hampshire anomaly, which she was in a position to solve.

She would make Archie proud.

Deb brought sandwiches and paper cups of iced tea from Group Therapy. Vanessa brought a blanket and sunscreen. They met at the trail head of Walcott Trail and hiked uphill to Lost Pond. During the climb, Pepper came upon a waddling porcupine. Emma called a warning, "No, Sergeant Pepper!" But her caution was unnecessary. Pepper was too wise to give a porcupine more than a disdainful sniff. Further along, Emma spotted a lonely *trillium erectum*. It's distinctive three-petaled flower poked through a bed of winter-brown dead leaves. Its leaves were the color of a fine burgundy wine. "Look, guys," she pointed. "Look at that gorgeous trillium."

"Wow," Deb said, "the flower of spring. It's beautiful."

Emma said, "It's common name, wake-robin, comes from the robin redbreast, the bird that truly heralds spring."

"How do you know that?" Vanessa said.

"Dad."

Pepper, running ahead, suddenly applied the brakes. She'd found some coyote pooh, over which she engaged in some concentrated, up-close sniffing.

Deb said, "Fuck. Gross."

Emma said, "Dog's don't know the meaning of the word gross. Anyway, that's what Will used to say."

Before rejoining them, Pepper squatted and covered the pooh with pee.

"Is it true your dad named Pepper for the Beatles' album?" Vanessa asked.

"I wish! Actually, Dad named her for Sergeant Pepper Anderson, the Angie Dickinson character in the '70s cop show, 'Police Woman.' I can't tell you how many re-runs we watched together ... so embarrassing."

"No way," Deb said. "My mom and I loved that show."

On the southern shore of Lost Pond, the threesome spread the picnic blanket. Nearby, spring peepers sang their sleigh-bell chorus, and the air had that heavenly mixture of the smells that spell spring.

It felt so good to be with friends she could trust.

Deb hadn't changed much since high school. She still wore her dark hair loose and long. Heavy make-up and high heels, which she usually wore, belied her steadfast feminism. Her figure remained buff and stunning, but Emma thought, not meaning to be unkind, most of Deb's beauty remained inner. Vanessa had changed a lot. Today, despite picnicking, she wore a Vineyard Vines seersucker dress straight from her job as the branch manager of Hampshire Trust. She styled her hair in a preppy do, complete with hairband. Pearl studs nailed the look. Vanessa was the Gwyneth Paltrow to Deb's Lena Dunham.

"Such a damn shame about Ethan Jackson," Deb began, sipping tea through a straw. "With only way-back-when to go on, I never would have thought he would take his own life. I don't know why I should know, though. I haven't seen him since high school."

Vanessa unwrapped her sandwich, which gave Emma a good opportunity to change the subject. She knew they would get to Will soon enough.

"The grapevine says you've got a new boyfriend, Deb," Emma said.

"So true! His name is Ernest, but he's not. Anything but. Since I split up with you-know-who, I've never met a funnier man. He makes me laugh so much I pee my pants. Swear to God."

"Lucky you. You deserve it. What about you, Vanessa? How's Dave?"

Dave was Vanessa's stolid husband. "Same-same," she answered. "Isn't it lovely here?"

"Yes, it sure is," said Emma.

Deb took a moment, looking pointedly at Emma. "Promise you'll tell me to shut up … if you don't want to talk about it … but how're you handling the Will situation? And, God, poor Archie, too? Two totally unfair blows almost at once."

"Emma doesn't want to talk about Will. Or about her dad," Vanessa said. "Jesus, it's only been—what?—a month since Will went missing."

"Actually, I do." Emma glanced across Lost Pond. In the distance, Mount Kaibab shimmered in the warm sun. She inhaled Kaibab's beauty before continuing. "The truth is, I think about him every single moment. Dad, too. I'm so alone. You know what really sucks? I don't even have the company of kids."

"I feel for you, babe. I really do." Vanessa said. Of the three, only she had kids.

It was classic Deb, though, when she cut the chase, "Do you think he's still alive?"

Vanessa said, *"Deb!"*

"No, it's okay," Emma said. "I would do anything to know. For now, all I can do is believe he is. On the other hand, I can't imagine Will just splitting. So unlike him. He could never help himself from being brutally honest. If he'd found someone else, he'd have just come right out and told me. You know, I despise the word *closure*, but guess what I need? I've never said this to anyone, but, one way or another, I need to get on with my life. It makes me feel incredibly guilty."

"I think that's a step in the right direction." Deb said. She added quickly, "Don't yell at me, Vanessa!"

"Anyway, you don't have to be alone," Vanessa said. "I don't mean now. It's way too early. But in the future. Look at you. You're smart, sexy, and you're the effing chief of police!"

"Yeah, but really look at me." Emma indicated her polyester uniform blouse and her navy-blue polyester trousers.

Deb said, "Hey, it's a well-known fact, real men *love* a woman in uniform."

Emma laughed. "Thanks. I doubt you're right, but thanks."

"You're welcome."

"The other problem is my new uniform and my new job are stressing the hell out of me." She couldn't tell them yet that Ethan had been murdered.

"How come? Gender resentment?" asked Deb.

"No, it's not that. I just feel like a damn rookie. Talk about on-the-job-training. I went to Ethan's autopsy the other day, and I puked."

"Jesus, who wouldn't? Don't be so hard on yourself," Vanessa said.

"Dad wouldn't have. Speaking of which, most everyone on the force agrees I shouldn't have the job. Remember Stella Weeks? She'd just as soon see me dead—"

"That sucks."

"Speaking of Archie," Deb said, "what are you going to do with his house?"

"I am so not dealing with that yet," she replied. "I haven't even been over there since Dad died. His old cleaning lady checks on it once a week—"

Vanessa said, "Maybe you should move in there. It's such a lovely place."

Emma's cell phone rang. "Damn!" She almost pushed End without answering, but habit made her glance at Caller ID.

Office of The Chief Medical Examiner.

"I'm so sorry, guys, but this is super-important. I've got to take this."

"Hello, Emma," Dr. Mittendorf said, "I have important news. How soon can you get here?"

"I'll be there fast as I can."

Her hand shook. Excitement or dread? She wasn't sure.

"I hope I didn't upset you, asking about Will," Deb said.

Emma called over her shoulder, "No, don't worry, you didn't upset me. But I've got to run. There may be a break in my case!"

15

Discouraging Words

At the Walcott trailhead, Emma sprayed pebbles driving out of the parking lot. Ignoring state law, she turned on her concealed emergency lights and fired up the siren. Weaving through traffic, she reached Mittendorf's in thirty-one minutes, nine less than the usual forty.

Emma was out of breath when she arrived.

"That was quick," he said.

"What's the verdict?"

"Looks like your case is now officially a homicide. Have you ever investigated one before? No, never mind, of course you haven't."

She shook her head anyway.

"What have you found?"

"Your Mr. Jackson was poisoned by a neurotoxin found in certain marine creatures, like tropical fish, called tetrodotoxin. Imagine a single crystal of salt. A dose that small, injected, can kill a man Ethan Jackson's size within a minute. And Jackson's dose was significantly larger. It works fast. Almost instantly, tetrodotoxin increases heart rate, decreases blood pressure—both of which accelerate the poison's distribution—and paralyzes the body. Breathing stops and so does the heart. I'm rather pleased to have picked this up. It's not something a pathologist sees every day."

Dr. Mittendorf smiled.

"Moreover," he continued, "there is no chance that someone could self-inject tetrodotoxin and proceed to climb a ladder and hang himself. Thus, the proximate cause of death is murder by poisoning. Q.E.D., as you might say."

All Emma could say was, "Wow."

"There was no mention of a suicide note in the police report," he said. "As you can probably guess, suicide notes can be, and often are, faked. But no suicide note, right?" Before she could answer, he continued. "Most people don't know this, but nationwide only about twenty-five to thirty percent of suicides leave notes behind."

"I didn't know that."

"Well, in Ethan's case it's moot. There's one more datum that I should have picked up on. The ligature marks on his neck are not consistent with a pre-mortem hanging."

"What about the mark on his ankle?"

"Sorry. Not a clue. I may be good, but I am not clairvoyant."

Emma asked, "Is there anything else I should know?"

"Indeed, there is, my young investigator. I've saved the best for last. I found a dried substance, comprised of fructose, proteolytic enzymes, citric acid, acid phosphatase, and lipids, in and about Mr. Jackson's anus. *Dun-dun*, as they say on 'Law & Order!'"

"Huh?"

"Those would be the ingredients of all-natural semen. Without being crude, it's a bit tricky to get your own semen into your own anus. In other words, Ethan Jackson had sex with a man, likely on Sunday morning."

"And that means he wasn't having sex with soccer mom but with someone else. Hmm, maybe Mary and Julian caught Ethan *in flagrante delicto* and killed him right there? But how could they be ready with the neurotoxin? And what happened to the lover? Where's he? Is he dead, too?"

"All good questions. By the way, I love a police chief who knows her Latin—"

"Just trying to keep up with you."

"Oh, and in addition, I found traces of C_3H_8O—isopropyl alcohol, to the layman—inside his mouth, on his ears and cheeks, and between his toes. Whoever did this was exercising an abundance of caution. No DNA except the semen. Which raises some puzzling questions ..."

"I'll say."

Emma said her goodbyes and thanks and hand-carried Dr. Mittendorf's report and a headful of questions back to headquarters. She was so jazzed that she violated protocol on the return trip: lights and siren, all the way.

B uzz Buzzucano called down to the front desk where Stella was serving a shift as Desk Sergeant. "The Saintly One wants us both to attend the six o'clock roll call, and damn if I don't have poker at 6:30."

"Hey, that's a good one, The Saintly One. I'll have to remember that," Stella said. "Anyway, I doubt she'll notice if you skip it. It'll probably be a big nothing-burger."

They both laughed. "I dunno about missing roll call. She said it more like an order than a request."

"Suit yourself. I'll be going 'cause I have to. I'm the duty sergeant."

E mma entered the meeting room before anyone else. She carried Mittendorf's full report. She stood behind the podium, which was emblazoned with the department's logo. Emma caught a faint whiff of her own B.O. There was not much she could do about it, except keep her arms down.

As with the rest of Hampshire's police headquarters, the meeting room was shabby. Some of the folding church basement chairs, stacked in a heap in the corner, no longer worked. There was no bulletin board, so the desk sergeants push-pinned wanted posters right into the walls. Mentally, she added *Clean Up Headquarters* to her to-do list.

Cops began to wander in, Max, Pete Sinclair, Chuck Smith, and Caroline Stoner. Buzz and Stella came in last. Emma waited for everyone to settle down. "Good afternoon. Stella, why don't you start roll call, and I'll follow up with an announcement."

Sergeant Weeks went through her usual roll call punch list, which included:

—Local outstanding wants and warrants.

—A new BOLO from the state police: "Be on the look-out for a brown Caprice, Massachusetts tag number 375-NQ4. Suspect wanted for armed robbery. Consider armed and dangerous."

—A burglary: "There was a B&E at 18 Sperry Drive in Northwood, last night. The Case residence. Standard junkie M.O. TV, laptop, and some Valium from the medicine cabinet. Same-same."

—A seventy-two-hour-old Amber Alert: "White female, 6-years-old, last seen wearing red hoodie and blue jeans. Believed to be a stranger abduction. Blue Honda. New York tag number begins with number nine." Stella looked up from her notes and smiled, "Wouldn't want to take a bet on that kid."

She glanced at Emma. "The Chief has a few words she'd like to say. I'm sure they'll be encouraging. Chief?"

The brassiness of Stella's balls continued to astound her.

"Actually, I have some discouraging words. I have received the full autopsy report on Ethan Jackson, who, as you know, was found deceased in his residence last Sunday. Dr. Herbert Mittendorf, Chief Medical Examiner, performed the autopsy. I was present. Dr. Mittendorf's findings point inescapably to homicide. Mr. Jackson did not take his own life."

The cops exhaled a collective gasp. There had not been a homicide in Hampshire in years. And that one was even before Archie's time. An obvious wife vs. husband murder.

"There is also evidence that Mr. Jackson had sex with a male shortly before his death."

A smattering of disapproving sounds ensued. Exclusively from male officers.

Emma quickly put the kibosh on that. "Guys, enough," she said. "I am assigning Detective Buzzucano to be the lead investigator. Sergeant Weeks will second him. We will have the resources of the Connecticut State Police at our disposal if we need them. However, for now at least, I have not called on C.S.P. to take charge of the investigation."

She hoped that that wouldn't turn out to be a blunder.

"Tomorrow morning, Buzz and I will re-interview Mrs. Mary Jackson, try to assemble a list of friends and/or enemies to question, and study the report from the forensics team. Meantime, Pete and Chuck should canvass the neighbors. See if anyone saw someone come or go on Sunday morning. Copy your report to Buzz and Stella, who can follow up if you get any hits. Caroline will check phone records."

She went on to summarize Dr. Mittendorf's findings including the poisoning and the mysterious mark on Ethan's ankle. "We may be looking for someone with medical or nursing experience. Someone who has access to syringes, although I suppose everyone does. Or possibly an ichthyologist—"

Stella groaned loudly, and, Emma thought, justifiably. Sometimes her vocabulary got the better of her.

"—by that I mean a person who knows a lot about fish."

Buzz muttered, "There's always something fishy about gay guys."

"Meantime," she interrupted the laughter, "the rest of you hit the streets and find out everything and anything you can about Mr. Ethan Jackson *and* his sex life. We will solve this case, but I need all of you to help us do it. One more thing: let's keep this out of the newspapers for now, give us some breathing room. Okay, guys? That will be all for now."

Stella stood up. "I think the Chief may have forgotten to say, 'Be safe out there.'"

Emma returned to her office. By not asking for outside assistance, she recognized that she was placing herself and her department in a precarious position should she fail. She decided to risk it. Pride? No doubt. A big part of missing Archie and Will was wanting them to be proud of her.

She also decided that if she responded to each one of Stella's affronts she would run out of oxygen.

Privately, she'd dubbed Stella with a Spoonerism: *Shining Wit.* Translation: *Whining Shit.*

She hadn't yet heard that Stella had nicknamed her *The Saintly One.*

16

Colonel's Secret Recipe

After I kiss Ethan Jackson on the lips—long, hard, and deep—I taste my own revulsion. But he responds hungrily, like he's never been kissed before. I think about his wife, pretty, useless Mary. She has no fucking clue.

Ethan is all decked out, from his tasseled loafers to his pink cable knit Brooks Brothers sweater. The sweater even has that stupid dead sheep logo in baby blue. I place my lips next to Ethan's ear. I can smell that he has product in his hair. He is an over-coiffed poodle, fresh from doggie beauty parlor. I whisper, "Let's go into the living room. I want to fuck you on the floor."

His voice is husky, pathetically so. "Oooh." He actually drools as he looks at my crotch.

Ethan is Phase One of my plan. As devilishly clever as it is, it is quite simple: I intend to right a wrong. A very big WRONG.

"If injury *must* be done to a man, it should be so severe that his vengeance need not be feared," said Machiavelli. Actually, I think I'm paraphrasing. Close enough, though.

I know exactly how this is going to end, the pain it will inflict, and the collateral damage (vapid Mary and her spoiled kid). Ethan is a weakling. He hasn't even had the balls to make Mary take the kid to baseball practice for a slew of wasted weeks.

In his over-decorated living room, I suddenly drop to my knees and rub his already swollen cock. It is almost sad when he moans. I undo his pressed chinos. Pop goes the weasel.

> Every night when I go out,
> The monkey's on the table,
> Take a stick and knock it off,
> Pop goes the weasel.

I remove the rest of his clothes, loafers and red socks included. I dump my coat and backpack on the carpet, seemingly with abandon, but I am careful that my coat lands with the correct pocket face-up.

"Lie down," I say, "you will never feel anything like this again."

I tell Ethan that I am going to start at his toes and work my way up. I begin to suck on his toes. He squirms with desire and emits another, ghastly moan. I reach into my coat pocket and retrieve the syringe. With my teeth, I pop off the plastic protector covering the hypodermic needle. I separate his big toe from his second toe. I jam the needle into the crotch between Ethan's toes. I push the plunger home.

He screams and bucks, kicking me in the face. My satisfaction obviates the pain. In a matter of seconds, he is gasping for breath. I can't believe how fast-acting my experimental concoction is working. I watch him writhe in panicked agony on the carpet. After watching him impassively for a moment, I leave him to his agonal respirations.

I find the door to the basement. At the base of the stairs is a step ladder, ideal for my plan, which I bring upstairs.

Ethan is now dead.

I check my watch. I still have oodles of time before Mary and Julian are likely to return home. I put on a pair of nitrile gloves and carefully swab the inside of his mouth, his cheek, his ear, and his toes with alcohol swabs. Everywhere I may have left some DNA. Not that I think that the Hampshire Police Department's experience with DNA is anything worth writing home about. Yielding to my obsessiveness, I fold his clothes neatly and leave them on the sofa. Everything but his boxers, which I manage to get back on him.

I mean, who kills themselves naked?

Now, for my *pièce de résistance*. I remove a small brown bottle from my coat pocket. I have harvested what is in the bottle from a prostitute in New Haven. The kid had all the earmarks of a junkie—facial abscesses, dirty hair, and a long-sleeved shirt—but I was prepared. I was double-gloved and had brought along a condom. After the kid learned what I wanted, and no doubt figuring me for a sicko, the kid had charged me a premium over the quoted price. Well worth it, I figure.

I run the faucet until the water gets hot and then add a few drops of water to the bottle. As I return to Ethan, I shake the bottle vigorously until, presto, I have a re-liquefied mixture. Still with gloves on, I roll him prone. I dribble The Colonel's Secret DNA Recipe around and into his asshole and roll him back supine. *Even a sub-standard medical examiner will find that!*

The Colonel's Secret Recipe® is a registered trademark of Kentucky Fried Chicken, a subsidiary of Yum! Brands, and the recipe remains locked in a vault in Louisville, Kentucky. But, by inserting DNA into it, I have not violated the Lanham Act (1946).

The noose, I had pre-tied at home. Measuring Ethan with the rope, I adjust its length so his feet will clear the ground by six inches or so. Getting the rope tied around the beam is easy. It is a bit of a job to carry Ethan up the ladder. Now I know what dead weight means. When I haul him about five feet off the ground, I release my grip. The rope makes a loud snap. Ethan's body jerks and sways crazily, like a spastic marionette.

> Every morn when I go out,
> Ethan's on the ladder,
> Take a noose and knock him off,
> Pop goes the second and third cervical vertebrae.

His body hits the ladder. Losing my balance while doing this, I am still able to jump clear of the falling ladder. Where it falls, it shatters a glass-topped coffee table.

Perfect, I think, *I couldn't have planned that detail better myself.*

I find a vacuum cleaner in a closet near the kitchen. I vacuum Ethan's body and the living room carpet.

I check Ethan one last time. No pulse, no respirations. The combined forces of the noose, the rope, and the plunge appear to have broken his neck.

The following Wednesday, I shadow Emma Thorne's friend, Deb Barger, into the Super Stop & Shop parking lot. I am in no hurry.

Ethan's suicide is percolating in the minds of the police, but they won't find any evidence to suggest his death is anything other than self-inflicted. As usual, my plan is perfect … and flawlessly executed. I, alone, will choose the moment to reveal that Ethan has been murdered.

I feel relaxed. I have time on my side. Boatloads of time. Before I drop the next bomb on Emma Thorne's head.

17

Crater Face

Emma drove Buzz and Pepper back to the Jackson residence on Hickam Street. Buzz rang the doorbell. Julian "JJ" Jackson, Ethan's son, opened the door. Understandably, he had not yet returned to school.

He was standing straighter than when she had seen him the day of his father's death. He also looked older. Closer to sixteen.

He said, "I hope you've come to tell us that my Dad didn't kill himself."

"As a matter of fact, we have." It was not the way Emma expected the interview to begin.

"Good," he said with no discernible affect. "You'll probably want to speak with my mother then. She's in the kitchen. Follow me." Buzz shot Emma a raised-eyebrow look, which she returned with a nod. She instructed Pepper to wait outside before entering.

They passed the living room, which had been tidied to the point of perfect. Someone had already replaced the glass table shattered by the ladder.

Mrs. Mary Jackson stood in the kitchen watching "Fox & Friends" on a wall-mounted flat screen TV. Emma glanced at the tube. Bill

Hemmer was interviewing Chris Christie. Emma was surprised he was still newsworthy. She hadn't heard him mentioned on NPR in ages.

Without being asked, Mary Jackson muted the sound. "Have you come to tell me that Ethan didn't take his own life? I damn well hope so."

"Mrs. Jackson, this is my colleague, Detective Larry Buzzucano. Again, very sorry for your, and your son's, loss. May we sit down?"

She sighed and pointed to the kitchen table. They sat, and Julian joined them.

Buzz said, "Okay if I tape our—"

"Do what you have to."

Buzz readied the digital recorder. "The medical examiner," Emma announced, "has determined that Ethan Jackson was murdered by the injection of a poison."

"Of course," she said with a thin, incongruous smile.

Emma quickly said, "Of course he was murdered or of course he was murdered by poison?"

She smiled again. "The former."

Emma took a moment to collect her thoughts. So, Buzz said, "Your husband, he have any falling out with friends, business acquaintances? Any enemies?"

Julian said, "Is that like saying, did Dad have any murderous friends?"

Mary Jackson turned to Emma. "Look, as I told you Sunday, Ethan was a happy guy. He didn't have any enemies. He was successful. Just look at our house! I loved him, and he loved JJ and me. I'm not sure what else I can tell you other than … I told you so."

As a street cop, Emma had heard every obfuscation, evasion, and lie. There were the obvious tells: flushing, changes in pupil diameter, reduced eye-contact. But Emma no longer relied on these clues. She could smell a lie like a hound smells a hare. Mary stank. Maybe she'd figured out that Ethan had stepped out on her … with a man.

Mary Jackson had just pole-vaulted to the top of Emma's suspect list. The creak of Buzz's chair and his attentive stare told Emma that he concurred.

"Did your husband know any doctors, nurses, or paramedics?"

"Oh, I get it. Because of the poison? Well, we don't socialize with paramedics or nurses, of course, but we know plenty of doctors."

Emma thought Hampshire's nurses and paramedics could count themselves lucky. "Do you have any Sharpies in the house?"

Mary asked, "The hell's a Sharpie?"

"I have a Sharpie in my desk," Julian said.

"May I see it?"

"Okay, I guess." He came back a moment later and handed the pen to Emma. She uncapped it and tried to draw a line across a page in her notebook. The Sharpie was as dry as an AA meeting.

Emma reached into her briefcase, removed Buzz's photograph of the mark on Ethan's ankle, and showed it to Mary Jackson. "Does this mean anything to you?"

"Is this a photograph of some part of Ethan's body?" Her voice became shrill. "What are you people trying to do to us? This is unconsciousable!"

Emma ignored the neologism and her protest. "Does this mark mean anything to you?"

Mary Jackson handed back the color photograph without further comment.

"Okay," Emma said, "let's move on. What about friends and work colleagues with whom we can speak? And where did Ethan work?"

"He didn't," Julian said. "He started spudger.com. In case you don't know it, it's an internet repair company. He sold his share for nine million bucks."

"Wow," Emma allowed, "that's a lot of money." She was beginning to hate these people. "Anybody in the company feel like they didn't get their fair share?"

Mary Jackson said, "Why would they? They're all as rich as Jews."

Now, she really did hate these people.

Emma took a moment. "I'd like to ask you a question alone, if that's alright."

Mary reacted the same way she had during their first interview. "JJ stays with me."

Okay, lady, your decision, Emma thought.

"I need to ask you when you and your husband last had sex."

Julian interjected, "Like, what's up with that, lady? Where do you get off—"

But Mary surprised them by saying, "I don't mind. I happen to be proud of our relationship. Let's see ... last week sometime. Yes, I remember. It was Wednesday night. We went out for a romantic dinner in Great Barrington ... just the two us ... and then, you know ..."

Emma glanced at Julian. His face gave nothing away. Neither confirmation nor disagreement. Emma weighed the advantage of revealing what Mittendorf had found and decided to keep seminal fluid stowed in her still-pretty-empty cubby of evidence.

She signaled to Buzz, and they both stood. "If you could prepare a list for us of Ethan's friends, people we could talk to, I would appreciate that. Particularly male friends. I'll send an officer over this afternoon to pick it up. We can see ourselves out. Thank you for your time." They headed for the door. "Oh, one last thing. Do you know anyone who raises tropical fish?"

"What possible relevance could that have to the death of my dear husband? If you don't mind my saying so, Emma, you might be a little inexperienced for a murder investigation. Shouldn't you call in the state police … people who have a little more practice with this kind of thing? And, no is the answer to your question. My dentist has a fish tank in her waiting room, but, really, do I look like the sort of person who has friends with tropical fish?"

Outside, Buzz followed Pepper to Emma's car. "I don't know about you," he said, "but I like her for the murder. Him, too. I really do. She's got motive: nine million is a lot of dead presidents. And opportunity: the creepy kid provides the alibi, and he's an athlete, easily strong enough to haul Ethan up a ladder. And, honestly, what rich 45-year-old says, 'the death of my dear husband' or 'I happen to be proud of our relationship?'" Catch my drift? What do you think?"

"I like them for it, too, but not enough to stop looking at other possibilities."

Emma was happy to be outside on a sunny June day, free of the Jackson family. She started the car. "I did learn something from Mary, though. Raising tropical fish is not something the upper classes do."

"Huh?"

"Not important."

Back in her office, Emma rubbed Pepper's head, which elicited a satisfied moan. "Well," she said to Buzz, "we did get elimination prints from Julian and Mary. The kid's prints were all over the aluminum ladder—"

"Which proves diddly-squat."

"You're right. So, we have a possible suspect or suspects in the family. Then again, they presumably already have the nine million. This afternoon, I'll send Caroline Stoner to pick up her list. After that, we start interviewing. Was she as happily married as she insisted? I agree with you, that was a little thickly applied. I felt like I was getting a PB&J with way too much jelly. Obviously, Ethan had a sweaty squeeze on the side and a boyfriend, to boot. Did she know? Did they catch them? Someone will talk. When it comes to affairs, someone always talks."

"Anything else, Chief?"

"No, I've got a guy coming in for a meeting," she glanced at her dad's old banjo clock on the wall, "in ten minutes."

Buzz rose. "Tell you what, I'll go talk to Jerry Rathbun at Paws & Claws. Maybe he's sold some tropical fish supplies to someone we'll want to interview."

"Good idea."

Emma's phone rang after Buzz left. "Hey Chief, Stella here. There's a guy in the lobby. A Mark Byrne. Claims he has an appointment with you? That so?"

Stifling a sigh, Emma said, "Send him up."

Mark knocked and entered. Pepper growled a low, don't-do-any-thing-funny growl and rose to check him out. Undeterred, Mark rubbed Pepper behind her ears and instantly made a new friend. "Mark Byrne, Chief. Pleased to meet you." His voice was as growly as Pepper's. They shook hands.

Mark was tall, lantern-jawed, and acne scars pitted his face, which he wore with rugged assurance. His hair was steel-gray, cut short, and curly. Crater-face aside, he struck Emma as handsome.

He sat without being asked, just as he had entered without being invited.

Mark dove right in: "So, we've got a missing person who happens to be your husband. One way or another, he vamooses like snow in June. And your department can't find him. Have I got that about right?"

Emma nodded.

"Let's go back to the day he disappeared. Tell me everything you remember." He opened a notebook, licked the point of his pencil, and prepared to take notes.

She told him about Will's depression. She told him about coming home from shopping and finding Will gone. There wasn't a lot to tell, but she filled him in on everything else she could think of.

"Do you still own the house?"

"Of course."

"I'd like to check it out."

"Sure, but it's been cleaned since his disappearance. Multiple times. It's already been a month. You know, I hadn't thought of this before, but I took some photos after Will disappeared. Some kind of emotional crutch, I guess. I was confused and panicky. In the days after Will disappeared, I had the notion that I didn't want to stay in my house anymore, that I might want to sell it. I've changed my mind since then.

I have the photos on my iPad. Want to see them?"

"Yup."

He scrolled through the photos. In the bedroom shot, Will's Bible was still squared off on the pillow. She wondered if Mark noticed. Then Mark looked at the images again, more slowly. He meticulously studied each one. He examined a particular one for a long time, zooming in with a touch gesture. Zooming back out, he rotated the iPad to show her the picture of the front hall. "What do you see in this picture?" he asked.

She looked at the image on the screen as carefully as he had. "I see my hallway, carpeted. The front door is at the end. The umbrella stand is full of umbrellas. The Arts & Crafts chair my grandmother left me has Will's hat on it. The side table has my keys, a lamp, my sunglasses … and … nothing much else. What am I missing?"

"Look carefully at the carpet. I see two faint, parallel marks leading to the front door—"

"Yes, I see them now. So?"

"I'll give you short odds that those marks were made by a hand-truck or something like a hand-truck carrying something heavy. I'm assuming you didn't vacuum before you took these photos?"

"Not that I remember, but I might've."

"Let's assume you didn't. If I am correct, I have to say that there are really only two possibilities. Get a grip now. Either someone hauled Will, the person, out of your house, probably in a large container. Or Will, the dead body, was similarly removed."

"God," she said. Her hand flew to her mouth. "This changes everything. If you're right."

18

A See-Through

Mark Byrne leaned over her desk and said, "I'm starving. Does Hampshire have a decent place to eat? You're the client. You buy."

Emma studied him. He certainly was direct, but he didn't seem to be hitting on her. The circumstances would hardly permit that.

"Sure, I could use a bite, too," she said.

At Group Therapy, Mark ordered a dry martini with olives. "Same for you?" he said.

"No."

Without asking, Phil Masters, wrote up her usual lunch order. She always had a Cobb salad and an iced tea.

"And for you?" Phil stared at Mark with unabashed curiosity.

"I'll have the rib-eye, well-done, a side of onion rings, and whatever veg you have today." He snapped the menu closed and handed it back to Phil.

While waiting for his midday martini, Mark said, "I know you have a lot of new information to swallow. Obviously, I don't know you very well. I know you are wealthier than the money you make as chief of police. Probably from Will's parents, the Fosters. I know you never expected to be chief of police. I know you never had children and that dog of yours, whom you adore, bonds you to your recently-deceased father. I know—"

"You seem to know a lot." Emma said, irritated.

"Google and deduction. Always a good cocktail," he said, sipping the martini which had just arrived.

"Before you get any more annoyed at me, let me repeat, I hardly know you. But, if I am correct that a person or persons unknown removed your husband from your house—either, to be completely brutal, dead or alive—you are at a critical juncture. It seems to me that your next decision could be the beginning of a new life. Or not."

Emma felt confused and frightened … and annoyed. "Okay," she said, "you know so much. Why don't you tell me about my next decision?"

She felt Ms. Perceptive rest her velvety muzzle on her thigh. Like dogs that detect cancer, Pepper could always sense her mood.

"Sure you won't join me in a see-through?" Mark asked.

She smiled in spite of herself. She'd never heard a martini called a see-through. But she said, "Nope."

He stared at her for a moment before continuing. She read his look as one of compassion yet not one of sympathy. "Here's my take on this. Emma, you are an intelligent woman (B.A., M.A.), an accomplished police officer ("Heroine of Hampshire"), and now a chief (success still to-be-determined). Plus, you are one hell of a looker. I'm assuming that your brown hair is natural. You're not wearing any make-up, because you don't need any—"

"Jesus, will you give it a rest!"

"Simmer down. The more you blush, the prettier you get."

"Drop it Mark. I mean it. You're pushing this routine too far."

"Look, I tell it like I see it," Mark said. "So, let me finish. What I'm telling you is obvious to anyone. Your decision, and you asked, is whether to move on with your life or to wallow indefinitely in the not-knowing." He paused, studying her again. "Okay, here goes: as soon as you face the fact that Will is dead, the faster you can live the life you deserve. If he was carried out of your house in a box, he was probably murdered. If a person or persons kidnapped him, why was there no demand for money? You don't need a private detective to figure that out. Will's parents have more than enough money to pay a ransom. So, then what have you got? Sexual pervert? I know Will was a good-looking guy. I've seen a picture of him on yale.edu. But who keeps a thirty-eight-year-old guy locked up as a sex toy? Nobody's that cute. Will's depression could've driven him to kill himself. Which he did in a place where no one would find his body. That was the gist of your dad's theory, right? Lastly, he could have run away. Perhaps with another woman. But who runs away without his wallet, his credit cards, his money? Doesn't provide some chick with a particularly desirable new boyfriend."

After all his sexist folderol, Emma understood where this was heading. As meanly as Mark had whipped her emotions, she recognized that she had been homing in on the same conclusion. Hadn't she had the stirrings of this conversation yesterday with Vanessa and Deb? And she trusted them. Mark? She wasn't so sure.

She breathed in a deep lungful of air and hoped that she wouldn't have to ask him again to stop. Thankfully, he down-shifted: "So, after all that, do you still want to hire me?"

Emma swallowed a forkful of blue cheese, bacon, and lettuce and sipped iced tea while she thought.

He was an over-confident son of a bitch. No question about that. Yet his arrogance had an effect. He had done more homework than she would've expected. He'd zeroed in on some truths. She had a hunch that he was good at what he did … despite his annoying presentation. The more she thought about it, the more she found his acidic pitch persuasive. Her own colleagues had failed and Archie, Archie had come up short, too. But she had to give it one last try. Didn't she?

"Yes," she finally said. "I'd like you to look into this for me. Do me a favor, though, take your swagger down a notch."

"Good," he said with a grin, "I'm not successful enough to turn down work."

"Jesus."

"Hey, I'm kidding. I'll get right on this. I'll give it my best shot. Just don't get your hopes up. No guarantees about my ego, though."

She reached into her purse. "I brought these along just in case," she said. She handed him a list of Yale contacts, faculty and a few students whose names she knew, and a separate list of Hampshire contacts with addresses and phone numbers. Reluctantly, she had included Frank, Joan, and Georgia Foster. She had to get at the truth, and, if including them, got her closer, well, so be it.

They discussed his fees, which seemed reasonable to her and to which they agreed.

"I want to give it one last shot," Emma concluded, "before I take your advice and moveon.com."

Mark put out his hand, they shook.

19

Gone Fishin'

While Emma was dining with Mark Byrne at Group Therapy, Stella and Buzz ate lunch together at Marco's Pizzeria. Extra anchovies on Stella's slice, none on Buzz's. Stella took a sip of her beer. When in uniform, Marco always served her Bud Light in a paper milkshake cup. Buzz sipped from a can of Coke. Both slid another slice of Marco's house favorite, Marco's Magic, onto their plates.

They sat across from one another in a window-side booth with a view of Main Street. The pizzeria wanted for a sprucing-up. Marco had nailed 1970s record album covers to the walls where the printed likenesses of Led Zeppelin, Sly and The Family Stone, and David Bowie were fading toward nothingness. There were holes in the Naugahyde benches, the table tops were sticky, but all the cops agreed that the pizza was the best in the county.

Buzz stared at Stella. He found her cute, but he had never had the nerve to hit on her. She was round-faced with an appealing ski-jump nose and fluffy blonde hair, worn that day in a ponytail threaded through the adjustable strap at the back of her Hampshire P.D. baseball cap. As always, she'd painted her eyes with blue eye shadow, her lips a color Buzz thought should be called fuck-me-red, and her lashes were teased out with black mascara.

As they often did, Buzz's eyes strayed south to Stella's chest.

"Jesus, Buzz, are you checking out my knockers again? You men are so pathetic. Haven't you ever seen a woman's breasts?"

Buzz blushed. He quickly averted his gaze.

"Pretty awesome we got an honest-to-God murder on our hands," he said in a clumsy changing-of-the-subject.

Stella smiled and said, "We did catch a murder 'bout fifteen years ago—"

"Before you and I were on the force."

"—but it was a slam-dunk. Jenny Prichard blew away her no-good, piece-of-shit husband and walked into HQ with her gun still smokin'."

"Doesn't seem like Ethan is going to be so easy to solve."

"Hmm, no," Stella agreed. "I still think the Saintly One is insane not to get the state police in. What does she know about investigating a murder? I even heard Mary Jackson wants them called in."

"Sure thinks she's God's gift. I'll say that."

Stella said, "I hope she falls smack on her snooty butt."

"Roger that!"

They finished their pizza and drinks. Stella stuck a piece of Juicy Fruit in her mouth to hide the smell of beer, and they thanked Marco, who, as usual, didn't charge them. "The Saintly One has Caroline Stoner doing something else today," Stella said. "She wants us to pick up some kind of list at the Jackson house. You coming with me?"

"Sure, but I've also got to stop at Jerry Rathbun's Paws & Claws. I told her I'd check who he sells tropical fish supplies to."

"Right. It's on the way." Buzz joined Stella in her black and white.

Paws & Claws was as seedy as Marco's. Puppy-mill puppies scratched at the front window. "Aw, look how cute they are," Stella cooed. Two kittens rolled in a bed of wood chips. Rathbun greeted them with a broad smile. Rathbun had a jaundiced complexion and a monkish fringe of brown hair around his bald pate.

"Looking for a puppy? Or maybe a gerbil for your kid?" Rathbun asked helpfully.

"Don't have kids," Stella said. "Actually, we're here about tropical fish."

"Great! They're in the back. Follow me."

Rathbun's hopeful face turned to a frown when Buzz asked, "We'd like to know who in town buys fish from you or, you know, tropical fish supplies, like fish flakes, aquarium filters, aerators, that type of thing."

Stella whispered, "I'm impressed."

"Truthfully," Rathbun said, "I don't sell many fish at all … or much of anything else, I'm afraid."

"Somebody at least must buy fish food," Buzz persisted.

"I guess I still have a couple of customers. Less than I used to. Mrs. Georgiade over on Nibang Avenue is my most regular, but, gee, she's getting on to ninety now, so I doubt she'll be feeding her fish that much longer." Buzz and Stella exchanged a look: not a promising lead. "Fern Davenport comes in every once in a while. Not too often. She's getting on, too."

"Anyone else?" Buzz asked.

"Couple of people used to buy from me, but now they probably go to Amazon or some other effing dot com."

"Names?" demanded Stella.

"Georgia Foster and Eileen Perria, but they haven't been in for ages."

Buzz whispered to Stella, "Ask him if he knows any fudge-packer fish-lovers."

Stella gave Buzz a withering look. In a normal tone of voice, she said, "No male fish buyers among your customers?"

Rathbun shook his head.

Back in the car, Stella said, "Jesus, Buzz. Fudge-packer? You are so retro. Hey, by the way, nice idea going to Paws & Claws. Big, fat waste of time. Let's go pick up Mary Jackson's list, do some real police work."

At 103 Hickam Street, Mary Jackson opened the door with a smile on her face. She acted like a different person. Buzz studied her carefully. He still had her high on his suspect list.

"Can I pour you guys a cup of coffee?"

"Sure can," Stella said. She removed her wad of Juicy Fruit with a Kleenex and stuffed it in her pants pocket. "I could use some."

They sat at the kitchen table. Mary distributed coffee, milk, and sugar and joined them. "Here's the list your chief wanted. I can't begin to imagine what use it will be. No one on this list knows who killed Ethan … let alone did it themselves."

Buzz was surprised when Stella said, "I'm sure you're right. Seems like a stupid idea to me, too."

"Hmm," Mary said, looking interested.

Buzz, knowing his partner too well, thought, *Don't go down this road, Stella. No good will come of it.*

Mary Jackson grinned. "So, do you agree with me that your boss is totally out of her depth here? That calling in the state police is the only way to catch the killer?"

Buzz shot Stella a frown, but she ignored him.

"I agree with you completely."

The conversation continued between Stella and her new pal, both trash-talking Emma. Finally, Buzz rose and said, "C'mon, Stella, we've got to get back to work."

Out on the driveway, Buzz lit into her, which was not something he often did. He said, "Stella, that was dumb. Like it or not, dumping on one of our own is just plain stupid."

With a smug smile, Stella said, "You can go fuck yourself, Detective Flip-Flop. Like it's not the truth? Like you don't feel like I do?"

20

Victor Blaine

On Friday afternoon, Emma decided to create an opportunity to speak with Julian Jackson without his mother present. Not strictly kosher to interview a youngster without a parent, but she felt it was worth the risk. Her suspect list was short. She hoped he might be able to provide some insight into his father, information he would be reluctant to share in front of his mother.

Emma drove back to the Jackson place and parked well down the street. She placed earbuds in her ears, opened Spotify on her iPhone, and settled back to wait.

An hour later, Julian appeared at the end of the driveway, riding his bicycle. Bingo. She followed, keeping her distance. He rode downtown and locked up his bicycle outside Rusty's Hobby Shop. Emma knew the store. It was large with multiple aisles of overstuffed shelves. It seemed like as good a place as any for an ambush interview.

Before she could buttonhole Julian, a florid man approached him and engaged him in conversation. He had white hair, and he wore a well-cut navy-blue blazer. She couldn't hear what they were saying, but their conversation appeared to become heated. After a few moments, which included spirited gesticulating and raised voices, the man spun on his heel and left the store.

On a hunch, Emma abandoned Julian and followed the man, who drove away in a brown Mercedes. She tailed him closely, not particularly worried about being spotted. On the radio, she ran his plates by her dispatcher. They came back to a Victor Blaine of 204 Hickam Street.

Hmm, she figured that was about a hundred yards from the Jackson house, where she had just been. She followed him home.

Emma and Pepper intercepted him before he made it to his front door.

"Mr. Blaine?" She held up her shield. "I'm Emma Thorne, Hampshire Police Department. May I have a word with you inside?"

Blaine studied the badge and said, "That dog. Is he really necessary?"

"She. And, yes, she's my partner. She goes where I go."

He led them into a room filled with, well, toys. On every surface—tables, shelves, and open cupboards—there were toy soldiers, model airplanes, model boats. Hence the hobby shop, she gathered.

Blaine was portly with thinning hair. Somewhere in his sixties, possibly early seventies. He wore a thin argyle cardigan under his blazer and khaki trousers. She thought she detected the remnants of an English accent.

"I happened to be in Rusty's Hobby Shop earlier," Emma began. "I noticed you speaking with Julian Jackson. As you know, we are investigating the death of his father."

Blaine raised an eyebrow. "Happened to be?"

"Buying a present for my nephew," she lied. "It looked to me like you and Julian had a disagreement. Can you tell me about that?"

"Happy to, because I am the person who made spudger.com a success, not Ethan Jackson."

"That's the company Ethan sold. Correct?"

"The way I see it, the Jackson family owes me $4,500,000. My payout from Ethan Jackson was $500,000. Just that ... after I built the entire company. Were it not for me, spudger.com would be no better than The Geek Squad, those fellows who drive those black and white Geekmobiles. I recruited every single one of the techies who made our company so successful that it sold for nine million dollars."

"Is that what you were talking to Julian about?"

"Yes," Blaine said, "and he told me to piss off."

Emma realized that she was speaking with her first truly viable suspect. She'd never been fully convinced that Julian murdered his dad.

And Blaine came complete with a financial motive.

"Do you mind if I sit, Mr. Blaine?"

"Of course," he said, "forgive my rudeness." He gestured to a club chair and took one himself. Pepper sat right next to Emma.

"That's a fine-looking bitch you have, Chief Thorne." He smiled, but the smile missed his eyes. "Is she a killer?"

Well, Emma thought, *he opened the door.*

"Yes," she said, "are you?"

Victor laughed wholeheartedly. "Unusual interrogation technique, Chief. Admirable. But, no, I did not kill Ethan Jackson."

"Tell me more about your relationship with Ethan."

"Safer territory, I agree. Ethan and I started spudger.com a while ago. To be fair, it was Ethan's idea. However, he could not have done it without me. All we had between us was a written contract, which we had prepared without the assistance of an attorney. I had one copy, and Ethan had the other."

"What does spudger mean?" Emma asked.

"A spudger is a tool computer technicians use. It's used to pry and probe electronics' parts. Since we repaired computers, it was the perfect name. I thought of it, by the way. Ethan was a clever businessman, but he was not particularly creative."

Victor rose from his seat and started pacing the room. "Then out of the blue, Ethan decided, unilaterally, to sell the company. In our agreement, either one of us could invoke that privilege. I didn't want to sell, but I had no choice. That night I went home to check the details of my contract, but it was not in my desk drawer where I had left it. There is no question in my mind that Ethan stole it. After he arranged the sale, he walked away with nine million, of which he gave me half a million. So, you can see why I detested the man. But I didn't kill him."

Emma said, "Why don't you sit down, Mr. Blaine? You're making me nervous."

He did. Emma continued, "Ethan was murdered on Sunday morning, the thirteenth of May. Can you tell me where you were between, say, 6:00 a.m. and 11:00 a.m.?"

"I was out photographing birds."

"But it was raining that morning."

"I know. But I photograph birds every Sunday morning, rain or shine. It's one of my many hobbies." He waved his arm to indicate his toys.

"Really? Did you run into anyone who could verify this?"

"No," he said, "but I can easily prove where I was and when I was there."

"How's that, Mr. Blaine?"

Victor rose again and left the room. When he came back, he was carrying a black camera with a light gray telephoto lens. "It's a Canon 7D Mark II DSLR," he said proudly. "I also use it to photograph my models."

"Models?"

"Plastic models, like these. Not nude women, if that's what you're thinking."

Victor pointed the LCD screen toward Emma. He scrolled back through a series of pictures. They were time- and date-stamped. Eventually he got to the series he was looking for. Sure enough, the date read Sunday, May 13. And the pictures clearly showed that it was raining.

Emma thought for a minute. She said, "What's to have stopped you from adjusting the date afterwards?"

Victor had a ready answer. He scrolled forward through the pictures and showed her last Sunday's date, five days ago. More bird pictures and no rain.

"This camera also has GPS-encoding. Let's see … ah, here's a good one: 9:33 a.m., Sunday, May 13. 41.9914° North, 73.0957° West. That's the latitude and longitude of Mount Pisgah State Park, which is about an hour away. You can check the lat-long if you want. Does that satisfy you, Chief?"

"Was there anyone else at spudger.com who felt cheated by Ethan Jackson?"

"There was The Kid," he said thoughtfully, "we always called him The Kid."

"What's the kid's name?"

"Joe Henderson," Blaine said.

Emma perked up.

"I know a Joe Henderson," she said quickly. "Mid-thirties? Short, dark hair? Good looking?"

"Sounds about right."

Emma leaned forward. "Tell me about him."

"Super bright kid. MIT. A real computer genius. He started his own company in college and sold it before coming to us. I understand he made a lot of money. Odd kid, though, he kept himself to himself, very much the loner. But I will say, when he engaged, he could be quite agreeable. Ethan used to say he could charm the habit off a nun."

Emma smiled. "What happened when Ethan sold spudger.com?"

Blaine picked up a model airplane from his chair side table and fiddled with it. He averted his eyes. "The kid was as furious as I was. He got a settlement from Ethan but not nearly what he deserved. The last day, he and Ethan were shouting at each other inside Ethan's office, but I couldn't make out their words."

"I'm sure you read that I arrested Joe recently," Emma said deep in thought.

"No, I didn't," he said. "I don't read the local newspaper. I find it provincial and amateurish. Why did you arrest him?"

She answered obliquely. "He's being charged with child abduction among other crimes. The girl went with him willingly. He had a weapon, but he had a permit to carry one. But he is in serious legal jeopardy for evasion and vehicular endangerment. That said, I'm told he was able to make bail."

"Gee-whiz!" Blaine exhaled. "Sounds to me like you should pay him a visit."

"Oh, I will. Thank you for your candor and your time, Mr. Blaine. We can let ourselves out."

Emma and Pepper left the house. She *would* check out Joe Henderson, because she found Blaine believable. She decided to ask Buzz to go back and check the camera over. He understood techno-shit. Maybe he could figure out if Blaine could have manipulated the metadata.

But she doubted that even the self-described hobbyist was that clever.

21

Leak

Officers Pete Sinclair and Chuck Smith wrote their canvassing report and left it on Emma's desk, where she found it Saturday morning. As she feared, none of the neighbors saw, or admitted seeing, anyone at the Jackson house. Not on Saturday night or on Sunday morning. No one reported hearing anything out of the ordinary either. One neighbor noticed Mary Jackson and Julian driving out the driveway, but she couldn't say what time. Not that it mattered. Emma already knew that.

Caroline Stoner stopped by the office.

"Chief," she said, "got a sec?"

"Sure, what've you got?"

"Two cups of coffee, for starters. Milk, no sugar for you."

"That's thoughtful. Have a seat."

"I also have Ethan Jackson's phone records. I'm afraid they're not gonna be much help. One call was made to the house on Sunday morning. No out-going calls. The incoming was made from a cell phone. We traced it to a Walmart store on Foxon Boulevard in New Haven. The buyer paid cash ... three months ago. No way anyone's going to remember who, but I asked the manager to contact everyone who was working a register that day. I got the carrier, AT&T, to ping the cell phone. No response. The tech said the phone is either destroyed, or someone removed the battery or the SIM card. Worst of all, there is no record of any calls made from this phone before or since. Smells like a burner to me."

Caroline continued, "True, but it tells us that someone called Ethan the morning he died. *That* smells like a killer to me. Plus, it makes Mary and Julian less likely suspects.

"So, Ethan knows the killer, who calls him in advance. Then Ethan willingly lets him into his house. They have what looks like consensual sex. The partner disappears after stringing Ethan up. Why? And why stage it as a suicide?"

"All good questions," Emma said. "I wish I had some answers."

Emma then told Caroline about her meeting with Victor Blaine and his mention of Joe Henderson.

"*Our Joe Henderson?*" she said in surprise.

"Yup! Our old buddy Joe Henderson. Count on my paying him a visit real soon."

Caroline nodded but didn't move to get up.

"Anything else?" Emma asked.

Caroline took a sip of her coffee. Her eyes wandered around the office and then back at Emma. She said, "Okay to speak frankly, Chief?"

"We've been friends a lot longer than I've been chief. I'm Emma, before and now. What's on your mind?"

"I just want to say that I always have your back."

"Shit, that sounds ominous. Why do I need your protection?"

"There's, um, just been a lot of talk. I mean, I hear people say things."

"I'm guessing not very nice things."

Caroline said, "Pretty hurtful, truthfully. I don't need to tell you that Archie's a tough act to follow ... for anyone. Like all good leaders, he had the unconditional support of his troops—"

"Is this about my handling of the Ethan Jackson case?"

"Um, partly."

"You were right, Caroline, to give me a heads-up. Go ahead and spit it out. I can take it." Emma meant it when she added, "Whatever you tell me will be helpful."

"Okay then, here goes. From what I can tell, there are two issues. Some of the guys ... well actually most of the guys ... think that Wardlaw may have been hasty in promoting you to chief—"

"They think that Stella should have been chosen instead of me?"

"Not exactly. Stella may think that, but I don't think most of the department agrees with her. She's not the most popular, to be honest. Did you know that she calls you 'The Saintly One?'"

Emma had to laugh. "Do you know what a Spoonerism is?"

"A what?"

She explained, "A Spoonerism is an accidental (or intentional) transposition of sounds in two or more words, such as ..."

Emma tried to remember a good example. "Oh, I know one that's perfect for a cop called Stoner: 'A hot pie would make me happy.' The Spoonerism would of course be 'A pot high would make me happy.' My Spoonerism for Stella is 'Shining Wit', AKA, 'Whining Shit.'"

Caroline gave a full-throated laugh. "'Whining Shit!' How perfect!"

Emma joined in, loud enough to wake up Pepper.

But it didn't take her long to get back on track. "You said two issues. What's the other?"

Caroline stopped laughing as quickly as she'd started.

"It's the Ethan Jackson case. People can't figure out why you're going it alone ... why you're not asking for help from the state police."

"Yes, the state police, the ones with all the experience. Truthfully, I'm not entirely sure either. I think about it a lot. I guess I think I'm trying to prove something to all three of us. To Archie, Will, and myself."

"I hate to sound like a typical cover-your-ass cop, but it would help to spread the blame if the Jackson case turns cold."

"I really appreciate your being candid with me."

"Yeah, sorry to be the bearer of crappy news."

"That's what it means to be friends. Thanks for sharing. I mean it."

Caroline went to the door, chuckling. "Gotta love Whining Shit!" She closed the door behind her.

After Caroline left, Emma turned to Pepper. "What the hell am I going to do? All my suspects seem to evaporate. Maybe, Joe Henderson will have legs." Pepper pricked her ears, stood, and placed her muzzle on Emma's thigh.

"What do you say we take a walk?"

Pepper raced to the office door.

In Broken River Park, Emma released Pepper from the backseat. Instead of running off, the Belgian Malinois glued herself to Emma's left thigh like a limpet and quivered with anticipation. Emma lowered her voice, as she always did when giving Pepper a command. Free, she said. A thoroughbred at Churchill Downs couldn't have made a faster start. Pepper bounded away, her scissor-stride accelerating as she ran. She tore past two kids who shrieked, but Emma had utter faith that

Pepper would never hurt anyone unless she was told to.

Emma sat on a park bench. Saturday was bright and sunny. The air smelled fresh. The puddles left earlier in the week had evaporated.

She wished she could ask Will about the Ethan Jackson case. Will was a super person to bounce ideas off. He'd listen to the conundrum and give some seemingly random response, which would send her mind spinning in a new direction, often toward a solution. But, alas, no Will. Her dad would, of course, have been the perfect person to ask, too.

Dad's death had been so sudden, so unexpected she still hadn't fully processed the hole he'd left. Then again there was Will. How could anyone process the hole he had left? Still, she was glad that she had thought of asking Will first.

None of these thoughts was making her happy.

After giving Pepper a half an hour of pure joy, she pushed the tip of her tongue back with her pinkies and produced an ear-splitting whistle. Pepper was back at her side within seconds.

Emma said, "How about we take the rest of the weekend off?"

Even for Pepper that was a little too much to interpret.

On Sunday morning, after a breakfast of café au lait and a croissant, Emma walked to Jiffy Stop, where she picked up the *Hampshire Chronicle*. She handed it to Pepper, who liked to carry the newspaper home.

So, it was not until she was back in her kitchen that she saw the banner headline:

Medical Examiner: Ethan Jackson Murdered

She had no doubt that it was Stella who had leaked the story. Furious, Emma read the lead.

By Virginia Hobson, Staff Reporter

According to a source in the Hampshire Police Department, Ethan Jackson, 37, of 103 Hickam Street in the Northwood section of Hampshire was found dead in his house last Sunday. Police initially suspected suicide. However, after an autopsy by Dr. Herbert Mittendorf, 71, Chief State Medical Examiner, Mr. Jackson's death is now being investigated

```
as a homicide. Mr. Jackson, founder of
the internet start-up company spudger.
com ...
```

Emma threw the paper on her kitchen table and reached for her cell phone. She had Stella on speed-dial. Her call went straight to voicemail. Stella's cell phone was her third hand. Emma knew that she was ducking her call.

Emma forced herself to read the rest of the article, but there wasn't much more to glean other than the leak itself.

To calm down, she read the rest of the paper. The broadsheet was only twenty-four pages long. On the Obit Page, she saw that Mary Jackson had scheduled a funeral service for Ethan in four days, on Thursday at ten o'clock.

At least that gave her something tangible. Like FBI agents who photograph license plates at a mobster's funeral, she would attend just to see who else was there.

22

Geriatric Chubster

At precisely 6:30 a.m., I turn off "New Day Sunday" with Christi Paul and Victor Blackwell. I go to my front door to pick up the Sunday *Hampshire Chronicle* and the *Times*. I take the papers in their plastic bags back to my breakfast table.

I open the plastic bags and place them in the drawer that I have dedicated for newspaper bags. On the first of each month, I leave them outside for the paper girl to recycle them. I despise unnecessary waste. I regularly donate to the Natural Resources Defense Council, Inc.

I sit at my breakfast table, open the paper, and the headline screams at me.

I let out a banshee shriek. I throw the *Chronicle* across the room. Its pages flutter to the kitchen floor like angry butterflies. My fucking plan! So fucking perfect and now … wrecked. I smash my formidable fists on the table. Dammit, I shout. I am breathing as rapidly as when I do my barbell squats.

Calm yourself, goddammit. Think!

Eventually, I get on my hands and knees to retrieve the front page. I look for the name of the reporter who has rat-fucked me.

There. Virginia Hobson. Never heard of you, but I fucking have now!

I go to my laptop on the kitchen counter. My fingernails clack on the keys. The letters of the key tops I use the most—etaoin shrdlu—have already been obliterated by past use. I can't help myself. I have a heavy hand on the keyboard. I find her on the interweb: Virginia Hobson Hampshire CT, and I find Hobson's home address: 7 Waldron Avenue. I know the place. It is a new development in south Hampshire. Tacky houses all mish-mashed together with no regard for individuality or aesthetics, in short, puke-worthy architecture.

My bedroom closet, however, is the epitome of proper order. I hired a professional team from California Closets to install it, under my supervision.

I choose simple clothes. From the trouser section of my California Closet, I choose a freshly-laundered pair of Tom Ford blue jeans. From T-shirts, I choose a navy blue one. I check myself in the full-length mirror. Perfect. Except for the designer blue jeans, I look casually normal.

In the basement, I cut off a hank of the same rope I used to hang Ethan. I have a revised plan—you have to adapt when circumstances change—which will give Emma Thorne something new to consider. "Adapt or perish," H.G. Wells said. In my sports closet, I find my scuba-diving knife and insert the knife and its sheath next to the small of my back, covering it with my untucked T-shirt.

Preparation lowers my respirations.

Lastly, I place a Sharpie in my jeans' pocket.

Seven Waldron Avenue is, as expected, a cookie-cutter, builders' house *sans* much-needed input from an architect. In a word, hideous. Just the kind of house I expect an impertinent reporter to own.

Waldron was once a fine open area with a line of old growth maples lining the avenue. It is a damn shame how developers have torn the heart out of the neighborhood. And the trees.

As I stroll inconspicuously past the house, I am still at a rapid boil. I can't believe the damage this nosy-parker has caused.

There are lights on in the living room. Unless Hobson is a climate-change-denier, there is someone home. I didn't intend to re-use the phone I'd called Ethan with so soon. But, really, what better time? Knowing that the same cell phone was used in the murders of both Ethan and Virginia Hobson will drive Emma bat-shit. I dial Hobson's number.

Through the living room window, I see a plump, elderly woman pick up her phone.

"Virginia Hobson."

I adopt a low-pitched, professional voice. I say, "Ms. Hobson, my name is Pat Roberts. I'm a reporter with the *Hartford Courant,* a professional colleague of yours." I try to sound super-friendly, butter her up a bit. Not like a person who is about to garrote a geriatric chubster who's poked her nose where it doesn't belong. Anyway, flattery always works on the elderly. "Congratulations on your scoop. You've blown the Ethan Jackson case wide open. I wonder if I can have a quick interview with you?"

"Since when does a journalist interview another journalist about the latter's scoop?" Hobson says. Her words are reasonable, but the tone is icy.

I realize I'm underestimating her. I try again. "This is a big deal, Ms. Hobson. Right now, you're in the limelight, and I would like my article to reflect that. What do you say?"

"It's Sunday, Pat. If you want to talk about my article, why don't you call me in my office tomorrow morning to set up an appointment?"

My full fury comes to bear. I will not be thwarted by this biddy-bitch. "Look, Hobson, I'm from the *Courant,* not the *Hampshire Chronicle,* a rinky-dink newspaper at the best of times. Right now, I'm outside your house—"

I immediately regret my error. Just before Virginia Hobson turns to look out her window, I step behind one of the few remaining trees. Hobson doesn't know me, but I have to be careful. I peek from behind the tree and see Hobson's fat face pressed to the window.

"Whoops, Pat, could you please hold on a minute? I have another call. I must be popular today."

The change in Hobson's tone makes me suspicious. Impulsively, I wait anyway. When Hobson comes back on the line, she is downright cheery. "That'll be fine, Pat. Just give me a moment, I'm not even dressed yet. I'll put some coffee on."

Again, I wait ... until I hear an approaching siren. First one, then another. I race around the corner to my car. I'm barely behind the wheel when I hear the first police car skid to a stop outside Hobson's house.

As I drive my car away, I begin to calm down. That was a close call. I have to give Hobson credit. She was craftier than I would have guessed.

I hadn't particularly wanted to off the old biddy. Collateral damage doesn't keep matters as tidy as I like them to be. Still, I would've done it if I'd gotten inside her house. *I'm* not the one who screwed up my plan. She was.

I wasn't alive when Eisenhower was president, but I studied him at Hampshire High. Except for D-Day, he never struck me as being all that smart, but he did say, "In preparing for battle I have always found that plans are useless, but planning is indispensable."

Words to live by, I say.

Re-analyzing the situation, I figure that I have accomplished my mission, since Emma will surely trace the call back to the same cell-phone I used at Ethan's. I wonder what Emma will make of that. I delight in toying with her. It adds an unanticipated, yet delicious dimension, to my scheme.

I look forward to getting to know *ma nouvelle amie*, Deb Barger. Any friend of Emma's is gonna be a pal of mine ...

Feeling more like my confident self, I follow Deb's car as she drives it into Super Stop & Shop. I grab a shopping cart. I now have on a Red Sox ball cap, a pair of Ray-Ban shades, and a loose wind breaker. I'm traveling incognito, like people hope to when they're surfing the web for porn.

I load my cart with random items until I blend into the supermarket scene. Then I steer the cart in search of Deb. I spot her in Dairy, but I don't let her see me.

She's not the prettiest girl I ever saw, but she has a curvaceous, sexy figure. Her dark hair is appealing, though, in an tidy sort of way.

I watch her, thinking for a minute about where I am. Shopping means different things to different people. For Deb it is all about granola ingredients, tofu, and La Croix sparkling water. It's different for me. I'm shopping for my next victim.

A man walks up to Deb. He is nondescript with a broad smile on his face. They kiss on the lips. He whispers something in her ear. Deb starts laughing. Soon they're yukking it up together. I know Deb's not married, so this guy must be a boyfriend. By his enthusiasm, I judge him to be a new boyfriend.

I hope he is not a live-in boyfriend. It will muddy the old waters if I have to kill him, too.

23

Suzy Szarkowski

On Wednesday, a gorgeous, breezy June day, Emma arrived at the office early.

Pepper, as she always did, entered the room with her snout aloft. Each morning, her three hundred million olfactory receptors sampled the air, a continuation of her search for Archie. After a thorough investigation, she made a beeline for the desk chair, placing her front paws on the seat. Although Pepper knew Emma like a sister, the loyal hound mourned her true love, her master, her Chief.

Emma threw open the office windows to let the air in, distracting Pepper with new smells to enjoy. Emma wasn't quite sure why she was in such a good mood.

She sipped her coffee, which tasted better than normal. Leaning back in her chair, she enjoyed the cool early morning breeze playing on her face. After a few indulgent moments, she opened her laptop and checked her calendar. Time for work.

In the phone book, she found only one Henderson. A Matthew Henderson on Meadow Drive. Joe's father? She knew the street. It was in a secluded area on the outskirts of Hampshire not far from where her sister-in-law lived. She was about to dial the number but stopped herself. Paying Joe an unexpected visit would better serve her purpose.

With Pepper in tow, she drove out to Meadow Drive and found the long driveway which wandered up to the Henderson house. She knocked on the door of an obviously expensive, modern house with expansive views to the south and west. Henderson House, as a sign at the foot of the driveway announced, incorporated a series of black slabs at right angles separated by floor-to-ceiling windows. A big swimming pool dominated the front lawn.

Joe Henderson answered the knock. He was better looking than she remembered. Taller than she, at about six-foot-one, his black hair was carefully barbered. He wore pale blue bathing trunks and no shirt. He had a monogrammed towel around his neck. Clearly, he worked out.

With a cheery smile, he greeted her like an old friend. Joe had even, white teeth.

"What an unexpected surprise! It's my arresting officer. Come on in." His words spelled sarcasm, but his tone didn't. "What can I do for you?"

Emma was nonplussed. She'd anticipated hostility.

"Want to go for a swim? I'm sure one of my mom's bathing suits would fit you."

This was too bizarre. "Your parents, are they home?"

"No, they moved out about a year ago. They moved to an assisted-living facility outside of Boston. I have Henderson House all to myself."

Emma found herself saying, "They must be quite young for assisted-living."

"My mom has early-onset dementia. And my dad's a dick. Honestly, I'm glad to see the back of them. Are you sure you don't want to go for a swim?"

Emma was tiring of this *faux*-friendly back-and-forth.

"No, I don't want to go for a swim. I'd like to ask you a few questions, though. About Ethan Jackson."

"Sure, shoot. But I can save you some trouble. I hated the dishonest, lying sonofabitch." Joe was still smiling. "However, I didn't kill the thieving prick."

"I see," Emma said mildly. "Can you tell me where you were on the morning of—"

"Sunday, May 13, yes I can," he interrupted. "I know exactly where I was, because I was elated when I heard the news. Unfortunately, I don't have an alibi. I was asleep, by my lonesome."

Emma looked around at his richly-appointed living room and the walls of windows. "You have a beautiful house." It really was gorgeous. She was about to ask him how he could afford it, decided not to, and then changed her mind. "How do you afford the upkeep?"

Joe graced her with another of his dazzling smiles. "I'm rich."

Emma shifted gears again. "Tell me about Sophie King. I figure that there are about twenty-two years separating you two in age. What were you doing with her the day you were arrested?"

"Hey, what can I say? I was showing the girl a good time. No law against that. I like to show my girlfriends a good time."

"Sophie told me that you were planning to take photographs of her and introduce her to some of your friends. What kind of photographs? And what kind of friends?"

For the first time, Joe averted his gaze and fidgeted with his towel. "Look, I'm trying to be friendly here, and you're making some unpleasant insinuations … which I don't really appreciate."

"Nude photographs?" Emma persisted.

"No way. She's just a kid. Just some portraits. Photography's my hobby."

Emma raised an eyebrow, making sure Joe noticed. "Why would you want her to meet your friends? Did you plan on sharing her?"

Joe took several menacing steps toward her, his face furious. He pointed at the door. "That's enough! Get out of my house."

She decided to leave it for now, but she added Joe Henderson to her suspect list.

At the door, she asked, "What's the address of your studio?"

"Get out," he said. She left.

From her lay knowledge of the subject, Joe had some of the earmarks of a sociopath: the charm, the menace, and an irrational take on the world. Going forward, she would keep tabs on Joe Henderson.

Back in her office, Emma reached for the telephone, but it rang before she could pick up the receiver.

It was her private detective, Mark Byrne.

"Emma? Mark," he said. "How are you? Listen, I've interviewed everyone on your list both in New Haven and in Hampshire. Got some time today?"

"I'm impressed," she said, but her heart started pounding. "Are you in Hampshire? If so, are you free to come over?"

"I am, and I will."

Like the last time, Mark opened her office door without knocking. "Hey Pepper! How're you doing, girl?"

Pepper wagged her tail furiously. She clearly considered Mark an old friend. He spent a moment scratching Pepper behind her ears.

Emma was impatient. "What have you found out?"

"Bad news and not-so-bad news."

"Great."

Mark sat, laced his fingers behind his head, and stretched. "The not-so-bad news is that I am no closer to knowing what happened to Will. Which, as I said at our first meeting, shouldn't come as much of a surprise to either of us."

Emma nodded.

"If that's your definition of not-so-bad news, I hate to think what bad news—"

"Have you ever heard of Suzy Szarkowski?"

"Of course," Emma said, "she was one of Will's teaching assistants—"

She looked across the desk at Mark, who dropped his eyes. She said, "Oh no! Please tell me no."

Mark met her gaze. "I'm afraid so. If it's any consolation, which I doubt it is, she never saw Will after his depression began. That much, she swore."

Emma felt dizzy, sick to her stomach, and angry. She lashed out at Mark. "So, you just marched up to Suzy Szarkowski and said, 'have you been fucking Will Foster?'"

"Not exactly. I know this sucks. No, I interviewed her because she was on *your* list. Remember? But, during the interview, I didn't buy her affect. I guessed she was lying. That's when I asked, to use your words, if she had been fucking your husband."

"Thanks, Mark, you just wrecked my day. Rather, my life."

Emma grabbed a pencil and tossed it up in the air. Surprising both of them, its point stuck in a ceiling tile and stayed there. "Well, I feel better now," she muttered.

Mark got up and came behind her and placed his hands on her shoulders. "Emma, I feel shitty about adding to your troubles—"

"Don't touch me," she hissed.

Mark's hands lifted off her shoulders like rockets. He went back to the seat on the other side of the desk.

"You can't possibly know how I feel," Emma said. "I have fucking mourned that guy every second since he disappeared. I have cried my heart out. Will was my world, my everything. You know what's funny? I would have forgiven him in a heartbeat if he'd 'fessed up. But to find out this way … really fucking stinks. I'm not feeling sorry for myself.

Well, yes, I am. I would still do anything to get him back. So much longing, waiting, so much heartache. What's the point?"

"You want me to leave?" Mark asked.

Emma surprised herself, when she said no. She didn't want to be alone.

"Want to hear some more not-so-bad news?"

"Sure, WTF."

Mark smiled. "On Monday, I enjoyed a martini with Mary Jackson—"

"Mary Jackson," she said incredulously, "as in Mary-I-haven't-yet-buried-my-husband-Jackson?"

"One and the same."

"What on earth were you doing with Mary Jackson? She has nothing to do with Will's disappearance."

"I just like to cover my bases."

"What is that supposed to mean?" Emma didn't like this. Mark Byrne had no right messing in the Ethan Jackson investigation. On the other hand, this came as important news. Maybe Mary *did* know about Ethan's other life. Emma filed that away, without any intention of sharing her thoughts with Mark.

She looked at him appraisingly. "Just a martini?"

Grinning, he said, "Two martinis, actually. But I'm pretty sure it could have ended with a nightcap somewhere else."

Emma found his smugness annoying. She changed the subject.

"Who else have you spoken with?"

"I called Georgia Foster, your sister-in-law. She gave me a weird runaround, so I decided to give her some space. Try her again after a day or two. Then I called the Fosters. They agreed to meet with me, saying they would 'do anything' to get Will back. When I got to their house—nice house, by the way—Georgia was there, too."

Emma said, "I'll bet you got an earful from that trio."

"So, you know how they feel about you ..."

"I don't have to guess what they said, if that's what you mean. Georgia, in particular, hates my guts."

"Then there's no need to rehash my conversation with them."

"Not really," Emma said. "So where does that leave us? Is Will out there somewhere banging Suzy Szarkowski?"

"I'm pretty good at this. I believed her when she said she had no idea where Will was."

Emma watched Mark across the desk. Again, he laced his fingers behind the back of his head as he stared back at her. She got the unmistakable vibe that his look had lost a certain professional distance. *Not gonna happen, Mark,* she thought. Never going to happen.

"Are you free for lunch today?"

Instead of answering, Emma got her checkbook out of her bag. "How much do I owe you?"

"That's it?"

"Yes, it is."

A s soon as Mark was out the door, Emma smacked her forehead on her desk. Her tears came as expectedly as a hard rain in April.

The phone rang again. Ruby Sato said, "It's Mayor Wardlaw on the line for you, Chief." Emma considered trying the runaround but decided that was cowardly.

Angrily, she said, "Put him on."

"Emma, my dear, how are you on this fine June morning?" His voice boomed. "What you say you and I meet up for lunch today, say around 1:00?"

"I've had a pretty crappy day already," she said. "I'm not in the mood for lunch."

"Oh, Emma," he said, "you would be making a big mistake to turn me down. Besides, this would be a business lunch ... although, of course, if it became more, that would be fine, too."

Emma could almost smell his bad breath over the phone. "The answer is still no."

"Listen up, Emma, I'm going to give you ten minutes. Then I'm going to call you back, and I will expect a different answer." He disconnected.

Emma called Pepper out from under her desk well. She leaned over and gave her a kiss on her forehead. "What the hell am I going to do, Sergeant Pepper? I will never let him touch me again. What do you think? Will that cost me my job?"

Pepper replied with an inconclusive moan.

She called down to the dispatcher. "Can you cut a tape of my last phone call? And send it to my iPhone?"

True to form, Dick called her back after ten minutes. He said, "I'll meet you at Group Therapy at 1:00. Why don't you call Phil and ask for a quiet table in the back?"

Before she could reply, he rang off.

Emma again asked Pepper for her opinion, but this time Pepper answered with a yawn.

"Well if losing our job doesn't matter to you, why should it matter to me?"

She wasn't sure what to do next. But then she did.

Joe, Mark, and Dick had put her in a confrontational mood.

She got Ruby on the intercom and asked her to send Stella Weeks up to her office. Emma waited impatiently. Ten minutes passed before Stella knocked on her door.

"Come."

"What's up, boss?"

Stella helped herself to a seat facing Emma's desk.

"I want to know how the *Chronicle* learned that Ethan was murdered. Before we had a chance to fully investigate and before the whole goddamn world knew. I made it very clear to the entire department, yourself included, what my wishes were. Someone inside our family leaked this to Virginia Hobson, and I want to know who. I think—"

"Um, Chief—"

"Let me finish. I think it was you." The chances that Stella was *not* the leaker were slimmer than an anorexic model.

"That's ridiculous. Why the hell would I do something like that?"

Emma studied her smug expression. Stella averted her eyes, and, at that moment, Emma knew she was lying. Trouble was, she couldn't prove it.

"I think you're lying to me," she said.

Stella smiled a nasty smile, arched an eyebrow, and looked at Emma square in the face. "You know what, it's shit like this that makes you such a crappy chief."

Angry as she was, Emma was stunned by the insult. She stood and went to the window, to conceal how she felt. She knew her face would give her away. Looking out at the alley below, she took a deep breath and said, "You and I are going to have to get on the same page here, or we are not going to be able to work together."

"Is that a threat?"

"Yes, it is."

"Are you firing me?"

"No, not yet. But I'm considering it."

Stella said, "If I were you, I would stop considering it. You don't know who you're dealing with. You fire me, and I guarantee that you will regret it."

Emma regained her composure. She said, "Now that is definitely a threat. Please leave."

Whining Shit stood. She pulled down her uniform shirt so that it was even tighter over her stare-at-me chest. She lifted her right hand, its back toward Emma, and raised her middle finger.

"Later, Chief," she said, slamming the door behind her.

Emma shook her head. Slowly but surely Stella was whipping up a storm, like the first rolling pebbles which telegraph a landslide.

She sat, staring at Archie's picture on the wall, until she decided to put Shining Wit on the back burner, for the moment. But she left the gas on High.

One o'clock came and went. She blew off Wardlaw, who didn't call her a third time. At least she had that for which to be grateful.

Shortly after 3:00 p.m., Emma slapped Pepper on the butt.

To the dog she said, "Fuck this," and they went home.

24

"Where are you, Chief Thorne?"

Dominating a hill above Main Street stood the larger of the two Catholic churches in Hampshire, St. Michael's. The tip of its copper-clad bell tower was Hampshire's highest point. Though its infrastructure was at risk, the interior was vast, ornate, and slathered with gold. Emma wasn't religious. But she had been inside the church many times, for weddings and, in this case, her second funeral in a matter of weeks.

She arrived early. She stationed herself inside a secondary doorway at the top of the stone stairway leading to the ogival-arched front doors. Concealed, but, she thought, not overtly furtive, she watched the arrival of Ethan's friends and relatives.

She still felt crushed by the previous day's body-blows, but she had resolved to bury her emotions until Ethan's funeral was over.

She saw Officer Larry "Buzz" Buzzucano watching from across the street. He'd clearly had the same idea as she. Good for him.

Mayor Dick Wardlaw arrived with his wife on his arm. Emma couldn't remember her name. Hizzoner glad-handed everyone within reach as he mounted the steps. Emma spied her sister-in-law Georgia Foster in the distance. She was surprised to see her there, since Georgia didn't get out much. Perhaps she was friends with Mary Jackson.

Vanessa Mack spotted Emma, and she came over and gave her a hug and a kiss. She was with her husband, Dave, who shook Emma's hand.

A lot of people she didn't recognize arrived. Ethan had drawn an impressive turn-out.

She checked her watch. It was time to go inside.

So far, her investigation had not advanced a millimeter.

Emma dutifully signed the Book of Condolences and took a pew in the rear.

She was beginning to chafe at the interminable service when Julian Jackson rose to speak. He thanked everyone for attending. He mentioned that all were invited to a reception in the Parish Hall afterwards. Emma's attention wandered until Julian paused for a long silence. His demeanor changed, and his expression grew hard.

"As you all know," he said loudly, "folks accused my father of committing suicide." Emma sat up in her seat. "That accusation was vile and despicable and hurtful."

Julian no longer seemed like the sniveling boy pressed against his mother's bosom. And he had the full attention of the congregation. There wasn't a cough or a fidget.

"My Dad was happy, loving, warm, and successful. He never did anything to hurt anyone. Then, out of the wild blue yonder, some vicious felon violated our home and murdered my Dad."

People gasped. Pews creaked.

"This criminal, who has not been caught, faked a scene to tell a different story. Only an ignoramus would have fallen for it. Guess what folks? Guess who bought it hook, line, and sinker? That's right folks. The cops. Hampshire's Finest. Led by Chief Emma Thorne. They questioned my mom and me while my dad's body was still inside our house." Julian wiped tears from his eyes. His voice rose. "We tried to tell them that Dad was a good guy, who would never hurt himself or us. But they wouldn't believe us. *They wouldn't believe us.* Do you know how much that hurt? And then—hold on people, it gets worse—they actually, like, accused my dad of fucking around!"

Louder gasps. People throughout the church were speaking aloud.

"And now we know how wrong and cruel they were," Julian bellowed from the pulpit. "And how sick. Well, I say, cops, it's time to do your goddamned job. Where are you, Chief Thorne? Oh, there you are…" He pointed his finger right at Emma. "…is there anything you would like to say?"

Emma was horrified. She felt her face turn a deep red. Nearly everyone in the church turned in their seats to stare at her. Since there was no place to hide, she kept her head high.

Dick Wardlaw, who was sitting in the front pew, stepped toward the pulpit and put his arm around Julian to guide him back to his seat. Emma couldn't hear what he said, but, as Julian shoved the Mayor roughly aside, everyone heard Julian shout, "You're no better than they are. Let me finish, you fraud!"

At that moment, Father Ben intervened and managed to shepherd Julian, now crying, off stage and into the privacy of his sacristy.

While every attendee's eyes stared at the sacristy door, Emma seized the moment and made a bee-line for her car.

She drove a few blocks away from church. She pulled into the anonymity of a Burger King parking lot. Julian's speech in church shook her to her core. He had a right to call her out. Just as he had the right to say that her search for the killer was no further along than it had been eleven days ago. Emma knew that she had caused the boy and his mother considerable pain.

She felt crappy. Worse, now, because she knew she owed Dick Wardlaw a word of thanks.

She restarted her car, forcing herself to attend the reception. She had to confront the firestorm head on. She drove to the Parish Hall and was one of the last to arrive.

Everyone stared at her when she walked in. None of the stares was friendly. She didn't meet the eye of a single person who communicated sympathy, or even empathy.

Too proud to appear to be hiding, Emma strolled over to the refreshment table where a churchwoman poured her a glass of punch.

Remembering why she was at Ethan's funeral in the first place, she forced herself to scan the room.

She spied her sister-in-law moving through the crowd. Why was she here? When Georgia stopped to chat with Deb Barger, Emma was further surprised. She felt certain that Deb would have mentioned it if they were friends.

Emma couldn't stop watching Georgia.

The next person Georgia huddled with was none other than Sergeant Stella Weeks. The surprises continued. Heads pressed together, they appeared to know each other well. They clinked punch glasses. What could they have in common? Emma decided that they must be discussing Julian's outburst. Everyone else was talking about it. Could it be more, though?

She looked for Julian. She spotted him through the crowd. He was standing by himself for the moment. His eyes were still red-rimmed. He took a quick slug from a flask, which he quickly replaced into his suit-jacket pocket.

While she was thinking, however inappropriately, that she too could use a pop, she felt someone's presence directly behind her.

In her left ear, she heard: "You never should have stood me up for lunch, Emma. I've warned you that there will be consequences."

Before she could turn around, Wardlaw goosed her right in her butt. Right up her butt, in fact. She couldn't believe it. Livid, she spun around to see his back moving through the crowd. The pig was actually holding his wife's arm with his other hand.

Emma tore after him, funeral be damned. Everything that had already happened be damned. She grabbed his free arm and wrenched him around.

"Don't you ever touch me again," she snarled.

Wardlaw's wife sputtered, "What in heaven's name is she talking about?"

Wardlaw ignored Emma.

To his wife, he said, "It's nothing, honey. I'm sure the chief is just reacting to being called out in public." He took his wife's arm and led her away.

No thanks for you then, perv!

Emma felt dirty and violated. She shuddered and freed the wedgie he'd inflicted. She felt more threatened than ever. Her job, her existence, her self-respect. *What should I do now?* Wardlaw could fire her as capriciously as he'd hired her. Maybe, she no longer wanted the job. Maybe, she really wasn't cut out for it. Maybe, she should call in the state police for help. Why hadn't she? Hubris, she ashamedly admitted. Misguided pride. Maybe Dad would have already solved Ethan's murder.

Maybe, maybe, maybe…a scribbled list of fucking maybes.

She couldn't go back to the office. Not now. Instead she drove home. She'd been doing a lot of going home early recently.

On the way, anger shoved her doubts aside. *I* will *solve this case! I* will *figure out who killed Ethan Jackson!* she told herself. *Screw the odds, I* will *prevail.*

25

Sherwood Forest

Although she was generally a beer and wine drinker, Emma bought a bottle of Lagavulin on her way home from the debacle at St. Michael's.

Pepper greeted her at the door with a welcome that would have cheered most anyone.

By sunset, Emma was sloppy-drunk. A half-empty bottle proved it. She remembered Phil Masters telling her at Group Therapy that being chief meant you could never get shit-faced. *Ha-ha!*

Next, she tried very, very hard not to think about anything. Without success. Every horror of the last month-and-a-half haunted every sip. At least, the scotch was good.

Deb Barger rang, but Emma let it go to voicemail. Deb offered to come over, "if you need a friend." Vanessa called to say that the whole funeral-thing had made her furious. That, Emma heard on voicemail, too. She wished they would leave her alone.

She paced, stumbled really, around her house cursing at anything and everything. She noticed that her glass was empty again. She poured another, not bothering with ice.

Emma passed a picture of Will hanging on her living room wall.

She raised her glass, bitterly toasting him, "Here's to you, my darling husband, for better or for worse, for richer or poorer, for whatever." She took the photograph off the wall and threw it into the fireplace. Pepper leapt to her feet, startled by the shattering glass. Pepper looked inquiringly with her soulful brown eyes. Emma looked away.

Despite the booze, Emma remembered inadvertently knocking the same picture off the wall the day Will had disappeared. She had replaced the glass and repaired the broken frame. This time, why fix it? What was there to fix?

The damn phone rang again. She checked caller ID. Caroline Stoner was calling. Odd.

"Emma Shorn speaking." She realized she was slurring, but she didn't give a shit.

"Chief, it's Caroline Stoner. I'm sorry to call you at home, but I thought you might want to hear some news."

"Didn't I tell you to call me Emma?"

"Um, Emma, have you been drinking?"

"You bet your ash I have. Didn't you hear about my latest humiliation?"

"Yes, I did. I'm sorry about that, what you had to go through. Maybe this can wait until morning."

Emma took another gulp. "You called. I answered. So, get on with it."

Caroline said, "Right. You'll remember that I told you about my interview with Virginia Hobson? After someone called her? She was convinced that that person meant to do her harm. I wasn't so sure, but I ran the phone anyway with my tech buddy—"

"It was the same phone used to call Ethan Jackson."

"How the heck did you know that?"

Emma felt a little more sober. But she said, "Probably because I'm drunk."

Caroline chuckled. "Maybe you should get drunk more often."

Emma couldn't summon a chuckle. "Shanks for the heads up," she told Caroline.

Then she hung up on her.

Emma didn't know what to make of Caroline's news. She knew it was important, but at the moment she didn't really care.

Emma turned the TV on. Good Christ, there was another school shooting, this time in Florida. She watched for a while, and then she decided to issue every teacher at Hampshire High with an assault rifle.

She looked at her watch. The hands looked like eels swimming in a round fishbowl. It didn't really matter what the time was. She half-walked, half-crawled up the stairs to her bedroom. Still in her funeral dress, she fell over the bed and passed out.

In the distance, Emma heard a hornpipe. It was "Sherwood Forest." Robin Hood was in her bedroom.

She lifted her head off the pillow and immediately regretted it. A chorus of pounding drums joined the tune. Except for the drumming, there was a brief moment of silence before "Sherwood Forest" played again and before she realized that her iPhone was telling her that she had an incoming text.

Supporting herself with her elbow, she reached for her iPhone and knocked it to the floor. Fuck it. She let her head fall back onto the pillow, which felt like she'd hit a sturdy piece of plywood. Ouch. But she was back asleep in seconds.

"Sherwood Forest" played a third time.

She leaned over the edge of the bed, sweeping with her outstretched hand, feeling for the phone. Eventually, she gripped it.

Holding it away from her, she blinked her eyes. Sawdust crunched. She squinted until the tiny little letters came into focus. Then they crackled out of focus. Holding the phone with her left hand, she rubbed each eye in turn with her right knuckle. She blinked furiously and was finally able to read the text. If she hadn't been so drunk, she would have been able to read it in the first place.

> Emma, your endless interference is really pissing me off. Stop looking for me. Stay out of my life.

The text was signed by her husband, Will Foster.

26

Christina's World

Barring the mosquitoes, it's a fine June night. The tree line lies about fifty yards from Deb's house. It is surrounded by woods. My car is nearly half a mile away, parked on Addison Road. I have changed into an all-black outfit, well-suited for surveillance. There is a moon out casting spooky shadows, but I'm unconcerned.

Deb must feel safe and secluded. Not a single curtain is drawn, and every light is lit. I am invisible, though. There is no way she can see me.

She is making herself something for a late dinner. I don't mind. Patience is my fourth **P**. Actually, that's not strictly true. There are only three **P**s: preparation, plotting, and pulling it off. But if you think there are four, then it must be true. Mustn't it?

She takes a plate into the living room and turns on the TV by remote control. I watch as she flips through the channels until she settles on something that piques her interest.

Time to move closer.

I creep-walk across her lawn. In spite of the night, I manage not to step on a single twig.

The lower part of the northeast window of her living room is blocked by a hedge. I tiptoe behind it and peep over the top through the window. Deb is only nine or ten feet away. The window is open. If the privet weren't so fragrant, I would be able to smell her.

She is engrossed in that insipid movie, "Forrest Gump." But I'm not going to get distracted by Deb's "cultural" proclivities. I am waiting until she gets ready for bed. I figure I've got about ninety minutes left of Tom Hanks pretending to be a retard.

I almost slap a mosquito before I stop myself. I am so close to Deb, she would definitely hear a slap. I let it bite me. Do you know how hard it is to watch a mosquito's proboscis burrow into your skin and not react? Did you know that if a mosquito finds enough blood to suck, avoids being squished, and gets enough water, she can live as long as three weeks. Only the females bite. Big surprise.

After nine more bites, I am finally forced to watch the interminable final scene, Forrest's monologue when he yaps to Jenny Gump's gravestone.

Deb remotely clicks off the TV and leaves the room after turning off the lights. She turns the kitchen and hall lights off, too.

I creep around the house until I find the southwest-facing window of her bedroom. She is standing next to her bed. Her hair has been done up in a messy bun. She removes some hairpins and lets it fall over her shoulders.

Hanging on the north wall, lined up one-two-three, I notice framed images: one, a rendering of the Rainbow Coalition flag; two, a poster of an extremely unattractive black woman, who I believe is Harriet Tubman; and, three, an antique Equal Rights Amendment poster, no doubt printed before Deb was born.

Against a backdrop of flying hearts, it reads:

Girls just want to have Fun– damental Human Rights

I grieve for her boyfriend, the one I saw at Super Stop & Shop.

After turning down the bed and fluffing her pillows, Deb begins to undress. I've looked forward to this part.

Underneath her shirt and shorts, she is wearing standard-issue, #MeToo underwear, high-waisted, white cotton panties and a white cotton bra. A complete turnoff. She unhooks her bra, and her large breasts tumble out. Like pancakes with too much batter, they flatten against her ribs. Her nipples stare at the floor. Sad!

She bends over and removes her panties. Then she turns and faces me. I am in the shadows, the bedroom is brightly lit. I don't think she can possibly see me, but at this point I am hardly going to stop watching. My new view of Deb is a significant improvement. She has shaved her crotch around her *labia majora,* but she has left a small triangle of wiry hair over her *mons pubis.* I stare hard. There is a Christina piercing where the *labia majora* meet below her pubic mound. A small diamond sparkles in the light.

Maybe, I shouldn't grieve for the boyfriend.

Deb lies down on the bed on her back, her head against the puffed pillows. Her sheets are black satin. *Who knew?* She adjusts a contraption which looks like a swing-arm desk lamp. Instead of a lampshade and bulb on the end, there is a clamp that holds an iPad. Ingenious. She punches some virtual keys and then settles back to watch. Another Tom Hanks movie? No! Through the open window I can hear a man and a woman saying naughty things to one another. Huh! Debbie does Dallas. Deb does porn.

She reaches into a drawer in the bedside table and takes out a squirt-container of personal lubricant. Then her left-hand drifts to her crotch. With two moistened fingers, she rubs her clitoris using a slow, gentle circular motion. I watch, mesmerized. It's all I can do not to touch myself.

She stops and squirts a generous dollop of Glide onto the fingers of her other hand. She slides those two fingers into her vagina. With the other hand, she resumes massaging her clitoris, varying her pressure and timing.

From the iPad comes the sound of some serious moaning. Deb joins the chorus. Her body spasms. She shrieks. No one can hear her but me. She has what I take to be a soul-striking orgasm.

Peeping is definitely underrated.

Deb goes into the bathroom and washes her hands. Seconds later, she's back in bed with the lights out. Apparently sated, she begins to snore softly.

I wait.

I time myself with my expensive watch. Precisely one hour later— it's now 10:45 p.m.—I walk around the back of the house to the kitchen door. As I expect from a free spirit like Deb, the door is unlocked. Gingerly, I open the door, prepared to stop at the slightest squeak. But it opens smoothly and quietly. I creep down the hall which I know leads to Deb's bedroom. The door to the bedroom is open, too. I tiptoe across the room to the edge of her bed. My special shoes have rope soles. I move soundlessly.

I indulge myself in a pleasant timeout to watch her sleep. She looks prettier asleep. I glide to the left side of her bed, lean over, and take a deep sniff of the smells emanating from her body. She wears a heavenly perfume. It smells more expensive than I expect. *Delicious.*

I snap the light on.

Deb wakes up and, with astonishing speed, sits up, fully alert.

"Hi Deb," I say casually.

"Oh, God," she shouts, "what are you doing in my bedroom?"

27

Nineteen Words

A cold, wet nose woke Emma up. She pushed it away. When that didn't work, she cracked an eye. Pepper and she were nose to nose. "No, Pepper, let me sleep."

If Pepper could speak, she would've said, "Wake up, it's nearly ten o'clock." Instead, she licked Emma's nose. Through gritty eyes, Emma managed to focus on her bedside clock. Jesus, it was nearly ten o'clock. She sprang out of bed. When her feet hit the floor, she instantly regretted moving at all. The shock went straight to her alcohol-ravaged brain.

An EMT had once told her that medical-grade oxygen is a miracle cure for hangovers. She had half a mind to drive over to ambulance headquarters, for which she had the key-code, and help herself to a tank.

Still in the dress she'd worn to Ethan's funeral, she went into the bathroom, stripped, and took a cold shower. Icy jets needled her body. Drying off, Emma realized that she couldn't remember anything except people constantly leaving messages on her answering machine. She knew that she had suffered a complete alcoholic blackout. She also knew something bad had happened after the funeral, which had been bad enough in the first place. She just couldn't remember what.

She reheated some cold coffee in the microwave and let Pepper out to pee.

While sipping bitter coffee, she scrolled through Caller ID on her landline. Deb, Vanessa, and Caroline Stoner had all called. It was the last call that caught her attention. Stoner had never called her at home before. She couldn't remember a thing about their conversation or the reason for the call, but she would check in with Stoner as soon as she got to the office. Vanessa and Deb, she would get to later.

Which reminded her that she was very late.

She dressed in a clean uniform, and she and Pepper hurried to headquarters.

Caroline Stoner was in the lobby when they arrived. They went up the stairs together, Caroline's ponytail bouncing flippantly behind her.

"Big news about the cell phone," Caroline said. "No?"

Emma grinned through her headache. "Would you mind replaying that conversation for me?"

"So, you were as drunk as you sounded."

"I sure was."

Caroline again told her that the same cell phone had been used to call Ethan Jackson and Virginia Hobson.

Up in her office, Emma gestured for Caroline to sit. For the first time, Pepper went straight to her den in the well of the desk. Emma wondered if her period of mourning for Archie was finally tailing off. She hoped so.

"So," Emma continued, "if Hobson is correct—that her Sunday caller was out to do her harm—then we have a potential multiple murderer on our hands. He just was not as successful with number two, thanks to your response."

"Sure sounds like it."

Emma fiddled with a stapler. "How certain are you that Hobson was really being threatened? Or was it the excitement of an old lady reporter who had just obtained her first scoop?"

Caroline said, "She's only seventy-one. I asked her age. And she seems pretty sharp. My bet is that she assessed the situation pretty accurately. First off, I checked. There is no reporter at the *Hartford Courant* named Pat Roberts. And then there's the part where the alleged reporter goes off on her. Hobson quoted him as saying something like, 'I'm from the *Courant*, not a rinky-dink newspaper like the *Hampshire Chronicle...*'"

"It's not exactly an I'm-going-to-kill-you moment, but I see what you mean. I hope you told her to be careful, watch her back, etc."

"Yup, I did."

"Well, thanks for the follow-up. I'm glad we have your source at the phone company. He is a godsend. Apologies again for last night."

"Not a problem," Caroline said, leaving. "I hear that Julian Jackson was pretty brutal at the funeral. Strikes me as a perfect time for a bender."

Emma snorted. "You wouldn't say that if you could feel the torture chamber inside my head."

As best she could, Emma concentrated on backed-up paperwork. After a time, she was interrupted by an incoming text. The notes of Sherwood Forest triggered some unpleasant yet irretrievable memory.

> **Let's try to reschedule lunch. I'm free tomorrow.**
> **Dick**

Yeah, like that was going to happen.

She deleted the text, which was when she noticed that there was another text she didn't remember reading.

Expecting a routine message, she casually scanned the text, date-stamped yesterday, Thursday, at 11:17 p.m.

The nineteen words buried her with the force of vertical wind shear. She sucked for air. How could it be that Will was alive and knew what was going on in Hampshire? She read the message over and over. How incredibly cruel! Why would he want to hurt her so? What had she done to deserve this? Her head pounded now with far more than just a hangover.

She tried to focus, to concentrate. She looked at the incoming number. She had a friend who lived in Massachusetts with the same prefix. Could Will have been living just across the border this whole time, keeping track of her, and knowing about the police's and Mark Byrne's search?

She reached for her desk phone to call Caroline Stoner. Stoner's phone company friend could track this in a flash. But she stopped herself.

A loud voice in her percussed brain told her no. This was no longer police business. This was personal.

She didn't want to, but she called Mark Byrne.

"Mark, I need to see you. This is Emma Thorne. I have a problem."

"Why, Emma, I thought you had terminated my contract," Mark said.

"Come on. I don't need cruelty from you, too."

"What's that supposed to mean?"

Emma spilled her guts, reading him the text from Will.

"Holy shit, I didn't see that coming. Tell you what, I can be at your office at noon. How about some lunch?"

What was it about men and fucking lunch?

"No lunch. Just come."

"Okay, okay. Read me the originating phone number again."

A t 12:45, Mark arrived, greeting Pepper first, then Emma. He took his usual chair. Without preamble, he said, "I've traced the cell phone. It has never been used. It's a prepaid jobbie, a Straight Talk Huawei Sensa, purchased from a Walmart in Pittsfield, Massachusetts, on April 11, a Sunday. Pittsfield is about an hour north—"

"I know where Pittsfield is," she said. "Oh my God, Mark, this is huge."

"How come?"

Mark didn't know about the Jackson/Hobson cell phone, also a Walmart purchase, albeit a different Walmart. What were the chances of this being a coincidence?

"You said it's never been used?"

"Uh-huh."

Suddenly, the whole weight of Mark's bombshell crashed down upon her.

Oh, Jesus, Will! she thought. Could it be? Could it possibly be? Her husband Will could be the one she was looking for … times two.

Emma averted Mark's eyes and openly wept.

She could feel him staring at her. He tried gently, "Emma? Tell me what's going on."

When she didn't answer, he added, "What did I say? Why are you crying? Are you thinking what I think you are? Please tell me how I can help you."

"You can't," Emma said with finality. She wished he could.

Mark came around the desk. He embraced her shoulders with his arm and hugged her.

Emma flinched. "Please, just leave!" She hated herself for her words.

"I can't leave you like this," he said.

Shrugging off Mark's well-meant attempt to comfort her, Emma

rose from her chair and pushed him away.

She said, "I need you to leave me alone. I have to figure this out on my own." Even she was aware of the paradox. She'd called him, after all.

Pepper accompanied Mark to the door, not as a guard dog, but as a friend saying goodbye to a friend.

At least one of us has manners.

28

A Pleasant Tone of Voice

I take my time staring at Deb against the backdrop of her sexy black satin sheets. I watch her shake. Her terror is evident, but, for the moment, she doesn't say anything more. My eyes reluctantly leave her crotch and wander up to her face. *Her* eyes are darting every which way. I understand that she is seeking an escape route. She looks around her bedroom, presumably for a weapon. I follow her gaze. The most threatening object I see is a comb on her bureau. *Whatever.* I'm not terribly worried. Deb is well-toned, muscular even, but I've worked out more than she has.

I adopt a reasonable, pleasant tone of voice. "First an apology, Deb. I have nothing against you personally, but I *have* come here to kill you."

Deb says, "You're insane. Get out, or I'll call Emma."

Then she starts to scream and thrash and plead. "Please, please don't hurt me. I beg you. I'll do anything, anything."

I remove my scuba diving knife from where I like to keep it, snuggled against the small of my back.

Deb howls and struggles to free herself from the sheets. With my left hand, I grab her wrist and twist it violently behind her back. Turns out, I am far stronger than she is. She calls out in pain, "Stop it! Please don't hurt me! I've done nothing to you!"

I grab a clump of Deb's hair. "Deb, my pet, we're going for a little walk."

She kicks out at me with surprising force. Her adrenal glands sure are secreting. Her heel catches my left kidney causing unexpected pain. I throw her back on the bed.

"Okey-dokey, bitch, let's try it another way."

I gash her wrist with my scuba knife. I don't know which artery I've severed—her radial or ulnar (maybe both)—but blood spurts all over her bottom sheet.

Deb screams even louder.

I grab her hair again and force her out of the house. I frog march her around to the back as she continues to plead with me. She's getting irritating, and I tell her to shut up. She doesn't.

When we reach the back driveway, I instruct her to kneel down. She refuses, so I kick her legs out from under her. With a shriek she lands heavily on the road.

Seizing her hair once again, I rock her head back until her neck yawns invitingly. Placing the blade against her left carotid artery, I cut through her neck, finishing the slice at the opposing artery. I jump away, trying to keep the geyser of blood from spraying my clothes.

"Number two, Emma dear," I say aloud. But nobody can hear me.

I return to the house and take the top sheet, which is now on the floor. Outside, I cover Deb's naked butt with the black satin sheet. I want to protect her privacy from a bunch of horny cops.

Finally, with a brand-new Sharpie, I inscribe my special calling card on her back. This time, though, it's a brand-new letter. Emma can figure out whether it's an **M** or a **W**.

So fun.

29

Another Sharpie

It was a fine evening when Emma drove home, but she didn't take much notice. She had a plate piled high with worries.

It wasn't until she'd poured herself a class of Sauvignon Blanc—no scotch tonight—that she thought to call Vanessa and Deb. She tried Deb. There was no answer. She got Vanessa on the second ring.

"Dearie," Vanessa said brightly, "How are you surviving that frightful funeral. How dare that brat Julian Jackson! He had no right at all. You're doing as much as anybody can possibly do. And shame on you for not answering my phone call last night. I knew you were home. Who would go out after such an appalling day? I was just calling to cheer you up—"

Emma succeeded in getting a word in. "If truth be told, I hit the scotch pretty hard last night and managed to get plastered. Strictly for therapeutic reasons."

Emma could hear ice clinking at the other end of the line. "Everyone deserves a bender from time to time," Vanessa said.

The airy banter was wearing on Emma. She would have loved to unburden herself to Vanessa and read her Will's hurtful message. But some stronger power, which she obeyed, kept telling her not to.

"I tried Deb. No answer. Do you know what she's up to tonight?"

"I haven't talked to her since the funeral. So, no idea."

"Look, sweetie," Emma said, "gotta pour myself another glass of wine. Bye-bye. Talk soon. 'Kay?"

In the kitchen, she treated herself to another full pour. She decided that "Hair of the dog that bit you" was not a foolish concept. From her distant past, she remembered that the expression came from an old wives' tale that someone bitten by a rabid dog could be cured of rabies by taking a potion containing some of the dog's hair.

Whatever. Hangover-helper was working.

She sat on her red sofa and took out her cell phone. For the umpteenth time, she clicked back to Will's message. Much as she wished otherwise, not a single word had changed. And every one of them communicated no small measure of hatred. Everything about the text was so unlike the Will she knew. The man she loved was kind, gentle, and generous. Not the man who would write such vile words. It made no sense.

Her Will could never murder anyone. That was preposterous. Hell, with his depression raging he couldn't even get out of bed and get dressed let alone murder Ethan Jackson. And why kill Ethan anyway? None of it made sense. And yet there was the text …

The real question was what to do next. That was the job for a clear head. Tomorrow.

Meantime, she re-dialed Deb's home phone. Still no reply. She also tried her cell phone, which went directly to voicemail.

The moderate amount of wine she had drunk combined with the remnants of her hangover were taking their toll. She was exhausted. She looked at her watch. It was just after midnight and time for bed.

No sooner had Emma fallen asleep, her phone woke her up. She didn't mind. She wanted to hear Deb's voice. But it was Vanessa. "I'm really worried about her, Em, she treats her cell phone like a bodily appendage. When was the last time you called her cell and she didn't answer? Never. Right? I think we should go over there, check on her."

"Hmm," Emma replied, thinking of her comfy bed. "No, you're right," she decided. "I'll pick you up in fifteen."

Pepper perked up as Emma dressed. She slipped on shorts and a short-sleeved blouse. She found a waistband holster in her chest of drawers, placed her Glock in it, and clipped it to her shorts. Connecticut law requires off-duty police officers to carry.

She stopped at Vanessa's house. Vanessa was waiting for her in the cool, clear evening. They drove to Deb's.

Deb lived in an attractive center-hall Colonial outside Hampshire's city limits. Her house was surrounded by woods. They drove up her gravel driveway. The house was ablaze with light. Vanessa said, "Since she's obviously home and still up, why the hell isn't she answering her phone?"

Emma said, "Let's find out."

They walked up the sidewalk to the front door, which, typical Deb, was unlocked. Emma opened the door and shouted for Deb. She didn't get a reply. She looked at Pepper. Her canine companion was on high alert, her withers twitching.

Emma always listened to Pepper.

Emma placed a hand on Vanessa's arm. "I'm not getting a good vibe here. Why don't you wait here while I check the house?" Emma drew her Glock and held it next to her thigh. Pepper knew the meaning of a drawn weapon, and she tensed in anticipation of a job.

"Jesus, Emma, aren't you getting a little ahead of yourself? You're scaring me."

"I'm a cop. This is what cops do."

Emma ordered Pepper to heel. She stepped into the foyer and again shouted Deb's name.

Emma's short hairs were sending warning signals. She added her left hand to the butt of the Glock and held the weapon out in front of her. The master bedroom, she knew, was in the back.

"Seek!" she commanded. The Belgian Malinois went down the corridor and looked into each room in turn. She didn't enter. She merely sniffed. She was trained not to taint a crime scene. When she looked into Deb's bedroom, she backed up two steps. Immediately, she sat down and stared expectantly at Emma. Pepper made no sound.

Emma knew right away that something dreadful had happened.

She went to where Pepper sat. She instructed Pepper to stay put. Emma entered the room carefully. Deb's bedroom appeared to be empty. Emma stared at the bed. The bottom sheet was mussed up. A struggle? Or maybe just energetic sex? Yet where was her friend?

She approached the bed. When a yard or two away, she spotted the pool of blood. It had already coagulated, which told her nothing, because she knew that blood clots outside the body in thirty seconds or so.

She left the room and shouted down the stairs. "Stay where you are, Vanessa. Do not come back here."

She heard, "What's going on? You're freaking me out."

Without answering, she quickly checked the other rooms. They were all untouched by the events that had turned the master bedroom into a bloody butchery. She didn't doubt Pepper's skills, but she had her own rules to follow.

Emma had neglected to bring her portable radio. There was an old rotary dial telephone on a table in the upstairs hall. Emma shook her head sadly. It was just the kind of thing that Deb would have saved. She dialed the dispatcher's line and requested the resources she needed be dispatched.

"Hot response," she instructed.

Downstairs, as kindly as she knew how, she told Vanessa what she had found. But there was no way to lessen the shock … for either of them.

"Oh God, I knew something awful had happened. Emma, you've got to find her."

"That's exactly what I intend to do."

She looked down at Pepper, who was shaking with eagerness. Emma figured the dog knew more than she did.

She said, "Pepper, Seek!"

Her partner disappeared faster than a buttered bullet, around the side of the house and toward the back.

30

Another List of Maybes

"Stay here!" Emma ordered Vanessa.

To which Vanessa retorted, "I'm coming with you. Jesus, don't leave me alone!"

They both followed Pepper's path to the back of the house. Emma immediately spotted her dog sitting in the moonlight next to a black and blue lump the size of a body.

She returned her gun to its holster.

Emma pointed her flashlight. Deb was face down. The blood pool began at her neck and spread widely, staining the road beneath.

Vanessa wailed, and Emma wanted to. Knowing the futility of doing so, Emma felt for a pulse. Then, with two fingers she pulled the sheet back.

There it was: a letter formed by a Sharpie. Depending from which side of the body one viewed it ... either a **W** or an **M**.

Now there was no way to shade the new reality. The same person who had murdered Ethan Jackson had murdered Deb Barger.

Emma guided Vanessa back to the front of the house to await the troops.

On the front step, they hugged and cried.

Stella was the first to arrive, her deafening siren blaring. Ignoring Vanessa, she demanded of Emma, "What's going on?"

Emma sighed. "Follow me." To Vanessa she said, "Wait here. I'll get someone to drive you home when I have a spare officer. "

"No," Vanessa said firmly, "I told you, I don't want to be alone."

Before Emma could lead Stella around back, Buzz, Caroline, and Pete Sinclair arrived. Buzz carried his camera.

Caroline looked at Emma, who was obviously red-eyed, and said, "Deb was a good friend of yours. Are you sure you want to be doing this?"

Emma led the way without answering.

Over the body she said, "Let Buzz approach first, keep the contamination to a minimum. Buzz, get me a complete set of photographs. And don't miss the Sharpie signature."

"Holy shit!" Stella exclaimed. "Mr. Sharpie strikes again?"

"That's the way it looks," Emma said.

She had a feeling that the name Mr. Sharpie would stick. Didn't all serial killers get a nickname?

Buzz's strobe fired dozens of times as he worked the scene. Everyone waited patiently except Stella, who paced the driveway. Eventually, she said, "Chief, you gotta swallow your pride. Now's the time to call in CSP—"

Stella couldn't hide her surprise when Emma said, "You're right. Why don't you get in touch with the state police?"

"I'll get right on."

Emma excused herself and walked off by herself.

Between Will, Ethan, Archie, and now Deb, she was so angry that her pride no longer mattered. *Jesus, a serial killer in Hampshire.* All that mattered was catching the killer, even if the killer turned out to be Will, which of course was impossible. She was sanguine with her decision, even happy. Calling in the state police might feel like a victory to Stella, but, now, for Emma, it didn't feel like it was a defeat.

Re-energized, she went back to be with Vanessa.

Caroline and Pete left the house to knock on doors. Stella stayed with Buzz. Emma could still see the strobe flashes bouncing off the trees.

Emma wouldn't stay bottled up any longer. She suddenly confessed to Vanessa, "I heard from Will."

Vanessa broke off a sob. "That's wonderful," she said, wrapping her arms around Emma. "I am so happy for you."

Emma freed herself from Vanessa's embrace. She pulled up Will's message on her iPhone and showed it to Vanessa, who read it slowly. Then she appeared to read it again. "I am so sorry for you, Em. I hardly know what to say. This is a god-awful disaster."

"That pretty much sums it up. I can only see this is a punctuation point in my life. Not a comma, a period. What am I supposed to do next? Except hate the son of a bitch."

Vanessa said, "How did you reply?"

Emma blinked her eyes in self-astonishment. "You know what? I was so shocked, it never crossed my mind to text him back."

"Are you going to now?"

"I don't know."

"Let me see that again," Vanessa said suddenly.

Vanessa read the text for the third time, this time out loud. She inflected the words with the same malice with which they had been written.

> Emma, your endless interference is really piss-
> ing me off. Stop looking for me. Stay out of my
> life. Will

"Christ, Emma," she said when she finished, "you do realize what this might mean?"

"Yes. I do."

At 1:45 in the morning, a large Ford truck arrived. Painted gray, white, blue, and gold, the vehicle looked like an over-sized ambulance with no windows. The decals on its side read Connecticut State Police Major Crime Squad.

Emma realized that she felt relieved. She greeted the lieutenant who was in charge. Pepper regarded him with suspicion. His name was Skip Munro. Unlike every trooper she'd ever met, he wore his blonde hair over his ears and long in the back. He gave her a pleasant smile, but the bags under his eyes and the wrinkles on his face suggested he had seen more than most people had or should have. Despite the bumpy road etched on his face, she guessed he was not much older than she. Early forties.

Emma fully briefed him, ending with: "So, Mr. Sharpie is responsible for at least two homicides."

Skip let out a whistle. "No shit."

"No shit," Emma echoed.

"How come you didn't call us when Mittendorf figured out that the first guy—um, what's his name, yeah, Jackson—was a murder victim?"

Emma ducked the question. "It's a long story, but I'll be very grateful for your help now."

"That's what we're here for. What's the situation?"

"Deb is lying on the back driveway. Her neck has been slashed, well, ear-to-ear. I'm guessing a large knife was used, but that's only a guess."

"You called her by her first name," Skip said. "Were you acquainted with the victim?"

"I was," Emma said haltingly. "She was my best friend."

"I am truly sorry to hear that. If you want, we can take over from here. Why don't you go home and get some rest?" He looked at his watch. "It's pretty late."

"No, I would like to stay. "

Skip appraised her. "Did you know the other victim?"

"I knew Ethan Jackson, too." She decided to be honest with Skip. "He and I had a brief physical relationship in high school."

He kept his face impassive.

"Did the two victims know one another?"

"Yes, but I don't believe they were friends, *per se*."

He removed a tube of Nicorettes from his pocket and popped one in his mouth. "Trying to quit," he muttered.

"Is there any evidence of a sexual assault?" Skip asked.

"She is naked except for a sheet, but the truth is I don't know. I only touched her twice. First, to check for a pulse. I guess I did that out of desperation. I loved Deb very much. Second—call it a gut feeling—I lifted the bedsheet to check for a Sharpie mark, which, as you know, I found. I wasn't wearing gloves, but I only used two fingers to lift the sheet."

"Thank you for your candor. Time we got to work. Will you show us the way?"

Emma finally convinced Vanessa to go home to her husband. She got Caroline Stoner to drive her.

She watched as the three-person team investigated the scene. Skip took more photographs than Buzz had. One tech used a SAFE kit, a sexual assault forensic evidence kit. The third Major Crimes trooper scoured the area. Emma doubted he would find anything given the sanitary nature of the Ethan Jackson crime scene.

About 4:30 a.m., the team packed up. She said goodbye and thanks to Skip and his guys.

Finally, a grieving Emma Thorne drove home, while Pepper slept in the backseat.

31

The Bombshell

Though exhausted, Emma knew she couldn't fall asleep. Wouldn't. A maelstrom of conflicting emotions and ghastly thoughts prevented any chance. She sat on her bed, her back propped up by pillows. She stared at her cell phone.

Nothing came to mind.

She had no idea how to answer Will, or, for that matter, whether she should. Should she beg him to come home? Should she damn him to hell? Should she ignore him, and try to continue her life as best she could? No bright-eyed solution popped into focus.

A tear splattered on the screen of her iPhone. She wiped it away and slipped the iPhone under her pillow like a child might. Out of sight, out of mind.

But Deb's merciless murder was all too real. Emma couldn't suppress the memory of her brutalized body. Deb, who didn't even kill flies, let alone hurt people.

She would miss Deb Barger terribly. Deb was gone forever. She would never come back. It seemed more and more likely that Will wouldn't either.

She reached for a pen and paper on her side table. She wrote down all of Mr. Sharpie's possible combinations.

$$\angle M \quad M\angle \quad W\angle \quad \angle W \quad M7 \quad W7 \quad 7W \quad 7M$$

Were the first four a person's initials? **W7** was a London postal code. The **M7** sounded like a foreign motorway. She Googled it. There was an **M7** in Ireland, which terminated in Limerick. Could this refer to a limerick? **7W** could also be a route. **ML** and **LM** were Roman numerals for 1050 and 950.

Emma was good at puzzles, but the solution to this one eluded her.

She had a more frightening thought. Were there still more letters or numbers to come?

Emma's mind was caroming around like a trick pool shot.

Her next thought: although *she* knew both Ethan and Deb, they barely knew each other. Hadn't Deb said, when they were picnicking at Lost Pond, that she hadn't seen Ethan since high school? So, what was it that tied them together in Mr. Sharpie's sick brain? It made no sense to Emma that she was the common link.

And, finally, what should she do with the knowledge that Will was alive, somewhere close by? Vanessa, earlier, had alluded to the same scenario. That Will was somehow a part of this nightmare. Emma remained convinced that Will's involvement was impossible, but the evidence suggested otherwise. Maybe. She also knew that it was vital information which she should be sharing, not hiding.

Emma shook her head. It was preposterous to think that Will was capable of killing anyone. Yet where had the viciousness in his text come from? It didn't sound anything like her Will.

Finally, she consoled herself that Joe Henderson cried out for more of her investigative attention.

Before leaving for the office, Emma, who had not closed her eyes all night, telephoned Skip Munro. She bet that Skip was enough of the go-getter-type to be at work already.

"Lieutenant Skip Munro," he answered.

"It's Emma Thorne from Hampshire, I'm anxious to hear whatever you've found out so far—"

"How are you feeling, Chief? I hope you were able to get some rest after we left. I know how much it sucks to lose a friend."

She was surprised that a hardened Major Crimes vet would trouble to ask. She was also pleased. "I'm okay, considering what happened. Didn't get much sleep though. Actually, none."

"Yeah, I feel your pain—"

"About the case—"

"How's this for a plan? Get your guys together for a noon meeting. I'll drive up from Litchfield and brief everybody all at once. In cases where we are called in to assist with an investigation, I like to start off on the right foot. Some folks resent our presence. Sometimes the Chief even does." He laughed. "We feel the same way when the governor calls the feds in."

Emma received two phone calls before Skip arrived. The first was from Mark Byrne, and the second was from Dick Wardlaw.

"Emma, Mark here. I've been thinking a lot about you and the creepy text you received from your husband. I'd like to try to help you out. What do you say?"

Emma thought a long time before answering. She shifted the receiver to her other ear.

"Emma? You there?"

"Help how?"

"For starters, I could try to track Will down. Would that help or hurt?"

Emma said, "That's a very good question. I'm not sure I know the answer. Anyway, how could you possibly find him? The bastard could be anywhere. Anywhere at all. Oh, I don't know Mark, part of me wants to wish this all away into oblivion."

"Not to be the bad cop, but that ain't going to fly."

"There's stuff that you don't know. Police business, but I'm going to tell you, if you keep your mouth shut. Deb and Ethan were killed by the same hand. Worse still, I can tell you that my friend Vanessa thinks that Will could be our killer."

"Whoa! Why would she say that?"

"First off, my heart tells me it's impossible. Setting that aside, common sense tells me something else. We're sure of the connection between Ethan's and Deb's deaths. We also know that I'm the only obvious link between the two. I knew both of them. They didn't know one another. Well, they did, but not for years. Then, all of a sudden, Will makes his presence known in an especially un-Will like way."

"It's a stretch," Mark said hesitantly, "but I get your point. Is your department searching for him?"

"Not really," she admitted.

"Because you haven't told them about the text?"

"True."

"Emma, I don't mean to be the asshole here, but you could be in a whole shitstorm of trouble if you keep withholding."

Emma's other line rang. She told Mark that she would call him back. Ruby Sato, her assistant, told her that Mayor Wardlaw was waiting.

Emma was in the mood to nail the son of a bitch.

"Put him on."

Once again, Dick Wardlaw invited her to lunch.

She told him that she couldn't make lunch but that she could meet him for a drink after work. He reacted with all the enthusiasm of an adolescent who has just figured out how to masturbate. He suggested they meet at Lizard's Lounge on the back side of town, a low-rent bar for a low-rent lizard.

She agreed.

It was nearly time for Skip's briefing, so she didn't call Mark back. She didn't particularly want to. He had a knack for flooding her open wounds with alcohol.

That day's dispatcher had called in all available units and personnel. Emma guessed most of them couldn't wait to hear what Skip Munro had to say. She knew most, if not all of them, thought that she had blundered by not calling in the state police sooner.

At the podium, she looked out at the sea of expectant faces. Everyone except for Caroline Stoner looked away.

Emma introduced Lieutenant Monroe and gave him the floor.

He began with engaging, friendly smile. "As the chief told you, I represent a team from the Western District Major Crimes Squad out of Litchfield. The chief has asked us for assistance in two difficult cases, both unfortunately homicides. I just want to say right off the bat that we are not here to step on your toes. We are only here to assist."

Stella Weeks piped up from the back, "We're *all* glad you're here."

Emma heard a rumble of approval from her colleagues.

"Unfortunately," Skip continued, "so far, we don't know much that you don't already know. We haven't had any luck at Ms. Barger's crime scene with fingerprints. The chief told me that you guys had the same issue at Mr. Jackson's scene. We also haven't had any success with DNA evidence. The state police have a consulting cryptographer. We've engaged her to examine the Sharpie marks on both victims. Which, by the way, is the only piece of evidence linking the one perpetrator to both crimes."

"What about Virginia Hobson?" Buzz asked.

"Good question. The chief told me about the incident at her house, that the same cell phone was used for both Jackson and Hobson. Officer Stoner, why don't you and I have a chat about that after the meeting?"

Emma sat in a chair off to the side of the roll call room, half-listening but also thinking hard. Skip Munro answered some questions. Then he gave a general briefing about serial homicide. She tuned out, hearing neither the questions nor the answers.

Should she, or shouldn't she? She weighed the pros and cons. In her mind, the cons outweighed the pros. And yet, wasn't it time to do the right thing and act like a team?

After a few more minutes of anguished mental juggling, Emma made up her mind.

Skip wrapped up his briefing and turned to her and said, "Anything to add, Chief?"

With lingering doubt—she hadn't fully completed her risk-reward analysis—Emma rose.

"I have something to add."

She hesitated and could feel the tears forming in her eyes, which she tried, unsuccessfully, to stanch. Stammering, she said, "On Thursday night, I received a text. The text was from Will. He is alive. I don't know where he is, but …" She paused. "… wherever he is, he is angry—"

From the back of the room, Stella shouted, "And you didn't think to mention this sooner?"

"Hold it! Who are we talking about? Who is Will?" Skip interjected.

"Will Foster is my husband. He disappeared forty-three days ago."

O n her way home, Emma angrily stopped at Petticoat Parlor and bought her first push-up bra. The salesperson called it The Bombshell. "Hot date?" she'd asked. Emma tried it on. She was aghast at her appearance but satisfied.

Later, Emma flipped through her closet looking for exactly the right outfit for her "hot date" with Dick Wardlaw.

She had left headquarters immediately after the meeting, avoiding everyone, especially Stella. Her confession about Will had left her bruised and broken. She was not sure what was next, but she had a pretty good idea.

She finally chose a wraparound dress with a plunging neckline. Ironically, the last time she had worn it was to a party with Will. With her new bra underneath, she checked herself in the mirror. She couldn't help but laugh. Damn if Bombshell didn't work as well as plastic surgery. Her boobs looked two sizes larger, and they puffed into the middle of the dress's **V**.

She overdid the makeup, too.

Leaving a surly Pepper at home, Emma drove to Lizard's. She arrived fifteen minutes late, intentionally. Outside the door, she pushed her boobs even closer together for maximum impact.

Wardlaw was sitting in a booth with red vinyl benches, the very last one at the back of the bar. He studied her, his eyes widening, as she approached.

She gave him a peck on the cheek and sat down across from him.

He patted the space next to him. "Why don't you sit here next to me?"

"I'm quite comfortable, but thanks." She gave him her best imitation of a Miss America smile.

"You look beautiful, Emma. I'm so glad we could get together. Drinks are so much more preferable to lunch, don't you agree?"

"Speaking of which," she said, "would you order me a dry martini? Dirty."

Wardlaw snapped his fingers, which made her cringe.

Two martinis arrived. The waitress, who knew both of them, couldn't help but stare. Emma rewarded her with a wink. The waitress smiled uncertainly and departed.

Emma held up her glass in the universal toasting gesture. Dick clinked glasses with her, grinning his yellow-toothed grin. She downed the entire martini in a series of greedy gulps.

"Oh yeah," Dick sputtered.

He proceeded to do the same with his drink.

He ordered a second round. They finished those, too.

They made innocuous small talk while Wardlaw's eyes darted back and forth between her face and her cleavage. Soon, she'd had enough.

With a taste of Dutch courage, she advanced the game.

She reached into her handbag and took out her badge. She shoved it into his face.

"Mayor Wardlaw, I'm here in my capacity as Chief of Police. If you ever so much as touch me again, you sorry prick, I will arrest your ass and charge you with sexual harassment and sexual assault. Is that plain enough for you? So keep your filthy fingers out of my ass, and go have sex with your goddamn wife."

She put her badge back in her bag and took out her iPhone. She found the Voice Memos app and pressed Play. She watched his face fall even further as he listened to the snippet she replayed from their phone conversation of just three days ago.

His voice was tinny, but the words were clear: *Oh, Emma, you would be making a big mistake to turn me down. Besides, this would be a business lunch…although, of course, if it became more, that would be fine, too.* Emma's voice: *The answer is still no.* Wardlaw, again: *Listen hard, Emma, I'm going to give you ten minutes. Then I'm going to call you back, and I will expect a different answer.*

Emma stood.

"Thanks for the drink, you *Dick*."

32

A Woman in Uniform

My property is an old farm outside of Hampshire. The driveway that leads to my house is one mile, two hundred and twenty feet long. There is an electric gate at the entrance. A key-code opens it. I feel secure in my privacy.

I am feeding my fish when I hear someone coming down the cellar stairs. I wheel on my heels, looking for a weapon.

Stella Weeks appears at the bottom of the stairs.

"Hi, sexy," she says.

Although she is welcome, I am annoyed. She has the key-code, but I have told her in the past that my cellar is off-limits. Stella usually does what I tell her to do.

"Upstairs," I say.

In the kitchen, she wraps her arms around me and presses her buxom little figure against my body. She is wearing her cop uniform, which I find erotic.

She has to tiptoe to kiss me on the lips. She kisses passionately and tonguefully. I respond in kind.

Before we know it, we are in my bedroom engaged in spirited oral sex. Stella is one hot pistol. The bitch really drives me wild. I can't get enough of her little bod.

Afterwards, exhausted and sweaty, we lie naked on the bed, cuddling each other. I trace my index finger around one of her nipples. It is the color and texture of a Brazil nut. Stella moans softly. So do I.

Suddenly, she props herself up on her elbow.

"Do you love me?" she asks.

I don't really like to share these kinds of confessional intimacies, but I lie to her, "Of course, I do."

Sometimes Stella can be quite needy. Anyway, a new plan is germinating in my mind, a possible substitution scenario. I think about that for a while.

We fall back into silence.

Then Stella says, "You can't imagine the scene at Deb's house. It was god-awful."

Casually, I ask, "How was she killed?"

"The perp opened up her neck from ear to ear. Whoever did it was a fucking sociopath. You've never seen so much blood."

"A fucking sociopath?"

"That's what I said. Lieutenant Munro calls him a sociopath, too." Stella sits up and stares at me. "I knew Deb. She was a nice girl, never meant anybody any harm."

"You don't know that," I say, unable to stifle my anger. I really do not like being called a sociopath. "She might've been a piece of shit, for all you know. Besides, she was a friend of Emma's. Need I say more?"

"Look, I know how you feel about Emma. I feel the same way. But what does that have to do with Deb?"

"So, your genius cop, Lieutenant Monroe, parrots a hackneyed psychiatric profile for you guys. Am I right? By the way, Stella, a serial killer, by definition, has killed three or more people. You should know that. This killer has only killed two people. Hence, no serial killer."

I feel a happy grin spread over my face and continue, "I'm guessing that he told you that the killer was a white male between the ages of thirty-five and forty-five, a loner. He's charming and manipulative. He grew up in an abusive family, was obsessed with fire setting, wet his bed, killed kittens, and blah blah blah. Am I right?"

"Not in all respects," Stella admits, "but that's the gist of what he said."

I say, "Well, la-di-da, don't you have an eidetic memory. I don't want to talk about this anymore. I need to take a nap. Why don't you get going and leave me be?"

Stella looks surprised.

"You're hurting my feelings. Why are you being so mean? We just made love, and now you are being … cruel."

Finally, I say, "I'm sorry. I didn't mean it. Don't worry, you can stay."

Relieved, she kisses me on the nose.

We spend the rest of the late afternoon lolling about in bed. The warm June air breezes through the open windows and cools our sweaty bodies. I start working on my unfinished *Times* crossword puzzle. It is pretty easy. The clue for twenty-four across is "death." The answer (thirteen letters) takes me a minute. I consider asking Stella, but she would be clueless (pun intended). Then "inevitability" occurs to me, and, of course, I'm correct.

Just before 4:00 p.m., Stella dresses back into her uniform. She has evening duty.

I have evening duty, too, but I can't share the details of *that* with Stella.

I go into my luxurious bathroom without saying anything further. I close the bathroom door to brush my teeth and to think. I use exactly seven-sixteenths of an inch of toothpaste.

Vanessa Mack's house is not dissimilar from Deb Barger's. It's also a Colonial. Unfortunately, she has painted it a hideous shade of green. I know that Vanessa lives there with her husband, Dave, who is an insurance actuarial. They have two kids, a boy and a girl, both cute as buttons. I'm not sure how old they are, but I have seen them in their school playground on a prior reconnaissance mission. I tell you, I like to be prepared.

I circumnavigate the house, ticking off boxes on my mental checklist. As Jon Stewart says, "I watch a lot of astronaut movies … mostly 'Star Wars.' And even Han and Chewie use a checklist."

I won't be entering the house tonight. I can see that the children are home. I won't harm children. Even though I don't have any, I love children.

Dick and Jane, as I call the kids, are watching television. I'm too far away to see what's on. I disapprove of kids watching too much television, but, then again, I'm not their mother. As Kurt Vonnegut once said, "Future generations will look back on TV as the lead in the water pipes that slowly drove the Romans mad."

Vanessa is in the kitchen preparing supper. The kitchen is cheerful with frilly curtains, red Formica counters, and is painted yellow. Not my hue for a kitchen, but it seems to suit the family.

I wonder what Vanessa is making for dinner. My guess is that it is something white bread. Maybe mac and cheese or chicken tenders. They'll miss her comfort food when she's gone.

Dave, who is balding and chubby and boring looking, is at the kitchen table reading his Kindle. The couple is not having a conversation. Why be married if you don't talk? But what do I really know about marriage? I decide to leave them to their conventional suburban life and retreat back to my car.

"I'll be back," I say. But they can't hear me.

But as I linger in the shadows on the edge of Vanessa's lawn, I think more and more about what I'm now calling Plan 3a. It came into my head earlier this afternoon when I was with Stella. Which would freak Emma out more? Plan 3 or Plan 3a?

I'll choose the one which will wreak the most havoc.

33

"Why didn't you tell me?"

Early Sunday morning, she picked up the *Hampshire Chronicle*, which Pepper carried home. Emma tossed the paper onto the kitchen table and began preparing a comforting breakfast. Scrambled eggs, sausages, and whole wheat toast. She cracked two raw eggs over the kibble in Pepper's bowl. Pepper hungrily slurped them down.

Over breakfast, she unfolded the paper. The lead article was, naturally, by Virginia Hobson.

TWO MURDERS IN HAMPSHIRE: POLICE STUMPED

by Virginia Hobson, Staff Reporter

Recently-appointed Chief Emma Thorne was forced to call in the State Police for assistance in the shocking homicides of Ethan Jackson and Deborah Barger, according to a source inside the Hampshire Police Department. The same source, who asked not to be identified, told The Chronicle that officers in

the department had been begging Chief
Thorne to seek outside assistance be-
cause their investigation was stalled.
Chief Thorne, under pressure from her
officers, contacted the Western District
Major Crimes Squad of the Connecticut
State Police for help . . .

Whining Shit strikes again. But this time Emma didn't bother to call her. Ever since Emma's cathartic rendezvous with Dick Wardlaw, she felt free to go her own way. She had a new attitude and new priorities. If she had to find Will on her own, that is what she would do. And, she realized, she might well have to go it alone.

Emma spent the morning wondering when she would hear from Dick Wardlaw. She was certain she would. She knew a call or a summons from Dick was inevitable.

Still, she was determined to regain her equilibrium. She texted Vanessa, "Want to go for a run? New Forest Lake parking lot at noon?"

She'd hardly pressed Send before her text tone sounded.

To clear the head? Meet u there.

Vanessa, Pepper, and Emma headed off along the path that bordered the shore of New Forest Lake. Thrilled to be out on a beautiful mid-June morning, Pepper was in a fine mood. Actually, it made them all feel good.

They ran hard to, as Vanessa had said, clear their heads. They didn't try to converse along the way. On the north cove of the lake, there was a three-sided forester's hut with a bench facing the water. It was rustically built with cedar wood and smelled delicious. Red-faced from two miles of running, they collapsed on the bench. Pepper was panting, too.

"What a spectacular day!" Emma declared.

"It sure is, but, I have to say, it does nothing to make me stop thinking about Deb. I miss her so much already. I just can't get her out of my mind. She was such an awesome friend. I really loved that girl."

"Ditto," Emma said sincerely. But, when she thought that wasn't quite enough, she added, "I loved her, too."

"I read about your calling in the state police. I hope that takes some of the pressure off."

"Actually, it does. I feel strangely relieved, like everything isn't crushing onto my shoulders."

Then, Emma told her about her encounter with Dick Wardlaw at Lizard's Lounge.

Vanessa bumped fists with her. "You go, girl! It's about time someone nailed that perv. I'm so proud of you. It must make you feel great."

"It was more than worth it, even if it costs me my job."

"The perv can't fire you. You've got that tape. If that's not sexual harassment, I don't know what is."

"I'm not so sure about that," Emma said. "I don't think threats faze Mayor Wardlaw."

"So, what's next?"

"*That* I can answer. Without having to devote all my time to the Ethan and Deb cases, I intend to find Will. After I've found him, I will either clear his name or I will arrest him."

"Wow."

Emma laughed mirthlessly. "Although it might end up being a citizens' arrest."

Vanessa frowned, suddenly serious. "Can I tell you something? Maybe something to do with Will? I don't have any proof, but I have the strangest feeling that someone is watching me."

"Shit, why didn't you tell me?"

"Like I said, it's just a feeling. I can't tell whether I'm so freaked about Deb that I'm imagining it."

"I'll pass the word to patrol, get them to check on your house every time they're in the neighborhood."

Anxiously, Vanessa asked, "Do you think that will be enough? I mean, has it ever occurred to you that I might be the next one to die? Don't laugh at me. I'm not being melodramatic. I've been giving this a lot of thought. You already said that you are the connection between Ethan and Deb. Well, I'm a friend too. What if Will *is* crazy? I'm not necessarily saying he is, but, don't forget, he did have that creepy depression. What if he comes after me?"

"Do you really think that Will is going around killing people?"

"Not to be a creep, but who's doing the killings is not as important to me as not being killed. Look, I'm sorry, I know how upset you are about Will—"

"No offense taken. You have every right to be scared. I have an idea. Why don't I move into your house until the dust settles?" Emma smiled. "I have a gun and a badge. I could be your live-in bodyguard. Pepper's no slouch either."

"If it were my decision, I would say yes right now. But Dave is kind of set in his ways. He doesn't really like it when people stay over."

Emma said, "You haven't told him your suspicions, have you?"

"No, and I don't intend to. Dave is an actuary. He would go berserk. He'd probably move us to Cleveland."

Emma smiled and looked at her watch. "I've got to head home."

They ran back around the other side, the west shore of the lake.

Back at the parking lot, the two friends hugged.

Emma said, "Stay safe, sweetie. If you change your mind about me moving in, give me a holler. Meantime, I'll be looking out for you every way I can."

The message light was blinking on Emma's answering machine. There were two messages. She pressed Play. Mark Byrne was inquiring about her well-being. He reiterated his offer to help her find Will. The second message was—no surprise—from Dick Wardlaw. He said that he would be in his office at Town Hall between 3:00 p.m. and 4:00 p.m. "I expect to see you, in person, in that timeframe."

Emma found one of Pepper's rope chew toys. She played tug-of-war with her until she became too tired to play anymore. Before making herself lunch, she refilled Pepper's water bowl. Pepper was still thirsty after the run and the tug-of-war bonanza.

Emma took her sandwich and an icy beer into the backyard, where she sat in the shade of maple tree. Pepper lay nearby, exposed her tummy to the sun, and promptly fell asleep.

In spite of the bumper car ride of the last two months, Emma felt surprisingly good. The weather made her feel even better. She lay back in her lounge chair. She worried for a few minutes about Vanessa before falling asleep with Pepper. She had another Will-dream.

She first spotted Will in the parking lot of the old bowling alley on Spruce Street, now shuttered. They had bowled more than a few frames there in the old days. Will got into an expensive looking sports car. She couldn't read the model, because he quickly drove away. She tailed him straight to Deb Barger's house ... into the house ... and into Deb's bedroom. Deb, who was dressed in a sheer baby doll outfit, greeted him as if they were lovers. Watching from the doorway, Emma saw her leer at Will.

Deb said, "Come to bed with me. Emma will never be the wiser."

"No," Will said, "I can't do that to Emma. I don't want to hurt her. She looked after me when I was sick. I owe her."

"I always knew you were a putz, Will Foster. What do you care what Emma thinks?"

"Oh, but I do."

When Will left Deb's bedroom, her smooth neck was unharmed and blood-free.

Emma was no longer in the shade. She awoke, feverish and sweaty, and she remembered every detail of her dream.

Wasn't this a good omen? she thought absurdly.

She went to take a sip of her beer, but the bottle was empty. She tossed it aside.

Suddenly, Emma remembered the meeting with Dick Wardlaw. Her watch read 3:30 p.m. *Damn!* She went up to her bedroom to change into her dress uniform. A moment later, she flipped a switch. Why proffer the respect he didn't deserve? She pulled on a pair of faded shorts and a T-shirt.

Leaving Pepper shut up in the house, Emma drove to Town Hall. Wardlaw's secretary was there, which surprised her. It was Sunday afternoon.

The secretary said, "Please wait, Chief, the Mayor is not ready for you."

Without comment, Emma took a seat on the sofa in a small waiting area. She stared at a cactus in a bowl on the coffee table and cooled her heels. A petty power play on Wardlaw's part. Twenty minutes later, the secretary's phone buzzed, and she could clearly hear Dick say to send her in.

She stood, opened the door to Dick's office, and marched in. Taking a sheet from Mark Byrne's playbook, she sat without being asked.

Dick was pretending to study some papers on his desk, and he did not lift his head. Emma looked around the over-decorated office. Antique furniture, chintz curtains, and a faux Persian carpet. Farrokhzad Oriental Rugs in The Lincoln Mall, she guessed. Tax-payer-paid.

After ten silent minutes, Wardlaw addressed her.

"You were very unpleasant last night. I won't forget that, but that is not why I called you to come in."

Emma said nothing.

"Are you taping this conversation?"

"No, I am not."

"I don't give a shit if you are," he said. "Recordings do not scare me."

"It's your behavior that should scare you."

Angrily, Wardlaw said, "Don't fuck with me. I'm warning you."

"You're wasting my time. Why don't you get to the point?"

Wardlaw leaned back in his chair. The corners of his mouth turned down in an ugly sneer. His yellow polo shirt was tucked into his trousers so tightly that his belly looked like he was carrying triplets.

"The point, eh?" he resumed. "Okay, I'll get to the point. Sergeant Weeks briefed me on the text you received from your husband. This raises a very specific problem, which I'm sure has occurred to you, too. If Will Foster is now a person of interest in these two dreadful murders, then you have a serious conflict of interest—"

Emma had already guessed how this meeting would end, but she surprised herself by feeling down-right cheery about it.

"I agree," she said.

"Oh, you do, huh?" he said, not concealing his irritation.

"Yes, I do."

"Do you agree about this, then? You're fucking fired!"

"Shall I surrender my badge and my gun to the Acting Chief?"

"How do you know who's gonna get the job?"

Emma smiled.

"You know what your problem is? You are an insufferable, arrogant fucking bitch!" he bellowed.

Emma closed the door behind her.

34

Ka-ching!

Call me brilliant.

This morning, I have decided to follow Dave Mack instead of Vanessa. Right now, he is in his office at The Hurley Insurance Agency. I patiently wait for him across the street. I will be here all day if necessary. I am wearing a brimmed hat, wraparound sunglasses, and a light windbreaker. I figure that makes me pretty hard to recognize. Pretty inconspicuous, too.

Today, by the way, is Monday, the twenty-first of June.

The summer solstice or, as some like to call it, the estival solstice (meaning "of or pertaining to summer") occurs when Earth's rotational axis, or geographical pole, is most inclined toward the Sun. Today, in Hampshire, at 11:17 a.m., the Sun will reach its highest position in the sky when its axial tilt is precisely 23.44°.

At 11:08 a.m., nine minutes before the solstice, Dave walks out the front door of the Hurley Agency. I thought that I would have to wait at least until lunchtime. Maybe he takes an early lunch. I follow him down the street. He is wearing a brown suit and a brown tie. I mean, who wears a brown suit? Dave steps into a storefront. The sign above the entrance reads Gulliver's Travels. What a lame name. And, anyway, who uses a travel agency these days?

I wait on the sidewalk a few doors down, ready to slip into a diner so he doesn't see me when he comes out. He's inside for about fifteen minutes.

After he leaves the travel agency, I step out of the diner and enter the travel agency myself. I have never been inside before. *I* would arrange my trips on the Internet if I went anywhere.

A stout woman in a dowdy, floral dress greets me like we're old friends. She's wearing a name tag, which says Helen.

"Good morning," she chirps, "and how may I help you today?"

"I'd like to book a flight out of Bradley to LAX for tomorrow. First class."

She gets even friendlier. Everyone knows that a first-class flight, booked at the last minute, costs a fortune.

While she's tapping away at her computer, I say, "Wasn't that Dave Mack I saw leaving just before I came in?"

"Yes, it was. He's an old customer, a good friend to Gulliver's Travels."

"Where's Dave heading off to?" I ask casually.

"He's taking the kids to Cincinnati to visit his mother next weekend."

"Vanessa didn't mention that she was going away."

Helen looked up from her computer. "Oh, she's not going. Dave's taking them by himself. Just three tickets."

Ka-ching! A window of opportunity gapes.

Before Helen can ask for my credit card and personal details, I pull my phone out of my pocket. "Whoops," I say, "I'm so sorry. I have to take this outside. It's rather personal. Back in a sec."

Poor Helen, another commission surrendered to the modern world.

I want to be fully up-to-speed for my week-end rendezvous with Vanessa. At dusk, I return to her house for more reconnoitering.

Dave is the kitchen table reading his Kindle. Vanessa is cleaning up after dinner. Dick and Jane are watching television in the living room. I'm grateful for a white-bread family with a predictable routine. I look forward to the weekend.

There's no point in sticking around. I return home, feeling optimistic and lucky.

I carefully set the table for tomorrow's breakfast. In the living room, I push Guide on the remote, searching for a relaxing crime drama.

I settle on a rerun of "Law & Order: Special Victims Unit." Mariska Hargitay, who plays Olivia Benson is wearing a tight T-shirt. She has great tits, which I study. Did you know that she is the daughter of Jayne Mansfield, who also had a pretty good set of knockers? Soon I tire of the show—it's another rape plot, which holds little interest for me (although I wouldn't mind a piece of Mariska)—and turn the television off. Rape is a crime of cowardice, perpetrated by men who are mentally defective. Rape has none of the finesse of murder.

My thoughts drift to Stella. I'm conflicted about our relationship. I've been giving it a lot of thought. I know she loves me and is wholly dependent on me, but I'm beginning to think that she might serve me better in another way. The more I think about it, the more convinced I am.

After I have the pleasure of dispatching Vanessa, I will have the time and energy to re-focus on Sergeant Stella Weeks.

35

A Continental Seven

Stella must've gotten her leak to the *Chronicle* on Sunday night, because Virginia Hobson's front-page story ran in Monday morning's paper. Emma found nothing surprising in the piece. Words and music by Stella Weeks.

Emma felt none of the rage that she had felt when Hobson's first story came out. She was oddly unperturbed. The duo of Wardlaw and Weeks no longer held sway over her worries.

She gestured to Pepper, who trotted over. She put the knuckles of each of her index fingers into Pepper's ear canals and gently corkscrewed her knuckles. Pepper moaned.

"It's just you and me, girl. We're on summer vacation, the permanent kind. Let's use the time wisely. Let's find Will."

Pepper wagged her tail in agreement.

They drove to headquarters through a rainstorm. Emma found Stella already sitting behind Archie's old desk.

"Okay if I clear out a few personal things?" Emma said. She'd brought a box with her. Pepper ignored Stella as she always did.

"Of course." Stella stood up and moved to the side of the desk. "Look, Emma, just want you to know that this had nothing to do with me. Actually, I'm sorry for you."

"No, you're not," Emma said happily.

Stella, clearly taken aback, didn't say anything for a moment. She probably expected a more chastened Emma.

But, true to form, Stella quickly bared her fangs. "You're right. That was a lie. What happened here is easily explained. Competence trumps incompetence. Fortunately, that's the way Dick Wardlaw saw it, too. And, be advised, no one is going to miss you around here."

"I wish I could say the same thing, but that's a discussion we'd better save for another day."

"Aren't you forgetting something?" Stella said.

Emma withdrew her service weapon and her badge from her handbag. She popped the magazine and laid all three items on the desk.

"I hope that being chief gives you a measure of happiness. I know it is what you have always wanted. If you don't mind my saying so, you have too much hate in your heart to ever be truly happy. I wish you the best. Good luck to you, Stella."

After leaving headquarters, Emma swung by Hampshire Trust to see if she could tempt Vanessa to join her for lunch. Emma found her in her branch manager's office. Vanessa said she could get to Group Therapy in three-quarters of an hour.

Emma decided to use the forty-five minutes for a leisurely walk. She strolled the familiar streets of her hometown and thought about her future. She might not be chief of police anymore, but that was not going to stop her from continuing her various investigations. She would miss the resources of the police department, but not being in charge of the Mr. Sharpie case give her a new-found freedom. She felt okay.

Emma arrived at Group Therapy at the same moment Vanessa did. They found their favorite booth at the back while Pepper patrolled the restaurant/bar looking for customers she knew.

Vanessa's first question was, "What are you doing in civvies?"

Emma chuckled. "That's a long story. Actually, not true, it's pretty short."

"Tell me."

They were interrupted by Phil, who greeted them and took their lunch orders. Instead of her usual iced tea, Emma ordered a bottle of Chardonnay. Vanessa giggled. "I'll have to buy some mints before going back to work."

Emma continued when Phil went back behind the bar, "So you didn't see today's newspaper?"

"No, I was getting stuff ready for the kids. They're going away this weekend. You know how I like to be prepared! Actually, I want to talk to *you* about that trip, but you start."

"A trip, huh?" Emma paused. "Okay, I'll start. Wardlaw fired me."

"Oh, you poor dear, after all that's happened." She paused for a moment. "Actually, I'm happy for you. That was a sucky job."

Emma laughed. "I thought you told me that I looked hot in uniform."

Vanessa said, "Actually, it was Deb who said that."

Then, Emma told her about having to surrender her badge and gun to Stella.

"That sucks, too."

"It's funny," Emma said thoughtfully, "it didn't bother me as much as I thought it would. Not to be trite, but it feels like I'm turning the page to a new chapter. And I'm feeling good about it."

"That's great to hear, sweetie. I'm really happy for you. You deserve it. Hey, I have an idea, why don't you use your free time to nail Dick Wardlaw, get him charged with sexual harassment and send him to jail. You've got him on tape. Nobody likes him anyway. Incidentally, Dave has a friend in the state prosecutor's office. I'm sure Dave could help set up a meeting."

Emma took a sip of her wine. "Nah, I don't think so. I'm done fighting for now."

"Then what *are* you going to do with your new-found free time?"

"Find Will."

"Oh," Vanessa said.

Emma waited, but she didn't elaborate.

"What's that supposed to mean?" Emma asked.

Vanessa looked down and swirled her wine

Emma said quietly, "Because you think Will is the man behind these murders."

Vanessa didn't respond. Instead, she said, "Look, can we talk about Dave's trip this weekend?"

"Of course."

"You know me. You know I'm not flighty. But I still have the feeling that somebody is spying on me. Frankly, Emma, I'm scared, and I don't want to be alone. Can I take you up on your offer?"

Emma gave her an encouraging smile. "I'd be more than happy. We'll spend the weekend with you. How long has it been since the two of us had a sleepover?"

"Um, you can't bring Pepper."

"If it's protection you're looking for, Pepper is a hundred times better than I am."

"The thing is, Dave is hyper-allergic to dog dander. He'll come home sneezing and wheezing. Sometimes he even gets hives. He would kill me."

"Well," Emma said, "the whole point is we don't want anyone to kill you. So, no Pepper."

They finished the rest of their lunch recalling old stories about Deb. Vanessa became teary. So did Emma.

After lunch, Pepper and Emma drove to Archie's house. Neither had been there since his death. On the porch, Pepper's entire body quivered. She looked up at Emma as if to say *I don't get why we haven't been here before.*

As soon as Emma unlocked the front door, Pepper shot inside. Frantically, she ran around, sniffing everything. While Emma stood in the living room gazing at Archie's familiar possessions, Pepper returned downstairs and sadly lay down beside her. As Pepper often did when in a contemplative mood, she crossed her front paws and sighed.

"I know, Sergeant Pepper, I'm as heartbroken as you are. We just have to remember him as the good man he was."

Emma started going through the house. It was tidy and clean. The housekeeper was doing her job.

In Archie's office, she went to his gun safe. She dialed in the combination. September 29th was Pepper's birthday. The combination was 929. Inside, there were quite a few weapons. Long guns, revolvers, and pistols.

She chose a Beretta Px4 Compact. Easily concealable, the pistol carried fifteen 9 mm Parabellum rounds. Sixteen, if you counted the one in the chamber. She also took two extra magazines and three boxes of cartridges. At the bottom of the safe, she found two soft holsters. One was an ankle holster, and the other could be concealed inside a waistband.

Emma again felt a new, steely resolve.

Stella might have her service weapon and badge. But, if Emma was going to go after a killer, she wouldn't go unarmed.

Pepper reluctantly followed as Emma went to the front door and locked it behind them. On the drive home, Emma thought that maybe she should sell Archie's house. Without a job, she would surely need the money. She had no idea how much it was worth, but it was a solid old structure. Archie had been conscientious with his repairs. He had even maintained the original shutters. He had been proud that they still worked.

It didn't take her long, though, to say to herself, "Not yet." Losing that last tie would be a little too much to face.

At home, Emma found the list she had made of Mr. Sharpie's "calling cards."

$$\angle M \quad M\angle \quad W\angle \quad \angle W \quad M7 \quad W7 \quad 7W \quad 7M$$

She studied the letters and numbers trying to decipher a meaning or pattern. Suddenly, she had a minor breakthrough. Will always wrote his sevens in the European-style, a continental seven: 7. She felt that that exonerated Will from having written the last four combinations. Which left

$$M\angle \quad \angle M \quad W\angle \quad \angle W$$

Could they be the killer's initials?

She still didn't feel like she was getting very far.

She studied the paper some more until she found herself doodling rather than concentrating. She sighed in frustration. Her mind went back to the day when Joe Henderson had kicked her out of his house and then, even further, to the day that she had pulled Sophie King from Joe's Escalade.

She found the cordless phone in the kitchen and dialed a friend of hers who was a detective in the Lincoln Police Department. Lincoln was about thirty-five minutes south of Hampshire. Despite being a larger town with American amenities like a Walmart, a Home Depot, and an Applebee's, Lincoln's financial future didn't look much brighter than Hampshire's.

She got Detective Dave Swanson on the first ring. Fingers crossed that the *Hampshire Chronicle*'s news of her firing hadn't yet reached Lincoln.

"Dave, this is Emma Thorne—"

"Chief Emma, long time no hear. What's up?"

Emma didn't correct the honorific. Her sin of omission would be revealed soon enough. Meantime, she needed a little breathing room.

"Is a Joe Henderson on your radar?"

"Hmm, interesting question. What's your interest in Joe?"

"As you know, we've been investigating several homicides—"

"Mr. Sharpie."

"Indeed. Henderson is not a suspect, not yet anyway. I'm interested in getting a little more background on him." She told Dave about her interview with him and what Sophie had told her after the pursuit.

"We have a, uh, highly confidential investigation ongoing. I'm not going to say a whole lot about, because my chief would have my ass. As a chief, you can understand that. Let me just say that we are looking into a sex trafficking ring involving female minors. They're using a photo studio as a front … and as a lure. It's in an old mill building on River Street. Yes, Lincoln's got a River Street, too. That's about all I can tell you, except, of course, your buddy Joe's name came up in flashing neon. We think he is the lease-holder through a shell company."

Emma said, "Thank you for sharing. I really appreciate it. Don't be too pissed at me when you hear the news coming out of Hampshire."

She hung up before Dave could ask what the hell she was talking about.

Emma felt guiltily satisfied.

Emma found the King family landline in the phone book. She dialed them and got Sophie on the phone.

"It's Emma, Sophie. How are you making out?"

"Fine. How come?"

"Have you seen anything more of Joe Henderson?"

"No way! Why would I want to see that creep? How come you're asking?"

"It's not important. Do me a favor. If you hear from him, will you let me know?"

Emma made Sophie promise she would.

She heard Sophie say, "Weird," before she hung up.

36

Walmart Shopper

Monday afternoon, Emma booked a pet-friendly motel room in Pittsfield, Massachusetts. On a splendid summer day with puffy cumulus clouds wafting against a picture-perfect blue sky, she drove with the windows open. Pepper thrust her head out the passenger side window, sampling the passing smells. Officially off-duty, she was now permitted to ride in the front seat of Emma's personal vehicle.

Pittsfield, where the second burner cell phone had been purchased, was only an hour and one-half north of Hampshire. It was a pretty and pleasant drive past Monument Mountain, in and out of famous towns like Stockbridge and Lenox, and through the Berkshires. While not as prominent, the Berkshires connect with the Green Mountains of Vermont to the north.

Emma's room at the Route 7 Motel smelled a lot like the last Fido to have slept there. It was cheap, though. $65 for a night with a $20 "pet deposit."

She found a decent burger joint in the middle of Pittsfield. She'd dressed Pepper in a black vest, which Archie had bought for parades. In white letters on both sides was the legend Police K-9 Unit. That way, Pepper wouldn't have to cool her heels outside. She washed her cheeseburger and fries down with a glass of Berkshire Blonde, thinking about her competing interests: Will and Joe.

She and Pepper went to bed early.

First stop, Tuesday morning, was the Walmart on Dalton Avenue. Although Stella had confiscated Emma's badge and gun, she had neglected to take Emma's laminated ID card, which identified her as a Chief of Police, complete with a photograph. As a *poseur*, she now had to think of such things. Pepper again wore her cop's vest, which she quite enjoyed wearing. Emma was confident that she would pass for an active-duty police officer.

Lastly, she packed the Beretta in her handbag and carried a photograph of Will. It was his last passport photo, a remarkably good one, and he looked very handsome in a tweed jacket and a blue and green tie.

The Pittsfield Walmart was as grim as the few other Walmarts she had ever entered. Ironically, Emma found the manager in the firearms department. She was wearing a blue vest with its stylized yellow star and standard-Walmart How May I Help You? stenciled on the back.

"How may I help you?" said the store manager.

Emma explained that a cell phone under investigation by the Hampshire Police Department had been purchased at her store. "Oh dear," she said, leading her to the section of the store where cell phones were sold. Patrons gave Pepper wide berth as they navigated the aisles.

Emma asked the on-duty salesman if he had been working on Sunday, April 11. He scrolled through his cell phone and announced, "As a matter of fact, I was."

She showed him Will's photograph and her ID.

"You have got to be kidding, Chief. That's more than two months ago. Do you know how many people walk in and out of this store even on a Sunday?"

"Please," Emma said, "just look at the photo."

To be fair to him, he did study the photograph. He even said, "Not a bad looking guy." But he shook his head. "The face doesn't ring a bell. I'm sorry not to be any help."

Emma asked if anybody else was working on that day, but again he shook his head. "Sorry."

"Are there any security cameras that cover your counter?"

He pointed at the ceiling directly behind her. She looked at the unfortunately-placed camera, realizing immediately that it would only capture the back of the patron's head.

"Crackerjack security system," she said.

She left the store after politely thanking him and the manager.

At the door, she noticed that the Pittsfield Walmart was open from 7 a.m. until midnight, i.e. seventeen hours a day. Checking the security tapes for one month would mean scanning the backs of peoples' heads for five hundred and ten hours. Less on fast-forward, but still … a tad too Herculean for her.

Their next stop was the Pittsfield Post Office on Fenn Street, a block and half off Route 7.

Emma stood in line at each window. Each time she got to the front, she showed Will's photograph to the postal workers. Negative all around. As she was leaving, one of those annoying women who greet all dogs with in-your-face enthusiasm started to coo-coo at Pepper. Emma warned the woman, "I wouldn't get near her if I were you. She's vicious."

Emma spent the afternoon visiting post offices in the towns of Lanesborough, Dalton, Lenox, Stockbridge, and Great Barrington, a waltz through the Berkshires of over eighty miles.

All her stops drew blanks.

On the way back to the Route 7 Motel, she parked at a package store and bought a couple of bottles of wine.

Before going to her room, she ducked into the motel office to tell the guy on duty that she would be checking out on Wednesday. The receptionist was a young man with dirty blonde hair, a ponytail, and a tattoo crawling out of his T-shirt and up his neck. The Notorious B.I.G. was printed on the T-shirt. Emma figured that he couldn't have been alive when Biggie Small died in a drive-by shooting. In addition, Emma thought that this ambassador for the Route 7 looked like a stoner.

"Man, that's some freaky lookin' dog you got lady," he said.

His eyes were red and his pupils, dilated. His weed was probably laced with something more than THC.

"She's a police officer."

Emma noticed that the Ambassador's hands were busy shuffling something underneath the counter. She realized that she couldn't bust him even if she wanted to, which she didn't.

On a whim, she pulled out the weather-beaten photograph of Will. "Did this guy ever stop here, spend the night?" she asked.

He picked up the photograph and looked at it. "Yeah, maybe."

Emma jumped. She watched him carefully. "What did you say?"

"Said I mighta seen him."

His eyes drifted from the photograph to a place on the wall somewhere behind Emma's right ear.

"How sure are you?"

"Like I said, maybe."

He looked like he was dissembling, but, *damn*, she couldn't be sure.

"Does the name Will Foster mean anything to you?"

"With faces, I'm good ... names, not so much."

"But this face, you remember, no?"

"Like I said," he repeated, "maybe."

Emma took a fifty-dollar bill from her purse and placed it on the counter.

The Ambassador suddenly looked nervous. "I thought you said you was a cop."

"I am. Have you ever seen this man? How about giving me a Ulysses S. Grant's-worth of the truth?"

"Lady, the fuck you talking about?"

She pointed to the picture on the bill. "*That* dude's Ulysses S Grant. What I want to know is," she said pointing to Will's photo, "have you ever seen *this* dude?"

"Ah," he said, "I get it." His pupils seemed to dilate further, but the fifty-dollar bill disappeared from the counter in a magician-like sleight-of-hand.

"Yup. I seen him."

"When?" she asked.

"A week ago? Maybe?"

She realized that both his sentences ended with a question mark and that she was fifty dollars poorer.

And yet she couldn't be sure.

She asked him when he went off duty. He answered, eight o'clock tomorrow morning.

"Later," she said.

In her room, Emma uncorked one of the bottles of wine. After struggling with the plastic wrapper of the plastic "glass," she poured herself a big one. She lay on the bed, briefly considered TV but decided against it. Pepper joined her, stretching the full length of her long body against Emma's thigh and leg.

As she lay there thinking, Mark Byrne popped into her head.

She found and dialed his number.

37

Re-Alphabetizing

She told Mark everything that had happened. Her job termination, her search for and suspicions about Will, Vanessa's concerns, the state police "helping" with the investigation, everything she could think of. It was oddly reassuring to speak with him.

"Where are you?" he asked.

She told him.

"I'm about an hour away. Why don't I come see you?"

Emma thought about that one. *Why not?*

She said, "That would be nice."

She was three quarters of her way through the first bottle of wine when Pepper growled. A moment later, Mark knocked on the door.

After giving Pepper some hearty pats on her withers, he said in his gruff voice, "Christ, this room stinks. Let's find a bar and get a drink."

Mark drove Emma to an Irish bar he knew. Pepper sat in back of the car wearing her parade vest so she could join them inside.

"Ah, here it is," he said, parking in the back of the building.

Erin Go Bragh was noisy, crowded, and a complete dive. The walls were covered with photographs of women in green T-shirts. "From the Erin Go Bra-less contest," Mark explained, "every year, the night before St. Patrick's Day."

Emma thought the place was perfect, such was her mood. They couldn't find a free booth. So, they squeezed into two empty stools at the bar, hips touching. Mark suggested they have a Guinness, and Emma readily agreed. The bartender was exacting in his pouring, and they were each served a pint with a creamy white head. Mark tipped his glass, plinking hers. He said, "Sounds like you've had a rough few days."

"I haven't had a Guinness in years. It's delicious."

"Tired of rehashing things?"

"Yup." She thought for a moment, studying Mark's life-beaten face, which, as before, she decided was quite handsome. "Actually, no. How the hell am I ever going to find Will?"

"What will you do when you find him?"

"As I told my friend Vanessa, I'm either going to clear his name or make a citizens' arrest."

Mark laughed.

"It's not funny." But she laughed along with him.

"Maybe I should give you a hand."

"For pay."

"Naturally."

Emma said, "I forgot to tell you about the night clerk at my motel. When I showed him Will's photo, he seemed to think that he remembered him. I emphasize *seemed*. Then I made the mistake of giving him a fifty-dollar bill which only made him positive. He really got my hopes up, but now … I don't know."

"I have quite a lot of experience with liars. Why don't we pay him another visit? But no need to rush. Another Guinness?"

Emma ordered two more and was beginning to feel a buzz.

"Tell me about yourself. I know nothing about you," she said.

"Hmm, I grew up in a shitty part of Boston, Jamaica Plain. Which is probably why I feel at home here." He waved his arm around. "My dad was a cop. Irish, of course. So, I became a cop, too. But the corruption wore on me. Every beat cop I knew was on the take. After a few years of collusion, shaking down the neighborhood bodegas with the other cops, I quit. Before quitting, though, I got to know the *crème de la crème* of Beantown's shadier types. So, becoming a private investigator was kind of a no-brainer. Right off the bat, I had plenty of well-paying clients. Eventually, I moved to Connecticut to start afresh and clean up my act a bit." He looked her in the eyes as if he was trying to gauge her reaction. "Married once, no kids, no girlfriend. I guess that's about it. And you?"

"Based on our first meeting, you seem to know plenty about me. I don't need to say anymore, other than I'm enjoying this evening."

"Do you still love Will?"

"That's a complicated question," she said truthfully. "But if you are asking if I am going to sleep with you tonight, the answer is no."

Mark closed the short distance between their lips and kissed her. She didn't mind. It felt great. Mark had learned more in Jamaica Plain than he'd let on. The tip of his tongue flirted with hers. She opened her mouth a little wider and returned the kiss. In the long months of Will's depression, Will had not felt any desire for sex. For her, it had been over six months of abstention.

After a few more minutes of blatant barroom necking, she gently pushed him away.

"Enough of that."

They each had a third Guinness before Mark drove Emma and Pepper back to the Route 7 Motel. Mark seemed to take the rejection in stride.

They stopped at the front desk, and Emma introduced Mark to the Ambassador. Mark stepped behind the counter. The kid said, "Hey, you can't be back here."

Mark took the Ambassador's arm and led him, protesting, into a small office behind the check-in desk and closed the door. Emma heard a loud ooof and a cry. Peppers hackles went up. Presently, Mark returned. In his hand was a room key and a fifty-dollar bill. On his face was a smile.

"The kid hasn't seen Will."

Mark politely escorted Emma to her room and said, "Breakfast at seven?"

The threesome spent the next three days canvassing Berkshire County. They stopped in stores and restaurants, showing Will's photograph over and over again. They tried hunting and sports stores. They stopped at pet stores to see if anyone resembling Will had bought fish food. Leaving one, Emma observed, "Will didn't even like to eat fish, let alone want to raise them."

They even made another stab at the Pittsfield Walmart.

They ate their breakfasts and lunches at diners. They ate their dinners at nicer places. Emma paid for all the meals. There was no more kissing.

On Friday morning, they drove back to Hampshire. Emma had to babysit Vanessa.

Mark, offering "backup protection" said he would be glad to join her for the weekend at Vanessa's house.

Emma turned him down, showing him her dad's Beretta. On the ride home she said, "I have an idea, though. Vanessa's husband is allergic to dogs, so Pepper has to stay home. Why don't you stay at my house and look after her?"

Saying he'd have to go home and get some more clothes, Mark agreed.

"Which bed should I sleep in?" he asked mischievously.

"Don't worry, I have a very comfortable guest room."

"Sounds lonely," he said. "What are you doing this afternoon?"

"I have one more stop to make," she answered ambiguously.

Mark dropped her off in front of her house on Deerfield Street and drove home to grab some weekend clothes. Emma fed Pepper, took a shower, and dressed.

Considering the vitriol that Will had spewed in his text, the only person Emma could think of that he would contact was his twin sister. As kids, they had been extremely close. Georgia, she knew, adored Will. Emma also knew that in recent years Will had carefully distanced himself. As sympathetic as he was to her, he found her "fixation" troubling.

Emma knew all about Georgia's distressing history. Beginning when Georgia was fourteen, her uncle, her mother's brother, had repeatedly molested her. Georgia, after more than a year of sexual abuse, had finally told her parents. Instead of protecting her, they had punished her. In Will's view, they preferred protecting their country club reputation rather than protecting their daughter. Eventually, Georgia had shared her secret with her twin. Will had confronted Uncle John. When the uncle told him to butt out, Will had threatened him. The abuse stopped. That was when, according to Will, Georgia "sort of fell in love with me."

Next stop, then, Georgia Foster's house. Emma wouldn't call in advance and give her a chance to duck a visit.

"Who is it?" Georgia shouted through the locked front door.

"It's Emma."

Nothing happened.

"For chrissakes, let me in."

The door opened. "What do you want?"

"To talk to you."

Beyond the hallway, Emma could see into the living room. On the floor, there were dozens of neat stacks of DVDs. Standing amidst them was Georgia's goddaughter, Sophie King.

"Hi Sophie, how're you doing?" She wondered if Sophie had mentioned their recent phone call. For some reason, she hoped she hadn't.

Sophie gave Emma a friendly wave.

Georgia said, "My sister-in-law is apparently paying me a social call. Sophie, why don't you head home and let us talk?"

Sophie looked surprised. She said, "Can't I help you some more?"

"What are you guys doing anyway?" Emma asked.

"Sophie spent the night, and she got some of my movie DVDs out of order. We're just re-alphabetizing them."

"Wow," Emma muttered.

Sophie gathered her things. She was obviously put out by her godmother's dismissal. At the door she whispered to Emma, "I couldn't figure out why you called me about Joe."

"I just want you to stay away from him. Remember your promise."

In a louder voice, Sophie said, "Sure do. Anyway, Joe's a bastard."

"Language, Sophie!" Georgia barking in her low-pitched voice.

Sophie ignored her. "I wouldn't have anything more to do with him anyway. He wasn't the right guy for me. My bad."

"That sounds very grown-up," Emma said, hoping she didn't sound condescending.

"I *am* fifteen."

Before leaving, Sophie patted Pepper on the head and gave Georgia a curt nod.

Georgia frowned. She was still blocking the doorway. Emma eased by her and walked into the living room, uninvited. She scanned the neat piles on the floor. There were too many DVDs to count. She picked one up.

Ridley Scott's "Black Hawk Down."

"I loved this movie." Emma said, "I didn't know you liked war movies." She replaced the DVD onto its stack of movies beginning with the letter **B**. Georgia, who had followed Emma into the room, immediately leaned over and re-adjusted the stack so that it was as perfect as it had been before Emma had touched it.

"I don't particularly like war movies. I bought it for my boyfriend."

"I didn't know you had a boyfriend. That's great news."

Georgia stood up. "You don't know anything about me."

"Who's your boyfriend? Do I know him?"

"That's none of your business."

Emma could see this wasn't going to go very well. She hadn't expected it to. She dropped any further effort to be friendly and got to the point.

"Has Will been in touch with you?" she demanded.

"If he had, I wouldn't rat him out. Least of all to you."

Emma swallowed a nasty rejoinder. "I have been searching for Will all over Berkshire County for the last week—"

"Berkshire County? Why?" Georgia seemed genuinely interested.

Emma explained, "It was at a Walmart in Pittsfield that a cell phone was purchased which has become part of our investigation—"

"*Your* investigation? You are no longer the chief, let alone a cop. What right do you have to search for Will?"

Emma lost her temper. "Georgia, you are a Class A bitch! You know that? If you have any idea where Will is, for God's sake tell me. I'm the one who's suffering. I love that man, no matter what he's done. So just fucking tell me!"

"*You* love him? I'm the one who loves him," Georgia shouted. "You're the one who ruined his life and drove him away." Georgia got into Emma's personal space. "Get out of my house and out of my sight. I never want to see you again. Stay out of my life!"

Her parting shot hit Emma like a body blow.

Indeed, an instant later—her left eye twitching, combined with that maniacal grin—Georgia shoved her, nearly knocking her over.

Pepper entered the fray, inserting herself between them. The dog snarled. Just in time, Emma shouted, "Stand Down!" Pepper obeyed.

Instead of Pepper, Emma snapped. She cocked her fist and unleashed a haymaker. She struck Georgia on the left side of her chin. The blow knocked her backwards onto the floor, sending DVDs skittering all over the room.

Georgia lay there stunned. There was hatred in her eyes. She rubbed her chin and said, "You will regret that."

Emma left. Her knuckles ached, but she was pretty happy about un-alphabetizing Georgia's DVDs.

38

Sleepover

Mark returned to Emma's house late in the afternoon carrying a bag of clothes and a paper bag full of groceries. He said, "Your living alone, I didn't know what I might find in your refrigerator."

She gave him a tour of her house, skipping her bedroom. She showed him how to use the TV remote, and, with a flourish, opened the door to reveal a fully-stocked refrigerator.

"If you can't find anything, I'll have my cell." She wrote down the number for him. "Thanks for doing this Mark. I appreciate it. And don't go peeking in my underwear drawer."

He looked genuinely affronted. "Not gonna happen," he said in his idling-chainsaw voice.

"Just kidding," she said airily. "Why don't I cook you dinner on Sunday night to thank you. I can tell you about the super-fun visit I had with my sister-in-law earlier this afternoon."

With a wave to Mark, she left. Pepper watched but didn't seem miffed.

Emma arrived at Vanessa's house at 5:30 p.m., the time Vanessa usually arrived home from her job at Hampshire Trust. Emma drove down Vanessa's long, narrow driveway. When she saw that Vanessa was not yet home, she backed out and parked down the street. Dave went bullshit when somebody parked on his Turf Builder grass. Carrying her overnight bag, she walked back to the house. She waited on the doorstep for less than five minutes before Vanessa drove in.

Vanessa greeted her with a hug and a kiss. She returned to the car and took a satchel of groceries out of the backseat.

"I stopped at Luigi's and bought two filet mignons, which we can grill on the deck, and some bacon to wrap them in. We'll be really wicked. I also have two expensive bottles of Bordeaux waiting for us inside."

"Aren't you the perfect hostess!"

Emma briefly wondered if they should rather be filets mignon, but she didn't say anything.

A few minutes later, they were on the back deck sipping pre-dinner chilled Chardonnay. Vanessa lit the charcoal. Then, they sat on comfortable lounge chairs with their feet up. Dappled sunlight filtered through the leaves.

They reminisced about Deb, a ubiquitous topic.

Vanessa poured them more wine, and Emma told her about her encounter with Georgia.

"Good on you, Em, for decking her. Sounds like she deserved it."

"Oh, she definitely did, but I have a feeling, however pumped it made me feel, I may have gone too far."

Vanessa, who was not prone to cursing, exclaimed, "Fuck her!"

Emma then told her about her Berkshire County-wide search for Will and how unsuccessful she and Mark had been.

Vanessa observed, "If he's managed to elude everyone for—what has it been?—almost two months, he's probably pretty good at it."

"Seems like it."

They never mentioned the reason that Emma was spending the weekend.

Warmed by the cool wine, Emma told her about The Kiss.

Vanessa scrunched her face. Emma knew her friend, despite slipping in a *fuck* earlier, had become more conservative since Hampshire High.

"Are you sure that was wise?" she asked.

"Hey, you and Deb were the ones who told me I should be looking for a guy."

"Not yet, we said, *and* that was before we knew Will was still alive," Vanessa said, not mincing words. "Not sure that was a really good move, Em. You know men, they get ideas, and they get hard to stop."

Emma said (with a high degree of uncertainty), "Mark's not that kind of guy."

"He's a private investigator. Exactly what kind of man becomes a private investigator?"

"Ouch. Now, I'm sorry I brought it up. Let's change the subject."

"Sure," Vanessa said. "This is making me uncomfortable, too."

Over the grill, as the sun was going down, their conversation turned to happier matters. Emma had placed herself in charge of grilling. She considered herself quite the grillmeister, having learned everything she knew about charcoal cooking from Archie. Grilling had never been Will's forté.

They ate outside with the mosquitoes.

Vanessa complimented her on the perfection of the steaks. They were delicious and so was the Bordeaux. They finished a bottle and a half. When they got up to do the dishes, they were both tipsy.

Emma, who had *not* forgotten why she was there, wondered how well wine and guard duty went together. But Emma was pooped after her trip, and Vanessa admitted she was always pooped after a week at the bank. After cleaning up, they agreed it was time for bed.

Vanessa led her upstairs to the bedroom she shared with Dave.

Emma, raising a mental eyebrow, noted there were two twin beds separated by a bed table with a pair of reading lights. As if reading her mind, Vanessa said, "Dave thinks I'm too hot to sleep with. Unfortunately, he doesn't mean *hot* the way I wish he did."

Emma smiled awkwardly.

"You take that one," she said pointing. "It's Dave's, but the sheets are clean."

Vanessa changed into a pair of pajamas. Emma got into her bed naked. It was a hot night. Vanessa had her back turned when Emma slipped the Beretta under her pillow.

With the lights out, they chatted some more.

"Just like old times. A sleepover. God, I wish Deb were here."

"So do I."

Moments later, the alcohol lulled them to sleep.

By her wristwatch, it was nearly 2:00 a.m. when Emma got up to pee. She took the time to recheck the house. There was just enough moonlight to maneuver. Downstairs all the windows, which they had closed and locked in spite of the heat, were all secure. The front and back doors were, too.

She returned to bed. Vanessa hadn't woken up.

It must've been about an hour later when Emma awoke with a start.

She was absolutely positive that something, a wet something, was touching her ankle.

39

Ever so Silent

The only nonstop flight to Cincinnati today is on Delta. The flight is scheduled to take off from Bradley International Airport in Windsor Locks, Connecticut, at 11:45 a.m. The perfect flight for a father traveling with two kids.

Guess what? I'm right again.

Since I want to make sure of the departure of Dave Mack, a.k.a. Mr. Bland, and his kids (*sans* Vanessa), I return to my usual observation post outside Vanessa's house at 7:30 a.m.

It takes about forty-five minutes to drive to Bradley, and I figure Dave will want to be at the airport to fulfill the two-hours-before-departure rule. Plus a safety cushion.

At 7:55 a.m., sure enough, Dave, Dick, and Jane drag rolling suitcases out of the house and load them into a brown Buick Verano four-door sedan, just the make, model, and color I expect an actuarial to own. Dave must be taking a personal day to manage this trip. If all goes well, he'll be needing a few more.

Dave hurries the kids into the car. I can hear him say, "We don't want to be late, kids! We don't want to miss our flight and disappoint Nana." And off they go with Vanessa waving.

I return home to feed my flock.

All day and all evening I wait inside my house, pacing the rooms with keen anticipation. Tonight, will be another nail in Emma's coffin. Crueler than the last because now there will be the combined demise of her two best friends.

At 2:12 a.m., I arrive on the edge of Vanessa's lawn on a sweltering, moonlit night. Only Vanessa's car is parked in the driveway. Once again, my perspicacity astounds me. Vanessa is alone in the house. In the terrorist movies I devour, she would be termed a "soft target."

Not a window is lit in her green Victorian. Outside it is easy to see. The moon is waning but still bright. Inside the house will be different. But I am prepared.

I am dressed all in black. My long-sleeved black T-shirt is already making me sweat, not out of nervousness, though. It's just hot as hell. I also have black jeans and black sneakers. I haven't forgotten to apply mosquito repellent either.

I am fully equipped. I have a night vision goggle device, an Armasight PVS7-3 Alpha Gen 3, head-mountable for hands-free usage. It cost a whopping $3,896.75, and I bought the gadget from, believe it or not, Amazon ("Export of this product outside of the United States of America is not allowed."). I agree with that prohibition. No sense letting tools of war get into the wrong hands.

I've brought other necessities, too. They are in a black backpack. I have custom-built a number of compartments into my backpack. Each of the additional tools in my quiver resides in a specially fitted space so I can find what I need instantly. I remove a black balaclava from one compartment and slip it over my head.

I have practiced with the night vision device at home. Tonight, I fit the straps around my head and tighten them. They fit snugly over my three-holed mask. For $3,896.75, they sure as hell better.

I creep softly across the lawn and around the back of the house. The goggles are unbelievable. Although green and grainy, the image is well-defined, high-resolution, and focused.

Unlike at Deb's house, I discover that the back door is locked. No problem. From my backpack I extract a double-suction glass puller—the kind car window installers use ("Safelite® Repairs! Safelite® Replace!")—which I attach to one of the four divided lights of the back door. I etch a rectangle with my never-used tungsten carbide glass cutter. A little tap tap tap, and I am able to silently withdraw a piece of glass large enough for my arm to fit through. I unlatch the door and find myself standing in a mudroom. Although the field of view of the goggles is narrow, I move my head left and right, up and down and scan the room. It is as bright as a sunny day after a snowfall. I listen for the telltale beep beep beep of an alarm panel. Even though I don't hear any beeps, I check the walls anyway. No alarm system. It makes no sense to me that someone would live without an alarm system. Hasn't Vanessa ever heard of "home invasions?" The mudroom is filled with skis, skates, life jackets, swimming noodles, flippers, and boots. Every object is distinct. I have in my possession an enormous tactical advantage.

I pass into the kitchen. The only sound is that of a ticking analog clock. Not a creature was stirring, not even Vanessa.

> 'Twas the night of a killing, when all thro' the house,
> Not a creature was stirring, not even a mouse;
> The kitchen was tidy and cleaned with great care,
> In hopes that Mr. Sharpie soon would be there;
> Vanessa was nestled all snug in her bed,
> While visions of a murder danc'd in my head.

I find the doorway which leads to the basement. Stairs are always a problem, particularly in an old Colonial. I widen my stance and place my sneakers on the ends of the treads. Hardly making a squeak, I duck-walk down to the cellar. Aided by the goggles, I have no trouble finding the breaker box. I press down on the main disconnect switch. It makes a loud snap. I freeze. After a few moments of intense listening, I can't hear any movement upstairs, which is where I proceed next.

I assume that Vanessa's and Dave's bedroom is on the second floor. (My English teacher used to repeat, tiresomely, "Assume makes an *ass* out of *u* and *me*.") Never mind her, I turn out to be correct.

I use the same duck-walk technique to mount the back staircase. I am trebly careful now as I get closer to my quarry. Four more treads (and four more risers) to go. This is when I hear the sound of a door opening on the second floor. My head and shoulders are above the floor level of the hallway, fully exposed.

Vanessa, naked, emerges but immediately turns the other way. She walks away from me, down the hallway, and descends the front staircase. I can't see her face, but the goggles give me a clear image of her ass.

I retreat down the back stairs, sit down, and listen. This is not the way I planned it. I never like to deviate from my plans. I am patient. I will wait.

Three minutes later, I hear Vanessa remounting the front stairs. I hear her walk halfway down the hall to where her bedroom is. I do not hear the bedroom door close. In fact, I hear nothing more.

I sit on the backstairs for a full hour, waiting.

I want Vanessa to be in REM sleep. Rapid Eye Movement sleep (hence, REM or R.E.M.) is sometimes called paradoxical sleep, which is physiologically similar to being awake. I want Vanessa to be in that state. Symptoms include: rapid breathing; an increased heart rate; rapid, low-voltage, desynchronized brain waves; and low muscle tone throughout her body. It is also the time when she will have a propensity for vivid dreams. If she has a sexual dream tonight, I somehow doubt she'll be dreaming about Dave.

It's just after three o'clock. I flex my fingers and stand. I am ever so silent.

Several quiet moments later, I'm outside her bedroom. I spy her immediately in the bed closest to the door. Her head is turned away. Her body is covered by a wrinkled sheet. Her feet and ankles are exposed to the hot night air. That is how well I can see with my priceless goggles.

I'm amazed that one person can snore so rapidly. Must be REM sleep, as I had hoped.

I take one step into the room. The floorboards do not creak.

I am in.

40

Between the Sheets

Wide awake, Emma felt a foreign object touch her ankle. It was not a bug. It was wet. She struggled not to flinch, and she managed to remain motionless.

The enemy was in the bedroom. She wished Pepper was.

She rolled over onto her stomach. To suggest that she was still asleep, she snorted. She heard Vanessa in the next bed breathing softly. As she rolled, she slipped her right hand underneath the pillow and found the grip of the Beretta. Emma stayed that way, frozen, for a few moments, lying on her stomach, trying to breathe slowly, feigning sleep.

Then she smelled an odor, the all-too-familiar smell of a Sharpie.

She rolled gradually onto her back and snapped her eyes open. No moonbeams shone through the window. The only light available to her was indirect moonlight. But it was enough to see a black, shadowy creature standing at the end of her bed.

The figure started. Emma heard a muttered oath: *"Shit!"* She couldn't be sure, but the voice sounded lower pitched than Will's tenor.

Emma's left hand shot for the light switch. Miraculously, she found it on first lunge. She snapped the switch on. Nothing happened. The half-light of the moon was all she had. Vanessa remained asleep.

Underneath the sheet, Emma aimed her Beretta at the intruder, trying to decide her next move. She had every right to fire her weapon, no questions asked. But what if it were Will? She really didn't want to shoot him.

She wished she could spring clear of the sheets. Although she had the gun, the balance of power would be a lot less one-sided if she could get to her feet. But she knew she wouldn't be fast enough.

Suddenly the black figure went airborne.

The full weight of the intruder's body landed on her, smothering her and her gun hand. The unyielding, and unmistakable, rigidity of a ballistic vest crushed her chest. The Beretta slipped out of her grip and, for the moment at least, was lost in the sheets.

A heavy fist clocked her in the temple, and her brain swam from the blow. Still, she was able to get her fingers around the intruder's throat.

She screamed, "Vanessa! Get up! Run!"

Vanessa shrieked, "What? What!?"

"Go! Get out! Get help!" Emma managed to bellow, although she could barely breathe.

Vanessa leapt out of her bed and ran down the hallway, screaming bloody murder.

The monster on top of her—heavy, tall, strong—was able to pry her fingers away, bending them back one by one. Emma knew she was not going to win a wrestling match against him. He was too powerful. Instead she groped for the equalizer, Archie's Beretta, trying to find it in the tangle of sheets.

She stole a glance at him. He looked like a sci-fi character. He had an all-black head and, where his eyes should have been, a single tube with a lens at the end. The blow to her head must have been worse than she realized.

His other fist walloped her other temple. The pain was incredible. She felt like she would vomit. She jammed the heel of her hand up her assailant's nose. She heard only a mild "ooof" for her efforts.

He punched her repeatedly, pummeling her eyes with his fists.

She kept scrabbling for the Beretta.

41

Knockout

It is only when Vanessa rolls onto her back and her eyes spring open that I realize that I have been sucker-punched. Vanessa is Emma. Emma is Vanessa.

Fucking Emma, my once and future nemesis. *How dare she?*

My plans never go awry. There is no way that I could have foreseen this ambush. That would have been beyond anyone's capability. Anyway, none of this is part of my plan. Rest assured, I will not apologize.

Emma is underneath me. I have complete control over her. I can kill her if I want to. But that is not the fucking plan! Killing her would be too easy, and it would defeat the purpose. Emma suffers while those around her die. *That* is the plan.

I box her eyes. She is moaning and crying. I know she is in great pain. Payback for insulting my intelligence. The only answer is to knock her unconscious. Only then can I pursue and dispatch Vanessa.

I wind up and deliver a shattering blow to the temple that I have already softened up. Emma's body heaves, and she is finally still.

I jump off her and off the bed. Outside the doorway, I scan both ends of the hallway. Vanessa must already be downstairs. I take the stairs three at a time. No need to be quiet now. The front door is wide open. I run outside. I can't see her anywhere. I circle the whole house. No Vanessa. I realize that when I come back for her I won't have the element of surprise. *Fuck surprise!* The cops will be all over her like maggots on a corpse. I refuse to apologize, but tonight has been a goddamn fiasco.

Fuuuck!

Rattled and frustrated, I can't decide what to do next. It crosses my mind that I may have inadvertently killed Emma. Maybe I should go back up and check on my punching bag?

I re-climb the front stairs. When I get to the top, I am shocked to see the same naked figure I once thought was Vanessa stagger through the bedroom door.

Emma is not only alive, she is armed. Of all the equipment I brought, it never occurred to me that I would need a gun to kill Vanessa. I have guns, of course, but I don't have one with me.

I freeze. I can't tell if she can see me.

She lurches down the hallway toward me. The hallway is pretty dark. I don't think she can see me yet, but I'm not sure. I ease backwards.

It turns out she *can* see me.

"It's Emma," she says in a surprisingly strong voice after the beating I've given her. "If that is you Will, it's time to stop this insanity. Give yourself up. I promise to do everything I can for you. I love you, Will."

I don't answer.

"Put your hands in the air and walk slowly toward me. I have Archie's Beretta, and I will use it if you force me to."

Emma kept shuffling unsteadily in my direction, narrowing the gap considerably.

I think desperately of ways to escape. But now, even though her gun hand continues to waver, I think that she is too close to miss.

Then I hear Emma say, "I'm sorry."

All of a sudden, the hallway lights up like the fucking Fourth of July. The explosion deafens me. Instinctively, I duck. The bullet, of course, is a whole hell of a lot faster than my reflexes. I take a slug in my arm. I scream. The pain is unbearable. I feel my upper arm. There is blood on both sides, anterior and posterior. It is a through-and-through, meaning there is both an entrance wound and an exit wound. I remember this from my combat medic days in Iraq. I nearly shout, *"You little shit!"* But I stop myself. Emma still doesn't know for sure who I am.

Emma is stumbling toward me. Her gun hand is wavering. Through the goggles I can clearly see a cloud of gunpowder still wafting from the end of the barrel.

I take my chance. I start to turn, and fuck if I don't lose my footing. Ass over teakettle, I tumble down the stairs. At the bottom, dazed, I stagger to my knees. I am temporarily blinded, because my night vision goggles have popped off my head in the fall. I still have my balaclava.

Emma appears at the top of the stairs, an indistinct blob in the dark. But I see her moving as she descends toward me. I can't believe she still has the wherewithal to crawl, let alone walk. At the very least, my beating must've given her a concussion. The woman has more steel than I gave her credit for.

Still she comes, lurching like she was in a B horror movie.

I manage to get to my feet. Wobbly, I aim for the front door. I hear her pace quicken on the stairs. I can't believe Superwoman is still after me. My arm is on fire.

I turn to face her and wait for come-what-may. She reaches the bottom of the stairs. We are only about five feet apart. She stops, but I can see that her unsteady gun hand is darting like a hummingbird. I smell equal measures of gunpowder and fear. There is enough ambient moonlight from the open doorway to see her naked body glistening. I wait to see what she will do. Advantage, Emma. Yet, all the while I am calculating my chances to take her down despite the burning agony in my upper arm.

In a weak, shaky voice, she says, "Take off your ski mask. I need to see your face."

I stare at her eyes, not at her gun.

That's what I learned in Close Combat Class. Close Combat Class (via the United States Marine Corps) is a required course, even for medics.

I shake my head, no.

She repeats her demand.

Again, I shake my head.

If you want to see my face, you will have to kill me first.

The stalemate continues. Her gun continues to float.

I develop a plan and try to summon the courage to execute it. My eyes dart from hers to her gun hand. I wait until her wavering hand is on an upswing. Then I bend over double and tumble onto my back rolling my body into her ankles. The moving blow sends her flying over me. I hear her weapon clatter across the floor. My arm explodes into the fiercest pain I've ever felt. I let out a shriek. I can't help myself. I hold my injured arm tight against my chest.

It takes all my willpower to raise myself to my feet. When I do, I take one step toward Emma's writhing body. With the full force of my leg, I kick her head. I am only wearing sneakers, but the blow is a knockout. Emma is finally motionless, but my arm is about to drop off.

I retreat to my car, nursing my bloody injury.

I have to assume that Vanessa is long gone and has probably found some way to telephone the police.

42

Dilated and Sluggish

Emma couldn't understand why she was cold and miserable. She felt her eyes flutter, then open. She realized that she was lying on the floor. *Where are my clothes?* The horrors of the night before came back. Where was Vanessa? Why hadn't she called the police? Maybe Mr. Sharpie had gotten her after all.

A hesitant light filtered through the hallway window. She looked behind her. Through the open doorway, she saw dawn driving the darkness from Hampshire. Her head felt sledgehammered. She was head-achy and nauseous. She touched her right temple. Her fingers recoiled. The simple, light touch caused intense pain.

From a sitting position, she glanced around. On the floor underneath a radiator she made out her Beretta. She remembered firing her weapon and hearing a scream. She remembered feeling his body armor on the bed, but the scream on the stairs told her that she must've hit him somewhere. She didn't want to kill anyone, let alone Will, and she had, to the best of her ability, at least, aimed away from his head. But the body armor confused her. Joe Henderson had worn a vest during the Escalade incident. Joe *must* have been the intruder. Maybe.

A few feet away from the Beretta was a black device which looked a lot like a set of night vision goggles. *So that's how he did it, whoever he was.*

She began to gather her thoughts together. Then, her actions.

First, her clothes. Second, a phone.

After a long time getting dressed, she found her cell phone on the table between their beds. She dialed, held the phone to her ear, and looked in the mirror over Vanessa's bureau. Both sides of her face had virulent black and purple contusions. Her face looked camouflaged for battle.

"911 operator. What is the location of your emergency?"

"Laura, it's Emma Thorne. Could you please dispatch police and an ambulance to 17 Highcroft Terrace, the Mack residence. We have a missing assault victim—"

"Jesus, Chief, is the ambulance for you? Are you okay?"

"Pretty banged up, to tell the truth. But I'll live."

"Units are on their way," she shifted to the matter-of-fact manner dispatchers affect. "Could the perp still be in the residence?"

"No," Emma said enigmatically, "he left hours ago."

"Stay on the line with me until they arrive."

"I'm okay, but thanks." She pressed End.

Emma sat on Vanessa's porch and watched the sun rise. She remembered doing the same thing at Deb Barger's house.

The morning was full of promise for another gorgeous day. For her, the day would be pain-filled. In the distance she heard the first warble of an approaching siren, soon multiple sirens.

Without knowing exactly why or how, the reason she had woken up in the first place popped into her head. She looked down at her ankle. Sure enough, a Sharpie mark. It was a single line. An **I**? Or a **1**? Or just a line?

The solution came to her like a slap on the cheek. She didn't need to write down any more combinations of letters and numbers to solve the riddle.

The killer was three quarters of the way. So far, he had spelled **W-I-L**. This meant that Joe Henderson was no longer a viable suspect. Either Will had killed Vanessa, and only one more letter would be delivered. Or, he hadn't caught Vanessa, and there would be two more victims. Emma shuddered. She felt cold in the warm sunshine.

Had Will morphed from an insular depressive into a sick killing machine? She didn't even know whether a depressed individual could become a sociopath or a psychopath or whatever the hell he was. And why would he be leaving breadcrumbs pointing directly to him?

Emma rubbed her eyes and tried to reassure herself for the umpteenth time that, if Will couldn't get out of bed, how would he have the wherewithal to murder?

She had the saddest feeling that Vanessa had not survived the night. When will it end?

Stella was the first to arrive in Emma's old chief's vehicle. Emma noticed that she had added more LED lights behind the grill, and that the headlights now wig-wagged. Emma was surprised that she even noticed.

"Whoa!" said Stella, standing over her. "You look like you had the shit kicked out of you. What the hell happened here?"

Within moments, other cruisers arrived. Soon Max, Buzz, Chuck Smith, and Caroline Stoner encircled Emma, looking down at her.

Caroline knelt beside her and put her arm around her. "You poor thing. The ambulance is on its way. We'll get you to the hospital."

"Yeah, yeah," Stella said, "but first I want to hear from Emma what happened. Like, why did you wait until morning to report this? And where's Mrs. Mack?"

"I think I was unconscious," Emma said haltingly. "Last time I saw Vanessa, she was running out of the bedroom while the intruder was on top of me."

"Jesus, were you raped?" Caroline asked.

"No." Emma shook her head. "But it might have hurt less if I had been." She tried to smile but couldn't.

"Buzz, make sure the house is clear, and report back," Stella ordered.

While Buzz was inside, Caroline stroked her back, making sympathetic sounds. All of a sudden, Pepper bounded toward her. For the first time, Emma was able to smile. Pepper sniffed her wounds, wagging her tail uncertainly. *How the hell did Pepper get here?* she wondered. When she looked down Vanessa's long driveway, she got her answer. In the distance, standing on the grass was Mark Byrne.

Buzz returned. "Clear," he announced. In one gloved hand, hanging from a pen were the night vision goggles. In his other gloved hand was Archie's Beretta, hanging from a pen by the trigger guard. "A pane of glass has been cut from the back door. There's a suction device still attached to the glass. Professional and quiet. Also, the main breaker was tripped. The power is back on now."

"Are those yours?" Stella asked Emma, pointing at Buzz.

"The Beretta belonged to Archie—"

Stella interrupted, "Do you have a permit for the handgun?"

"No. And the intruder brought the goggles. Surely, they are traceable. Not everyone walks around with military grade hardware."

"You leave the police work to us," Whining Shit said. "You and I will discuss the permit violation later."

Emma decided that she might as well get the Sharpie discussion over with. She explained to the assembled cops what had caused her sudden awakening in the middle of the night. "He clearly mistook me for Vanessa, who, equally clearly, was his intended target. He had multiple opportunities to kill me. He didn't take them." She pointed out the line drawn on her ankle. "The message already reads **W-I-L**. Only lacks a final **L**. You will all have to come to your own conclusion."

"I figured Will was good for it all along," Stella said.

An EMT and a paramedic arrived and began to fuss over Emma. Meanwhile, Pepper disappeared. The paramedic applied Steri-Strips to the laceration on Emma's forehead, which the intruder's kick had caused. The EMT obtained a set of vitals. When she checked Emma's eyes, she reported to the paramedic, "Eyes dilated and sluggish. She should get a CT scan."

She spoke as if Emma wasn't capable of hearing.

Emma heard barking inside the house. She knew that bark.

"Help me up," she demanded.

The paramedic said, "You're not going anywhere except to the hospital."

Emma struggled to her feet, without their help, and shambled into the house in the direction of Pepper's bark. Pepper was sitting with her shoulder against a door, which, Emma knew led to the basement.

She shouted for Max, "Someone's in the basement!"

Led by Pepper, Max Beyersdorf raced down the cellar stairs, gun drawn. Two minutes later he returned. He was supporting Vanessa, who was shaking so hard she could barely walk.

"I found her behind the oil tank," Max said. "She needs EMS."

Thank the Lord, Emma thought, *Vanessa made it.*

Stella said, "Nice job, Buzz, securing the house."

43

The Pleasures of Morphine

Vanessa and Emma rode to the hospital in the same ambulance. After a tussle with the paramedic, Emma convinced him to allow Pepper on board, too. Vanessa sat in the captain's chair swaddled in a blanket. Emma was strapped onto the stretcher. The paramedic started an IV line and gave her 2.5 mg of morphine.

"This should take the edge off," he said.

From her position on the gurney, Emma couldn't see Vanessa, who was sitting behind her head. But she could hear her teeth chattering. She wanted to ask her why she hadn't called for help, but she didn't have the heart. When Emma started to tell her what had happened after Vanessa had ran from the bedroom, Vanessa said she didn't want to talk about it. Then she started to cry.

"Would it help if I got Dave on his cell?"

"Please," she whimpered.

"Dave," Emma said when he answered, "this is Emma Thorne. Hold on, I'm going to put Vanessa on."

Vanessa immediately erupted into a volcano of tears. Emma could hear Dave's shouting through the phone trying to find out what she was so upset about. Eventually, after hearing the entire tale, Dave insisted that she take the next flight to Cincinnati. Without hesitation, she agreed.

Vanessa tapped Emma on the shoulder, and, proffering the phone, said, "Dave would like a word with you."

Emma held the phone so that it did not touch her bruised cheek. "Yes?"

Emma wasn't expecting a clap on the back, but she didn't expect a full-throated tirade.

"Dammit, Emma, how could you expose my wife to such risk? You nearly got her killed. Why don't you just do your damn job? Find your wacko husband and lock him up! Vanessa is joining us in Cincinnati, and none of us is coming home until Will Foster is where he should be. In jail.

Emma said, "Thanks, Dave."

She used her thumb to touch the End button.

Blissfully, the morphine was beginning to still her rampaging brain. She didn't much care what Dave had blathered. His words hurt, but she didn't feel them.

At the hospital Emergency Department, Vanessa and Emma were separated.

As Emma was being wheeled to the CT suite for a brain scan, she reflected that Vanessa, whose wounds were entirely psychological, would be discharged sometime later that morning. Emma didn't entertain the same hope for herself. Meanwhile, she reveled in the haze of the morphine, that heavenly, miracle drug, not looking forward to when its sublime effects cleared.

After her scan, an orderly returned her to Room 9 on the main corridor of the Emergency Department. A young doctor arrived carrying Emma's chart.

She said, "Good morning, I am Dr. Emma McKay. How are you feeling, patient-of-the-same-name?" She had an infectious grin and lively blue eyes. Her black hair was tied into an artful chignon.

"Great … for the moment."

"I'm sure," she said, still smiling. "I had to read your paramedic the riot act. Concussion—you have one, by the way—and morphine are generally contraindicated."

"Then I'm glad that he made a boo-boo."

"I'll bet you are. Unfortunately, you also have an epidural hematoma. It's a small bleed, and we are going to keep an eye on it—"

"I've heard of a subdural hematoma, but what's an epidural?"

She worried it sounded serious.

"Epidural bleeding occurs between the skull and dura; whereas subdural bleeding occurs between the dura and arachnoid. Subdural is usually more serious. Yours is relatively minor. Sometimes surgery is called for, sometimes aspiration. But, for the time being, we're just going to monitor yours, make sure the pressure on your dura doesn't increase. I am going to prescribe some medicine which should reduce the swelling."

Wow, Emma thought, *that's a lot to digest*. She asked the doctor, "How long will I be here?"

"Overnight, minimum. Longer if the bleed grows." She closed the privacy curtain around Emma's bed. "Now, I'm going to give you a full head-to-toe and make sure everything else is as it should be."

Dr. McKay carefully removed her hospital gown. She gave her a thorough examination, poking and prodding, yet causing little pain. She checked absolutely everywhere. Emma was glad she was not modest.

"You sure took an unholy beating," the doctor observed.

"This is where you're supposed to say 'And what does the other guy look like?'"

"I'll play along," McKay bantered. "What does the other guy look like?"

"The other guy has a hole in him."

McKay's eyebrows soared. "You shot your assailant? With a gun?"

"I sure did. You haven't admitted anyone with a GSW, have you?"

She laughed. "I'd remember if we had, and I'll be sure to tell you if we do."

She and Dr. McKay joked around some more until she had to leave to attend to other patients. Emma liked her.

An hour or so later, Caroline Stoner arrived carrying a bouquet of flowers. Roses.

"These are from the gang."

Emma was glad to see her. She smelled the roses. They smelled a lot better than the ubiquitous stench of hospital disinfectant.

Caroline said, "Shit, you look worse than when I saw you at the house. You looked in the mirror recently?"

Emma nodded. "If it weren't for the morphine, which the doc said the paramedic shouldn't have given me, I'd be feeling a lot sorrier for myself." She thought for a moment. "I trust there's a full manhunt on for Will."

"Yup. Whining Shit is all over it. Like a dog with a bone. You know how she gets."

"I can't believe that Will would beat me so viciously. None of this makes sense. I'll tell you, though, I'm glad I'm no longer in charge of this whole shitstorm."

"That reminds me. I want to apologize for not reaching out to you after Wardlaw sacked you. I don't feel like I was a particularly good friend."

"Don't beat yourself up." Emma laughed at her own joke. "Just find Will and protect him. That's all I ask."

"You got it, Chief." Caroline air-kissed her. "Back to work," she said, leaving the cubicle. "I'll come see you when you get home."

Emma's eyes followed the plastic tubing which connected her vein to the drip chamber of an IV bag. She watched the steady drip drip drip. It was hypnotic, and she soon dozed.

When she woke up, Vanessa was standing at the end of her bed. She was still dressed in her pajamas, but they were now covered with a borrowed lab coat.

"They're discharging me," she said without coming closer. "Stella Weeks offered to drive me home."

"That's nice of her," Emma said sincerely.

"But I'm not spending the night. I'm not sure I will ever be able to spend the night in the house again. It's ruined for me." She stared at Emma. Her expression was not particularly sisterly.

"What?" said Emma.

"I thought I knew you. Now I don't know what to think. What could've happened between you and Will to make your relationship so utterly poisonous? What did you do, Emma? Was it you? Did you drive him mad?"

Emma couldn't believe her ears. She'd just risked her life for her friend.

She lifted herself up in bed. "I am truly sorry that that's the way you feel."

With unmistakable finality, Vanessa said, "Goodbye, Emma."

Emma slumped back onto the pillow.

What did she have left? She'd lost her two best friends, her job, any feeling of safety going forward. All she had was one faithful dog. And a horny private investigator.

Who, to her surprise, was her next visitor.

"Pepper is still standing watch outside the ambulance entrance. She seems a little annoyed. Do you want me to take her home?"

"I am so selfish! I forgot all about her. I'll bet she's pissed."

"By the looks of you, you have every right to a little self-involvement."

"You don't know the half of it." She told him about her visit with Vanessa.

He listened sympathetically, but without comment.

Then Emma asked, "You interested in hearing what happened at Vanessa's house? Last night?"

He nodded soberly.

Emma told him every detail that she could remember. From awakening to the wet tip of a Sharpie, to the shot, the scream, and, finally, the assailant kicking her unconscious.

Mark took her hand. She didn't resist. He kissed the back of her hand and told her, "You can count on me, babe."

"Thank you, Mark, and thanks for looking after Pepper."

After he'd gone, Emma wept. For no credible reason and despite all evidence suggesting she was a fool, she still loved Will Foster.

44

Home Remedies

I maintain at all times a plentiful supply of medical equipment, supplies, and drugs. I keep them in a large, locked storage unit at the opposite end of my basement from my Tsunami 300-gallon aquarium. Each cubby is self-contained and labeled. I know exactly where to find the cubby labeled Narcotic Analgesics. Obviously, I cannot waltz into an Emergency Department with a gunshot wound and not be asked a couple of questions.

From a plastic tube with a child-resistant, pop-up plastic top, I remove two 20 mg OxyContin tablets. On my kitchen counter, I crush the pills into a fine purplish dust. The prescription expired three years ago, but that is just big-pharma bullshit. They are fine. In fact, they're better than a new prescription, because Purdue, which makes Oxy (their headquarters are in Stamford, Connecticut, which isn't very far away), caved to the anti-opioid crazies and changed the way the pills are manufactured. Now, they are designed to turn into goo in the moist environment of the nostrils, which makes snorting them an unpleasant experience. I hate the Sacklers.

I have 40 mg ready, crushed and lined up, on the counter.

I roll up a bill and snort each line until there's no Oxy left. I know that I could overdose, but I am not getting anywhere near my gunshot wound without a boatload of painkiller.

Fucking Emma!

I remove my shirt. The entrance and exit wounds are weeping blood through my stop-gap dressing. I have various suture kits ("retired" from the US Navy). The problem is I am right-handed. I know I will not be able to stitch the holes with my left hand. The wound is approximately 12 mm medial to my right humerus. The entrance wound looks like it was made by a 9 mm slug, and the exit wound is larger.

Before beginning, I wait a full hour until I get super-stoned.

First, I run warm water right into the hole on the anterior side of my upper arm. In a contortionist's pose I flow tap water into the posterior hole. In paramedic school, my instructor said, "Don't put anything in a wound that you wouldn't put in an eye."

I have to get back to work, and I don't need an infection to delay me. I select a 10-60 cc irrigation syringe and fill it with medical grade isopropyl alcohol. I insert the tip of the syringe into the bullet hole, grit my teeth, and push the plunger.

Turns out, 40 mg of OxyContin is not enough.

I scream. My arm is on fire.

Contorting my arm again, I disinfect the exit wound, which for some reason hurts even more. As the alcohol evaporates, so does some of the sting.

With a pair of Kelly hemostatic forceps, I squeeze the anterior wound closed and lock the forceps. The forceps flop over and hang off the wound, because I only have one hand to work with. The pain is indescribable.

I open a box of Nexcare Steri-Strips. They have their own built-in adhesive, but I need to close these holes, so nothing gets in or out. I add a drop of Krazy Glue to each end of the Steri-Strips and press each one into place. I pull them as tight as I can, after which I unlock and remove the Kelly forceps. I don't look forward to ripping off the Steri-Strips.

Shaky and sweaty, I swallow a tumbler full of bourbon, a dividend to my analgesic cocktail. Finally, I indulge myself and go to bed, although it is Saturday morning.

Midafternoon, I wake and, still hurting, swallow an OxyContin. I don't bother to snort this one. I'm feeling marginally improved, and the bleeding has stopped.

I call Stella on her cell phone.

"It's me. I heard all the brouhaha on my scanner this morning.

What the hell happened at Vanessa Mack's house? Sounded like the entire Police Department responded."

"Someone tried to murder Vanessa. The same person killed Ethan and Deb. But Emma Thorne was in the house. She shot him. She says she hit him, but she doesn't know where."

"No shit."

"Actually, I'm at Vanessa's house right now. She's packing to leave town." Stella lowers her voice. "Between you and me, she's an ungodly wreck. I mean, psycho-city."

"Can't say I blame her."

"Anyway, I'm just about to head back to headquarters. A taxi's coming to pick her up in about an hour and take her to the airport. Do you want to get together tonight?"

"I'm afraid I can't tonight, sweetie. Rain check?"

"That's too bad." She sounds disappointed.

As soon as I am ready, I drive right over to Vanessa's house on Highcroft Terrace. I park directly in front. Cool as a cucumber, I knock on the front door, being careful to use my left arm. When she answers the door, she looks surprised and confused.

Then, in full-on panic mode, she squeaks, *"What do you want?"*

She is even more horrified when I pull my Smith & Wesson .38 Special (it has a Crimson Trace upper grip-mounted laser sight integrated into its handle).

The Crimson Trace laser beam is available in red or green. I chose green when I purchased it.

I see the green dot dancing on Vanessa's face.

45

No-Show

Late Saturday afternoon, Dr. Emma McKay found Emma a bed on a Med-Surg corridor on the fourth floor. Like so many others, Hampshire Hospital was built on a hill. Although she shared the room with another woman, the bed that was empty had the window view. She looked out over Hampshire toward the west. In the distance, side-lit by the June sun, she could see the densely-forested Litchfield Hills. A comforting sight; it was, after all, home.

The morphine had worn off. Dr. McKay had proved stingy with additional painkillers. She recommended Tylenol, which was wholly inadequate. A harried nurse's aide served her dinner-on-a-tray, the high point of which was Pomegranate Jell-O.

Right after the same aide collected her dinner tray, there was a knock on her door. She assumed it was a visitor for her roommate, so she didn't answer. Following another knock, Lieutenant Skip Munro from Major Crimes poked his head in.

"Hello, Emma, mind if I come in for a moment?" He took a chair next to her bed and studied her face. "As my daughter would say, 'Ouchy-ouchy. Poor you.'"

She managed a laugh. "You don't sound like a Major Crimes cop."

"Do you feel up to answering a couple questions?"

"Anything to relieve the boredom." She jerked her thumb at her roommate, who was watching a well-amplified Fox News program. "My companion doesn't seem to know I exist."

Skip began, "Chief Weeks filled me in on some of the events of last night at Mrs. Mack's house. What a horror show. You showed a lot of guts getting a shot off after what looks like a damaging beating."

Emma frowned. "Maybe, but I might've shot my husband."

Skip said, "That's kinda why I'm here. How sure are you that Mr. Foster is our guy? I've been looking into your husband. Pretty thoroughly, actually. What his friends say, his family, his history. Either some component of his personality went seriously haywire, or we're looking for the wrong person. What do you think?"

"That you are the only person around here who doesn't have a bull's-eye on Will's back."

"Ha! Why don't you walk me through last night? Did—let's call the intruder the 'suspect' for now—did the suspect say anything to you?"

Thoughtfully, Emma answered, "I'm pretty sure the only word he said was 'shit.' He sort of muttered the word. I remember thinking at the time that the suspect's voice sounded lower than Will's."

"That was all he said, during the whole encounter?"

"Yeah, funny that, no? There were a lot of obvious times for him to say something, but the suspect chose not to."

Skip shifted in his chair and thought for a moment. He said, "That would make me think that the suspect has a voice you would recognize and intentionally didn't give you that opportunity. Make sense?"

"Hmm, makes sense."

"Assuming that Will does not wear perfume," Skip smiled, "did you catch a whiff of the subject? In my experience, most people have a distinctive smell, and if you know them well you can pick it up."

"The only odor I remember smelled like bug spray. And BO, but I'm afraid that the latter was mine. Sorry."

"How about the way the suspect felt? I understand he was on top of you. Did that feel like Will's body?"

"Now, don't go kinky on me Lieutenant," she said. "But now that you mention it, the suspect didn't feel like Will. Same height and about the same weight. It was hard to tell, though, because, as I'm sure you heard, the suspect was wearing a bulletproof vest. Which is another bizarre anomaly. I simply can't imagine my husband choosing to wear body armor, no matter what the circumstance. Too weird for words."

"Anything else?"

"No, I can't think of anything more that might be helpful."

"Well, in that case," Skip said, standing, "I better be off." Before he left, he added, "I'm not going to rule out your husband, but him being the killer doesn't add up to me. How could a man so well known in Hampshire be skulking around murdering people, and yet not a soul has laid eyes on him. Huh?"

Emma was deep in thought when Skip Munro pulled the door closed behind him.

After Skip left, she turned over in her mind all the doubts that the investigator had raised. The most obvious of which was, if not Will, who? Emma hadn't given much voice to one daunting construct. To wit, she couldn't think of another link between Ethan, Deb, and Vanessa other than herself. It felt like a circle of murders with her at the center. But who, and for what possible reason, would someone be so against her to do the things they had done. That left her with one final thought. Archie had taught her to be, above all, kind.

Hadn't she tried her damnedest?

A little after nine o'clock, Emma's cell phone rang.

"Emma!" a panicked voice shouted. "I'm at the Cincinnati airport, at baggage claim. Vanessa was not on the flight. Checked with Delta. She was booked, but a no-show. What the hell happened?"

"Oh God, Dave. This is horrible."

"You're damn right it is! And I expect you to fix it."

"Have you called the Hampshire police? I'm still in the hospital."

"Of course, I've called the goddamn police. I spoke with a, a woman—"

"Stella Weeks?"

"Yeah, her!" Dave said, still shouting. "She said that she drove Vanessa home from the hospital to pack and called her a cab to take her to the airport. Wait! There's another call coming in. Hold on."

Emma waited fearfully.

Dave came back on the line, wailing. "Jesus, Emma, Weeks just talked to the taxi driver. He told her that he went to our house, banged on the door a bunch of times, and NOBODY ANSWERED. What am I going to do? *This is on you, Emma.*"

46

An Inattentive Guard

Grinding pain kept Emma awake most of the night. Finally, in the predawn hours of Sunday morning, she finally found a fitful sleep. At precisely 6 a.m., however, "Fox and Friends" ruined what became a short nap. The hospital provided cheap personal TV speakers for each patient. Her roommate's lay on the pillow right next to her ear. She was definitely deaf, because the volume was way too high to be close to a properly functioning ear. The crackling speaker was as distorted as Fox News itself.

There was nothing Emma could do about it. She waited patiently until she thought it was not too early to call Mark Byrne. She hoped that he was still at her house looking after Pepper. By seven o'clock, her patience crumbled. She got Mark on the phone and asked him to bring her iPad and the Sunday *New York Times* crossword puzzle to the hospital. She asked him to bring her some clothes, too.

"Any particular underwear you need from your underwear drawer?" he asked, harkening back to her comment from Friday.

"*Touché!*"

Mark told her that he would give Pepper a long walk and would then come to the hospital "bearing gifts."

"What's that noise in the background?" Mark asked before ringing off.

"'Fox and Friends,' I'm afraid."

"I can see why you are going crazy. Right-wing rubbish. I'll lend you my Bose headphones. Be there soon as I can."

Emma only knew one private investigator, but she couldn't imagine there were too many others out there who viewed Fox News as rubbish. She was pleased that he was one of them.

Outside her window, battleship-gray clouds threatened. A June thunderstorm was on its way. She looked forward to the diversion. If she accomplished anything today, it would be to persuade Dr. McKay, who had promised to stop in, to discharge her. Meantime, she looked forward to seeing Mark.

He arrived during her perfect English breakfast, scrambled eggs and cold toast. She handed him her plate and asked him to dump it in the trash. Mark sat in the seat that Lieutenant Munro had occupied the night before. He had two shopping bags with him. From one, he produced a headset, the complete Sunday *Times*, her iPad, some fresh fruit, and an Elizabeth George novel she was halfway through.

"I found this," he said handing her the book, "in the living room."

How thoughtful, she thought.

"Thanks," she said.

"I don't mean to add to your burdens, but have you seen this?" He withdrew the *Hampshire Chronicle* from his busy shopping bag and held it up for her to see.

> Hampshire Police Investigate
> Disappearance of Vanessa Mack

Emma read the article.

> By Virginia Hobson, Staff Reporter
> According to David Mack, 37, Vanessa Mack, 36, both of 17 Highcroft Terrace, failed to board her ticketed flight to Cincinnati yesterday. She was expected to join her husband and children there. Police say that she is missing and that they are investigating. Foul play is feared. On Friday night, there was a major police action at her home

on Highcroft Terrace. At this time,
police are not providing any details
about Friday night. However, the Chronicle has learned that Mack and former
Hampshire Chief of Police, Emma Thorne,
were transported to hospital. Mack was
released on Saturday. Thorne remains
hospitalized ...

Emma finished the rest of the lengthy front-page story, which con-
tained lots of verbiage but no further information.

She handed the newspaper back to Mark. "I heard about it, because
Dave Mack telephoned last night from Cincinnati and reamed me a
new asshole."

"Just what you needed, huh? It's like with my ex-wife ... everything
was my fault."

"But, seriously, it's horrible about Vanessa, and that *is* my fault."

"Don't beat yourself up, kid. Judging by the way you look, you did
everything humanly possible to protect her. According to what I heard,
your friend Stella Weeks drove her home and just dumped her there.
None of this would've happened if she'd driven Vanessa to the airport.
I place the blame right on her doorstep."

Emma nodded tentatively.

Changing the subject, Emma said, "I don't think I can stand another day in here."

A new idea occurred to her.

"You know what, Mark, I'm just gonna check myself out. Screw
this. Did you bring me some clothes?"

He handed her the other shopping bag. "Sorry I didn't think to
bring you a raincoat." Rain was now pelting the window.

Wearing a skimpy hospital johnny, bow-tied in the back, Emma
shuffled to the bathroom. Over her shoulder she said, "Don't you be
sneaking a peek at my tush."

Mark scouted the hospital corridor. When the coast was clear, he
and Emma made it to the fire stairs without being spotted.

Pepper went mad with excitement when they arrived back at her
house. While reveling in their reunion, Pepper rolled onto her back
and demanded a tummy rub.

Mark cooked them a proper breakfast, brunch really. Eating together, she declared, "Ah, finally some decent food."

Chewing some toast, Mark spoke with his mouth full. "I want you to take it easy. You're probably still concussed. Unfortunately, I have to visit my mom today. So, I won't be around to keep an eye on you. I try to go every other Sunday. She's not doing too well."

"That's nice," she said. They finished eating a cheese omelet, bacon, toast, and coffee. Mark said goodbye to Pepper and Emma, giving the latter a peck on the cheek.

The second he left the house, Emma prepared to leave too. With an umbrella and a rain jacket, she waded through a cloudburst to her car. Pepper jumped through the open door and thoroughly shook her coat, drenching Emma all over again.

She drove directly to Highcroft Terrace and parked around the corner from the house and away from the driveway. She figured that Vanessa's house would still be considered a crime scene and probably guarded by a Hampshire officer. She and her dog stole through the wet woods behind the house. Sure enough, Officer Pete Sinclair was sitting in his cruiser, parked near the front door, with the windshield wipers on. He was reading a book. Anyway, he couldn't see the back door from where he was parked.

There was crime scene tape crisscrossing the doorway. Emma found the key that Dave always kept above the lintel of the back porch. She let herself in, telling Pepper to be quiet. They passed through Vanessa's cluttered mudroom and into her thoroughly suburban, yellow kitchen. The living room, like the kitchen, was neat. There was no evidence of mischief.

Back in the kitchen, she opened the door to the basement and instructed Pepper to search it. Pepper returned to the kitchen seconds later wagging her tail, eager for a more fruitful assignment.

They went upstairs to Vanessa's bedroom, the scene of the horrors of Friday night. In a laundry hamper in the bathroom Emma found the pajamas Vanessa had worn that night. She let Pepper smell them.

"Search, Pepper."

Leading a frenzied tail, the dog sniffed each room methodically. Emma followed her. Downstairs, Pepper suddenly sat and looked to her master for approval. Emma couldn't see immediately what Pepper was signaling that she had found. She got down on her hands and knees. She ran her hands over the patterned carpet. Partially underneath the sofa, she found a hoop earring. She remembered that it was the same style as the earrings Vanessa had worn on Friday.

As Pepper's tail thumped the carpet next to her, she picked up the earring. The kidney-shaped ear wire was bent into the open position. There was blood on the wire and on the earring.

This suggested an abduction. Still, there was no overturned furniture or any other signs of a struggle. Vanessa must have been swiftly overwhelmed. She found a Ziplock in the kitchen and a fork. She lifted the earring with a tine and dropped it into the baggie.

"Good job, Pepper!"

47

Nine Criteria

Dark wood paneling sheathed the lobby of the Hampshire Police Department headquarters, which reflected its nineteenth century heritage. It was far from grand however. Bolted to one wall was a metal box with a slot on the top. The sign on the box said: Leave Your Expired and Unwanted Drugs Here. Next to the box, there was a poster advertising Hampshire's Gun Buyback Program. "You can get $50 to $100 for certain handguns and up to $200 for assault weapons."

The wall facing the entrance doors was glass. Archie had changed the original plate glass to ballistic glass-clad polycarbonate as befitted the twenty-first century. The dispatcher who sat behind the glass doubled as the receptionist.

That Sunday it was Laura Hester, who greeted her with genuine warmth. "I'm so glad to see you back on your feet. I can't tell you how freaked I was when you called in on Friday night."

"Thanks. Still achy and creaky, but I'm doing okay. Is Stella in?"

"Yup. She's called a meeting about Vanessa Mack—they're about to start—in the war room."

Emma asked, "What's the war room?"

"That's what Stella's renamed the roll call room," Laura said. She repeated the new name, enclosing it in ironic air quotes.

"Really?"

"Kid you not! Maybe she thinks she's Winston Churchill." Laura's phone rang. "Oops, gotta go. 911 coming in." She buzzed Emma in as she answered the 911.

Emma and Pepper headed down the corridor to the roll call room. They waited outside the door. She told Pepper to Stay. Otherwise, Pepper would have happily proceeded inside to greet her old friends. Emma debated whether to enter and hand over her new evidence to Stella when the meeting started.

Emma heard Stella rap the podium and say, "Okay, everyone, listen up." In a lengthy presentation, she brought the team up to speed on the disappearance of Vanessa Mack. Like Virginia Hobson's article in the *Chronicle*, there wasn't much meat.

She continued, "I am confident that the man we are looking for is Will Foster. The mark on Emma's ankle, which he mistook for Vanessa's ankle, proves it. Many of you, probably most of you, knew Will. So, how hard could it be to find him? Let's hit the bricks and get this sonofabitch behind bars, where he belongs."

Emma recognized the voice of Skip Munro.

"Um, okay if I say a few words?"

"Of course, be my guest."

"With all due respect, Chief Weeks, my team hasn't come to the same conclusion. Not yet, at any rate. I'll explain why in a moment. But first let's discuss some basics.

"The term 'serial killings' means a series of three or more killings, having common characteristics such as to suggest the reasonable possibility that the crimes were committed by the same actor or actors. At least, that's what the FBI says. Do we have a serial killer in Hampshire? Yes, I believe we do. If you count Vanessa Mack's attempted murder and the Sharpie marks on three different individuals, it tastes like serial to me."

Emma heard a few chuckles.

"Pun intended," he said.

It sounded to Emma like Skip was skillfully disarming his audience in anticipation of bad news to come.

"So, let's look at some commonly accepted traits linked to serial killers. And which of these apply to Will Foster ... and which don't."

Emma couldn't resist any longer. She stepped into the room and stood at the back. She made Pepper wait outside. Skip moved to the whiteboard at the front of the room and began writing:

1. White male in his mid-20s to mid-30s.
2. Antisocial Behavior.
3. Arson.

Skip turned back to the room. "I read that childhood friends of the 'Son of Sam' killer, David Berkowitz, called him 'Pyro.' The police in New York said that he may have set as many as a thousand fires."

4. Torturing small animals.

"Jeffrey Dahmer, the cannibal killer, dismembered his own puppy and later mounted its head on a stake."
Officer Pete Sinclair said, "Yuck."
Skip said, "Agreed."

5. Poor family life and childhood abuse.
6. Substance abuse.
7. Voyeurism, sadomasochistic pornography, and fetishism.

Skip turned to his rapt audience. "As an adolescent in Tacoma, Washington, Ted Bundy cruised his neighborhood at night looking for windows without curtains and women without clothes.
"And, finally, the last component of an 'organized' serial killer, which I think our killer certainly has, is …"

8. Intelligence.

Skip placed the dry-erase marker he had been using onto the tray at the base of the whiteboard.
"Despite subsequent doubting research, let me also introduce you to the Macdonald Triad, because it remains a widely taught theory. It is also known as the 'homicidal triad' or the 'triad of sociopathy.'
"In 1963, a psychiatrist from New Zealand named John Macdonald suggested a link between fire-setting, cruelty to animals, and persistent bedwetting after the age of five to homicidal and sexually predatory behavior.
"So, that adds bedwetting to our list.
"Thus, we have nine criteria. How many of these apply to what we know of Will Foster?" He looked out over the room.
Nobody spoke.
"Exactly one," he said forcefully. "By all accounts, Will is an intelligent man. From what our investigation has uncovered, none of the other criteria fit. Well, I suppose, he could have been a teen-aged peeping Tom. But I kind of doubt it. Also, his parents told me that Will stopped wetting his bed at a very young age and that he treated

the family dog as his best friend."

Emma watched the whole room erupt. Everyone chattered at once. But in her own mind, Emma felt, if not vindicated, at least cheered.

Wouldn't it be wonderful if they weren't looking for Will?

Emma heard a loud Ahem. "Are you done, yet, Lieutenant?" Stella said to Skip with evident hostility.

"Actually, not quite." He smiled at Stella. "I'd like to make a few more points, if you'll indulge me. He said to the assembled cops, "Can I have your attention for a minute or two more?"

48

Yahoos

Lieutenant Skip Munro continued, "The best friend a serial killer has is a cop who makes erroneous assumptions. That bears repeating. The best friend a serial killer has is a cop who makes erroneous assumptions. Has anyone heard of Henry Louis Wallace, aka 'The Taco Bell Strangler?'"

Hearing nothing, he continued, "Wallace killed eleven women over a four-year period. Why did it take the Charlotte, North Carolina, police so long to catch him? A couple of reasons. Most serial killers kill strangers. So, betting on the standard assumptions, they searched for a white male in his mid-20s who didn't know his victims. Wallace turned out to be an African-American who had connections with all his victims. The only thing they got right was his age—"

Stella stood. In a loud voice she said, "Well, Will Foster knew Ethan Jackson, Deb Barger, and Vanessa Mack. Aren't you just proving I'm right?"

"Bear with me, Chief, I just have a few more points to make, after which we can discuss your case." He waited for Stella to settle down. Emma could see how rattled she was.

"Here's another scenario. Imagine you're called to an active shooter incident at Hampshire High. As you arrive on scene, what are you looking for? Instinctively, you're looking for a white male high school student, probably dressed in black, carrying an AR-15, who is going to shoot himself before you can take him out. Right? Don't forget that Iranian-born nut job who shot up the YouTube headquarters. She was a woman.

"In 1998, Roy Hazelwood of the FBI infamously declared, 'There are no female serial killers.' Guess what? He was wrong. About fifteen percent of serial killers in the United States have been women. It is believed that there are more who were never caught. Among conventional murderers, about ten to thirteen percent are women. While it is true in the active shooter/mass murderer scenario—that is, shooters who aim for multiple victims at once without a cooling-off period between kills—only three percent are women.

"What I'm trying to get across is simple. Follow the evidence and let the evidence inform your conclusions. Don't allow your presumptions to get ahead of the evidence. Okay, I'm done now. Thanks for letting me say my piece."

Stella stepped up to the podium. Huffily, she said, "I think I speak for all the officers present when I say that it would be nice for you to remember that you're not talking to a bunch of yahoos here."

A couple of cops clapped. She said, "See what I mean."

Munro smiled enigmatically and retook his seat in the front row.

Stella wasn't finished.

"I am more than happy to follow the evidence," Stella said. "Don't forget that the killer left his calling card, his signature, three separate times. That evidence spells **WIL**. If anyone cannot see that there is just one **L** missing, then I say *you're* not paying attention to the evidence. In my opinion, the killer has signed his work."

"I'd like to add something, too." Everyone turned in their seats. Mayor Dick Wardlaw was standing in the back of the room with his hand up in the air. "You should all be aware that the entire town of Hampshire is affected by these, um, incidents. My phone has lit up like one of your police light bars." He paused. Emma thought he was waiting for a laugh. When he didn't get one, he continued, "Folks are scared, people. They ask me why the police haven't caught the serial killer yet. I'm forced to wonder the same thing. Be advised, the pressure is on ... both on me *and* you."

"We are well aware of that, Mayor Wardlaw," Stella said. "Okay guys I think that's enough for now. Thank you, Lieutenant Munro, for giving us the benefit of your wisdom and experience. We sure appreciate it. But I think, going forward, we will be running parallel but equal investigations." Stella glanced at a note card on the podium. "We have distributed a recent photograph of Vanessa Mack to all area departments and, of course, to the state police. Just as we did previously with Will Foster. We've issued areawide alerts for both individuals. Her husband, Dave Mack, is flying back from Cincinnati. Although doubtful, it's possible he will be able to provide us with some useful information."

She stared directly at Skip in the front row. "The Hampshire Police Department's priorities are to find Vanessa Mark and bring her home safely and to find Will Foster and bring him home in handcuffs."

Emma looked around the room, trying to gauge the reaction of her former colleagues. There seemed to be broad approval for Stella's pushback. Emma saw Stella walk over to Munro and shake his hand.

Emma seized the opportunity. She hurried to the front of the room. It was purely an instinct, but she wanted to hand over Vanessa's earring to Stella while Skip was present.

"Hi, Emma," Skip said, friendly as can be and seemingly unfazed by Stella's remarks, "are you feeling any better? And where's that fine dog of yours?"

"She's waiting outside." Without raising her voice over the hubbub in the roll-call room, Emma said, "Pepper. Come."

Pepper ran into the room and came to a screeching halt by Emma's side.

"Well I'll be damned," Skip said. "That's amazing."

Stella followed the conversation, frowning.

"I was really interested in your remarks," Emma said. "I find it so hard to believe that Will would harm anyone, let alone Deb and Vanessa, who are nearly as close to him as they are to me."

Stella said, "Well, I *can* believe it." Emma thought she sounded, at the least, petulant.

Emma removed the baggie from her purse. "I'm afraid I have a new piece of evidence which suggests that Vanessa was forcibly abducted." She showed them the earring.

Stella didn't waste a nanosecond. "Where the hell did you get that?"

"Your team missed it. It was under the sofa in Vanessa's living room. Pepper found it."

"The Mack house is a goddamn crime scene," Stella sputtered. "You had no right to go in there. Anyway, we haven't finished processing it yet. You're not a cop and neither is your goddamn dog. I could charge you for breaking and entering *and* for illegal possession of Archie's gun!"

"Don't get your panties in a twist," Skip interrupted. "This is important evidence. Let me see that." He carefully examined the earring in the baggie. "Definitely looks like blood. I'll get this to our lab. Good work, but I agree this doesn't look very good for Vanessa." Turning to Stella, he said, "My advice to you is to worry a little less about imagined slights and find Vanessa Mack on the double."

As her face reddened, Stella straightened her uniform blouse and glared at Skip, but she kept her mouth shut.

Lieutenant Monroe said a polite goodbye to Stella, gave Pepper a friendly pat, and headed toward the door. Stella spun in the other direction.

Emma found herself briefly alone. Again, her heart went out to Vanessa, and her instincts told her not to expect a happy ending.

A tap on her arm caused her to turn around. She found herself nose-to-nose with Dick Wardlaw.

49

Revolver

Dick Wardlaw's smile bared his stained teeth. "What a surprise to see *you* here!"

Emma could not bring herself to say hello. The slime ball repulsed her with his bulbous face and asymmetrical, leering eyes.

She waited.

He studied her face and said, "Gee, you really suffered a beating. Somebody worked you over pretty good. But you're still beautiful. Bruised but beautiful."

Emma looked for an escape route. She tried to catch Buzz Buzzucano's eye, but the bastard turned away. She didn't blame him. Who'd want to get sucked into a conversation with Dick Wardlaw?

"I found Lieutenant Munro to be pretty impressive," Wardlaw continued. "He made some very cogent points, and he seemed to be exonerating your ex-husband."

Emma didn't fall for the "ex" trap.

"In comparison, I found the acting chief lacking. She seems to be a prisoner of her own theory, her only theory. I may have made a mistake about you, Emma. I'm considering reversing my decision. You see, I prefer to work with people who can keep an open mind."

No one could have misconstrued his words.

"There's a new French restaurant in Great Barrington. It's called Chez Max. Why don't we dine there sometime this week and discuss making you chief again? It's very expensive."

Although she tried hard, Emma couldn't come up with an appropriately withering response.

"Oh c'mon," he wheedled, "stop being such a stick in the mud. I just want to be friends. Don't forget, I could do a lot for you in this town …"

Still unable to come up with the perfect rejoinder, Emma turned on her heel.

She and Pepper made tracks for the exit.

Emma felt sick to her stomach. Dick's persistence insulted her.

When they arrived back at the house, Pepper raced into the kitchen, her tail wagging. Emma followed. Mark was sitting at the kitchen table reading the *Times* that he had brought to the hospital. He seemed quite at home. Emma wasn't sure how she felt about that.

"Where have you been? I was worried about you."

Emma countered with, "How is your mother?"

"Fine. But where were you?"

Emma was beginning to feel that Mark's concern—she had no doubt he was sincere—was intrusive. She never liked feeling boxed in. On the other hand, it was a welcome change that *someone* cared.

She tried for a gentle yet firm tone. "I'm not a baby, Mark. I need to do things—"

"Understood. But you need to look after yourself. Look at you. You've sustained a serious head injury. What did the lady doc call it?"

"An epidural hematoma."

"Exactly! I probably should never have let you leave the hospital."

More firmly this time, Emma said, "That was *not* your decision."

Her newfound popularity was claustrophobic. Not that she would ever compare Mark to Dick Wardlaw, but she needed to cool his ardor.

Emma sighed. "We need to get a few things straight. I like you Mark, and I'm grateful for the help you've given me. And for your concern, too. But I'm not ready for a relationship. This is not the time."

"What's all this about a relationship?" he replied angrily. "Who said anything about a relationship? You're sounding pretty presumptuous."

"Let's just agree," Emma said, less in anger than in exhaustion, "that I need some time alone to nurse my wounds. I also have a headache."

"Message received! I think it's time for me to go."

He got up and left the house.

Emma said to herself aloud, *Smooth work, Emma,* you just lost your last friend.

She went upstairs with the Sunday *Times* crossword puzzle, swallowed two Tylenols, and climbed into bed. Pepper looked at her quizzically but joined her. Her headache was becoming more intense, but she was determined to do something alone and for herself.

She puffed herself up with four pillows, two of hers and two of Will's. She balanced the magazine section on her thighs and grabbed a ballpoint pen from her night table. She worried briefly about her selfishness. About how she had hurt Mark's feelings. But she felt like being selfish. She pushed him, and the rest of her worries, out of her consciousness. For the moment, anyway.

That day's theme was "The Long and Winding Road."

She started solving from the lower right corner. It was not the usual way she did it, but the easy way.

The bottom right clue was simple: "Hospital opening."

Answer: "stent." The lower right corner always has common letters like **S** and **T**.

In time, she'd answered enough clues to reach 116-across. There were twenty-one spaces for the answer, which ran the full width of the grid.

The clue was "Revolver love song?"

Puzzle therapy was working. She smiled as she penned in the answer.

"Got to Get You into My Life."

Pepper started barking, her someone's-at-the-door bark. She got off the bed and went downstairs. A big part of Emma hoped that Mark hadn't returned. A small part of her hoped he had.

Pepper was sitting in the hallway, no longer barking. Strange, Emma thought, her head pounding. She opened the door. There was a package on the porch. It was an ordinary cardboard box, but, oddly, it was tied closed with a red ribbon like a birthday present. Pepper gave the box a thorough sniffing before Emma picked it up and took it into the kitchen.

Emma didn't know what to expect, but she had a strong feeling that she was not going to like what was inside. She sliced the ribbon with a kitchen knife.

50

Follow my Instructions

I do not intend to use the .38 to shoot Vanessa Mack. I have in mind a more pleasurable scenario.

I've only brought the weapon to compensate for my injured arm, although I'm sure I can take her with one arm tied behind my back. *Tee-hee!*

But I'm shocked by the speed with which Vanessa spins and flees. I have to take a moment to jam my Smith and Wesson into the waistband of my jeans to free up my good arm.

I chase her through the living room. She is not as fast as I initially thought. I stretch out my arm to seize her neck. Instead, my gloved hand snags her earring and tears it from her earlobe. She screams. I feel sure a torn earlobe is painful. It must be, because it stops her in her tracks.

I slap her face hard to let her know who is in charge. And I re-aim the gun.

"Please," she begs, "I have two kids. They can't live without their mother. I don't know why you are doing this, but please don't hurt me."

"You let your kids watch too much TV. That's bad for them. You should also give them better food instead of the crap you feed them."

"Whaaat?"

I can see that Vanessa realizes that I have been spying on her. This seems to terrify her even more.

But she shouts, "You're crazy!" anyway.

She can see that that makes me very angry.

"No, wait, I didn't mean it," she says, whimpering now. "I'm just so scared. I don't know what I'm saying."

I feel calmer after her apology.

"No offense taken."

Personally, I don't know if I really mean what I just said, but it seems to take her hysteria down a notch. Always a good thing under such circumstances.

I look around for the missing earring. I don't like to leave an untidy scene, but I can't find the damn thing.

Vanessa stares at me, cowering.

I say, "Now, my dear, I'd like you to remove all your clothing and your earring."

"I…I can't do that." She shakes visibly. She wraps protective arms around her breasts. "Please?"

Although the snub-nosed .38 is a small gun, it makes a satisfyingly loud click when I cock the hammer.

"Why are you doing this. I don't understand," Vanessa pleads.

"Follow my instructions, and you won't get hurt."

Vanessa can't be sure whether I am lying.

I am lying.

She takes off her blue travel dress. She slowly removes her bra and really stalls when it comes to removing her black thong. Isn't Dave the lucky one?

I admire her. She has a nice figure. I'm surprised to see that she shaves her crotch. I wouldn't have thought that she was the type, but like Deb, she has left a small, downward triangle of pubic hair.

Girls' Club?

I point to it with my gun. I say, "Just like Deb huh? I wonder if Emma has joined your club."

Vanessa covers her privates and wails. Her terror is complete. At least that's what she thinks.

"Shut up!" I command. Her wailing gradually morphs into a loud sniffle.

I shift gears, adopting a friendly, everyday tone of voice. I'm not into sexual assault or rape, as I believe I've stated. Rape is for the weak and the inadequate. Revenge is for the powerful.

"Say, you don't have a box and some ribbon, do you? I need to give someone a present."

I find I am getting tired of Vanessa. Her abject hysteria is rewarding but also annoying. I decide to keep things moving.

"Do you have any personal stationary, Vanessa?"

She nods numbly. I follow her naked backside into the living room, where she opens a faux-antique drop-front desk. It's very Bed Bath & Beyond. She removes a pad with her name printed in pink script on each sheet.

"This is all I have," she says.

No surprise there. "I want you to write down exactly what I tell you to." I dictate seven words. "That shouldn't be too hard."

"I can't do that. I don't even know who it's to. This is cruel. You *are* sick!"

I control my temper. "If I tell you who it's for, will you write it?"

Vanessa stares at me. Tears stain her cheeks.

"How about this?" I recite the salutation.

"I won't do that!" she shouts and strikes her fist on the desk top.

Vanessa appears to have found a modicum of courage.

"How about I shoot you in your left arm," I say, thinking of what Emma did to me, "and then you write what I'm asking?"

I think that sounds reasonable.

"I can't do write this. It's too cruel."

I press the barrel of the .38 against the back of her head.

"I have a good idea. Why don't I blow your brains out first, and we skip the note altogether?"

"Oh, God," she says, as she scribbles the message, "please don't hurt me. I beg of you. You've seen my children. They are beautiful. They are innocent. Please don't take their mother away from them!"

"Give me the note."

Vanessa turns in her chair and hands me the note. I let it drop to the floor.

"Pick it up," I order.

Her face is contorted with fear. When she leans over to pick up the piece of paper, I bash her head with the handle of the .38. The blow knocks Vanessa unconscious, and it sends a searing pain down my wounded arm. It is, in the moment, worth the agony, because I have to take Vanessa with me.

51

Aspiration

Emma looked into the open box. At first it made no sense. Just some clothes stuffed inside. She pulled out a blue dress and held it up. Emma didn't recognize it. Although it was her size, that didn't make any sense either. She looked back into the box. The next item was a black bra, which she could instantly tell was too big for her. Finally, there was a thong which was pinned to a piece of paper with the twin of Vanessa's bloody earring.

Emma cried out.

The clothes told a horrifying story.

Emma held the note by its edges. For a long while she didn't have the courage to read it.

She sat at the kitchen table, her pounding head in her hands. Her battered head had hurt when she'd left the hospital, but it hadn't throbbed like it did now.

With a heavy sigh, she read the note.

Dear Emma, This is all your fault. Vanessa

She remained at her kitchen table weeping bitter tears. Poor, sweet Vanessa. Emma couldn't bear to imagine the horrors she must have suffered. She thought of Dave and their kids and how devastated they would be. Between the clothes and the note, Emma couldn't find any part of her to hold out hope for Vanessa.

When her eyes were dryer and after she'd blown her nose, she didn't call Stella. Instead, she dialed Skip Munro's cellphone.

"Hey Emma, how are you feeling?"

"Not great ... on two counts."

"If it's your head, you should see a doctor," he said.

"Yeah, probably should. Listen, I need to see you. I need to show you something."

"I'm at home."

She could hear the reluctance in his voice, but she asked, "Can I come there? It won't take long."

"Sure, I guess. Well, I don't see why not." He gave her his address.

She drove directly into the sun to get to Skip's house. She began to experience double vision. She shouldn't be driving. But when she glanced at Vanessa's note and the box on the seat beside her, she knew she had to.

Skip's pretty wife, a redhead with a wide smile, greeted her at the door.

"I'm Lorna, Emma. Skip's in the backyard. And who's this?"

"That's my partner Pepper," Emma said, "she's friendly."

Lorna studied Emma's face. "You appear to have suffered."

"You're not kidding!"

Skip was sunning himself on a chaise lounge. It was late afternoon, warm but not too hot. There was a riding mower on the back edge of the yard. The lawn was half-mown and smelled delicious. Skip had a moisture-beaded beer can in his hand. "Can I get you one?"

"Thanks, but no. I don't want to wreck your day off."

"Don't worry about it," he said, sitting up. "Have a seat. It's good to see you."

Emma sat opposite him, perched on the edge of another chaise. She handed him the note, but he didn't take it.

"Is it evidence?"

Skip was pretty quick. She nodded yes.

He gestured. "Just put it there on the table."

He read the note standing up.

"Aw, shit," he said shaking his head.

He went into the house and came back with a Ziploc. "Put it in here," he said. "What's in the box?"

"A blue dress and underwear. I assume they are Vanessa's, but I must admit I don't remember the dress."

"I'm not going to open the box. I'll call somebody from the lab for pick-up. But, I have to say, our unsub has been so careful in the past, I doubt we'll find anything."

"What are you going to do?" Emma asked.

"I really don't know," Skip replied. "Whoever is responsible is consistently three steps ahead of us."

Emma felt, and must have looked shaky, because Skip put his arms around her and gave her a hug.

Lorna came outside. "Are you sure I can't get you a beer? Feels like you need one."

Emma refused again and thanked both of them.

She drove toward home feeling awful on every level.

Along the way, her head started to feel like it was about to explode. She knew she should listen to her body. As she drove through Hampshire toward her house, she took an unplanned detour. She went to the Hampshire Hospital Emergency Department.

Luckily for her, Dr. Emma McKay was on duty and saw her without delay. She ordered another CT. Emma was promptly taken to Imaging in a wheelchair.

Later, McKay arrived to explain her findings.

"I don't think you're the type of person I have to pussyfoot around. So, I'm not going to. Unfortunately, the medicine I prescribed hasn't worked as I'd hoped it would. Your hematoma has expanded, and it is putting pressure on your brain. You suffered a harsh beating. To put it bluntly, your brain bounced around inside your skull. We call it a coup-contrecoup injury. Judging by the CT scan, you must have a whopping headache."

"Sure do," Emma said. "What happens next?"

"The go-to treatment involves pretty major surgery. In this procedure, a neurosurgeon will open up part of your skull—a craniotomy— so she can remove the hematoma and reduce the pressure on your brain. However, there is a less invasive method called aspiration. The decision, of course, will be up to the neurosurgeon. I can recommend a good one. But I would start with this second option. The neurosurgeon will drill a small hole in your skull and use suction to aspirate the blood. A small hole versus a craniotomy will make a big difference in your recovery time."

"Neither sounds particularly appealing," Emma said with a weak smile. "But I definitely vote for aspiration."

"Dr. Michaela Parker is a great neurosurgeon with privileges here.

Do you want me to contact her?"

"Gotta be done, right?"

"Okay. I'll call her first thing tomorrow morning. Meanwhile, you will be sleeping here tonight," she said sternly, "and you will *not* be checking yourself out like you did yesterday."

"Roger that," Emma said. "Now will you give me some morphine?"

"You're funny. Here's some Tylenol. It's extra strength."

Forty-eight hours ago, Emma couldn't have imagined that she would be adding brain surgery to her list of woes. She resolved to stay upbeat.

The investigation was at an impasse. Emma was committed to changing that.

First, she had to get her house in order. Not just her brain, she had to think of Pepper.

She swallowed her pride and called Mark.

52

Impasse

Judging Emma's epidural hematoma to be sufficiently critical, Dr. Parker drilled a burr hole into her skull the next day. A few hours later, she pronounced the operation a success. The blood had been suctioned and cleared. Emma came out of anesthesia with an even bigger headache and a patch of shaven scalp. Dr. Parker assured her that she would soon be on the mend.

Emma would not be discharged until 3:00 p.m. Thursday afternoon. That timing, it turned out, was critical.

In the meantime, several things happened.

Late Monday night, Parker moved her from the post-op ICU into a single room, where she spent the rest of the night.

Tuesday, she was allowed to have visitors.

Her first visitor was wholly unexpected. Fifteen-year-old Sophie King knocked on her door.

"Hi, Sophie, this is a pleasant surprise," Emma said. "How on earth did you know where to find me?"

"Long story. My mom's friends with Caroline Stoner. She told her that you had to have some kind of yucky operation."

"So much for HIPAA!" Emma laughed.

"What's HIPAA?"

"It's a law that says, among other things, you're not supposed to talk about other people's medical issues."

"Whoops," Sophie said, "am I, like, in trouble?"

"No of course not. But what brings you here?"

"I sorta thought I owed you."

"You don't owe me anything, but I'm glad to have a visitor. And see you again. Come, have a seat, and tell me what's going on in your life."

"Oh, pretty much same-same. I passed the course, and I got a job as a lifeguard at New Forest Lake," she said proudly.

"Congratulations!"

"I'm thinking about becoming an EMT or even a police officer. When I get older, of course. What's it like to be a policewoman? Is it scary?"

They were interrupted by a nurse who rolled in a cart with tiny cans of soda. Emma chose an off-brand ginger ale and asked, "May my friend have one too?"

The nurse said, "Be my guest."

Sophie took a root beer.

"It can be scary, but most of the time it isn't. It's a good job. Plus, you get to help people. I guess you've heard about the unsolved killings that have been going on?"

"It's all my parents talk about. It sure is creepy. The kids I talk to at the lake are all pretty spooked."

"They shouldn't be, unless they happen to know me."

"What's *that* supposed to mean?"

"Never mind," Emma said regretting her words.

"Tell me," Sophie insisted. "I'm not a kid, you know."

Emma stifled a smile. Oh, to be a teenager again! "Are you sure you want me to explain?"

"Yup."

"The unhappy truth is that I know all the victims."

"That's awful!" She suddenly stood up and stared at Emma. "Hey, you don't think I could be his next victim, do you?" She looked genuinely scared. "I mean, *I* know you, too."

"No, sweetie, you have nothing to fear. I'm sorry I said anything. I just feel so awful about the killings."

Sophie appeared mollified.

Emma had a sudden thought.

"I know Joe Henderson knew Ethan Jackson. Do you happen to know if he knew Deb Barger and Vanessa Mack?"

"No clue. Joe's friends don't interest me."

Worth a shot, Emma thought.

Sophie said, "I'm a little worried about my godmother, you know, Georgia."

Teenagers have a startling way of changing the subject. Emma guessed it was because of social media. One *non sequitur* after another.

Emma said, "I know Georgia. She doesn't like me very much."

"Yeah, I know. Remember when you came over that day?"

"Uh-huh. What's bothering you about Georgia?"

"Every Sunday, I go see her. It's our special time together. Usually, she takes me out, and we do fun stuff. She doesn't have any kids, you know. Except that time when you came over. Alphabetizing DVDs is not exactly my idea of a laugh-riot although it sucked when she made me leave."

Emma grinned. "So, what's happened between you and Georgia?"

"On Sunday, two days ago, Georgia called me and said she didn't want to see me for a while. She really hurt my feelings," Sophie said, suddenly pouting. "She didn't sound herself. She sounded, um, mad."

Emma didn't care a hoot about Georgia. But, to be nice to Sophie, she said, "Angry mad or crazy mad?"

Sophie surprised her by saying, "Both, I think."

That interested Emma. She'd long thought that Georgia was a little screwy. Georgia had often been unpleasant toward Emma, but she wouldn't have thought that she would be mean or even crazy-mean to Sophie, who was clearly a good kid.

"I'm truly sorry to hear that, but I'm sure she'll get back to you and smooth things over. She must've been in a bad mood, or maybe she has a headache like I do."

Sophie shifted gears again and giggled. "Yeah, I guess you're right. I'm not gonna let it get to me. I better run. I sure hope you feel better."

She scooted out of the room.

Emma thought about disagreeable Georgia for a moment. She soon found that disagreeable. She picked up her iPad, found the on-line version of Tuesday's *New York Times* crossword puzzle, and started tapping in the answers.

The next few days passed agonizingly slowly.

She telephoned Caroline Stoner a few times to learn if there was any progress in the search for Vanessa and/or Will. Each time, Caroline returned bad news. She reported that the entire department was sickened by their ongoing failure to nail down a single clue. She also told Emma that Dick Wardlaw was bearing down on Stella and had even threatened to remove her. She asked about Skip Munro. Caroline told her that he stopped by headquarters every day, growing more frustrated each time he did. She said that, according to Munro, the only fingerprints on the note were Emma's and Vanessa's. The lab found a couple of hairs on the blue dress, but both matched those taken from a hairbrush in Vanessa's bathroom.

Mark paid her a short visit on Wednesday. She admitted to herself that she was glad to see him, but he remained cranky. He did say that Pepper missed her, that she was getting plenty of exercise, and that he promised to look after her until Emma was discharged.

Thursday morning, Dr. Parker stopped in to tell her that she would probably be free to go home that afternoon after a final CT scan.

Later, as Emma was getting dressed to leave, she heard her phone's text tone.

Assuming that it was Mark, who had volunteered to drive her home, she casually checked the incoming text. What she read shocked her.

> Meet me in Ella T. Grasso State Park at six, sharp. Come alone. No Pepper. Take the Pequot Trail exactly three quarters of a mile until you see an oak tree with a black X. I marked it with a Sharpie. Take a left at the oak. I will meet you in the clearing, one hundred and twenty-five yards into the woods. Will

While her shaking hands held the phone, lightning struck the back of her neck, traveled down her spine, and through her legs to the hospital floor below her feet. Along the way, the bolt thrashed through her stomach like a rabid snake. She gagged, feeling like she would never again be able to breathe.

53

A Button

The specter of coming face-to-face with Will after fifty-six days was unnerving. He'd ordered her to come alone. Should she defy him and bring back up? Pepper? Should she call Mark? Caroline Stoner? Or even Skip Munro?

She stood in her hospital room, half dressed. Shaking, yet paralyzed. She had three hours. Strangely, Emma didn't feel afraid. Fearful but not afraid. She realized she should, but she didn't.

It was time to end this madness. If resolution required this showdown with Will, so be it. She couldn't begin to guess his intentions. She had to allow for the possibility that Will was the serial killer ... and that he intended to kill her, too. She had no intention of going unarmed. She had already shot at someone in the dark. Maybe Will, maybe someone else. Whoever it was, she believed that she had winged her target. There was an angry, probably wounded person out there who did not wish her well. During her time in the hospital, she had had plenty of time to think. More than ever, she was now convinced that she was the focus of the killer's wrath.

Nonetheless, the last thing she wanted to do was shoot the man she still loved.

She also knew that she was going to respond as the situation demanded.

Resolute, she began to stop shaking and was able to finish dressing. She felt an eerie sense of relief that the finale was so close. However it went.

Hospital rules required an orderly to wheel her to the front door. She had already decided not to wait for Mark. Instead she took a taxi directly home.

She looked out the open cab window. The sights, sounds, and smells of her hometown whizzed by. There was a light rain falling. She had the macabre thought that this otherwise mundane trip through Hampshire might be her last. But she was too focused to let her imagination get the better of her.

She used the remaining time to decide whether or not to tell Mark what was happening. She knew that if she told him he would insist on protecting her. Although she had never thought of Will as Mr. Action-Man, he had a cunningness about him which she knew not to underestimate. He would've figured out a way of ascertaining whether she came alone or not. That helped her to make her decision.

Pepper and Mark greeted her at the door. Pepper showed unbridled enthusiasm. Mark appeared miffed that she hadn't waited for him. "I was just about to pick you up," he said. "How come you didn't wait?"

"I just couldn't stand to stay there another minute." The lie tripped off her tongue.

"How are you feeling?" Mark asked.

"Way better. Thanks. But I didn't sleep at all last night, so I think I might go up and take a nap. Hey, thanks a lot for looking after Pepper." She added, "You've been a good friend."

That seemed to settle him, more so when she said, "Would you like to come over for dinner tonight? I'll make something good."

"That would be great," he said.

"See you at 7:30, then."

Mark left.

If she didn't make it home by then, she doubted she'd make it home at all. At least there would be somebody there for Pepper.

If it developed that she brought Will home with her, she would deal with that eventuality when the time came.

After Mark left, Emma did take a nap. She amazed herself that she could fall asleep. She figured it was testament to her resolve. She set the alarm for 4:30 p.m. to give her time to prepare.

Later, in her bedroom with Archie's Beretta, she first made sure it was safe and clear. She field-stripped the pistol down to its component parts: frame, slide, barrel, recoil spring, and cam block. She carefully lubricated each piece before reassembling the gun. She remembered watching her dad clean his guns. The pleasant odor of Hoppe's gun oil was a deep-seated memory. Archie had wanted her to feel comfortably knowledgeable about weaponry. Thanks to him, she did. Emma ratcheted the slide back and forth. It was smooth as silk. Finally, she loaded fifteen 9 mm Parabellum rounds into one clip, which she snapped back into the Beretta's polymer grip. She loaded a backup clip, too. If thirty cartridges weren't enough, she was in more trouble than she cared to imagine.

The kitchen windows were awash with rain. It was a July thunderstorm, a classic, with thunder and impressive displays of lightning.

Upstairs she found a pair of sneakers which would maintain traction when wet. She'd had them for years. She wasn't quite sure what difference it would make, but she dressed all in black, including a black hat. Her darkest windbreaker was navy blue, but it was dark enough, and, more importantly, long enough to conceal the holster she clipped to her belt.

Now came the hard part, waiting. She was sorely tempted to have a shot of whiskey, but she knew that would be weak, if not foolish. She needed all her strength, determination, and clear-headedness going forward.

At five o'clock she turned on left-wing television, MSNBC. Chuck Todd was anchoring "MTP Daily." Instead of distracting her from clock-watching, the political news raised her blood pressure. She turned it off.

With a deep breath and tears in her eyes, she gave Pepper a long, affectionate hug goodbye. She retrieved the Beretta from the kitchen, loaded her holster, said another good-bye to Pepper, and drove to Ella T. Grasso State Park.

The parking lot was typical of an under-funded Connecticut state park. Overflowing garbage barrels and vandalized picnic tables. There were no cars in the parking lot, probably due to the rain. If Will had driven there, he had concealed his vehicle somewhere else. Maybe he hadn't arrived, or perhaps he would be a no-show.

She delayed leaving the comfort of her car while she watched the windshield wipers try to beat the downpour. She wished that Pepper was sitting beside her. Eager to protect her. With a sudden stab at courage, she pulled the hood of her windbreaker over her head and kicked open the front door. Before she reached the trailhead of Pequot

Trail, she was soaked. Wind-driven rain stung her eyes. She couldn't hear anything other than the racket of raindrops hammering her hood.

Rivulets of water streamed down the uphill trail, and her usually reliable sneakers slipped on rocks and roots. Occasionally, out of nervousness, Emma felt for the grip of her Beretta under her windbreaker. She told herself she was simply getting prepared. The canopy of trees bridging the trail, combined with heavy thunder clouds, darkened her path. Although it was a quarter 'til six, the path was inky.

Emma figured she was about half a mile up the trail. She began her search for the Sharpie-marked oak tree. Not sufficiently mindful of her steps, she tripped on an aboveground root. She went down hard. Her knee caught a rock and added a new, sharp pain to her catalog of complaints. She swore and used a low branch to lift herself back to her feet.

She continued looking for the tree Will had described. She didn't think that her knee was seriously injured, but it ached like a sonofabitch and forced her to compensate with a limp.

Upon identifying each oak, she would stop and inspect it. Between the rain and the paucity of ambient light, she wasn't sure that she would spot a black **X** on tree bark. She did not want to miss it, or all would be for naught.

About ten minutes later, she found it. She was surprised how easy it was to spot and how sinister it looked.

There was no obvious trail where she was supposed to turn.

She took a left, as instructed, and had to bushwhack through face-high branches, heavy with water. She was already soaked, but the prospect of fighting through one hundred and twenty-five yards of branches and scrub was disheartening.

With another quick check of her Beretta, she soldiered on.

Soon she saw the clearing. Still dark, but brighter than the woods.

She hesitated at the edge.

If Will was nearby, he wasn't obvious.

She withdrew her Beretta before stepping out from the relative safety of the forest. She held it barrel-down at her side. Black against navy blue, which, she thought, would be hard to see even in the lighter clearing.

"Will," she called, "it's Emma. I'm here. Are you out there?"

Her answer was more rain.

She walked slowly into the middle of the clearing, doing frequent 360s to watch her flanks and to see if he was following her. In the center of the circular clearing was an old charcoal pit. Emma studied the tree line around her. Still, she couldn't see him. She called again.

No answer.

Maybe Will had gotten cold feet. The whole premise of his text was so bizarre in the first place. And hurtful, too. Emma wasn't sure what to do. She thought about Pepper. If she had been here, she would have been able to flush Will in a matter of seconds. Compared to her partner, Emma was effectively blind. And, of course, she didn't have Pepper's nose.

Suddenly, despite the rain, she heard the noise of twigs snapping behind her. Rattled, she lifted her gun and assumed the shooter's stance. She couldn't see anything, but the noises kept getting nearer. Someone was moving through the woods. After a few tense moments of staring at nothing, she saw a black face appear under an evergreen bough.

She almost laughed. She had never before been relieved to encounter a black bear in the woods. The bear showed herself, an adolescent, and peered at Emma curiously. It appeared unaggressive and made a calm about-face and wandered back into the woods.

Emma watched, lowering her weapon. That was when she saw something that shouldn't have been there. It was right where the bear had been sniffing. Something purplish against the dark, wet bark of a maple tree. She approached cautiously, limping, with her gun at the ready.

She was about ten feet away when she realized what she was looking at.

Emma's heart broke.

54

The Investigation Takes a Turn

Two discolored human hands were tied together at the wrists around the tree. Emma couldn't see what was on the far side of the trunk, but she knew. There was a line of duct tape encircling the tree above the hands. There was another strip of duct tape above the first.

At about six feet away, a gust of thunder-wind blew her way. The horrible stench carried by the waft made her gag. She covered her nose and her mouth, but that did not stop the rotting smell from entering her nostrils.

She put her Beretta back in its holster.

Steeling herself, she moved into a position where she could see the other side of the tree.

Oh, sweet Jesus, she muttered to herself. *How could anyone be cruel enough to do such a thing?* The human depravity on display was beyond civilized comprehension.

The sweet, svelte body of Vanessa Mack was bound to the tree by duct tape. Underneath her armpits and around her forehead. Her open eyes stared at Emma. Her throat had been slashed like Deb's.

Vanessa's face and body were nearly unrecognizable. She must have been in the forest for all of the five days since she'd disappeared. Her bloated body had ballooned to twice its size. In some places, her skin was purplish; in others, a dark brown-red; and some parts of her body were coal black.

Putrefied flesh had sloughed off in sheets. There was a pile at the base of the tree.

Emma was too furious to be afraid. She stared at her old friend's face and watched a fly walk across her eyeball. There was a maggot mass between her thighs. The flesh eaters entered and exited her body at will. Angrily, she tried to swat them away, but there were too many.

Emma was surprised she didn't feel sick to her stomach. She was too angry. She did feel her body sway a bit. She found a tree a few yards away and sat on the ground in a puddle of water, her back against the trunk. She stared at Vanessa, weeping. Emma's hand still covered her nose … to little effect.

She heard herself say, "I swear to you Vanessa, and to you, too, Deb, that I will find the savage who did this."

She kept staring at the body hoping to see something that would give her some hint, some clue. But she knew that that would be a hollow hope. She reached for her iPhone in her pocket. It was time to call 911.

Before she did, she used the flashlight feature and studied the body some more. In the light of the flash, she noticed that Vanessa's right hand was closed into a fist. She stood and approached the body. Taking a deep breath, she reached for Vanessa's hand. She didn't have any gloves. Vanessa's hand opened easily. *Rigor mortis* had long since released its deathly grip.

Along with some skin and flesh, a button fell to the forest floor.

She found a Kleenex in her pocket and picked it up. With the help of her iPhone, she examined it carefully. It did not look like a button that Will would own.

Unless her marriage had been a complete fraud, she now felt more confident that Will could not be the killer. This death scene seemed to prove it. Yet, doubts remained.

Before dialing 911, she put the button, wrapped in Kleenex in her pocket. She intended to keep it there. She still had a fingerprint kit at home.

Emma gave 911 the directions to her location and explained the nature of the call. A new dispatcher blurted rather unprofessionally, "Jesus H. Christ!"

She agreed to wait at the oak tree on the Pequot Trail for the police to arrive.

And arrive they did. An army of cops and, lastly, Skip Munro and the Major Crimes team. Everyone except Stella.

Detective Buzz Buzzucano had called the fire department. They set up quartz halogen floodlights powered by portable generators. The scene suddenly became the night-time set of a horror movie. The responders had to shout over the din of the generators.

They cordoned off a wide area around Vanessa's body. No one was allowed in while Buzz and the Major Crimes photographer took photographs from all angles. When the overall photographs were completed, Skip's crew, dressed in white Tyvek suits, gingerly approached the body. Before each step, they searched the ground in front of them with powerful flashlights.

When they were right next to Vanessa, one of Skip's guys called out, "Lieutenant, you better see this."

Skip looked where the trooper pointed his flashlight. A flap of skin lay on the forest floor at Vanessa's feet. There was a black **L**. Emma had missed it.

Skip said, "Holy shit."

Buzz and Skip joined Emma on the perimeter.

"I'm sorry for your loss. I know she was a friend," Buzz began, "But how the hell did you find her?"

She showed them the text which he had received.

Skip said, "Well I'll be damned. I was steering away from your husband. But with this, I no longer can."

"I still don't think he's our man," Emma stated. "Will could never do this to Vanessa. He was as fond of her as I am ... was."

Buzz said, "I completely understand why you don't want to believe that your husband is Mr. Sharpie. With all due respect, it's good that you're off the case. But you better know, though, the Hampshire Police Department will continue to search for Will."

"Where's Stella?" Emma said. "I felt sure she would be the first to arrive."

Buzz looked uncomfortable. "She told Max that she had a date tonight. She's not answering her cell phone."

Skip took a sudden step backward. He said, "What's that on your hand, Emma?" He directed his flashlight.

Emma looked down. Her hand was covered with bits of Vanessa's hand. In the havoc, she hadn't even noticed or felt it. She thought quickly. She had already taken the decision that she, and no one else, would find the owner of the button. *Foolish?* Perhaps, but she was angry. She needed the satisfaction of bringing Mr. Sharpie to justice. For

Deb, Vanessa, and even for Ethan.

She said, "I didn't bring a flashlight. I had to make sure that Vanessa was actually dead. I felt her carotid artery. That must be where the stain came from."

Both Buzz and Skip looked skeptical. Skip said, "But she's been dead for, well probably five days. That doesn't make sense. Here, let me see your hand."

She held out her hand, palm down.

"Turn it over," Skip said. It sounded more like a command than a request.

Emma complied.

Skip and Buzz examined her palm closely.

"That looks like human flesh … and skin," Skip said. "Did you touch anything else?"

She lied. "Nothing."

"I have to say, you seem awfully calm for someone who has just found a dear friend basically crucified to a tree. How do you account for that?" Skip said.

"Simple. I'm no longer afraid. I'm too angry to be scared. This whole series of killings is aimed directly at me, and I intend to find out why."

"Would you wait here for a moment?" Skip said.

He pulled Buzz a short distance away, they conferred quietly. A few moments later, they came back.

Skip said, "I'm sorry to say that we're going to have to bring you in for questioning."

"Why?" Emma demanded angrily. "I've done nothing wrong."

Buzz said, "Don't make this difficult."

"I tell you what, we're going to be here for most of the night. Why don't you meet us at headquarters tomorrow morning at 8:00 a.m.?" Skip said, throwing her a bone.

She recognized that she had no choice. She probably would be doing the same thing they were, had she still been chief.

"Fine," she answered. "Right now, I'm going home. Is that okay with you guys?"

55

Coup de Grâce

It is time for my *coup de grâce*.

But first, I take stock. Despite a few very minor setbacks—the nosy reporter, Virginia Hobson, and Vanessa Mack's first escape spring to mind—my plan has unfolded brilliantly. Emma is being crushed. I'd love to be inside her head for a moment, just to savor her discouragement and failure.

Summary: in cosmic lockstep, Emma is losing everything she holds dear.

There has been one other minor snafu, which might turn out to be not-so-minor. When I returned home from Ella T. Grasso State Park, I was missing a button. Vanessa's survival instinct, as she realized she was about to die, kicked in. *Whose wouldn't?* I must've lost the button in the struggle.

Although Stella has given me no indication that it is so, I have a hunch that the cops are staking out the death scene to see who shows up. I'm too smart to go back.

That aside, the finale or *coup de grâce* for Emma Thorne is nigh.

My favorite example of a *coup de grâce* is the beheading of a Samurai to end his agony after *seppuku*. *Seppuku* is also known as *harakiri*, the

Samurai ritual of auto-disembowelment.

Gotta give it to those little bastards!

I get Stella on speed-dial.

She answers on the first ring.

Stella says, "Hi, lover. You're not still mad at me, are you?"

I laugh, disarmingly. "Of course not!"

I invite her over. I dangle sex. She is pathetically eager to accept. "I'll bring a nice bottle of wine," she assures.

Stella arrives in a light floral-print summer dress, carrying a useless umbrella. She runs to the front door where I am waiting for her. Her dress is soaked, but it looks great clinging to her curvaceous figure. I don't know what she's thinking.

I have to say, I do love her curvaceous figure and her poignant eagerness to please me in the bedroom.

"Let's get you out of those wet clothes *tout de suite*," I say.

She grins and turns her back to me. I unzip the long zipper, and her dress puddles at her ankles. She spins back, stretches out her arms, and says, "Ta-da!"

I have to say that she looks incredibly desirable in her lacy lingerie. I tell her so. She beams. I lead her to my bedroom.

She gives me one great payload of an orgasm. In due course, I return the favor. While Stella is still moaning, I smother her to death with a king-sized pillow.

It's been seven days since Emma shot a hole through my arm. The exertion of suffocating Stella re-ignites stabbing pains. But I don't mind.

I have nearly completed the Final Act.

I examine Stella carefully. I have managed to end her life with no visible marks on her body. I know that Stella loved me, but I just never really felt the same way about her. She was more of the pawn than the queen in my life. Chess is one of my favorite games, played both on a board and in life.

You can buy anything on the Internet. From a website called crimescenesupplies.net, I have purchased a "FEMA blue" body bag for $29.99 and had it shipped to one of my several PO boxes. Crime Scene Supplies also sell other items like casting kits, crime scene tape, evidence bags, and something called an infidelity test. The latter, a semen detection kit, was on sale. Minus 26%. Reduced from $65.00 to $48.00. But I have little need for one.

I load Stella into her pretty summer frock. Her dress is still damp. It won't make any difference.

I zip the stylishly attired and undamaged corpse into the body bag.

My car is in the garage, which is where I will carry Stella and put her in the trunk.

56

"Wicked Little Girl"

Pepper came to the front door in a frenzy of wriggling happiness. True, she hadn't been out in a while. There was that. But her emotion was genuine. Emma appreciated her loyalty. It was especially restorative in times like these. She promised Pepper that she would take her out soon. She had something to do first as soon as she changed out of her wet clothes.

In her basement, she found her old fingerprint kit. Wearing a pair of nitrile gloves, she carefully examined the button under a bright light and through a magnifying glass. She held the button by its edges. Even magnified, she couldn't see a latent print, but that didn't mean there wasn't one there.

Using an old cop trick, she mixed some of the black powder with some white powder until the shade of the mixture was approximately the same as the gray-scale density of the button. She swirled her favorite brush, made from the hair of a squirrel's tail, in a delicate circular motion. Using lifting tape against the surface of the button, she pressed out all the bubbles and bumps before removing the tape and sticking it to a white index card.

"*Omigod!*" she exclaimed.

It was Emma's eureka moment. She could discern a print. It was a partial, but still …

She didn't readily know if it would be sufficient to get a match through IAFIS, the Integrated Automated Fingerprint Identification System, but she sure hoped so.

Finally, she had a break, and, finally, the killer had made an error.

The partial print was so important to her that she took the precaution of storing the card in her basement safe.

Pepper, who was sitting next to the front door, whined and gave Emma the hairy eyeball. It was time to look after her. Emma needed some fresh air, too. The rain had stopped, the clouds were thinning, and she took Pepper for a long, head-clearing walk. The air smelled clean after the thunderstorms. Not a soul was out. They had the streets of the neighborhood to themselves. They had to avoid the many puddles.

She decided she would call Caroline Stoner in the morning and ask her to run the print. It would be a big ask, but she hoped that Caroline would be willing to break the rules for her.

When she arrived back at her house and while she was unlocking the front door, Pepper started acting strangely. The dog sniffed the crack under the front door. Her snout moved quickly back and forth along the bottom of the door.

Suddenly, Pepper sat.

Uh-oh, Emma thought. She'd left the Beretta on her bedside table before going out. She wished she hadn't. She considered calling the cops for some backup, but she didn't. She'd had enough of cops for one night. Besides, she had Pepper.

She cracked the door, and Pepper pressed the door fully open with her head. She raced into the house. Emma made a split-second decision. She ran up the front staircase and retrieved the Beretta.

Back at the bottom of the stairs, she called Pepper, who came immediately. The dog looked her in the eye and barked.

Pepper was not a barker.

If she'd had any doubt before, Emma knew that someone was in her house. Yet why had Pepper answered her call to return? Pepper's training, when faced with a threat, was to strike, subdue, and guard a suspect until ordered to stand down. So, why did she come back?

Holding the Beretta in front of her, Emma snapped up the safety lever and inserted her index finger inside the trigger guard. First, she cleared the living room; then, the dining room. There was no one in either room. She proceeded down the hall to the kitchen.

The shock made her gasp. Having no more need for a weapon, she placed it on the dining room table. She kept her distance, but she knelt to get a better view. On the kitchen floor lay the body of Stella Weeks. A carving knife, which Emma recognized as one of her own, protruded from her chest at the level of her heart. No blood had pooled around the stab wound. Emma knew, intuitively, that Stella had been stabbed postmortem. And likely somewhere else.

Most importantly, though, she had been stabbed with Emma's knife.

She checked Stella's ankles. On her left ankle, the killer had written an **X**. Black Sharpie, naturally. For the first time, the letter couldn't be read upside-down. Perhaps, it signified the last murder.

Stella's arms and legs were splayed away from her body like da Vinci's *Vitruvian Man*. Emma found another pair of disposable gloves. She reached out and attempted to move Stella's left arm. As she suspected, *rigor mortis*. Emma knew that *rigor* occurred between two and six hours after death.

Since she couldn't prove when she'd left for Ella T. Grasso State Park, that would place Emma smack at the top of the suspect list. She couldn't believe how ballsy the unsub was. The body had been dumped while she was walking Pepper.

She stood and drew out a kitchen chair.

As she had with Vanessa, Emma sat staring at the body. *Jesus,* she thought, *two corpses in one night.*

She considered her future.

She hadn't forgotten that she had been summoned to headquarters for an interview the next morning. Nor had she forgotten that Skip and Buzz had not been subtle about their new-found suspicions.

Pepper watched her carefully. The dog didn't seem to know what to make of a dead body in her kitchen. Emma didn't either.

A moment later, Emma sprang into action. She went back upstairs to her bedroom and packed supplies. Clothes, toiletries, and ammo, among other items she would need. In the pantry, she packed dog food.

She couldn't imagine a scenario in which the Hampshire Police Department and the Connecticut State Police wouldn't arrest her for Stella's murder. That is what her nemesis had intended all along. If she were still chief, she would do likewise. Everything that had occurred in the lead-up to this night was a prelude to framing her for murder. Actually, four murders.

If she wanted a chance to capture the real killer, she had no choice but to run. The only remaining question was where. She didn't have many choices. Her two best friends were dead. She figured that Dave

Mack would sooner spit on her than harbor her. She knew that Phil Masters would give her sanctuary, but it would put him in too much jeopardy. He could lose Group Therapy for hiding her. Mark Byrne came to mind. He would do it. He would be thrilled to have her. *Bad idea,* she thought. She would need to be much more desperate to further complicate her already messed-up life. On the other hand, Mark could be a big help. Besides muscle, she was convinced he was a good investigator. No, still a bad idea.

She suddenly had a wildly impractical idea. What about Georgia Foster? It was true that Georgia didn't like her very much. The feeling was mutual. But Georgia might be iconoclastic enough to say *Screw everyone* and let her stay. The more she thought about it, the more plausible the idea became. Georgia lived in a remote location. She didn't appear to have any friends except her goddaughter, Sophie King, and her parents. Possibly Georgia's dislike of cops was limited to her and Archie, but Emma had a hunch that her aversion extended to all cops.

What's the worst that could happen? Georgia could refuse. She could even report her to the police, but Emma would have time to get away. Then she would still be on the run, so what difference would it make?

She loaded the supplies and Pepper into the car, and they drove away. She checked her watch. It was 9:30 p.m. She knew that the Staples in Lincoln was open until ten o'clock. She hurried there. Not too fast to attract the attention of a trooper, but fast enough to beat closing time.

Staples was empty except for bored staff members checking their watches. She bought four disposable phones. Two could play the burner phone game. In the Staples parking lot, she pressed 911 on one of her new phones.

She didn't beat around the bush. What would be the point of that? She said, "There is a dead body at Emma Thorne's house." She immediately clicked End.

Keeping to the speed limit, she drove to a spot near Georgia's house, where she waited to make certain that there was no untoward activity. In time, Pepper grew impatient. She took her for a walk in the woods. When she returned to her car, she still waited.

Soon after 2 a.m., Emma pressed Georgia's doorbell, fully anticipating an unpleasant reunion.

They'd have to set their past troubles aside; Emma *had* punched her a couple of weeks ago.

Georgia opened the door. She was dressed in men's pajamas, but she didn't look like she had been sleeping. She was carrying an iPad. To Emma's surprise, she was grinning.

"I've been expecting you," Georgia said.

Completely taken aback, Emma said, "What?"

"Guess you haven't seen the e-edition of tomorrow's *Hampshire Chronicle*," she said smugly. "Here."

Still standing on the threshold, Emma took the proffered iPad.

> *Extra! Serial Killer on the Loose:*
> *Two More Murders in Hampshire*

> By Virginia Hobson, Staff Reporter
>
> Responding to an anonymous 911 tip, po-
> lice found the body of Acting Chief
> Stella Weeks, a veteran of the Hamp-
> shire Police Department. The body was
> discovered Thursday evening at the home
> of Emma Thorne. Ms. Thorne was recently
> called the "Heroine of Hampshire" by
> The Chronicle for her part in the res-
> cue of abducted teenager Sophie King.
> Thorne was the Chief of Police until
> she was fired on Sunday, June 20, by
> Mayor Dick Wardlaw.
>
> Police are searching for Thorne, who
> was not at home when they arrived at
> what one officer described as "a grisly
> scene."
>
> Earlier this evening, police were di-
> rected to Ella T. Grasso State Park,
> where they found the partially-decom-
> posed body of Vanessa Mack, bound to
> a tree. Ms. Mack of 17 Highcroft Ter-
> race was the wife of David Mack and
> two young children. It is reported that
> Thorne led them to the body before dis-
> appearing. Police are investigating
> both crimes.
>
> Lieut. Skip Munro of the Connecticut

State Police Major Crimes Squad told
this newspaper, "We are considering
Emma Thorne as a suspect in the murders
of Ethan Jackson, Deb Barger, Vanessa
Mack and, tonight, Chief Weeks. A warrant has been issued for her arrest. If
anyone has any knowledge of her whereabouts, please call the Hampshire Police Department. All information will
be kept strictly confidential."

The Chronicle will provide more details
as they become available.

After Emma finished reading, Georgia said, "Why you wicked little girl! What have you been up to?"

To Emma's further surprise, Georgia gestured for Emma to enter
her house.

57

Presumed Guilty

"I'll bet you need a drink," Georgia said cheerily, like she was hosting a party. "I know I do if I'm going to be harboring a fugitive."

Utterly confused, Emma watched her pour two massive whiskeys, no ice. Georgia handed her one. Emma had expected, and was prepared, to have to beg. She couldn't understand her sister-in-law's reaction to her arrival. Georgia had never hidden the fact that she despised Emma.

After a sip, a gulp, really, of some smoky, expensive-tasting single malt, Emma asked, "Why are you helping me?"

"I would do *anything* for Will."

Emma absorbed that explanation, but she was still puzzled.

"Sister-in-law to sister-in-law," Georgia said with teasingly arched eyebrows, "why did you do it?"

"I didn't *do* anything," Emma said. "How could you even think that?" As she said it, she realized that the whole town would be asking the same question. The cops, her former colleagues, would surely presume her guilt.

"Until tonight," Emma said, "the cops thought that your brother was the killer."

"I know."

Emma took notice. "How did you know?"

"I'm a good guesser." Georgia stood. She drained her whiskey and said, "You're welcome to stay here as long as you need to. I've prepared my best guest room for you. The sheets are clean, and I laid towels out on the bed. It's all ready for you. Let's get some rest, and we can talk more in the morning."

"But how did you know I was coming?" Emma said, more perplexed than ever.

She stared at Georgia. Her left eye had started its idiosyncratic tic, coupled with her strange grin.

"Just a guess," Georgia said. She headed for the stairs.

Georgia showed her the way to the guest room, said good night, and left her alone.

The tiniest of whispers told her to lock her door, which she did. Although she didn't feel completely safe, despite having Pepper with her, she decided that she was as safe as she was ever going to be while on the run. She knew from experience that every cop in the state would be carrying her photograph. Cops took manhunts for serial killers seriously.

The guest room was elegantly appointed. Georgia had already drawn the ceiling to floor curtains. The Persian carpet was anything but threadbare. Dominating the room was an antique, chestnut sleigh bed. It looked comfortable and inviting. A stack comprised of a bath towel, a hand towel, and a washcloth lay on the bed, perfectly folded at a meticulous forty-five-degree angle to the bed. She remembered a years-ago conversation in which Will had said how obsessive his sister could be.

Emma kicked off her shoes and lay back on the bed. It *was* comfortable.

The full impact of the events of the night hit her, as did the deep sadness she felt for Vanessa. The image of her, savagely bound to that tree, would stay with her for the rest of her life. The same was true of Deb. *What madness.*

There were so many, many voids in her life.

How did Georgia know that the police had suspected Will? She must have a source in the department. Who? Emma remembered Georgia and Stella having a conversation at Ethan's funeral and how chummy they had appeared. It wouldn't shock her in the slightest if

Stella was the leak. She had certainly leaked to Virginia Hobson. And how did Georgia know that Emma would show up at her doorstep for refuge?

She concluded that Georgia knew way too much.

Emma couldn't risk using her own cell phone—the police would be all over *that*—which was why she'd purchased the disposable phones. Using one of them, she logged into her iCloud account and download-ed her texts before quickly logging out. She was shocked by how many there were, all time stamped earlier in the evening. She read them with mounting dread. Hampshire's ether had been crackling.

> Come in, Emma. If you are innocent, it is the only way we can clear you. Lieutenant Munro

> If I ever see you again, I swear I'll rip your heart out! Feel free to share this text with the cops when they catch your psycho ass. Vanessa loved you. Think about that while you rot in pris-on and wait for the electric chair. Snap, crackle, pop. Dave Mack

> Emma, Julian Jackson here. Damn you to hell for murdering my father. I'd like to torture you like you did those women. You will pay for this.

> Emma, I need to talk to you. We can meet someplace secret. I swear I won't tell the police. Please? Sophie King

> I care about you, Emma. Running will only make matters worse. Contact me, and I can arrange for your safe surrender. Your friend, Caroline

The strangest one of all was from Joe Henderson:

> Since you fucked up my life, I was glad to learn that your life is way, way more fucked than mine will ever be. I was a good influence on Sophie. She was just too young to realize it. Joe (Hen-derson, in case you've forgotten)

Despite the kind words from Caroline and the odd request from Sophie, Emma was devastated.

En masse, people had prejudged her. They hated her. They were convinced that she was guilty. She had half a mind to get in her car and drive to police headquarters.

But she couldn't.

She reached for Pepper, but the dog was asleep. Emma knew she would get no sleep herself that night. She took all her clothes off, toweled herself off, and climbed into the crisp sheets of the sleigh bed. She tried to sleep, but she kept thinking about Georgia.

Had she stupidly waltzed into the lion's den?

Was there a shirt with a missing button hiding in this house?

Next, she thought about Joe Henderson, the man Lincoln Detective Dave Swanson suspected of running a "sex trafficking ring involving female minors." Why was Joe texting her, and how did he know her number?

58

On the Lam

Friday morning, Emma came downstairs to the smell of frying bacon. Georgia had a neat table set in the breakfast nook. Complete with ironed, linen napkins. A bay window framed her sunlit garden. As she had been the night before, she was bright and cheery. Emma couldn't figure out what to make of this odd change in Georgia's behavior.

"I hope you like bacon and eggs. I have some scones, too."

Emma was too polite not to thank her. She added, "I do like bacon and eggs. Thank you. Listen, Georgia, we need to talk."

"What about?" she said. She drained the bacon on a paper towel and brought the bacon and eggs to the table. Pepper whined, and Emma shook her head, no. Forlornly, Pepper lay at her feet wishing for her own breakfast.

Emma concentrated on Georgia as she said, "You need to know that I have not hurt anyone. I am only responsible to the extent that whoever has committed these vile acts seems to be targeting me. My sole goal is to find out who the killer is and stop him … or her."

Georgia's face and body language betrayed nothing. She said, "It's going to be a bit tricky to continue your investigation while every cop in the state is looking for you. Isn't it?"

Even her characteristic left eye tic didn't erupt.

Emma changed the subject. "You make a reasonable point. If I am going to continue, I can't go around in my own car, and I can't clear my name from prison. Can I borrow your car?"

"No, but I suppose I could borrow Dad's pickup truck for you to use. Not, of course, telling him whom it is for." Georgia grinned.

They agreed to a plan. Georgia would call her dad and get him to come pick her up so that she could fetch the truck. Emma and Pepper would stay out of sight upstairs.

The rest of their conversation was about Will. Not, however, with its usual attendant rancor. Georgia even conceded that Emma must miss Will very much.

Emma fed Pepper while they waited for Frank Foster. When they heard his car arrive, Georgia said she'd be right back with her dad's pickup.

The second Georgia left the house, Emma began searching it.

She started in Georgia's bedroom, rifling through her closet and drawers. Georgia had a lot of clothes for someone who didn't go out much. But Emma couldn't find a single shirt missing a button. She continued searching the room, but she didn't find anything unusual. She went back downstairs.

In the kitchen, she noticed that Georgia hadn't taken her cell phone with her. She turned it on and was surprised (and relieved) to discover that it was not password-protected. Pressing the button for Contacts, she noted that there were very few. Forty-two, in all. Georgia didn't seem to have many friends.

Under **F**, she found Georgia's parents, of course, Frank and Joan Foster. There was also an entry for Will, but it was the number of the cell phone he had left at home when he had disappeared. She scrolled down and was shocked to see Ethan Jackson's name under **J**. *What on earth was he doing there?*

She scrolled further not expecting to find anything more of interest. Was she wrong!

Under **H**, she came across Joe Henderson. Why would his name be in Georgia's phone? She was flummoxed. *What could those two have in common?* Georgia and Joe? Or Georgia and Ethan, for that matter? She sensed that this was a critical piece of intelligence, but she didn't yet understand why or how the couples were linked.

Hoping to find even more clues, she scrolled through the rest of the names.

She recognized a few names, but none appeared relevant to the case.

Deb Barger and Vanessa Mack were not on Georgia's list.

Emma checked her watch. Georgia had been gone for twenty minutes. She would be back soon. Emma wondered if she had time to search the basement. She decided to risk it.

Georgia had a large workout room installed in the basement. It was a complete unit built within the larger basement. She owned a lot of exercise equipment. The room was finished with a bead-board pine ceiling and wall-to-wall gray carpeting suitable for a gym. All four walls had custom, built-in bookcases. There must've been a thousand books, many with elegant leather bindings.

Emma looked around. Pepper walked over to the bookcase opposite the only door, which had been ajar when they'd entered. Pepper didn't make a fuss, but she carefully sniffed the middle section of the bookcase. She spent quite a bit of time sampling with her nose, but she didn't give her trained signal that she had found something. Whenever Pepper sat, Emma took notice.

Suddenly, Pepper give a short warning bark. Too late, though, for Georgia was halfway down the cellar stairs.

"What the fuck are you doing snooping around my house?" Georgia shouted.

Emma's first thought was: *Something to hide?*

"I'm really, really sorry," she said without delay. "The last thing I want to do is infringe upon your hospitality. It's just that you once told me that you worked out. Since I do too, I wanted to check out your equipment."

"I never told you I worked out!"

Emma thought quickly. "Maybe Will mentioned it…"

"I would appreciate it *if you kept out of my basement.*"

In the relative safety of the kitchen, Georgia relaxed a tad.

She tossed Emma the key to her dad's pickup truck.

"Thanks a lot. I really appreciate it," Emma said, "and I apologize for going downstairs without asking." She attached it to her own key-ring on which she kept her house key, Archie's house key, and her police handcuff key. "Don't want to lose it."

"What are you going to do now?"

"Wait for dark, I guess. I might go upstairs and read, to kill time. Okay with you?"

"Hey, girl, it's a free country! For most people, anyway." That witticism caused Georgia to laugh out loud. *Her sister-in-law hadn't changed that much.* Indeed, her left eye exploded into full-on spasm mode.

Tic-tock, Emma thought.

Later, in the guest bedroom, Emma locked the door and retrieved another of her disposable phones from her bag. She'd have to buy some more, she realized. Probably from a different store.

From memory, she dialed Caroline Stoner's cell. Although she was concerned, she didn't think the police would have time to triangulate her location if she kept the call short. Anyway, who would expect her to telephone a police officer?

"Caroline Stoner. Who is it?"

"It's me. I need your help."

There was a long pause. Caroline said, "Jesus, Emma, what are you thinking? I know you didn't kill anyone, but I am in a *distinct* minority. You have got to surrender. It's your only way out."

"I can't do that. If you believe in me, you can prove it by helping me. I've lifted a fingerprint from a button, which I found next to Vanessa's body—"

"Now you're concealing evidence, too." Her voice raised in pitch. "You do know that everyone is hunting for you? You could get shot!"

"All I'm asking is for you to run a single print. If it comes back to the person I think it belongs to, we will know the identity of Mr. Sharpie. What do you say?"

Caroline didn't say anything for what seemed like minutes.

Finally, she exhaled audibly. "Okay, but I don't want to see you personally. I need to protect myself, not to mention my job. Come to my apartment tonight. Leave the goddamned button outside my door and then scram." Caroline disconnected the call.

59

Night for Day

That evening, Emma offered to prepare dinner. Georgia refused, saying, "I don't like people messing up my kitchen, but, hey, thanks all the same."

She mixed an elaborate Cobb salad and served a bottle of white wine, which turned out to be as chilly as their conversation. After various attempts at small talk, they finally gave up. They finished the meal in silence. In her controlling way, Georgia wouldn't let Emma help clean up.

Emma short-circuited the evening's end. "I'll be going out tonight. Late. I'll try not to make too much noise."

Georgia harrumphed, and Emma retired to the guest room.

She waited until 2:00 a.m. before leaving. The less cars there were on the road, the better her chances of making the round-trip unnoticed. Unfortunately, Caroline lived in downtown Hampshire. Emma had no choice but to go. She had to get the fingerprint to her.

She and Pepper drove into town. Emma wore a baseball cap, borrowed, tacitly, from her hostess. It was a hot night, and she had the windows open. Pepper sat beside her on the front seat.

Traffic was comfortably light. She did pass one Hampshire police cruiser driving in the opposite direction. She recognized Officer Pete Sinclair. He glanced at Frank Foster's pickup truck but paid it no mind. She realized how tense she was.

Caroline lived in an apartment building on a street perpendicular to Main Street. The building stood between a liquor store and a thrift shop. She parked directly in front of 111 Essex Street and left Pepper in the truck. The street was empty. There was no buzzer system on the front door, so she was able to walk in.

Caroline lived on the third floor; Emma had been to her apartment before. Outside the door to 3B, she left the envelope containing the precious fingerprint, per her agreement with Caroline. She assumed the envelope would be safe. Despite a serial killer in their midst, Hampshire remained a relatively secure place to live.

Back downstairs, the main door to Caroline's building, the one through which she had entered, had an old-fashioned lace curtain covering its window. She parted the curtain with a finger and peered outside. Essex Street remained empty and asleep. She walked confidently to her loaner, secure in the knowledge that Caroline would live up to her side of the bargain. If the partial print yielded a hit, via IAFIS, they would have their killer.

Pepper's nose was outside the truck window, and she was wagging her tail. Emma noticed for the first time that Frank's truck was a Dodge Ram. It wouldn't do for Frank and Joan Foster to own a foreign vehicle.

She gave Pepper a pat on the head before rounding the front of the Dodge to the driver's-side door. All of a sudden, a gazillion-watt floodlight turned Essex Street into day. Emma froze. Although temporarily blinded, she realized that the floodlight was mounted in a second-floor window across the street.

She heard footfalls as two people exited the facing building.

A shouted voice.

She instantly recognized—but still couldn't see—that it was the voice of Detective Larry "Buzz" Buzzucano.

"Emma, let's not make this harder than it needs to be," he bellowed. "If you have a weapon, remove it slowly and place it on the ground in front of you."

Emma turned and headed back to the front door.

Instinctively, she sought cover over full exposure.

A second shouted voice.

Officer Max Beyersdorf. Another of her ex-colleagues. He yelled, "The building is surrounded. You have nowhere to go. Time to talk,

Emma, not to walk."

She kept walking toward the door. When she got close, the curtain parted revealing Caroline Stoner in full uniform and a tactical vest. Her expression was hostile and unforgiving.

Emma turned back to face Buzz and Max. Out of the corner of her eye, she saw a flash. Pepper launched herself out the truck window and hurtled toward Buzz. By now, Emma's eyes had adjusted to the brightness. She saw that Buzz had drawn his weapon. When Pepper recognized a threat, she responded.

She screamed, "No! Pepper, no!" Pepper ignored her. The dog knew Buzz well. She didn't aim for the arm holding the gun. Instead, she drove her front paws and the full inertia of her body weight into Buzz's chest. He went down with Pepper on top of him. He cried out as his head hit the asphalt. Max automatically went to his partner's aid.

Emma saw an opening. Max and Buzz were bunched together, and Caroline was still guarding the door. There was an alley to the right of the building across the street. She sprinted.

As she ran past the cops and Pepper, she heard a shot. Next, a horrifying canine yelp. Then, silence.

Emma wailed, but she kept running toward the cover of the alley. Would they shoot her next? Her eyes stung with tears. Jesus, not Pepper. *God, she loved that dog.*

She banged into a trashcan. Recovering her balance, she continued on, which was when she realized that she was not alone in the alley. She heard boot-steps pounding behind her and a voice, Caroline's staccato words, "Emma. You're a fugitive. Don't make me shoot."

Caroline wouldn't shoot her. Would she?

Still, she picked up her pace. She struck another trashcan. Pausing for a split second, Emma tipped the trashcan over and rolled it back toward the street. The tactic worked. Caroline tripped, flew over the trashcan, and landed with a loud thud. Emma didn't look back. And she no longer heard anyone following her.

Two streets later, she found another alley. She ducked into the entrance to give herself a moment's rest. *Pepper*, she agonized, as she sucked air.

Emma figured that, if she could escape, the police might still run the partial print. There would be a lot of pissed off cops, Caroline and Buzz in particular, but, if they identified the print, the payoff would be the same.

The payoff worked for everyone except Pepper.

She heard sirens crisscrossing the neighborhood as she resumed her flight.

She ran a further mile or two until she was near the city limit. She had to hide repeatedly as strobing cruisers narrowly missed spotting her. At the edge of town, she was able to use wooded areas for concealment. For the first time since leaving Essex Street, and, as she reminded herself with despair, Pepper, she thought she might actually make it back to Georgia's.

Exhausted and blistered, Emma finally arrived at the foot of Georgia's driveway. She wasn't running anymore, she was limping. The time: half past four in the morning. When she was within sight of Georgia's house, she stopped. There was a light on in the living room. At 4:30? She knew she hadn't left a light on. She'd been so surprised to escape that she realized she wasn't taking normal precautions. She decided to approach the house obliquely.

She had developed a suspicion that Georgia was somehow involved. Somehow guilty. But of what she still wasn't sure.

She retreated to the base of the driveway, took a left, and walked up the street which framed Georgia's property on the east. In the distance, she saw a parked car. *Strange*, she thought, *in this sparsely populated area.* When she got closer, she saw it was a nondescript black Chevy. The car sat empty, yet, barring Georgia's, there wasn't a house anywhere near.

Despite being fed up with branches snapping her in the face, she soldiered through the woods. She worked her way all the way around the house until she was able to approach a living room window while still remaining concealed by a bush.

Lit by a single lamp, Georgia, fully dressed, sat at the end of the sofa. Her elbowed arm supported her head. She was sipping a whiskey. A man sat opposite her. They were chatting amiably. Emma thought Georgia's body language suggested flirtatiousness. *Maybe she* did *have a boyfriend.*

Emma was so tired. She tiptoed to the next window, through which she hoped to identify the visitor. She was shattered to recognize Officer Chuck Smith. Without a doubt, he was on duty. Chuck loved whiskey, but he had a glass of ice water in his hand. While she watched, Chuck moved onto the sofa next to Georgia. Emma thought, *How big is this conspiracy?* Or was her sister-in-law just a slut?

She couldn't imagine being more discouraged. She had no reason to expect any loyalty from Georgia. But was Chuck involved, too?

Emma was so tired …

With no options left, she skulked back into the woods, where she spent the remainder of the night.

60

Heart of Darkness

Emma found a small clearing twenty yards or so behind the tree line of Georgia's yard. She collected handfuls of pine needles and mounded them into a makeshift bed. She tested it. Wet, but not horrible. Her back and legs cried for rest. She tried to run regularly, but tonight had been too much. She was too tired not to be able to sleep.

Sleep didn't come quickly, though. It was impossible not to remember Pepper. Emma relived the gunshot and the shriek of pain, and she shook. Only Archie would understand how she felt.

In time, she tried to think more positively. Emma remembered Pepper's curious behavior in Georgia's basement. What had her keen nose picked up? Emma's mind flew back to the scene of Ethan Jackson's "suicide." Like watching a replay, she could see Pepper storing Ethan's scent into her olfactory memory. Had Ethan once been in Georgia's cellar? Had a faint residue of him lingered there? Or had Pepper smelled something else which generated her attention? Somehow, Emma would have to get back into Georgia's basement.

Exhausted, hungry, and thirsty, Emma watched the dawning sun play on Georgia's house. Overnight, she had contracted chickenpox. Dozens of itchy, red mosquito bites poxed her bare arms.

Emma considered her predicament. In brief, she was fucked.

She had lost Pepper. First and foremost, Pepper was a service dog. Emma knew that Pepper would have gladly died for Archie if it meant saving him. She hadn't been so sure about herself, but Pepper hadn't hesitated.

Whichever was true, Emma felt honored to have spent the time she had with Archie's courageous K-9.

On a more pedestrian level, she had lost her wheels, and she had lost her hideout.

She had the strength left to think ... how important *is* a truck and a sanctuary? Those were potentially surmountable losses. She had escaped, and she was still alive.

Not surmountable, however, were Will, Deb, Vanessa, Ethan, and Pepper.

A lot was wrong with Emma Thorne's life.

She moved closer to the tree line and watched the house. Her empty stomach protested. She needed water. A full two hours passed before Officer Chuck Smith opened the front door and left. Georgia was nowhere in sight. Chuck must've telephoned or radioed headquarters and been called back.

Emma kept waiting. Lunchtime passed. Still, no Georgia. She looked at her watch. Tomorrow was the Fourth of July. Would it be Independence Day for her, too? She didn't think so. Miracles were too much to hope for.

The fourth, and last, of her disposable phones was in her pocket. Should she use it? Of course.

"Georgia, it's Emma, I'm in trouble!" It wasn't hard to sound scared. "The police ambushed me last night. They shot Pepper. I barely got away. Can you pick me up? I'm in the parking lot behind Group Therapy. I'm in the back of Phil's car."

There was a moment of silence on Georgia's end. Emma wondered if she was calling 911 on another line. She finally said, "What happened to my dad's truck?"

"Never mind that! You have to help me. Please come!"

"Okay, okay. Take it easy. I'll be there in about twenty minutes."

Emma watched Georgia's front door.

Ten minutes later, Georgia emerged and drove away.

Emma raced to the kitchen door, which was locked. She found a suitably hefty stone and smashed a hole in the glass. She proceeded directly down to the basement. Georgia had locked the door to the exercise room. *Good, that means I'm on the right track.* The door was hollow-core and easily kicked in. She busted through.

She went immediately to the section of the bookcase that had interested Pepper. Realizing she hadn't a clue what she was looking for, she examined the books. All of them were neatly shelved, their spines in lockstep. She put her index finger on the top of a random spine, but it wouldn't budge. She tried another. She couldn't move that one either. The books were apparently glued together and formed a solid wall. *Well I'll be damned!*

She scanned some titles. Many were the classic standards served up in high school and college. *Heart of Darkness, Hamlet, Crime and Punishment, Lord of the Flies*, and Plath's *The Bell Jar.*

Pretty gloomy fare.

She kept looking and feeling other books.

On the top shelf, there was a row of more modern titles. She came to a nonfiction section. True crime. She froze when she spotted the Bugliosi book, *Helter Skelter.*

The day that Will disappeared, Georgia had given him a copy of the same book. She remembered his revulsion … as if it were yesterday … not two months ago.

Why would she think to give me such a dark book at the depth of my despair, he'd said.

Emma was convinced that she was onto something.

For some indistinct reason, she was sure that, unlike the other books, *Helter Skelter* would pull free.

It didn't.

What it did do was more momentous. At her urging, the book triggered a mechanism that caused the entire wall to move soundlessly toward her. *Helter Skelter* incorporated some kind of ingenious door-opener. The bookshelves were hinged on the left. She went to the right end, which was ajar, and pulled the entire bookcase slowly forward. For a brief moment, she stopped, afraid to continue. The book wall might be hiding something she would regret exposing. She knew she had to see what was on the other side, *but what if?* Channeling Pandora, she understood that whatever horrors she unleashed, at least Hope would remain. Anyway, that was the point of the myth.

Her heart pounded crazily.

Immediately thereafter, her head did, too. Just for an instant.

A violent, agonizing blow knocked her senseless. She promptly lost consciousness.

61

Happy Fourth of July

Emma tried to open her eyes, but why should she? She just wanted to sleep, like forever. Her head felt like she had drunk a case of Thunderbird wine. She had no idea how long she had been out. She realized she might never know. She wasn't remembering a lot.

Memories gradually stirred. Her first wish was that her favorite paramedic would give her more morphine. Then she wondered if the blow to her head had exacerbated her brain bleed. After Georgia had boxed her temples at Vanessa's house—had to have been Georgia, right?—she had Googled *epidural hematoma*. Wikipedia had solemnly declared, "Without treatment, brain damage typically results. Death often follows."

Something more to look forward to.

Wherever she was, it was dark except for a nightlight.

Wherever she was, she knew she was Georgia's prisoner.

She felt a surprisingly comfortable mattress underneath her, and clean sheets covered her to her chin. She attempted to turn over and cuddle in, but her head screamed in protest.

She was still profoundly tired. She let herself drift off, not back into unconsciousness, but into a deep sleep. She wasn't sure how long she remained in that state.

When she awoke for the second time, she looked around the dim room.

The far wall, where the nightlight shone, included most of life's essentials: a toilet, a stall shower, and a kitchenette with a sink and a refrigerator but no stove. All were open to the room.

The rest of the room was dark.

She thought she heard something.

As her eyes grew accustomed to the limited ambient light, she made out a second bed. She couldn't tell if anyone was in it.

There was movement in the bed.

Suddenly, she recognized her husband in the gloom.

"Oh my God, you're alive!"

She thought, but didn't say, *You didn't kill anyone!*

Will *wasn't* Mr. Sharpie.

Will stared at her. She could just make out his open eyes, but he didn't speak a word.

"Will?" she tried again.

Still, he did not answer. All she could hear was a moan of despair.

62

Questions and A Few Answers

She leapt out of the bed, which triggered another agonizing brain implosion and stopped her short. She stumbled to Will's bedside. She knelt on the floor and put her arms around him.

She heard an abject voice: "Emma? Is that you?"

"Yes, my darling," she answered. She kissed his cheek.

Will's body spasmed, and he cried, "Where have you been, Emma? Why did you leave me here to suffer?"

She had no idea how to respond. Emma had never been fully convinced that she would ever see Will again. Now that their reunion had happened, she expected it to joyous.

He continued, "You can't believe the hell I've been through! I counted on you ... I believed in you ... but you never came."

Emma's life had never taken her to the abyss of depression. Consequently, it was hard for her to fathom the depths of Will's. How could his wonderful, caring personality have descended to a degree where he could speak so cruelly?

But she said, "Shush, I'm here now."

Before she knew it, Will was asleep in her arms.

The day Will had disappeared, he had been a man in pain.

But now?

Was he a man destroyed?

Emma cursed her psycho-sister-in-law. How insane does a person have to be to imprison her brother, the one she claims to love the most? And to what end? Torture equals love? She watched her husband sleep, realizing that the moment for which she had dreamed was just another landmine in her path.

Dispiritedly, she climbed back into her own bed and lay facing the wall. She closed her eyes. As if the Hoover Dam had failed, pent-up questions flooded her mind. Since there were no answers, she amazed herself by falling asleep, too, oblivious to everything but the tranquility of oblivion.

Hours passed. Maybe it was minutes. She had no idea. She looked at her watch. It was a couple of minutes before noon. Could've been a couple of minutes before midnight, too. There were lights on in the room now. She glanced to her side. Will was still napping. Or maybe he was sleeping the night away. Again, who knew?

Emma sat up and leaned her back against the headboard, careful not to let her head touch. So much had happened. The reality of their reunion made her heart ache.

She now knew with total certainty that Will wasn't Mr. Sharpie. That made her happy. What didn't make her happy was that Georgia held their lives in her hands.

What else did she know about Georgia? She thought way back to when Will had told her about her Uncle John molesting Georgia as a child.

She remembered him, when they'd first married, saying something akin to … *After I was able to stop John from abusing her, I believe that she fell in love with me. Probably as some kind of needy compensation for what she had been through. I don't think she ever thought of me in sexual terms, but I know that for our entire adult lives she has been obsessed with me. Sadly, for you, after we got married, she became obsessed with you, too.*

He'd also explained that Georgia had raged against Emma since that moment. Georgia had wanted a child, too, but she would have settled for a niece or a nephew. When Emma and Will couldn't conceive a child, that added to her rage.

Emma decided that in Georgia's perverted mind imprisoning Will was saving Will.

Emma glanced around the cell. Classic Georgia, it was over-decorated. Custom-built bookcases, laden with books, lined three sides, similar to the ones which concealed the entry. Two cushy easy-chairs were separated by a table, on which stood a large china table lamp with a Chinese motif. A luxe Oriental rug covered the floor.

She shuffled over to the door, a hollow-core like the door to Georgia's gym, and tried the knob. Locked, naturally. The door also had a peep hole and, below it, a large custom-built pass-though, large enough to pass a tray through. She opened the flapper and reached through. Her knuckles struck steel. Another door, she presumed. That door was anything but hollow.

She went back across the room and used the toilet. Afterwards, in the refrigerator, she found a green plastic bottle of Perrier with its distinctive juggling club shape. She suspected that Georgia didn't permit glass. She hadn't realized how thirsty she was until she downed the Perrier in one nearly continuous glug-glug-glug.

As she tossed the empty into a bin marked Recycling, she heard Will's voice behind her.

"Get me one, too. I'm thirsty." His voice sounded as empty as reverb on an old record.

Emma was so glad to hear him speak that she tried to overlook the other-worldly timbre of his voice.

"Coming right up," she said cheerfully. "You've slept a while. How do you feel?"

"Shitty," he said, "like I always do."

She brought him a cold Perrier and sat down next to him on the bed.

She handed him the plastic bottle and gazed into his eyes. They were unfocused, and he averted her gaze.

"Will, please talk to me."

"You want to know how I feel?" He took a sip of water. "I tried to hang myself—to end my useless life—but my sister saved me. According to her, that's what she's been doing ... saving me."

Emma looked on, appalled. She wanted to say something soothing, but he interrupted.

"My world is a black fucking hole. No, not that, it's a long tunnel with no lights. Far, far down the tunnel, my demons have sealed off the other end. You can't even imagine the hell I've been through, Emma."

What about me? she thought sadly.

She tried a different approach. "We have to get out of here. We have to escape."

"Don't you think I've tried?"

"Do you ever just scream bloody murder? I know Georgia's goddaughter, Sophie, comes over here every now and again. Maybe other people do, too."

Emma suddenly remembered the cryptic text she had received from Sophie: *I need to talk to you … Please.* Had she wanted to talk about Georgia? Moot point, though, because Emma doubted her jailer allowed the traditional phone call.

"I tried making a racket in the beginning," he said bitterly. "Until Georgia told me that there is a foot of sound insulation—walls, floor, and ceiling. This place is built like a professional sound studio. We'll never get out of here. Georgia will never permit it."

Emma shifted gears again, anxious to keep him talking.

"How the hell did she even get you here?"

"That night, while you were out—why did you even leave me alone?—Georgia came to our house and let herself in. She must've been watching, seen you leave. That zolpidem had zonked me cold. How she got me out of there I don't know. Apparently, my sick-fuck sister works out way too much. However she accomplished it, I never woke up. Maybe she gave me something for a kicker. I don't know. The next thing I knew is I woke up in here. You realize I've been here for the last fifty-nine days, don't you?"

Emma kept her forward motion. "But why would Georgia kidnap her own twin?"

"How should I know? She's sick. My sister's got serious mental health issues—more than I ever shared with you. My parents worry, too."

"Do your parents know you're here?"

"God no," Will snorted. "They may be dysfunctional alcoholics, but they would never be a party to this madness."

Emma took a deep breath. "I'm afraid there's a lot that you don't know about. Brace yourself. First, Dad died. A heart attack—"

"Aww, shit. I'm not sure I want to hear this."

"There's more," Emma said.

"Huh?" Staring at the floor, Will appeared distracted. No doubt, he was still absorbing the news about Archie

"Will, you better listen. There is more you need to know."

His head snapped up, but his eyes still stared behind her.

"Deb and Vanessa are dead. They were murdered. So are Ethan Jackson and Stella Weeks—both murdered, too. The police believe that I killed them. I believe that the killer left Stella's body in our kitchen to frame me for all four murders."

For the first time, Will looked her in the eye. "Stop! That's enough, I don't want to hear anymore. Are you trying to make me more miserable than I already am?"

Emma wasn't ready to stop. "Well try this out for size." She told him about the text she had received, purportedly from him. "Obviously, your twin sister sent it."

Will shook his head.

Emma concluded her litany, "You need to hear about one last atrocity. The police shot Pepper. It was my fault. She died protecting me. Pepper made it possible for me to get back to you."

Will turned his back on her.

He said, "I'm sorry Emma, but there's nothing I can do for you. I still love you, you know." Then, he either went back to sleep or pretended to.

Emma left his side and sat on one of Georgia's two over-stuffed arm chairs, weeping. She looked at the cherry table between the two chairs and dreamed that a tumbler of Lagavulin single malt scotch awaited another sip. She had to settle for Perrier.

She drank as if the fizzy water would somehow replenish her empty spirit.

63

Caroline and Skip

Despite it being a Sunday and the Fourth of July, Caroline Stoner called a meeting at headquarters. Dick Wardlaw had yet to appoint a new chief of police. Skip Munro was the last to arrive. Buzz, Pete Sinclair, Chuck Smith, and Max were already seated in the roll call room.

Lieutenant Munro took the podium, saying to Caroline, "Okay by you?"

Caroline didn't mind at all. She was so upset about the confrontation with Emma and her role in it that she wished she had never been involved in the first place.

"I'm not picking on you guys, but she's *got* to be somewhere," Munro said, not troubling to bury his exasperation.

Buzz took the heat. He told Munro that officers had run a grid all over town, all night long. He described how Chuck Smith had reached out to Georgia Foster, Emma Thorne's sister-in-law. She denied having seen Emma but let Smith stake out the house for the night. Buzz told Munro that she had not shown. "So far we've got bupkis," Buzz said.

Max raised his hand. "Did we hear anything on Stella's forensics?"

"Still preliminary," Munro said. "Mittendorf said his report should be finalized by tomorrow afternoon. He did tell me that there is evidence that Stella wasn't stabbed in Emma Thorne's kitchen, but we already figured that. On the other hand, there is no doubt that the knife belonged to Emma."

Buzz said, "Which means that Emma might have been set up."

Munro said, "Maybe, but, except for her husband, she is the only suspect who has a direct connection to each of the victims."

Murmurings filled the room. It was hard for Caroline to tell whether they were in support of Emma or against her.

Caroline called them back to order and said to nobody in particular, "What's next?"

"Who were Thorne's friends?" Munro asked. "Besides Deb Barger and Vanessa Mack."

Caroline said, "I guess I knew Emma the best. She was closest to her dad, Archie, but he's dead of course." Caroline noticed her colleagues staring at her as if she had just said the stupidest thing in the world. Her face flushed. "It's possible that she is holed up with Deb's husband, Dave. They were pretty close. Dave might've taken her in. And, actually, Vanessa's house is vacant. Emma would certainly know how to get into Vanessa's."

"What about this Georgia Foster? Why was Officer Smith sent there?" Munro asked.

"That was my idea," said Caroline. "The pickup truck parked in front of my apartment building last night came back to Frank Foster, Georgia's father. Staking out Georgia's house was just a hunch … which didn't pan out."

"Anyone else?"

"The only other person I can think of is Phil Masters," Buzz said. "He runs Group Therapy, the bar. Emma and he are friends."

"Okay then. At least we have some possibilities," Munro said. "Buzz, you and Officer Beyersdorf take Deb's house and Vanessa's house. Stoner and I will make three stops: Masters, Foster's parents, and Foster herself. The rest of you keep patrolling town. We'll meet back here later."

Caroline realized that Lieutenant Munro had just usurped their investigation. She was glad. Last night had been way too stressful. She hated that she'd turned on Emma.

The Sunday brunch crowd filled Group Therapy.

"May as well grab some food while we're here," Skip said. They sat in one of the few free booths. Caroline told the waitress that they wanted to speak with Phil when he had a free moment.

Skip ordered a roast beef sandwich *au jus,* and Caroline had the Southwest salad. Phil joined them at their table while they were eating.

He was visibly agitated.

Phil said, "You're here about Emma, right? I heard she's on the run, and I hope you don't find her." He stubbed a finger against Skip's chest. "Who're you? Another cop?"

"I'm Lieutenant Munro, Connecticut State Police, and I'd cool your jets if I were you."

"Says you." Phil sneered.

"Yes, we are looking for Emma Thorne. Do you know where she is, or have you seen her?"

"No to both. But I wouldn't tell you anyway. There is no fucking way that Emma killed anybody. You are so far off base you could get picked off by any half-assed pitcher."

Caroline said, "Phil, take it easy. We're only doing our jobs."

He turned on Caroline. "You don't believe in Emma either, do you? Some friend you are. You cops are wasting your time and my taxpaying dollars. I have nothing more to say to either of you. Finish your meal and get out of my joint." He stormed off.

Phil's dig about friendship rankled Caroline. She was conflicted. Yet if Emma were innocent, why had she fled? People who aren't guilty don't do that. Do they?

As if reading her thoughts, Skip said, "I know how hard it can be to think the worst of an old friend, but in my book a runner is usually guilty. Our job is to arrest her and find out for sure if she's Ms. Sharpie."

Frank and Joan Foster's lake house was next. They found the couple on a terrace facing the lake. They both had glasses in their hands, and there was a bottle of white wine in a cooler on the table. Frank rose. He greeted Caroline and looked at Skip Munro expectantly. Munro identified himself and asked, "Mr. Foster, do you know the whereabouts of your daughter-in-law?"

"No, I don't. We're still hoping that you guys will find our missing son. Why do you ask?"

Caroline was surprised that he didn't know that Emma was missing. Word had spread around town like a brushfire on a windy day.

Skip said, "Mr. Foster, do you know the whereabouts of your Dodge Ram?"

"That I can answer," Frank said. "I loaned it to my daughter yesterday. She had some trash to take to the dump."

So, Georgia had lied to her father, Caroline thought. She must've loaned the pickup to Emma.

"Thank you, sir," Skip said, "we won't disturb you any further."

Back in Caroline's police cruiser, Skip said, "Interesting development, huh? Next stop, Georgia Foster."

"Maybe we should get a search warrant."

"Nah, let's pay her a visit first. Catch her vibe. Know what I mean?"

Caroline drove past the town line to Georgia's residence.

Driving up Georgia's impressively long driveway, Skip observed, "Pretty swanky. Pretty remote, too. Good place to hole up, don't you think?"

"I guess so. That's why I thought to send Officer Smith here last night. The problem is that Emma and Georgia don't get on very well. In fact, they pretty much hate each other. Anyway, as you heard, Chuck's stakeout was a waste of time."

Caroline parked in the circle outside Georgia's front door. They got out.

Skip said, "Place this size, there'd be plenty of cubbyholes to hide a sister-in-law. Let's see what we can find out."

Georgia opened the door before they knocked.

In formal cop-mode, Skip flashed his shield. "May we have a word with you, Ms. Foster?"

"Absolutely." She treated them to a broad smile. "Won't you please come in?"

They followed her into the living room.

"Can I get you some juice or soda? I could make a pot of coffee or brew some tea? It's no trouble."

Caroline thought that she seemed awfully anxious to please.

"Nothing for us," Skip said, taking the liberty of answering for both of them.

"Well, if you change your mind—"

Caroline was impressed when Skip took a tack she didn't expect. He said, "Why did you borrow your father's pickup truck yesterday?"

"That's an odd question, Lieutenant." Georgia was still smiling. "Dad loaned it to me so that I could take a big load of trash to the dump."

"Where's the truck now?"

"It's in the barn. That's where I keep my vehicles."

"May we see it?" Skip said.

"Of course," she said, "I'll show you the way."

Georgia slid open an enormous sliding door. Caroline thought, incongruously, someone keeps that door as greased as a North Korean dictator's hairdo.

The three stared into the barn. Inside were two cars but, as they already knew, no truck.

Georgia reeled. "Oh my God, someone's stolen Dad's Dodge." She looked at Caroline, who noticed a tic in Georgia's left eye. With a screwball grin, she said, "I guess I'll have to report this to the police. No, wait, you are the police! Officer, I'd like to report a stolen vehicle."

Skip and Caroline looked at her with incredulity. Caroline wasn't sure what Skip was thinking, but it was clear to her that she was staring at a nut job ... with a ticking time bomb eye. Caroline felt that they were in the right place.

Skip said, "Ms. Foster would you give us permission to look around your house?"

"What are you looking for?" she said.

"We're looking for your sister-in-law."

Seemingly unsurprised, she blithely replied, "She's certainly not here. I don't even like her. But I have no objection to your looking around."

"Thank you," Skip said, "we'll start upstairs."

They checked all five bedrooms, closets included. They found no evidence that Emma was or had been there.

"What are you going to do about my father's truck?"

"We'll find it," Skip said opaquely.

They searched the attic, not finding anything more than the usual attic detritus. Old furniture, cardboard boxes, and the like. Caroline asked what was in the basement.

"It's where I exercise. I have quite a workout room. Want to see it?"

They followed Georgia to her basement. After Skip scoured the perimeter of the basement, looking behind the oil tanks, hot water heater, and furnace, they entered the exercise room. Caroline noticed a subtle change in Georgia's demeanor. The tic was still present, but there were other tells. Georgia's hands were now behind her back. From the movement of her arms, Caroline thought that she was wringing her hands.

Caroline also noticed Georgia's large aquarium. *Interesting*, she thought, but she said, "Wow, you have a lot of books. You must read a lot."

"I love to read," she said. For the first time since they'd arrived, Georgia avoided eye contact.

Perhaps Skip found the "vibe" he'd been looking for. He walked over to the bookshelves and studied some titles. "Ah, *Lord of the Flies*. That was one of my favorite books in high school." He reached to take it down, but the book didn't budge. "What's up with this? The book's stuck."

Georgia giggled. "Well this *is* embarrassing. The decorator I hired to do this room sold me on the idea of buying books-by-the-foot—"

Caroline stared hard at Georgia. "So these are all fake?"

"Well, um, they're real books, but—"

Skip interrupted, "I think we're done here, Ms. Foster. Thank you for your cooperation."

Walking back to the car, he said to Caroline, "Either my cop nose is shot, or Emma is somewhere in that house."

"I agree," Caroline said. "Did you notice the fish tank? Remember how Ethan Jackson was killed? Think we can get a search warrant and tear that place apart?"

"Pretty flimsy on the probable cause front, but I do know a friendly judge."

64

Georgia's AmEx Bill

A loud buzzer sounded. Emma jumped out of the chair. Will did, too. He sat up straight on the edge of his bed, feet on the floor, and palms on his thighs. "That is my crazy sister announcing lunch."

Emma thought he looked like an automaton.

But he explained, "Food is the only thing I have to look forward to."

What about me?

The buzzer sounded again, longer and seemingly more insistently.

"That's because you're standing. She won't come in until you sit down."

"Crazy," Emma muttered.

"Yup, Georgia is nothing if not crazy, but she's also careful."

Georgia opened the door. She carried a tray one-handed. On it was one bowl of soup, one sandwich, and juice in a plastic cup, which she placed on the kitchenette counter. Slung from her belt was a holstered pistol.

Georgia turned on Emma. "No lunch for you, you conniving bitch." She stepped over to the bed. Before Emma could react, she slapped one side of her face with the palm of her hand and back-slapped the other side. Georgia's ring cut her cheek. Emma screamed. The force of the blow triggered intense pain to her already-injured skull. She pressed the corner of her sheet to her cheek to stanch the bleeding.

"Because of you, the cops were here," Georgia said. "That's another black mark against you, Emma. I haven't yet decided what to do with you, but I can assure you that you are not going to stay here and ruin my beautiful relationship with my brother. Right, Will?"

Emma interrupted, "You call kidnapping your brother your idea of a beautiful relationship—"

"Shut up!" Georgia cocked her arm for another blow. This time, Emma ducked out of the way, but her sister-in-law pulled her punch anyway.

All of a sudden Georgia stepped back. The lunatic adopted a bizarre dreamy expression. She looked at the ceiling as she spoke. "Will and I have wonderful evenings together. Don't we, darling? We play chess, listen to music, dine together. Sometimes we watch a movie. When I think about it, I don't know why I didn't save him before. Don't you agree, Will?"

Will remained silent.

"Did you notice that I even cured his depression? True happiness can do that."

Will murmured, "Yeah, right."

Georgia spun toward Will. Her eyes lost their ruminative look and snapped to steel. She hissed, "Don't disappoint me, brother. You know I have to hurt you when you let me down."

Emma shouted, "Your beautiful relationship compels you to punish your brother? And to viciously murder four innocent people?"

"What are you talking about?" Georgia demanded.

Emma answered with a question. "You mean having to beat up your brother to make him love you?"

"Not that, asshole. The part about 'four innocent people.' What is that supposed to mean?"

"Come off it, Georgia. Why should we three be keeping secrets from one another?" Emma was winging it. She had no proof that Georgia was the killer. Was it even possible that one person could focus on imprisoning her twin and have the spare time to murder people?

"I really don't know what you're talking about," Georgia said.

"Do the names Stella, Vanessa, Deb, and Ethan ring any bells?"

"Of course. They're all dead. What are you suggesting?"

Georgia looked genuinely shocked. Her sociopathic skills were astonishing. Will gaped at her, too, and at Emma.

"I'm not *suggesting* anything. I know that you viciously murdered each one of them."

Georgia shouted, "You're the crazy one. I didn't kill anyone!"

"You're good, really good," Emma goaded her further. "Even if you lie to us, you should be truthful to yourself. The police think that I am the serial killer. I am not. You are!"

"I repeat, you're nuts." She stared coldly at Emma. "I haven't killed anyone, but, if I have to, I will start with you."

She stormed out, slamming both doors behind her.

"After all that's happened, do you think she *will* kill me?"

Will said, "Probably."

"Thanks for that."

Wordlessly, Will attacked his lunch, inhaling his food quicker than a Labrador. He didn't offer to share.

If it was possible for Emma's heart to break again, it did.

When he was done, he balanced the tray in the middle of the door slot and lay back in his bed, his back toward his wife.

Emma said to his back, "What the hell are we going to do? She could kill me. Ditch my body where it would be easily found. I'd be scratched off the suspect list. You would remain prisoner-for-life. And no one would ever know that Georgia is Mr. Sharpie. We have to figure some way out of here."

He didn't respond.

Emma and Will had no way of knowing that on Monday morning Lieutenant Munro had obtained a search warrant for Georgia's home. The police scoured the house, the barn, and the surrounding property. They never found the secret room.

Ignorant of the police department's fruitless search, they spent the next four days and nights in relative silence. Georgia had taken to delivering their food—rations for two, now—through the slot. She had stopped talking to them.

On the fifth morning after the breakfast buzzer sounded, the tray appeared through the door slot. There was an envelope underneath the plastic plate.

Emma greedily seized the envelope. Inside were copies of an airline ticket on Spirit Airlines and an American Express bill. The ticket, with Georgia Foster's name clearly printed, was from Hartford/Bradley to Dallas. The AmEx bill showed charges posted in Dallas between Friday, June 25 and Sunday, June 27.

Emma had no trouble remembering that Vanessa had disappeared (and was probably murdered) on Saturday, June 26.

Ironically, the AmEx posts were circled with a black Sharpie. But the police department—at her insistence—had never revealed anything about the Sharpie marks to the public.

Holy shit, she thought.

Still, how hard would it be to download an AMEX logo, place it in any garden-variety word processor, and type in some charges from Dallas? Georgia was nothing if not resourceful.

Emma knew that Will, despite his PhD, was no computer whiz. So, she didn't bother to ask his opinion.

Emma said thoughtfully, "You don't suppose that Hampshire is big enough for two whack-jobs, do you?"

65

A Sharp Crack

On the same day that Georgia had delivered the AmEx bill, Emma began to formulate an escape plan.

As dinner hour approached, Emma used her teeth to begin tearing her bed sheet into strips. She braided three strips together until they formed a strong rope of about four feet. The plan was simple but by no means foolproof. She tied one end of the sheet-rope to her wrist. Sitting in her proscribed spot on the bed, she waited.

Like many plans—especially those that are the brainchild of desperation—hers wouldn't progress hitch-free.

The buzzer sounded. Emma tensed. She knew she would have only the briefest moment in which to succeed. Georgia opened the slot and went through the routine of making sure they were both on their beds. Again, saying nothing, Georgia slid the tray through the gap.

Emma struck.

She lunged forward and gripped Georgia's right hand as hard as she could, yanking it through the slot. The unexpected force of her attack pulled Georgia off balance. But Emma wasn't able to lash Georgia's wrist with the other end of the sheet-rope before Georgia regained her footing. She was much stronger than Emma. Like losing a game of tug-of-war, Georgia pulled Emma's arm inexorably toward the slot. Emma had to drop the sheet and grab Georgia's wrist with both hands. She placed one foot against the door and heaved with all her might.

Even one-armed, Georgia was winning. If she did, Emma had no doubt that Georgia would return and shoot her.

Will watched in silence.

Georgia's arm poked through the slot at an angle. Her upper arm, below her elbow, touched the top of the slot. The part of her arm just above her wrist touched the bottom. Emma suddenly had a new idea. Instead of continuing to pull, she shifted gears and placed all her weight and strength on the top of Georgia's wrist and pushed sharply downwards.

Emma heard a sharp crack and a banshee scream. Georgia's arm hung limply in the slot, deformed and unquestionably broken.

Emma stooped and picked up the sheet-rope. She got one end lashed around Georgia's wrist and wound the other end around the doorknob. During a brief spell when Georgia stopped screaming and paused to gasp in pain, Emma calmly said, "If you let us out, I will call an ambulance."

Emma glanced at Will. She was shocked to see such a satisfied look on his face. Georgia had turned them both into savages.

Georgia alternated between screams and threats, curses and homicidal promises. She kept up her tirade for three hours. Finally, there was silence on the other side of the door. Emma looked at Will who pantomimed the snapping of a stick.

Emma felt bad enough breaking Georgia's arm. She knew she couldn't torture her further, but she said, "If you don't open the door, I will have to twist your arm. Which I'm afraid will cause you considerably more pain."

The latch clicked. Emma gently drew the door open, trying to minimize Georgia's suffering. But her howl was deafening.

To Emma's surprise, Georgia wasn't ready to quit. With her left fist, she slugged Emma in the jaw, shrieking in pain as she did so. Emma reeled.

Then Georgia cross-drew her pistol with her unbroken arm. She shrieked again. Her aim wavered as she tried to get a bead on Emma.

To Emma's utter shock, she was knocked aside by Will, who had finally sprung into action with a terrifying wail. He grabbed Georgia's gun hand. As they wrestled, Georgia continued to scream, and Will continued to wail.

Emma lurched backwards against the steel vault door. As she fell, her body pushed the door open further. The inertia of the blow made her roll over. The steel door began to close on its own. She heard the deafening sound of Georgia's pistol discharging. The steel door closed fully, with a solid thunk.

There was silence.

Emma lay on the floor to recover her wits, not knowing who was hit. Her head hurt now more than ever. Eventually, she was able to get to her feet and see the door which had imprisoned Will and latterly her. It looked exactly like the door to a bank vault, complete with an electronic keypad and a handle. She pulled on the handle, but it didn't budge.

To a certain extent her plan had worked. She had escaped. But her gut told her that she had left a dead body inside. Whose? she didn't know. And there was nothing she could do about it. She made sure to leave the bookcase/door wide open for responders to see.

Holding her battered head in her hands, Emma made her way to Georgia's bathroom. In the medicine cabinet, she found a drug called Fiorinal C, which rang a bell. She thought it was Canadian. She read the ingredients: codeine, aspirin, caffeine, and butalbital, whatever that was. At least the codeine would help. She swallowed three tablets. Two more than the recommended dosage.

In the kitchen, Emma found Georgia's landline, two cell phones, and the keys to her BMW.

She found a phonebook in the kitchen drawer and dialed the number for Karen and Henry King.

Sophie's mother answered, "Karen King."

"This is Emma Thorne. I'm looking for—"

"Emma Thorne? What do you want with Sophie?"

"She texted me some days ago, and I don't have her cell phone number."

"She texted you?" the mother said in horror. "The police say that you're a serial killer. It's all over the papers and the TV news. Please don't hurt my daughter."

Karen hung up.

Emma knew one truth. She would once again be the lead story on the evening news.

She found Georgia's BMW M6 in the barn and tried the key. She didn't want to call the police and not have the means to escape. The engine caught and purred. She left it running while she hurried back into the house and dialed 911 from Georgia's landline. The Hampshire Police Department had recently adopted the Enhanced-911 system, which incorporated automatic number and location identification. She knew that the dispatcher would see the name and address of Georgia Foster and a map pin-pointing her house.

"What is the location of your emergency?"

Emma quickly said, "Listen carefully, Will Foster and Georgia Foster are locked in a vault in the basement of this house. One of them requires an ambulance. Georgia is guilty of kidnapping if not murder. Bring a safe-cracker."

The dispatcher demanded, "Emma? Is that you? You're not making any sense."

Emma wasn't ready to throw herself on the mercy of her former colleagues.

She replaced the receiver, grabbed Georgia's two cell phones, found a floppy hat on a peg in the hall, and hurried back to the M6.

66

"I'll get it, Dad!"

Although her head felt like a balloon about to burst, Emma had the BMW's windows lowered. The breeze, blowing through her hair, enhanced her bitter-sweet freedom.

She was confident that the entire police force would be responding to 36 Roughland Road.

She returned to her nagging feeling that Sophie King had an important message for her. Maybe she should try to go to the King's house and ...

... and what?

Who opens their door to a serial killer?

She could wait for Sophie to leave, but it wasn't likely that the girl would be allowed out at 10:30 p.m.

She pulled the BMW to the side of the road. She opened both of Georgia's cell phones. In the Contacts section, she quickly found Sophie's cell number. *How dumb of me.* She noticed that neither Ethan Jackson's nor Joe Henderson's numbers were in either phone. How many cell phones did Georgia own? Or maybe she had guiltily deleted both names.

Emma called Sophie, who answered, "Georgia?"

"No, Sophie, it's Emma Thorne."

"How come you didn't text me back?" She sounded petulant. "It was … it *is* important."

"Sorry. I was busy."

"I was just trying to help you with your investigation, like you helped me."

Emma said, "What *did* you want to tell me?"

"Wait a second! That's weird. Someone's at our front door."

Emma heard her shout, "I'll get it, Dad!"

Emma shouted, "Do not answer the door, Sophie!"

She got no reply.

A moment later, Emma heard a terrified scream and what sounded like the cell phone landing on the floor.

Then dead air, as if the phone had stopped working.

"Sophie? Sophie!" Emma called.

Emma looked at Georgia's mobile screen.

Call Terminated.

Emma put the BMW in gear and skidded into a U-turn. The King house was roughly ten minutes away. She made it in five.

The front door was open when Emma jumped out of the car. Karen King was on the phone. With 911, Emma assumed. She heard Karen say, "Come quickly! Please!"

Emma saw tears streaming down her cheeks. Her husband stepped into the doorway and put his arms around her shoulders. He looked at Emma. "Oh God," he said, "what are you doing here? Did you have something to do with this?"

"What happened?" Emma asked, although she was sure that she knew the answer.

Karen started blubbering. "I can't talk to you. They say *you're* the killer!"

"For fuck's sake," Emma said, "just tell me what happened to Sophie."

Mr. King said, "Hold on, Karen, I've got a feeling about this. I'm going to tell her. We were upstairs … oh, Jesus, this is terrible …"

"I'll help you," Emma said firmly, "but I need to know exactly what's going on. Tell me."

Karen said, "Like Henry said, we were in bed. We heard the doorbell, and we heard Sophie say that she would get it. Then we heard a scream. Then we heard a muffled scream. Next, a car drove away really fast. We ran downstairs. The door was open like you see it. And, oh my God, my baby …"

"So, you didn't see who was at the door?"

"No," Karen said hollowly.

Emma heard a siren. Her heart started to pound. Before running back to the BMW, she paused long enough to tell them, "I know who did this, and I'm going to find Sophie and bring her home."

Henry firmly closed the door. She heard the deadbolt snap home.

Somehow, Emma found the courage to believe her own words.

At the end of the driveway, she turned in the opposite direction from the approaching siren. She saw the flashing lights of the arriving cruiser in her rearview mirror as she sped away.

Sophie wished she hadn't been such a bitch to her mother recently. She had been so *teen-aged*. She would do anything for a hug from Mom right now.

God, would she ever see her parents again?

In the back of the car, she was terrified. Way more scared than she was when Joe Henderson had led Emma on that asinine wild-goose chase and when the Escalade had flipped. Her wrists and ankles were zip-tied together. There was a smelly rag stuffed in her mouth, bound with duct tape. Scariest of all was the black hood covering her head.

Would Emma be able to save her again? Emma must certainly know that something truly hideous had happened, but would she be able to figure who her abductor was?

Prayers didn't come easily to Sophie, although her parents never missed a Sunday mass. Tonight, she prayed earnestly that ... somehow ... she would make it home again.

67

"Welcome Home"

What wasn't even remotely clear was how the hell Georgia had escaped from the vault. Did she have otherworldly powers? It sure seemed like it. And in what condition had she left Will? Was he wounded, in need of medical care? Or was Will dead? Emma shuddered.

The only other possibility was that the police had opened the vault, and Georgia had talked her way free. Emma dismissed that scenario as absurd.

No, actually *neither* was possible. The timing simply didn't work. If not Georgia, there could be only one other suspect. Joe Henderson. And, if Joe had abducted Sophie, was she headed to sex-slavery? Could Joe be Mr. Sharpie? Was sex-trafficking the gateway drug to serial murder?

She stopped the BMW and made a call to Detective Dave Swanson of the Lincoln Police Department. She did not expect a warm welcome.

"Dave, this is Emma Thorne—"

"Jesus, Emma, there's a murder warrant out for you and you conned me into thinking you were still chief of police. If you're calling me because you're scared of the Hampshire PD, I can set up a meet where you'll be safe. Turn yourself in—"

"Shut up! I don't have time for this. How long have we known each other? I murdered fuck-all!"

"I've known Skip Munro a long time, too. Skip's no dummy—"

"Listen to me! One question. Did you guys ever bust that photo studio front for the trafficking ring?"

"I *can* answer that. Don't you read the newspapers?"

Not lately, she thought.

Dave continued, "We arrested three male adults and freed six minor females."

"Okay, second question, then. Did you arrest Joe Henderson?"

"He wasn't on scene when we busted that hell hole. The D.A. says that one of the guys we charged is likely to flip. Then we'll get a warrant for Joe. We believe he's the money—"

"Thanks Dave. You're a true friend." She disconnected.

Gunning the BMW, Emma sped to Archie's house.

She needed a gun.

Regrettably, Lieutenant Skip Munro had out-thought her on that score. During the time she had been on the run or in Georgia's basement, Munro had emptied the gun safe. Inside was an official CSP form listing the weapons which had been confiscated.

Frustrated, she drove home. She needed some kind of weapon before confronting Georgia.

Where she expected to see a dark house, instead she was alarmed to find brightly lit windows throughout the downstairs. She had underestimated the persistence of the Hampshire PD.

Why were her former colleagues still hunting her? Between her 911 call asking them to respond to Georgia's house and Sophie having been snatched … wouldn't they be a tad busy?

And surely, they could see that she, Emma, couldn't be responsible.

She drove past and left the BMW around the corner. She reconnoitered on foot. She sneaked through her neighbor's backyard as silently as she knew how. Not silently enough. She peered through the kitchen window and came face-to-face with a large, barking dog, whose front paws were balanced on the edge of the counter. The dog was a Belgian Malinois—who bore an uncanny resemblance to Sergeant Pepper. The dog's bark morphed into ecstatic yip-yips.

Emma was the happiest she had been in recent memory.

She ran to the door and flew inside. Pepper greeted her in spasms of wriggling joy. She jumped up, placing her paws on Emma's chest, and licked her face. Strict no-nos at any other time. Emma couldn't care less. She kissed her repeatedly, unable to believe she was alive and well.

"Who is there?" she heard Mark Byrne shout from the living room. He came running into the kitchen. "Hey! It's you! Welcome home!"

"It's good to be home."

Mark asked, "May I give you a hug?"

"Sure can."

They hugged, and Mark kissed her on the ear.

Emma said, "I was so sure that Pepper was dead. I can't believe this. I'm so happy."

Mark's explanation tumbled out. "She was at the vet for three days and two nights. You're going to get a whopping bill. But Pepper never gave up. She was determined to survive and to heal. She took a bullet in her hindquarters, but it missed her femur and went right on through. By the way, Buzz feels terrible about it. Caroline Stoner called me when Pepper was discharged, and I've had her ever since. I hope you don't mind that we've been staying here. At my place, Pepper wouldn't stop bitching, if you'll pardon the pun. As it is, she's been sitting by your front door for the past five days. Still, she's made incredible progress." He concluded, "We just got back from a long walk."

Emma knelt to inspect Pepper's wounds. The dog was still so excited that Emma had to rub her ears to calm her. Where Pepper's fur had been shaven, she could see neat sutures closing both the entry and the exit wounds. "The vet did a great job. So, did you," she said.

Mark said, "Where on earth have you been hiding out?" Of course, he knew nothing of her imprisonment.

Emma explained where she had been.

"Shit on a stick," he exclaimed. He studied her face as he said, "So Will is still alive ..."

Emma then explained why she wasn't sure.

He thought for a moment before saying, "But Georgia has to be Mr. Sharpie?"

"I don't think it's possible, unless she's a magician. I feel pretty certain that we're looking at Joe Henderson."

"The guy you chased and rescued that girl from, Georgia's goddaughter. Jesus, how bizarre can it get?"

"The very same guy to whom you, Pepper, and I are going to pay a visit. Because I think he snatched Sophie King earlier tonight."

Mark's eyes bulged. "Whaat?"

She nodded and told him of her visit to the King household and about the sex trafficking ring in Lincoln.

He shook his head and sat down at the kitchen table. "And I thought my home had all the villainy a town could offer. Jamaica Plain doesn't hold a candle to Hampshire."

"C'mon," she urged.

He checked his wristwatch. "It's two in the morning."

"Now's the time."

"You're right," he said seriously. Mark's usual flippant demeanor seemed to have deserted him. "I have to get a couple of things from my car before we go."

Emma hoped those would include some heavy weapons.

She had a bad feeling about Joe Henderson.

68

Crazy Bitch

Mark, Pepper, and Emma piled into Emma's car and sped toward Henderson House in the early hours of the morning. Near the end of his driveway, they found an overgrown farm road off Meadow Drive to hide the car, and they proceeded up the long driveway on foot. Emma put her key ring in her back pocket and carried the policeman's friend—a four-D-cell Maglite flashlight. It was switched off.

She counted on Mark to be carrying, too.

On the way, Mark observed in a quiet voice, "This place must have set Joe back a shit-load."

"Trafficking in virgins," Emma whispered back, "must be good business."

Although it was nearly two in the morning, there were plenty of lights on in Joe's house.

Emma and Pepper proceeded to the front door while Mark took the back.

Emma pounded on the door and waited to the side. Pepper was a quivering mass of anticipation. There was no answer. She found a doorbell and pressed that. Inside, "La Cucaracha" played loud and long. Emma hadn't credited Joe with a sense of humor. There was still no answer.

Behind her, Emma suddenly heard a car screaming up the driveway. It was a Corvette. She remembered Sophie telling her all those weeks ago at the conclusion of the car chase that Joe owned a Corvette.

Indeed, Joe pulled to a stop in front of the front door, jumped out, and slammed the car door behind him. Sophie wasn't in the passenger seat.

"What the fuck are you doing here?"

Emma felt amazingly calm. She also felt brave. She was confident that, one way or another, Joe would lead her to the end of this madness.

Wagging warily, Pepper kept her brown eyes fixed on Joe.

"Where have you been, Joe, and where is Sophie King?"

"None of your business is the answer to the first question. And no fucking idea is the answer to your second. You're not a cop, so get off my land and out of my life." He took a menacing step toward her. Pepper tensed. "You've caused plenty of trouble, already," he added.

"Not going to happen. We're not going anywhere until we see Sophie and bring her home—"

Joe said quickly, "Who's we?"

"I meant Pepper and me."

Emma wanted to bet that he had accepted her lie. But then he pulled a gun from his waistband.

She took a step backward as Pepper went rigid. "No need for that, Joe. Give me Sophie—I know you snatched her—and we'll be on our way."

"She isn't here." In that, Joe had made a blunder similar to hers earlier. She took him to mean that Sophie *had been* there.

Suddenly, Joe looked confused, but his anger quickly returned.

Emma pressed: "I know about your dirty little operation down in Lincoln, selling under-age girls. I know that it got busted. And I know that the Lincoln PD plans to come after you—"

For a skilled sociopath, Joe's reaction surprised her. His face immediately betrayed surprise and fear.

He waggled his gun in front of her face.

Emma continued, "I can't prove it … yet … but I believe you murdered Ethan Jackson, Deb Barger, Vanessa Mack, and Stella Weeks. You're standing in some deep shit, Joe. I wouldn't want to be in your shoes. Waving that gun around is only going to make matters worse."

"You crazy bitch, I didn't murder anyone!"

"Okay, I'll settle for Sophie. Where is she?"

And where the hell was Mark?

"Like I said, don't know. Anyway, you're the murderer. You knifed Georgia's girlfriend in your kitchen—"

"Georgia's what?"

"You heard me. Georgia was having it on with Stella, the sexy sparkplug. You didn't know that? Some detective."

Emma needed a moment to regroup. She remembered seeing them together at Ethan's funeral. But *lovers* hadn't crossed her mind. Finally, she said, "You seem well-informed."

"Yeah, Georgia told me all about them. Every so often, I fuck Georgia, too."

"Didn't you just claim she's into women?"

Joe got the same snarky grin he'd had when he'd greeted her in his bathing suit. "What can I say? Women just can't resist me."

In her peripheral vision, Emma spotted a fleeting shadow at the corner of the house. She willed her eyes to stay focused on Joe. Unfortunately, Pepper wasn't able to do the same.

Joe read the situation correctly. He whipped around, spotted Mark, and shouted for him to come forward.

"I'm armed whoever the hell you are, and I won't hesitate to blow your brains out. Drop your weapon, raise your hands, and walk slowly toward me."

"Take it easy, big guy," Mark said flippantly, "I'm unarmed."

Mark stepped out of the bushes. He joined our little gathering on the driveway with his hands above his head.

Joe said, "No wisecracks, asshole. Lie on the ground face down. Spread your arms and legs wide."

"Well, aren't you Mr. Book 'em, Danno." Mark muttered.

Emma chimed in, "More like Mr. Sharpie."

"Both of you, shut the fuck up!"

Joe searched Mark thoroughly. Within moments he found a snub-nosed revolver in Mark's ankle holster and a pair of black matte handcuffs looped through the back of Mark's belt.

Without warning, Joe smashed the back of Mark's head with his own, larger weapon. Except for the crack of the pistol striking his head, Mark lost consciousness soundlessly.

Pepper whined and waited for a command from Emma.

Joe pointed the gun at Pepper. "Keep control of that dog, or he's gonna get shot again."

Emma said, "*She*, goddamnit! The dog's female."

Nonetheless, Emma was not going to let Pepper take another bullet for her. She told Pepper to stand down.

Joe tossed Mark's handcuffs to Emma. "Handcuff yourself to your buddy."

Emma did as she was told. Joe came over and tightened the cuff until it bit into her wrist. He searched Emma. He quickly found her key ring. While patting her down, he paused to goose her crotch.

Joe smirked when she spat, Pig!"

He threw the key ring deep into the woods. He left the Maglite on the driveway.

Keeping the gun pointed at Pepper, Joe said to Emma, "I'll be back, deal with you later."

Joe Henderson walked back to his Corvette and sped away.

Emma examined Mark's head wound. There was copious blood, and the gash at the back of his head would need sutures. Nothing life-threatening, and she didn't think he would be unconscious for long. With brute strength aided by adrenaline, she managed to rip off a good part of his shirt, which she used to reduce the bleeding.

Handcuffed to Mark, Emma's days on the run were over.

She maintained steady pressure on Mark's laceration.

After a few moments of direct pressure, she tried rubbing her knuckles over his sternum to stimulate consciousness, but Mark remained unresponsive.

Suddenly, Emma had a crazy idea.

With her uncuffed hand she opened her back pocket where her keys had been—her car key, house key, *and* her police-issued, universal handcuff key. She instructed Pepper to smell her yawning pocket.

Search, she ordered.

Pepper, who had been watching the events unfold, tore into the woods in precisely the same direction in which Joe had thrown the keys.

While Pepper furiously trampled the undergrowth, Emma recovered her Maglite and wondered, *exactly how clever is my dog?*

Moments later, Pepper was back, proudly dangling the key ring from her front teeth.

Omigod! "Good girl, Sgt. Pepper," she said, showering her with pats.

If the key fits, you must convict popped into her head.

Blessedly, the key fit.

She unmanacled herself and Mark. With another strip from his shirt, she tied her makeshift bandage tightly to his wound. "Help is coming," she promised.

With the help of the Maglite, she found Mark's gun in the bushes.

With Pepper at her heels, she reached her car in seconds ... but *not* in time to see the distinctive taillights of a Corvette speeding away.

In the car and for the umpteenth time, she dialed 911 and requested an ambulance and a BOLO for the yellow Corvette.

She ignored the dispatcher's urgent questions.

69

Too Pervy

With only a hunch to propel her, Emma headed south.

What if Joe, having snatched Sophie, had thrown her to his wolves—Lincoln's pervy predators?

Sophie's life might depend on her.

Emma had no trouble remembering that Detective Dave Swanson had told her that Joe operated his sleazy business on River Street in Lincoln.

Nor did she have any trouble remembering that Hampshire's River Street had been the beginning link of this entire murderous chain.

She drove the thirty-five minutes to Lincoln. On River, which was only a few blocks long, she searched for Joe's Corvette. She didn't spot it, but, as she rolled down the street, she did notice a burly bouncer-type standing in front of the door to an old mill building. His arms were crossed, and he watched her pass. Emma took the next turn and parked her car.

Why would a man be loitering in front of a former mill at this time of night unless he was guarding something within?

Emma had never been a fearful person, thanks largely to Archie. That night she felt fearless. And close to resolution.

She grabbed her Maglite and fashioned a makeshift leash for Pepper using her belt. Although River Street wasn't exactly residential, she didn't think the guard would worry about a woman out for a late-night dog walk. On the other hand, everyone got nervous when Pepper approached off-leash. She needed to get close to him without him becoming defensive or, worse, offensive.

She turned the corner, on which there was a streetlight. He immediately spotted her. Dropping his arms to his sides, he turned and faced her, watching carefully. Emma's mouth was dry, but she managed to whistle a tune—"You Can't Always Get What You Want"—while she strolled at a leisurely pace. Pepper helped the illusion by sniffing next to a fire hydrant and squatting to pee.

When she was about ten feet away, Emma said, "Nice evening."

The thug glared at her and didn't answer.

She pulled Mark's gun from her waistband and pointed it at his bloated belly.

"Have I got your attention?" she said.

He still didn't reply, but he nodded his head, yes.

"Put your right hand on top of your head, and empty your pockets with your left hand. Slowly."

"Crazy bitch!" he muttered.

"You know, you're the second guy tonight to call me a crazy bitch. It's beginning to wear on me."

"Fuck you, lady. You chose the wrong dude to rob. And what's with the dog?"

She repeated, "Empty your pockets."

He removed a key ring, a cell phone, a pack of Marlboros, and an old Zippo engraved with the Harley-Davidson logo. He reached out to hand them to her.

Emma took a step back. "No way." She told him to place them on the ground. He complied.

"Is Joe Henderson inside?"

That caught his attention. His head snapped up. "You a cop?"

She said, "Not exactly."

"The name isn't familiar."

"Oh, come on, man, it's late, and I'm getting tired." She cocked the hammer and pointed the gun of the guy's head. "Is Joe inside? And who else is with him?"

She expected him to continue to stonewall, and she wasn't sure exactly what you would do about it. She wasn't going to shoot him. But then he said, "Yeah, Joe's inside."

"Who else?"

He sighed. "Fuck it," he said. "One customer and the new girl. The other girls are locked up. Asleep, I guess."

She retrieved the keys and his cell phone, leaving his smokes and lighter on the sidewalk. "You and I are going to take a walk around the corner. Keep your hands on your head. Walk slowly."

At the corner he stopped. She could feel him tense like he was about to make his play. She took a few steps backward, released Pepper. When he turned, Pepper snarled and bared her fangs.

His hand flew to his mouth. He sputtered, "Christ, lady, keep that fucker away from me! I'll do what you say."

She used Mark's handcuffs to secure him to a stop sign. "One peep out of you, and I send my partner back to rip your face off."

The third key she tried opened the mill's steel door. There were low-wattage bulbs which barely illuminated a dim corridor. She used her Maglite. She couldn't hear anything. She ordered Pepper to keep silent. Together they crept down the corridor, at the end of which there was a **T** with two additional corridors branching off. Each had rows of doors on either side like the floor of a hotel. They were numbered. All of the doors had heavy slide bolts locking the occupants inside.

Except one.

The "office?"

Unlike the other doors, this one was hinged to open outward.

She looked at Pepper and mouthed the Ready command.

Next, she grasped the knob and threw open the door. Pepper charged inside.

When she heard a cry, Emma followed Pepper into the room.

Pepper's jaws were locked around Joe's right wrist. He was screaming for help. His weapon was on the floor. Emma picked up his gun and told Pepper to Stand Down.

Joe shrieked, "Goddamnit, your dog broke my fucking arm."

"Tell me where Sophie is," Emma said quickly, "or I'll tell her to break your other fucking arm."

"Fuck you. You busted me for DUI. You kneed me in the balls. My lawyer says I may go to prison just for taking Sophie on a date. Ethan Jackson fucked me over, too. He fucking robbed me," Joe ranted. "I fucked Georgia but in a different way. I despise all your friends. What do you fucking think I want? I want you to pay for what you've done."

"Enough!" Emma shouted. "Where is Sophie?"

She stared at Joe. He glared back at her. She couldn't decide whether his expression reflected fury, pain, despair, or all three.

Finally, with his useless right arm dangling at his side, Joe said, "Room Nine."

"Is she alone?" Emma said, fearing the answer.

"Of course not!"

Unbelievably, Joe then staggered toward her with his left fist cocked.

"Jesus, Joe, don't you ever learn from your mistakes?" Before he finished speaking, Pepper's powerful jaws seized his left wrist. Emma heard at least one bone snap. He screamed.

Emma ordered Pepper to guard him while she ran down the corridor to Room Nine.

By now, the john *must* have heard the commotion.

She snapped open the slide bolt and burst into Nine.

Emma took in the whole scene in the time it would take a camera's shutter to open and close.

Sophie was naked, spread-eagle on the bed, wrists and ankles tied to bedposts. The thin, balding customer looked to be in his early sixties. His trousers and underpants were around his ankles. He was masturbating, and Sophie was weeping.

The john stared at Emma, terrified.

Apparently, Joe's screams hadn't penetrated his concentration.

For Sophie, of course, the situation was horrific, but Emma took the long view. Sophie's first perv was too pervy to perform what john's usually pay for.

With the barrel of her Maglite, Emma clocked his penis. A full four D-cells worth of pain. The john fled the room, screaming.

She hugged Sophie for a long time before untying her. The girl couldn't stop shaking and moaning. Emma knew it would take her some time to recover from the night's events. She felt for her.

With Sophie dressed, they ran back to Joe's office.

Pepper was a good, brave dog, but she wasn't smart enough to know that a phone could be a weapon, too. Emma heard Joe say, "I don't give a shit what time it is. Get your ass down here and blow this cunt—"

"Give it up Joe. Put the phone down and come with me." To Sophie and Pepper, she said, "Best we be getting out of here."

At the corner of River Street and Blackberry, she uncuffed the goon from the stop sign, saying, "Get lost."

She made Joe sit on the sidewalk and shackled his ankles together around the same stop sign. No matter what he had done, she didn't want to cause him any more physical pain by 'cuffing his broken wrists. His real pain would come soon enough.

She still didn't know for sure if Joe was Mr. Sharpie.

They hurried back to Emma's car and flew away before Joe's other goon arrived.

70

"Is Joe our guy?"

Emma found a quiet street and pulled over. She assured Sophie, whose arms were tightly wrapped around Pepper, sobbing, that she would be taking her home to her parents after she made a phone call. Sophie's muffled voice told her that she understood.

Emma wasn't quite sure whom to call—Detective Dave Swanson, Buzz or Caroline, or Skip Munro. After a moment, she settled on Lt. Skip Munro. She expected to wake him up.

"Skip, it's Emma Thorne—"

"Are you okay?" he interrupted. "Jesus, you've been through hell. We are all so sorry—"

She interrupted him right back. "No time for apologies." *Although I'll make time later.* "You can find Joe Henderson at the corner of River and Blackberry Streets in Lincoln. I left him ankle-cuffed to a stop sign."

"Hold on." Emma could hear Skip bark orders into a portable. "I'm back. Is Joe our guy?"

"What do you think?"

"Honestly, we're still not sure. Either Joe or Georgia. We're still in Georgia's basement, still processing the scene."

Emma's heart skipped. She had to take multiple deep breaths before asking, "Is … is Will okay?"

"Jesus, you don't know? We thought you were still here when it happened." His voice went quiet for a moment.

"Skip, tell me about Will. Right. Now."

"Prepare yourself. Your husband was hit. Will took a head shot. Emma, he's, um, in very rough shape. They choppered him to Hartford Hospital, and, last we heard, he was still in surgery. He is gravely injured."

"I see."

Emma cursed Georgia.

"Any word on Mark Byrne?" she asked.

"Caroline Stoner got an update on Byrne. He's okay. A few stitches, but they're insisting he stay overnight at Hampshire Hospital for observation."

"I see," she said again in a hollow voice. "Look, I've got to go."

Before she pushed End, Skip was shouting into the phone, begging her to tell him where she was.

Emma was having none of it. She had to find Georgia.

Meantime, Emma drove Sophie home. "How're you holding up?" she asked her. She was still in the backseat hugging Pepper. "Do you want to talk about what happened? It must have been truly scary."

In a clear voice, Sophie said, "If it's okay with you, I'd rather talk to my mom."

Emma thought that sounded eminently grown-up and continued in silence to Sophie's emotional reunion with Karen and Henry King, her grateful parents. They were so profuse with their thanks that Emma had to cut them off.

She had to find Georgia Foster.

71

Not Particularly Proudly

It was nearly three in the morning by the time Pepper and Emma arrived in Emma's driveway. They were about to exit the car when a text arrived.

Emma gasped as she read it.

> If it weren't for you, Will would be safe and happy. We were so joyful. Living together was what we both have always wanted. Now, I have nothing. I'll have to leave Hampshire, leave my parents and my fish behind. You have destroyed everything I ever cared about, which is why I am going to kill you.

Insanity.

Like a graphite-lubricated lock, the tumblers in Emma's brain snapped into place. Everything was now clear.

Yet, she was left with a void.

She still didn't have Georgia.

Her thumbs flew over the virtual keyboard.

> Georgia, we need to talk. Where r u?

She stared at the Messages app on the phone, but no text appeared. She scoured her brain for all the places Georgia might hole up. Her parents' house? Stella's empty apartment? Somewhere in a stolen vehicle … unfindable?

A new text in a gray thought-bubble populated Emma's screen.

> Get out of my car. There is some rope in the trunk. Do you know how to tie a bowline? It's the King of Knots. Tie Pepper to the tree right next to the southwest corner of your house. Strip down to your underwear and come inside.

At least she didn't have to look any further for Georgia.

She obeyed the orders. She considered faking the knot, but Georgia aimed a powerful flashlight out the window fully illuminating her knot-tying. On the front stoop, Emma stripped and entered her own house in a bra and panties. Even so compromised, Emma walked inside with a wellspring of anger so cavernous nothing could frighten her. She knew that whatever happened this was their end-game. One of the two would likely not survive. She faced Georgia alone. No Skip. No Mark. No Hampshire PD. And, most perilously, no Pepper.

She entered her house, instinctively leaving the door open behind her. Would someone come to help her? No, of course not.

The hallway was dark. From the living room, also dark, she heard Georgia say, "Come in, and don't do anything stupid." As Emma entered the living room, Georgia turned on a table lamp and told her to stand still. Her sister-in-law was wearing a T-shirt and shorts. She must have changed after shooting Will. She held a chrome revolver, doubtless the same one she'd used on Will. Emma immediately noticed the bandage around Georgia's upper arm, the wound she'd sustained at Vanessa's house. The other arm, which Emma had broken in the vault, was in a sling. Georgia's pupils were constricted, probably from pain-killers. She was sitting in an armchair.

Georgia gestured with the revolver and said, "Take off your panties and let's see if you have the Girls' Club triangle like your buddies Deb and Vanessa."

"Take off my panties? Are you completely insane? Forget that, I already know the answer."

It was obvious to Emma that she couldn't take Georgia's admission into a court of law, but it was equally obvious that Will's twin sister was Ms. Sharpie.

"Why did you do it?" Emma asked. "Why did you kill all those innocent people? For what conceivable reason should they have died? Do you know that Will is still in surgery? He may die, Georgia. Did you want that, too?"

"Shut your sniveling face! I intend to enjoy this moment."

"Enjoy?" Emma asked incredulously. "What about Will?"

Georgia lifted the pistol with her bandaged arm, aiming it at Emma's face. Emma could see that the muzzle was pointed at a spot directly between her eyes. Pain killers or no, Georgia's gun hand was steady.

"Why don't we start," Emma said, "with Will, then."

For the first time, Georgia's gun hand drifted away from Emma's face. "Will was *not my fault*. That one's on you, Emma."

Not a very productive back and forth, Emma decided. Time to poke the snake.

"Let's stop playing games—"

"You call Smith & Wesson a game?" Georgia cried.

Emma pressed on. "What about Sophie? Let's talk about her. You must have known Joe Henderson intended her harm. Why didn't you try to protect her? She's your goddaughter, for heaven's sake."

"I said, shut up, you useless blob of Play-Doh."

Keeping her eye on the S&W's muzzle, Emma continued as calmly as she could. Although she was barely dressed, she felt sweat begin to run. She hoped Georgia didn't notice. "But you loved Sophie. Why let Joe take advantage of her?"

Georgia's eye began to spasm, but, incongruously, she smiled. Yet hers was a demonic smile. "I never cared a lick about Sophie. She only served me as a companion when I got lonely."

Omigod, Emma thought. But she bore on, hoping for an opportunity to overpower Georgia. "You once said to me that 'Sophie being rescued from abduction was a life-changing event.' What did you mean by that?"

Georgia giggled. "That's what gave me the whole idea. But you were too stupid to understand the ingenious web I spun. You're always bragging about your crossword puzzle expertise. But you couldn't solve my puzzle, could you?"

"What about Ethan Jackson then?"

"He was just to prove to everyone what a worthless police chief you were." Her hand covered her mouth. The lunatic was laughing.

"One more question: why point the finger at Will? Particularly since you already had him locked up."

"I don't want to talk about Will!" she shouted.

"I do," Emma said steadily.

"You are so idiotic. Don't you see that by implicating Will with the Sharpie letters everything would point to you. That's why I had to kill Stella. Don't you see?"

"No, I don't, and you know what? Your brand of insanity disgusts me. You don't even understand what you've done. You are worthless!"

Emma readied herself. She'd pushed Georgia to the limit, and Georgia's left eye told the story.

Georgia leapt to her feet. Emma watched her carefully, tensing her knees. When the revolver briefly pointed at the ceiling, she dove forward. The force of her lunge drove Georgia back over the top of the chair in which she had been sitting. They landed on the floor with Emma on top. But Georgia managed to keep the revolver in her hand.

The struggle continued on the floor.

They rolled back and forth. Emma tried to wrestle the gun away from Georgia. While Georgia tried to aim the gun in the direction of any part of Emma. Amid the grunts and groans, Emma felt the muzzle of the revolver pressed against her thigh.

Not proudly, Emma drove her free fist into Georgia's broken arm.

Georgia screamed.

The revolver discharged.

72

"How may I help you?"

Emma was hit. A white-hot poker had entered her body. In agony, she rolled onto her back. Seemingly indestructible, Georgia got to her knees, then to her feet. She clutched her arm with the wrist of her gun hand. She still had control of the weapon.

Each time her heart beat, Emma watched bright-red blood spurt from her thigh. Knowing that if she didn't stop her bleeding she would die, Emma couldn't even look at Georgia.

But she could hear her.

"Look at me!" Georgia shouted. "Look at what you have wrought! You have destroyed all that is dear to me. My God, who will feed my fish?" Her face was contorted with pain. "And now you must pay." Her left eye spasmed in hatred. She shifted the gun to the hand which emerged from the sling, because she needed to support that arm with her other hand. Still, she was able to aim at Emma's head.

"Anything to say, Emma dear?"

Emma was sure she was seconds from death. She had her right hand over her thigh wound, pressing as hard as she could, but the bleeding wouldn't stop. She struggled to speak. Before she could say anything, she saw a flash out of the corner of her eye.

It was not a muzzle flash. It was a fur flash.

Pepper sailed over Emma's body and seized both Georgia's wrists in her jaws. The gun discharged again.

Emma gasped.

This time the discharge missed. Georgia went down screaming, and she couldn't stop.

Emma tried to lift herself to one elbow to see what was happening and to see where the gun was. The latter had skittered across the floor, out of reach.

Where Emma had felt guilty about attacking Georgia's broken wrist, Pepper hadn't had the same inhibition. Pepper stood over Georgia, guarding. Tied to her collar was a hank of chewed-through rope.

Against the background noise of Georgia's shrieking, Emma tried to control her own cries of pain. Using her good leg to propel her, she slowly slid into the kitchen on her back. Her kitchen wall-phone had an extra-long coiled cord which she was able to reach from the floor. She flicked the cord until the handset popped off the switch hook and crashed to the tile floor.

She heard Georgia shouting from the next room, "Emma help me! I can't stand the pain!"

Next, she slid one of her kitchen stools over and, holding it upside down, tried to press the 911 buttons with its leg. After multiple, frustrating attempts, she dropped the stool. It landed painfully on her shoulder. She'd hit some buttons but not the right ones.

Pepper padded into the kitchen, her face a mixture of confusion and concern. She sniffed the blood coming from Emma's wound and sat down next to her.

After resting for a moment, Emma angled the chair leg so that she could pull the switch hook down and start again. She didn't know if dialing zero still worked, but, this time, she only tried for the zero. She succeeded in pushing in the button on the fourth try.

In Hampshire, Connecticut, dialing zero still connected one with a live human operator.

A man answered the phone. His "How may I help you?" might have been the sweetest words she ever heard.

73

No and No

Very quickly, an invasion force of state troopers, Hampshire cops, and two ambulances arrived at Emma's house. The EMTs loaded Emma into the first ambulance after applying a tourniquet to her thigh. They marked her forehead with a **T** and the time, 0243. They used a Sharpie.

In the ambulance, the paramedic on call administered morphine. She quickly felt relief. Enough to reflect on what had happened. She appreciated the irony that she and Pepper had sustained nearly identical gunshot wounds. Somehow that made her feel better that Pepper had already taken a bullet for her.

The paramedic directed that the crew proceed to a Level 1 Trauma Center. Lt. Skip Munro rode in the rig with her to Hartford Hospital, the closest one to Hampshire. They had plenty of time to talk, thanks to the analgesic and the fifty-minute drive.

Her first question was about Will. "Is my husband going to live?"

Skip was silent for so long that Emma felt she already had her answer.

"I need to know, Skip," she said. "No bullshit."

"Will made it through surgery, but he is currently on life-support.

That is honestly all I can tell you. At least, you'll be in the same hospital. You'll be able to see him."

Emma was quiet as she absorbed the news. Archie had always told her not to worry about the future until she had reason to do so. Nonetheless, her mind raced ahead to a dead Will ... or a brain-dead Will.

She sighed deeply enough to make Skip ask if *she* was okay.

"Let's talk about the case," she said suddenly.

"You sure?"

"I keep trying to wrap my head around Georgia hating me so much to kill my two best friends and possibly her own twin brother. Ethan almost seems like an afterthought ... a forethought, actually. Faking his suicide is almost the craziest part of her plan—"

"So, you're convinced it was Georgia and not Joe?"

"Yes, I am," she said unequivocally. "She spun a fatal web, which in her deranged mind made logical sense."

"You accused her," Skip said, "I assume?"

"Yup. She did it."

Angrily, Skip said, "We still have no proof—no forensics, no witnesses, no other evidence—nothing."

"We have two bits I can think of. Neither will convict her in court, but ... the first is her fish. Surely, some expert can trace the neurotoxins Dr. Mittendorf found to her fish."

"That works for me."

"The second," Emma said, "is her AmEx bill."

"Huh?"

"Georgia showed us her AmEx bill while we were still prisoners in her cell. It purportedly proved that she was in Dallas over the weekend Vanessa disappeared. Can you subpoena her AmEx records?"

"I don't think I'll have to. It's a murder investigation. I'm sure they'll provide copies."

"Great, but it still won't give us the ammo to send her away for a life sentence ... times four."

Skip said, "Well, assuming the gun recovered from your house is the same one she used to shoot Will, we have her for attempted murder. That's a start—"

"It's not enough for me," Emma said fiercely. "I want her for everything."

"There has to be something to nail her with—"

"Wait one second! Did you guys ever run the fingerprint from the button I gave Caroline Stoner?"

"What button?"

"The one I found next to Vanessa in the woods!"

"She never gave it to us."

"I left it outside her apartment … the night of the ambush … the night Pepper was shot."

"I'm sure it wasn't intentional on her part."

"I hope not," Emma said. "But what if Georgia's fingerprint is on that button? Wouldn't that fry her big ass?"

Skip chuckled. "I suppose so."

After surgery, Emma remained in the hospital for five days. On her first evening, she telephoned Mark Byrne to make sure Pepper was being looked after. Emma knew that Mark had developed a crush on her. She felt for him. She was grateful for his loyalty and friendship, but Will was her man.

Hartford Hospital provided Patient Advocates. Emma had informed hers that she did not wish to receive any visitors. It took Emma one post-op day to recognize the extreme stress that Will's critical status was causing and that the full Ms. Sharpie investigation had engendered. And she thought of other matters, as well. Emma was doing a lot of thinking. More than anything else, she thought about the possibility (likelihood?) of going forward without Will. She thought, too, about Deb and Vanessa and what a void they left in her life. You don't make new friends much better than the ones you loved in high school. Both of their families had opted for memorial services at the end of the summer instead of funerals. She didn't look forward to those. She also thought about Archie. What would he have thought?

On the second day, an orderly wheel-chaired her into the ICU. Will was hooked up to a million contraptions—most importantly the ventilator which was keeping him alive. It was a shocking sight. Emma was filled with despair. She couldn't help but worry that a life-or-death decision might soon devolve to her. For the moment she shook that out of her mind.

On the third day, a doctor, whom she had never seen before, knocked on her door.

"May I come in?" he said.

"More prodding?" she asked, feigning lightheartedness.

"No, not that," he said. "I am your husband's neurosurgeon. I've come to tell you that Will went into cardiac arrest this morning. We were unable to resuscitate him. I'm truly sorry."

Emma blinked and stared.

"Is there anything I can do, any questions I can answer, anyone I should call?"

Emma fought back her tears until she was able to speak. "If you had been able to resuscitate him and get him off the ventilator, would he have been … normal?"

"I believe that the answer is no. The bullet damaged the temporal lobe of his cerebrum. That is the part of the brain associated with perception and recognition of auditory stimuli, emotions, and language functions, among other important processes."

"Thank you, doctor," she said.

Will, she knew, would rather have died than be what he would have called a vegetable. That thought didn't provide much solace.

After the doctor closed the door behind him, Emma gave full voice to her grief. By nightfall, she had cried herself out. That Will hadn't written that hurtful nineteen-word text—obviously Georgia had—did give her a measure of relief. So did the catharsis of knowing that the man she loved was not a serial killer. Admittedly, she had let other people's doubts affect her, but she had always, deep inside, believed in him.

Lastly, she was humbled that Will—despite his chronic depression, despite Georgia, despite all he had suffered—had sacrificed his life to protect hers.

On the fourth day, Emma awoke to a morning thunderstorm. She realized for the first time since Georgia's bullet had torpedoed her thigh, that she didn't have as much pain. The loud claps of thunder didn't bother her in the slightest. It was July 14th. Four days had passed since the arrests of Georgia and Joe. Bastille Day, she remembered.

Her cell phone, which Mark Byrne had dropped off, had rung nonstop since she'd been in hospital. She had been in bunker mode and had liked it that way. The messages, all un-played, had piled up.

Today, though, she felt different. Will's death made her feel ready.

She knew that there were a few things she would never know. As far as full closure went, she would never know if Stella had knowledge of Will's imprisonment or of Georgia's murderous rampage. She would probably never know whether Joe and Georgia had a sexual relationship, and, if they had, if Joe knew what Georgia was up to. And why, at different times, were they both wearing ballistic vests? Did that tie them together? Finally, if Will had recovered, would she have confronted him about his affair with his teaching assistant, Suzy Szarkowski? Probably not, she decided.

It was time to listen to her messages.

Sophie King had left three voicemails of the I'm-thinking-of-you sort. Emma had been thinking about her, too.

Virginia Hobson was the winner of the persistence prize. She left four messages each containing similar content: "I am very anxious to get together with you for an interview with the *Chronicle*. Everybody in Hampshire is dying to hear your story." That was never going to happen.

Julian Jackson left an earnest and quite moving apology, which she appreciated.

As for the messages from Caroline Stoner, Dick Wardlaw, and Dr. Mittendorf, Emma knew she had to reply to all three.

She called Caroline first. Caroline's cell went to voicemail. Emma left her a message telling her not to worry … that they would remain friends and that she bore no ill feelings. It wasn't strictly true, but it needed to be said. Just as Emma was about to hang up, Caroline picked up. "Oh Jesus, Emma, I'm so sorry. What a cluster-fuck. I mean, what with your injuries and poor, poor Will. I don't know what to say—"

Emma needed to ask … and she needed an answer. "Why didn't you deliver the button I left outside your door to the lab, as you'd promised?"

"Um … I owe you an apology. More than one, I guess. Look, all I can say is I got swept along by the group. It's no excuse, but it's the truth. I'm sorry Emma that I doubted you. Can you forgive me?"

If there would ever be any normality in Emma's future, harboring grudges wouldn't get her there.

"Apology accepted." She said it a little curtly, but she'd said it.

She telephoned Dr. Mittendorf next. He said, "Emma, I gather you're in some pain. I'm truly sorry about that. I hope you're on the road to your future. What I called to say is that you're Archie's girl after all! Well done to you!"

She replied, "You don't know how much that means to me."

Lastly, Emma called Dick Wardlaw at home. Dick was not the sort to be in his office at eight o'clock in the morning.

In fact, she could tell that she had roused him from sleep.

A grumpy voice answered, "Dick Wardlaw. Who is this?"

"Dick," she said cheerily, "I hope I'm not disturbing you. It's Emma Thorne returning your call."

He pulled himself together. "How *are* you? I am so relieved to hear from you. What a dreadful mess! But you are Hampshire's heroine once again. I never doubted you for a minute. Locking up those two is nothing short of a triumph. Congratulations."

"But you fired me. Remember?"

"Well, that was just because of the conflict of interest. What with Will being—"

"Will's dead."

"Oh."

She plowed ahead, "Why did you call me?"

"To ask you to resume being my chief of police, of course! And to be my friend, too. What do you say?"

Emma was barely able to contain her delight.

She said, "I say *no* to being Hampshire's chief of police, and I say a definite *no* to being your friend. Thanks for the call, *Dick*."

Click.

Emma knew she hadn't done the most bang-up job as a rookie chief, but she did have the arrests of a serial killer and a sex trafficker to her credit.

That must count for something, she figured.

She made one further call.

As heavy rain pelted the windows of Hartford Hospital, she phoned Mark Byrne.

He immediately said how sorry he was about Will. She thanked him. He didn't sound himself.

He stammered, "I, I—"

His voice held none of his normal cockiness.

"—I guess I've fallen in love with you. That's stupid. I *have* fallen in love with you. And there's something I need to get off my chest. I lied to you. When I told you that Will and Suzy Szarkowski had an affair, well, that wasn't true."

Emma could tell that Mark was surprised when she said, "That's wonderful news. Thanks for telling me. It makes me feel better. And thank you for all you've done for me and Pepper."

While Mark seemed at a loss for words, she said, "Speaking of which, would you hold the phone to Pepper's ear? I need to thank her, too."

Acknowledgments

Readers first: Betsy Gill, Betsy Kittredge, Byron Tucker, John Garrels, and Amy Harren, who overcame her alone-in-the-woods fears to critique several versions. Thank you all. I am equally grateful to my publishing guru, Michael Selleck. Courtney Maum pitched in with special advice.

I am appreciative of the time and assistance provided to me by the following:

William T. Fitzgerald, Jr. Chief of Police, Winchester, CT

Marisa Edelberg, Medicolegal Death Investigator, Office of the Chief Medical Examiner, State of CT

Matt Ludwig, Chief, Norfolk Volunteer Fire Department

Dr. Richard S. Childs, Emergency Medicine, Charlotte Hungerford Hospital.

Any and all errors are, of course, on me.

Thanks to Mark Scarbrough's writing group. Helen Baldwin, Laura Didyk, Amy Harren, Molly Hinchman, Joyce O'Brien, Emilie Pryor, Frances Roth, and Tony Thomson steered me through the first chapters of this book with warmth and encouragement.

Note from an Indie Author

In the long run, Kindle and the ebook craze did not destroy the printed book as was widely expected. When Amazon released its first e-reader twelve years ago, it sold out in five-and-a-half hours. I bought one. Instead what happened is that readers of mass market paperbacks, especially in genres like Romance and Mystery/Thrillers converted to reading on ebooks, and that decimated the sales of mass market paperbacks. Only the big-name, established authors—and I say this without rancor—find their books on the shelves in airports, supermarkets, and Walmart.

For indie authors to survive, we rely on reviews and word-of-mouth. If you enjoyed this story, please take a moment to leave a review and recommend my book to friends and family. Thank you for reading.

•

Stay in Touch

I would love to hear from you. You may contact me via an email form on either of these two websites: **honeysucklepublishing.com** or **christopherlittle.com** [No spam, no list-selling]

•

Production Notes

This book was prepared for print using Adobe InDesign CC.
The body font is Adobe Caslon Pro.
Title fonts are Adobe Garamond Pro.
The cover was produced using Adobe Photoshop CC.
I guess I should thank Adobe, too.